The Self of the City

The Self of the City

Macedonio Fernández,
the Argentine Avant-Garde,
and Modernity in Buenos Aires

Todd S. Garth

Lewisburg
Bucknell University Press

© 2005 by Rosemont Publishing & Printing Corp.

All rights reserved. Authorization to photocopy items for internal or personal use, or the internal or personal use of specific clients, is granted by the copyright owner, provided that a base fee of $10.00, plus eight cents per page, per copy is paid directly to the Copyright Clearance Center, 222 Rosewood Drive, Danvers, Massachusetts 01923. [0-8387-5615-8/05 $10.00 + 8¢ pp, pc.]

Associated University Presses
2010 Eastpark Boulevard
Cranbury, NJ 08512

The paper used in this publication meets the requirements of the American National Standard for Permanence of Paper for Printed Library Materials Z39.48-1984.

Library of Congress Cataloging-in-Publication Data

Garth, Todd S., 1958–
    The self of the city : Macedonio Fernández, the Argentine Avant-Garde, and modernity in Buenos Aires / Todd S. Garth.
      p. cm.
    ISBN 0-8387-5615-8 (alk. paper)
    1. Fernández, Macedonio, 1874–1952—Criticism and interpretation. 2. Postmodernism (Literature)—Argentina. 3. Self in literature. 4. Identity (Psychology) in literature. 5. Buenos Aires (Argentina)—In literature. I. Title.
PQ7797.F312Z693   2005
863'.62—dc22
                                          2004063841

PRINTED IN THE UNITED STATES OF AMERICA

For Gary,
who made it possible to do this,
and in memory of my mother,
who made it impossible not to do.

Contents

Thanks	9
Abbreviations and Copyright	11
Biographical Note	13
1. Departures	17
2. The Myth of the Accidental Author	32
3. An Avant-garde Apart	48
4. The Political Is the Personal	89
5. Minding the Body	119
6. The Self of the City	162
7. Continuities	192
Notes	198
Works Cited	211
Index	221

Thanks

FIRST AND FOREMOST, ACKNOWLEDGMENT GOES TO THE LATE ADOLFO DE Obieta, whose selflessness was matched only by his kindness and his enthusiasm for his father's genius. Adolfo's heirs and Alejandra Valente, former curator of the Macedonio Fernández papers, and now the Fundación Palermo, where those papers have found a home, have continued to extend that kindness to grateful scholars. Among the innumerable other people in Argentina who helped realize this project, I should at least mention: Ana Camblong (who deserves much more than thanks), Nélida Salvador, Ricardo Piglia, Dora Barrancos, Noé Jitrik, Washington Pereyra; Nicolás Helft, and his gracious mother, of the Fundaciones San Telmo and Palermo; Juan Molina y Vedia, Alejandro Vaccaro, Hugo Biagini, Horacio González, Ricardo Kalimán, Sonia Vicente de Alvarez, Mónica Bueno, Germán García, and Alvaro Abós.

At Johns Hopkins University, thanks go to the Spanish faculty of the department Romance Languages and Literatures: Sara Castro-Klarén, a wise and dedicated advisor; Eduardo González, Paul Olson, Harry Sieber, and Ana María Snell. Thanks as well to former Hopkins colleagues Noël Valis, María del Rosario Ramos González, Miguel Fernández, Marcy Schwartz, Heather Dubnick, Laura Beard, and Viki Zavales, all of whom have had a hand in this at some point. At the University of Maryland, Ineke Phaf, Charles Caramello, and Susan Lanser gave me an exceptional start.

Elsewhere in the world: Jo Anne Engelbert, Naomi Lindstrom, Alicia Borinsky, Daniel Balderston, Gwen Kirkpatrick, Donna Guy, Christopher Leland, Scott Link, Laura Dahlmann de Toledo, Michael Gerli, Thomas and Carol Reese, Julio Prieto, Carlos García in Hamburg, and the remarkable Peter Johnson of the Princeton University Libraries. Librarians, who surely merit their own Executive Club in heaven, deserve special mention here. Among them are the librarians and staff at the Harry Ransom Center at the University of Texas at Austin; those at the special collections departments of the University of Virginia and the University Pittsburgh libraries; Paul

Dzyak—a true gentleman—of the Pennsylvania State University archives; and at the U.S. Naval Academy's Nimitz Library, Patti Patterson, and especially Florene Todd, who I am convinced possesses magical powers. In Buenos Aires, the library staff of the UBA Facultad de Medicina proved patient and helpful; also deserving mention are the librarians of the Museo de la Ciudad and the astonishing Asociación Amigos de Tranvía; most extraordinary of all are the expert librarians at the Biblioteca de la Mujer.

Projects culminating in the publication of this book were made possible by the generous grants from the Johns Hopkins Latin American Studies program and the Naval Academy Research Council. My colleagues in the Language Studies department at the U.S. Naval Academy have been exceptional in their encouragement and their efforts to afford me the time to see this book to completion.

And extra thanks to Vicky Unruh, truly a scholar's scholar.

Abbreviations and Copyright

FREQUENTLY CITED WORKS BY MACEDONIO FERNÁNDEZ ARE REFERRED TO by the following abbreviations. Unless otherwise indicated, citations refer to the editions listed below.

Adriana	*Adriana Buenos Aires (última novela mala)*. Buenos Aires: Corregidor, 1988.
Epistolario	*Epistolario*. Edited by A. Borinsky. Buenos Aires: Corregidor, 1991.
Museo	*Museo de la Novela de Eterna*. Critical edition. Edited by Ana María Camblong. Paris: ALLCA XX/ Colección Archivos, 1996.
Papeles Antiguos	*Papeles Antiguos: Escritos, 1892–1907*. Buenos Aires: Corregidor, 1981.
Recienvenido	*Papeles de Recienvenido y Continuación de la Nada*. Buenos Aires: Corregidor, 1989.
Relato	*Relato: Cuentos, Poemas y Misceláneas*. Buenos Aires, Corregidor: 1987.
Teorías	*Teorías*. Buenos Aires: Corregidor, 1990.
Vigilia	*No toda es vigilia la de los ojos abiertos y otros escritos metafísicos*. Buenos Aires: Corregidor, 1990.

Ediciones Corregidor, which holds the copyright for Macedonio Fernández's published works, has granted permission to quote from them here.

Collección Archivos has graciously consented to allow quotation from the critical edition of *Museo de la Novela de la Eterna.*

Portions of chapters one and two first appeared in March 2001 as "Confused Oratory: Borges, Macedonio and the Creation of the Mythological Author," *MLN* 116 (2): 350–70. They are included here with the kind permission of the Johns Hopkins University Press.

Biographical Note

Macedonio Fernández and his Complete Works

Macedonio Fernández was born in 1874 in Buenos Aires to a well-to-do landed family belonging to Buenos Aires's relatively small, closed creole society. He attended law school with the father of Jorge Luis Borges, graduating in 1896. In the years following, he married Elena de Obieta, set up a law practice, and lived a more or less conventional life. During this time, however, Macedonio enthusiastically read philosophy, engaged in utopian anarchist discourse and wrote iconoclastic libertarian articles on society, economics and politics. He also began to write poetry and his characteristic experimental narrative.

In 1920, Macedonio's wife suddenly died. Unequipped to care for a family of small children, he dismantled his household, set up his children with nearby relatives, and took to living in a succession of economical in-town boardinghouses and, during summers, in modest quarters on the ranches of family friends. Within four years, he also gave up his law practice. He soon came to be known as much for his peculiar lifestyle and unorthodox friendships—which included prostitutes and impoverished musicians as well as socially prominent artists and government officials—as for his original ideas.*

In 1921, Macedonio renewed his friendship with the Borges family, newly returned from nearly a decade in Europe. With the young Jorge Luis Borges, Macedonio immediately entered a decades-long dialogue on avant-garde thought and art. Buenos Aires's coterie of avant-garde writers and artists, later identifiable as the *Martinfierrista* generation, quickly adopted Macedonio as their mentor and as a father figure. The following year, 1922, Macedonio wrote his first novel-length book, *Adriana Buenos Aires*, which was to remain unpublished for decades.

---

*In addition to Abós's biography (2002), a straightforward capsule biography can be found in Engelbert's introduction to the sole volume of English translations of Macedonio's writings (Engelbert, 1984, 5).

But Macedonio's primary narrative project, which he often referred to as *Novela de la Eterna* (The Novel of Eterna), was in more or less constant development throughout the 1920s, 1930s, and 1940s, evolving along with Macedonio's radical poetics and singular philosophy. While he gave the rare address and published the occasional short piece in Buenos Aires's avant-garde literary journals (including *Martín Fierro*, for which the Buenos Aires avant-garde generation is named), for many years Macedonio resisted publishing anything in book form. In 1928, urged by Raul Scalabrini Ortiz and others, he finally published his book-length philosophical tract, *No toda es vigilia la de los ojos abiertos* (Open Eyes Are Not All Wakefulness). In 1929, fulfilling a promise to Borges and others of a book-length literary work, he consented to assembling several short, previously released pieces, publishing them under the title *Papeles de Recienvenido* (The Newcomer Papers). In 1941, under the initiative of Luis Alberto Sánchez, he published in Chile the short book *Una novela que comienza* (A Novel that Begins), written twenty years earlier and then revised.

The long-promised masterwork, however, never materialized in print in his lifetime. Macedonio fell largely silent during the 1930s. In the early 1940s he briefly renewed literary activity, largely under the encouragement of his youngest son, Adolfo de Obieta, who from this point on would be Macedonio's promoter, editor, and later, literary executor. In 1944 Macedonio published a second edition of *Papeles de Recienvenido*, amplified by *Continuación de la Nada* (Continuation of Nothing). Macedonio lived with Adolfo from 1946 until his death in 1952. Throughout the years, he worked on *Museo de la Novela de la Eterna*, producing several variants of the novel. Only in 1967, primarily as a result of Adolfo's tireless efforts, was *Museo de la Novela de Eterna* (Museum of the Novel of Eterna) published, its form determined partly by Adolfo's editorial decisions. In 1974, *Adriana Buenos Aires* finally saw the light of day. In succeeding years, Adolfo, under agreement with Ediciones Corregidor, published the greater part of Macedonio's work, including many of his letters, short stories, and philosophical and theoretical musings. Adolfo de Obieta died in 2002 and the bulk of Macedonio's papers, manuscripts, and notebooks, some of them still undeciphered, passed to the Fundación Palermo in Buenos Aires, to be maintained there as an archive.

The Self of the City

1
Departures

"Paradox" is the word that best summarizes the impressions left on scholars and critics by the works and life of Macedonio Fernández. The conclusion—or presumption—that paradox is the primary characteristic of Macedonio's corpus is reflected in commentary that persistently emphasizes qualities seen as corollary to paradox: whimsy, irrationality, confusion, arbitrariness, antilogic, disorderliness and, above all, irreducibility. With limited exceptions, scholarly criticism has implicitly accepted and perpetuated this assessment. Usually, scholars take these qualities as a given and thus a point of departure. Rarely does a study question them.

To a degree, the implied consensus on this irreducible paradox is understandable, and it has certainly been productive. For decades an underappreciated and neglected writer, Macedonio has been rehabilitated in large measure by two simultaneous efforts: the tireless work of his youngest son and literary executor, Adolfo de Obieta, and the dedication and enthusiasm of a handful of scholars. These scholars share a serious fascination for Macedonio's texts as well as an attraction to his persona, often more mythological than biographical. They also have the advantage, over earlier generations, of the insights of postmodern literary theories. These theories have been an important catalyst, both directly and through their influence on the way literature is read, to a better appreciation of Macedonio's writing.

But this postmodern theoretical foundation has made for some limitations and biases in approaches to the works of Macedonio Fernández. The predisposition to postmodern interpretation is evident in almost all of the major studies accomplished to date. It has, in fact, limited scholarship to two basic kinds of analysis: discussions of Macedonio as precursor or visionary, anticipating the aesthetic and philosophical advents of both the avant-garde and postmodernity; and comparisons of Macedonio's works and ideas with a modernist or postmodernist movement or idea. Aside from the value of their bringing attention to a neglected literary genius, many of these studies have great merit. But they also share the encumbrance that contemporary theory can place on art when applied to a retroactive appraisal.

It is worth summarizing their merits here. The first book-length study in English of Macedonio's works, Jo Anne Engelbert's *Macedonio Fernández and the Spanish American New Novel* (1978) is an articulate summary of many of Macedonio's innovations and their bearing on—or anticipation of—the more inventive aspects of Latin American boom literature. Engelbert is also the first to construct a lucid narrative correlating salient aspects of Macedonio's life—and legend—to those literary innovations. Naomi Lindstrom's 1981 study, also a pioneering effort in English, looks more closely and systematically at Macedonio's techniques and their effects, considering also their place in literary history. One aspect of Lindstrom's approach, however, which she in turn acknowledges is in keeping with Noé Jitrik's perspective, is illustrative of the outlook that has provoked the present study. Both Lindstrom and Jitrik (1973) believe Macedonio's "philosophical" pronouncements on the nature of aesthetics to be inconsistent with his art and an inaccurate reflection of his true approach to writing. Demonstrating the overall consistency of Macedonio's work is fundamental to the argument offered in these pages.

Among other important contributions to the study of Macedonio Fernández is Nélida Salvador's highly readable 1986 *Macedonio Fernández: Precursor de la antinovela*, which remains the first and best synopsis of Macedonio's poetics. Alicia Borinsky (1978) has given a particular focus to the analysis of those poetics through the lens of contemporary theory. Flora Schiminovich (1986), in an even more detailed analysis, elaborates the resonance between Macedonio's works and classical surrealism. As such, Schiminovich is also the first to touch on a greater contextualization of Macedonio's writing.

Several other book-length studies, all by Argentines, build on an integration of the texts and the anecdotal legend of Macedonio. The most noteworthy of these is Germán Leopoldo García's 1975 *Macedonio Fernández: La escritura en objeto*, which examines both legend and texts, applying the principles of psychological, mainly Lacanian, literary analysis. Although unconcerned with context, García's work contributes a perspective on the reason for being of some of the most enigmatic aspects of Macedonio's writings. Juan

Carlos Foix's similarly psychoanalytic study (1974) is distinctive in its efforts to clarify and understand some of Macedonio's most perplexing treatments of the human body and its desires, questions most pertinent to this study. José Isaacson is almost unique in tackling a political reading of Macedonio's aesthetics. Responding to contemporary conditions more than historical ones, Isaacson's reading is unavoidably affected by the difficulties of publishing such an analysis in the highly repressive Argentina of 1981. Other, shorter, studies have, for the most part, taken similar perspectives, generally adopting contemporary theoretical conceits or, less successfully, established anecdotal sources. Numerous insightful articles, often associated with editions of Macedonio's prose, use these sources to formulate questions in ways that prove provocative and fruitful. Among the more substantive contributions are studies by Noé Jitrik, Lydia Díaz, César Fernández Moreno, Sonia Mattalía, and Andrea Pagni.

Several noteworthy exceptions to these noncontextual studies support this present effort. One is Sonia Vicente de Alvarez's little-recognized analysis of Macedonio's system of philosophical thought (1982)—and she shows it to be a system indeed. Another vital contribution is made by Ana Camblong, whose herculean accomplishment of the critical edition of *Museo de la Novela de la Eterna* is matched by her exhaustive and incisive commentary on the history of its composition and on Macedonio's attitude toward publishing. Finally, Horacio González's 1995 monograph, though lacking scholarly apparatus, contains invaluable insight regarding Macedonio's relationship to his own literary creation, to social and political context, to literary and intellectual history, and to the mythology woven from all three of these phenomena.

In the past few years, some important additions to Macedonio Fernández studies have been published. Alvaro Abós (2002) is the first to compile an "impossible" but very readable biography of Macedonio, shedding light on several key aspects of his life that have until now been obscured. Mónica Bueno (2000) has written a sound analysis of Macedonio's early writing, emphasizing three vital points: the genesis of Macedonio's poetics in turn-of-the-century cultural and philosophical movements, the centrality of Macedonio's assault on the concept of self and the empirical bases for Macedonio's metaphysical inquiry. Nélida Salvador (2003) and Germán García (2000) have added to their initial work with updated monographs. Julio Prieto's impressive 2002 study, researched and written at about the same time as this book but published in a more timely fashion, arrives at many of the same conclusions regarding Macedonio's relationship with the *martinfierrista* generation and Borges. Where Prieto, however, emphasizes Borges's "obscuring" or "misunderstanding" of Macedonio, the present study tends to regard Borges and the avant-garde as misreadings and inversions of Macedonio. Prieto's analysis, inspired by Lacanian approaches such as García's, makes invaluable observations about the revolutionary and transgressive nature of *Museo* in particular. Diego Vecchio's 2003 monograph is a scrupulous analysis of Macedonio's dissolution of the self, a concern most pertinent to the present study. Finally, Ana Camblong has recently released (in 2003) an extensive and painstakingly documented book that will likely prove to be a bedrock foundation for future work on Macedonio Fernández.

The preponderantly noncontextual character of the bulk of all other studies, while not necessarily compromising their value, limits their potential to elucidate the more evidently paradoxical, deconstructive aspects of Macedonio's work. The reason for this limitation lies in the fact that these studies tend to take for granted the "postmodern" nature of Macedonio's poetics, having found confirmation of it in contemporary theory. An important distinction must be made here between postmodern *method*, which makes use of postmodern theory to question texts, and postmodern *readings*, which find evidence of postmodern thought in the texts themselves. The latter case, so compelling when dealing with Macedonio's extraordinary prose, has proven limiting and at times misleading. A large part of the problem is that when formulating questions with postmodern theories in mind, Macedonio's texts themselves sometimes appear to respond to those questions so directly and tidily.

It is crucial to recognize that postmodern theory itself is associated with a particular cultural context, as are the aesthetic literary phenomena grouped under postmodernism. It is too easy to lose sight of this context, failing to remember Jameson's insistence at defining postmodernism in terms of cultural and social context. The result of this failure is a tendency to regard postmodernism as a mode rather than a moment. Michel Foucault tells us that paradox is a fundamental characteristic of modernity; but his *valuation* of the preponderance of paradox in modernity is a function of postmodern thought. The most extreme result of the confusion between these two phenomena is highly anachronistic discussion of the more innovative works and authors of the modern age: the analysis of

Sterne or even Cervantes as "postmodern." Such approaches have the benefit of opening texts to new and interesting readings, and in the case of Macedonio have succeeded in drawing much deserved attention to an overlooked author. These valuable gains can be balanced by the complementary study of how innovative texts may be responding to social and cultural forces that have nothing postmodern about them. A handful of the studies mentioned above do, at points, attempt to assess the weight of such forces with regard to Macedonio Fernández.

The impulse to postmodern readings is especially problematic in the case of Macedonio Fernández because it abdicates analysis of some of the most fundamental—and defiant—aspects of his writing. Schiminovich is right to object to the commonplace that Macedonio's thought was disordered and asystematic (1986, 74). By accepting Macedonio's poetics and philosophy as purely deconstructive and negating of all system—a pure "pastiche," in Jameson's terms (1991, 16–17)—critics overlook one of the most fundamental of Macedonio's challenges: to recognize that elaborating an aesthetic and ethical *system* does not validate the existence of an objective *reality*. In Macedonio's thinking, the practice of a systematic poetics demonstrates the falseness of that reality.

Nor do we mean "systematic" in the purely deconstructive sense. Macedonio Fernández did not merely want to dismantle objective reality; he wanted to replace it with something better. Naomi Lindstrom's emphasis on Macedonio's efforts to make prose "less communicative" similarly loses sight of the fact that Macedonio wanted not to frustrate communication but to improve it. The paradox in Macedonio's work has a purpose; merely to observe and accept the paradox is to ignore the purpose altogether. Overall, the observation and acceptance of postmodern paradox in Macedonio Fernández's writing has, among other things, led some critics to value either his "intuitive" philosophy or his "ludic" prose without ever seeing them as integral. The assumption of this study is that by simultaneously considering problems of context and focusing on the issue of self, the integrity of Macedonio's fiction and philosophy will be made evident.

Much of the misjudgment of Macedonio's prose is in keeping with the substantial, at times overwhelming, mythology Macedonio has engendered. Here too the marriage of contemporary theory with established text is terribly seductive, especially since in this case the text in question is anecdotal, fragmentary, and highly intertextual.

The question of self is central to the problems posed by postmodern readings of Macedonio Fernández, and central as well to the readings imposed by the mythology about him. This mythology relies on a basic misreading of Macedonio's campaign against the self and a misinterpretation of its actions. It is because a critique of the self is so essential to Macedonio's poetics that a misconstruing of that critique has been able to gain such ascendancy. For Macedonio Fernández, the issue of self is an eminently ethical one, and a mere dismissal or dissolution of the self would fail to engage the real conflict. I would argue that Macedonio's corpus comprises approximately sixteen hundred pages of engagement.

Until very recently, assessments of his work did not see it that way. The general conclusion has been that Macedonio's dissolution of self is similar to one attempted by Jorge Luis Borges or other modernist writers of at least a generation later. This posture is in keeping with Octavio Paz's observation that contemporary Western literature dissolves the identity of the poet in a subjectless voice (Paz 1974, 207). It is also, as Schiminovich points out, in concert with Borges's early Ultraist negation of the self, a stance, she implies, in sympathy with Macedonio's own pronouncements (Schiminovich 1986, 59–60). The contention of the present study is that if Borges indeed got his early ideas on the fallacy of self from Macedonio, he got them wrong.

Lucille Kerr (1992) reinforces the observation that Borges, in keeping with the orientation of modernity, fragments and dissolves individual identity, the idea of self and the concept of subject, into a subjectless poetic voice. This subjectless voice effectively forces a redefinition of the concept of author. Writing on the famous vignette, "Borges y yo" ("Borges and I"), Kerr argues that the voice "effects a disappearance of the author as a univocal and stable authority or origin" but that "(T)he suggestion that the author cannot be found in any single site potentially situates the author's figure everywhere" (1992, 2). According to Balderston, that voice, in Borges's poetics, has history as a constant referent, irreducibly beyond the text yet accessible only through text (Balderston 1993, 16–17).

Vicky Unruh tells us that one hallmark paradox of the avant-garde is its search for a "pure national voice" at once culturally unique yet completely original and independent of historical and institutional forces (Unruh 1993, 208–31). Beatriz Sarlo argues that a primary motivation of Borges and other Martinfierrista writers was to establish a mythological foundation, free of historical contingency and responsive to Argentine modernity, for Buenos Aires, a city without "ghosts" (1988, 43).¹ This amounts to a kind of spontaneous generation of territory-specific myth and culture. James Holloway, Jr. details this "mythicization of Buenos Aires" in Borges's poetry and narrative. The conversion into a "mythological framework" (1988, 19) of a singular historical moment and "block" of the city is personally attested to by Borges's lyric voice and accomplished by means of the poet's "retracing" or "reascension" of time to a "prehistoric" point, along the lines of Mircea Eliade's conception of myth (31–33).

This mythological rendering is, in turn, fundamental to Borges's project of integrating the Argentine poetic voice into the cultural discourse of Western modernity. In other words, the stories told by that voice, whose identity is constituted entirely by the stories it tells, are in turn reducible only as far as history and mythology. With the self thus dissolved in the stories told, Borges must attribute genius to the voice itself in its success at expressing these fragments of Argentine identity. This conceptualization of poetic-voice genius could find no better incarnation, no better figure for demonstrating and anchoring Borges's idea of poetic voice, than Macedonio Fernández.

The Contexts of Paradox

The "discovery" of Macedonio by Borges and the accompanying generation of writers is often cited by these same writers and reiterated by critics. This discovery is perfectly in keeping with their need to establish a distinctively Argentine myth. In the paradoxes personified by Macedonio they saw a sort of metaparadox worthy of Foucault's characterization of modernity: a mythology that is always reducible to history, and history that is mythological by virtue of being irreducible. This revelation of historical mythology in Macedonio Fernández is abetted in many ways by Macedonio himself, but it requires a fundamental misinterpretation of both his writings and his lifestyle. To mention here just one example of such a misreading, Macedonio's admirers often note his words on the "Argentine character" as being especially suited to evolving completely new forms of human relations. For Macedonio, the point of this observation is to assert the aptitude of Argentines to transcend the very idea of nationality (*Teorías*, 95). But the responses of the *generación martin-*

fierrista to Macedonio's remarks are characteristic of their zeal to create a national mythology: they cite his ideas as demonstration of an Argentine "type" that is simultaneously specifically national and generically international.

The basic problem with this take on Macedonio's words is its misunderstanding, either intended or ingenuous, of his interest in dismantling the accepted concept of self and its corollary concept of character. It is a misunderstanding also maintained by an alacrity to welcome and adopt Macedonio's paradoxes without considering his motivations for elaborating and promoting them. To his admirers, Macedonio's paradoxical ideas, ludic prose, and championing of passion over intellect are his only reason for being. For Macedonio, paradox, play and above all, passion, are components of inventions for a new century, instruments for change. They are components Macedonio finds already present in his context. They can transcend history only because they respond to it. To put it in even more basic terms, Borges's dissolved self, a voice constituted largely by textual and fictional history and its figures, serves to manage history for the benefit of the Argentine *polis*. Macedonio's fragmented individual has the express purpose of repudiating history in order to beautify the city. The Martinfierrista generation and much of the scholarship that follows them thus neglects, or ignores, the social, political, and material components of Macedonio's explorations of individual identity. The Martinfierristas disregard the importance of Macedonio's inventorying the components of the individual in order to repudiate the concept of self. By ignoring this aspect of Macedonio's poetics, they disallow his investment in his own texts.

As to that abstract term, "self," central as it is to Macedonio's writing, a working definition of it will remain, for the first hundred pages, purposely rather vague. As the goal here is to examine in detail the conceptions of self Macedonio is working against, the actual components of that conception will be considered in their turn, as relevant contextual issues are discussed. From the outset, however, we can assert that the self Macedonio challenges is a direct product of Cartesian philosophy. Descartes's self, conceived in thought, and thus affirmed and analyzed by intellect (or to paraphrase, "one thinks, therefore one is a subject"), constitutes the model of subjectivity on which the modern individual identity is elaborated. Just as this definition of self will be more clearly rendered as we progress, a clearer sense of the "maximum individual" that Macedonio proposes to supersede the self will emerge piecemeal, over the length of this examination.

Each section of this book takes on one of three essential paradoxes that have gone largely unexamined. Chapters 2 and 3 consider the literary and intellectual context in which Macedonio elaborated his extraordinary poetics. One objective is to demonstrate that Macedonio was very much in step with both artistic and intellectual concerns of the time. His poetics, rather than being the "pastiche" work of a hermetic genius ("hermetic" being yet another postmodern quality), responds not only to the philosophical and artistic movements that precede him but also to those contemporary to him. Chapter 3 argues that Macedonio's ideas on the individual and his rejection of self are in part a reaction to what he sees as the utterly inadequate treatments of these problems by contemporary writers. And his motivations for taking on his contemporaries are closely related to questions of individual power that are fundamental to his relationships with social and material context as well.

This perspective on Macedonio's literary and intellectual connections also tackles the first of the three paradoxes (Díaz 1990, 498). On the one hand, Macedonio appears to eschew the status of author, refusing to publish or to associate with literary institutions of any kind. On the other hand, his prose is saturated with discussions on the nature of authorship, the process of writing, and most curiously, the fate of his own texts. Prior to the more general discussion of literary and intellectual context in chapter 3, chapter 2 focuses on the elaboration and repercussions of this particular paradox. The key to the paradox is Macedonio's constant preoccupation with replacing the concept of self with a thoroughly renovated, *and widely disseminated*, concept of the individual.

We go on, in chapter 4, to examine in detail some of the social and political conditions contributing to Macedonio's conception of individual identity, always focusing on his reasons for wanting to repudiate, ultimately, the concept of self. Not only do observations in this study support the notion, now widely accepted, that the so-called *grupo Florida* who befriended Macedonio were far from apolitical; we assert that Macedonio surpassed nearly all of his contemporaries in the social nature of his underlying motivations. In this respect, Macedonio Fernández shares more in common with Roberto Arlt than with Jorge Luis Borges.

The issue of politics tackles a second paradox. Reputedly shunning politics in favor of metaphysics, evidently always rejecting the social in favor of the aesthetic, Macedonio nonetheless fills pages, written throughout his life, with largely overlooked commentary on social, economic, and political institutions of his day. We shall see that his obsessive advocacy of libertarian principles is clearly based on a reaction to social environment and not in spite of it, and has everything to do with affirming, not negating, individual power. Part of his goal is to upend the valuation of power, thus reconstituting the social and political components of the individual. Macedonio's objective of reforming the conception of individual identity is central to this obsession.

In chapter 5, we take on the most perplexing paradox of all, Macedonio's obsession with health and physiognomy. His reputation as uncompromisingly metaphysical and uninterested in material conditions or in physical being, and most importantly, his negation of death, seem utterly contradictory to his fascination, at times verging on perverse, with the corporal. How can a purely metaphysical mind also be a nonstop hypochondriac? We examine in detail Macedonio's own words concerning health and body in light of recent historical research on these issues. The explanation for this ostensible paradox comes back to the problems of self and identity. Macedonio's apparently contradictory polemic—disdaining medicine and hygiene yet obsessing on sickness and cures—reflects his determination to restore to the individual the power of the body, partly by reconfiguring what constitutes corporal integrity. The key to understanding this corporal power rests heavily on a reconsideration of the relations between men and women and the institutions and practices supporting those relations. Macedonio's profound exploration of the paradoxical interdependency of body, sensation, and passion is integral to his attempt to rescue the individual from myriad institutions subjecting his or her body.

Overarching all three of these paradoxes is that of the city, where in fact Macedonio's confrontation with the aesthetic, the social, and the material come together. While never ceasing to repudiate the modern city as ugly, inhuman, impossible—in effect a living absurdity—Macedonio kept himself bound to it. The city, Buenos Aires, is both metaphorically and actually the crux of the dilemma he tries to solve and the world he attempts to reform. Metaphor and reality are indistinguishable for Macedonio, and his insistence on conflating them—a procedure fundamental to his whole poetic endeavor—is not merely an iconoclastic metaphysical conceit, but a function of his solution to the absurdity of the polis.

Polis is a term Macedonio never uses, but his treatment of Buenos Aires throughout his writings responds to this classical conception of the city as an entity that integrates and subsumes the aesthetic, the social, and the corporal. In chapter 6 we argue that Macedonio's "metaphysical vision" is no more nor less than a vision for the city that supersedes the polis and the powers it comprises. In this respect a brief comparison of Macedonio's treatment of the city with those of his contemporaries reveals how, as in the case of the literary avant-garde, Macedonio is motivated by many of the same concerns and shares many of the same methods as his contemporaries, yet differs fundamentally in his elaboration of solutions. These last two chapters, 6 and 7, return us to the irony that serves as the fulcrum of this entire study: the enshrinement of Macedonio, by his contemporaries, as mythology.

This irony is bitter in light of Macedonio's civic objective. His "selfless individual" is Macedonio's vision for the kind of populace that should constitute, inherit, and perpetuate this alternative to polis: in effect, the city's only possible salvation. In the final analysis, Macedonio Fernández's crusade against the self is integral to his campaign against "maximalism" (a term he adapts to his own purposes with characteristic defiance and abandon). He regards the self as an *institutionally* constituted falsehood pervading all aspects of the polis. Selfhood to Macedonio is a "maximalist" attack on the integrity of the individual body and its corporal power, the individual citizen and its political and economic power, and the individual artist and its aesthetic power. Macedonio's goal is to replace "self" with his "maximum individual," an entity defined in these very concrete terms and able to act with an ethically committed—not institutionally inspired—passion, a passion that must be gauged by renovated relations between men and women. Thus, the eradication of the self is tantamount to the liberation of the individual, and the only means to an ethically—or humanly—viable city. In this respect, Macedonio was intensely interested in relations of power.

Foucault's Shadow

The underlying assumptions of this study are unreservedly Foucault inspired. They are founded on Foucault's observation that cultural discourses both constitute and are constituted by, among other things, competing strategies for power (Dreyfus 1983, 184–88).

They also take for granted Foucault's assertion that these cultural discourses are all-encompassing, and that all modes of analysis and communication, from the most emotive to the most empirical, are ultimately driven by these evolving and competing discourses. Foucault's concept of episteme, accordingly, also figures in this approach to Macedonio's work. The conceit that all relations of a cultural period, including its scientific, or supposedly purely objective, activities of analysis, make up a coherent system is an essential component of our perspective on Macedonio's thought (Foucault 1972, 191).

Indeed, this study bases much of its strategy of analysis on the assumption that Macedonio's works and life are, ultimately, an integrated response to just such an episteme. Thus even Foucault's notion of rupture, the abrupt and inexplicable gap separating epistemes, is also supported by this analysis; another of its assumptions is that Macedonio Fernández was attempting what Foucault might call an epistemic revolution. Finally, many of Foucault's challenges to previously unquestioned categories of thought, such as the autonomy of author, are seen as prefigured by Macedonio Fernández. This prefiguring, I would argue, is simply a result of Macedonio's determination to create a renovated conception of the individual, necessitating a rethinking of the nature of categories such as author.

In effect, Macedonio is undertaking a resistance to power very similar to the one posited by Foucault in his discussion of the definition and study of power as discursive relations:

> They are struggles which question the status of the individual: on the one hand, they assert the right to be different and they underline everything which makes us truly individual. On the other hand, they attack everything which separates the individual, breaks his links with others, splits up community life, forces the individual back on himself and ties him to his own identity in a constraining way.
>
> These are struggles not exactly for or against the "individual," but rather they are struggles against the "government of individuation." (Foucault 1983, 211–12)

For Macedonio, the resistance to power entails devolving power onto the goodwill of individuals; the creation of a city constituted by ethical relations among individuals. These relations are so radically resistant to the polis and its discourses that they can only be articulated in a new invention of the novel: *Museo de la Novela de la Eterna*.

The persistence of subsequent generations in reading Macedonio as a mythological persona, disconnected from context and yet woven into history, is a perpetuation of the same kinds of power dynamics Macedonio resisted. Macedonio identified these discourses of power in specific practices and institutions: literary, social, and political, medical and corporal. And this resistance to them was a systematic attack on their definition and maintenance of the human subject, under the guise of, in Foucault's words, "salvation" (1983, 215). To cite Foucault again, Macedonio's goal is:

> to liberate us both from the state and the type of individuation which is linked to the state. We have to promote new forms of subjectivity through the refusal of this kind of individuality which has been imposed on us for several centuries. (1983, 216)

It is important to recognize here that the present study does not propose to examine power relations in interwar Argentina through the lens of Macedonio Fernández's prose: this is not a study of culture as such. On the contrary, the analysis of context throughout this book serves to elucidate the nature of Macedonio's writing, particularly as a means to address concepts previously regarded as irreconcilable, and to rescue Macedonio from the mythological persona imposed upon him, at odds with his purpose.

Of course, such a reliance on a set of contemporary theories annunciated by one person runs the risk of hypocrisy. How does one avoid repeating the same sort of anachronistic reading that prior critics stand accused of? The answer lies in taking care not to ascribe to Macedonio the same cultural perspective as Foucault. While Macedonio's poetics bear out many of the principles Foucault observes, Macedonio never performs an analogous "archaeology" on culture. Rather than attempting to study and manage cultural context, Macedonio Fernández confronts it. He would have had no inkling as to what an archaeology of culture might mean, or how to go about it. Nor would Macedonio accept Foucault's empirical and historical analysis of power relations. In fact, Macedonio's raison d'être runs completely counter to Foucault's observation that "a society without power relations can only be an abstraction" (1983, 222–23). Such is *exactly* the society Macedonio strove for.

In the same vein, one must keep in mind the Achilles' heal in Foucault's analysis: the fact that the archaeologist is unavoidably informed by the culture in which he or she operates. This weakness is revealed, for example, in Foucault's idea of epistemic rupture, which bears too close a resemblance to the avant-garde's own assertion of rupture with artistic tradition. It is for this reason that Foucault turns to archaeology—the study of empirical evidence. Accordingly, this study attempts to base its assertions, as much as possible, on textual evidence and on historical documents or studies citing historical evidence. In this respect, we are but one more link in the chain of thought informed by empirical method. Macedonio too, while not interested in reading or writing history, was convinced of the indispensability of empirical method for questioning the ascendancy of empiricism.

A similar caveat applies to our use of Lacanian terms, if not exactly Lacanian conclusions, in our consideration of Macedonio's conception and reworking of the self. The Lacanian approach to self and identity, while clearly relevant to an analysis of Macedonio's works, must also be employed with caution as to its anachronistic aspects. An important detail often cited but seldom investigated is Macedonio's fascination with the work of William James, who was devoted to the empirical, scientific analysis of consciousness and character.[2] The attractiveness of Lacanian readings of Macedonio's work and life may have more to do with Lacan's own debt to William James than with any inherently Lacanian approach, in Macedonio's works, to the paradox of self-constitution in language. While we acknowledge the usefulness of Lacanian concepts in reading Macedonio, the paradox of self and body, so integral to Lacanian interpretations, will not be allowed to stand unquestioned. Macedonio's conception of identity has more in common with Gertrude Stein—another disciple of William James—than with Borges, with whom Lacanian approaches may have more resonance. Macedonio's motives were analogous to Stein's, leading to the virtually diametric opposition between their conclusions (Garth 1991). This analogy helps elucidate the reasons for Macedonio's obsession with the physical as well as social components of self, an obsession Borges never fully understood. Those studies of Macedonio's writing that do undertake a Lacanian reading—Germán García's in particular—draw a portrait of a Macedonio Fernández who is not only hermetic, but who necessarily fails in his project to achieve a liberated, selfless "jouissance." Our objective in applying Lancanian ideas is to reveal quite the opposite—that Macedonio persistently regarded writing as the only means to an alternative constitution of the individual, without a self.

Macedonio would be repelled by Lacanian conclusions that he might have died anything other than a supremely contented man.

Finally, this apology for method leads to one final—but imperative—consideration. By attributing both motive and method to Macedonio Fernández's works and acts, we effectively endow him with an authorial self, one of the very things he most energetically fought. Such an infraction, we hope, is excused by the fact that no more satisfactory vehicle exists for the study of literature in context. Dispensing with the author altogether leads to attributing to "the text" all responsibility for meaning, or for response to context. While such a privileging of text may satisfy convinced deconstructionists, it does not really answer basic questions about how that context, or even prior texts, are being read.

The solution to this dilemma is provisional: the postulating of an author, both inferred and deduced, who is a reader of context and of other texts. This postulation is analogous to Pascal's wager on God's existence. This posited author purposely takes into account Kristeva's notion of author—myth elaborated by subsequent generations. If this projected author fails to correspond faithfully to either a biographically deduced entity or a textually inferred phenomenon, at least it incorporates some of the merits of both. It also reflects the same conundrum Macedonio himself confronted: how to repudiate the static, autonomous category of author and liberate text without sacrificing the individual's *investment* in text. Macedonio's solution, also perpetually and forcibly provisional, was to endlessly posit an individual, always in concrete terms, whose slippery relationship to text was proof of authorship without selfhood. Our solution is not so different, except that it extends that slippery relationship to context as well as text.

2
The Myth of the Accidental Author

CRITICAL TO THE UNDERPINNINGS OF THIS STUDY ARE MACEDONIO'S ATTItudes about his own individual identity: his sense of physical presence, his feeling of engagement in or irrelevancy to civic life and, most crucial here, his stance as author and his relationship to his own texts. This last question is the one critics and Martinfierrista writers rely on most heavily to maintain Macedonio's indifference to all aspects of material existence: his lack of interest in disseminating his own writing. Yet Macedonio himself was acutely aware of the potential consequences of his evident ambivalence toward publishing. Ironically, he reveals his awareness in a comment often cited by scholars as evidence for his absolute indifference:

> Nací porteño y en un año muy 1874. No entonces enseguida, pero sí apenas despúes, ya empecé a ser citado por Jorge Luis Borges con tan poca timidez de encomios que por el terrible riesgo a que se expuso con esta vehemencia comencé yo a ser el autor de lo mejor que él había producido. (*Recienvenido* 90; Lindstrom 1981, 16; Rodríguez Monegal 1952, 177)[1]

> [I was born *porteño* in a year very 1874. Not right away, but very shortly afterwards I began to be cited by Jorge Luis Borges with so little restraint of praise that through the terrible risk to which he exposed himself with this vehemence I started to become the author of the best of what he had produced.][2]

Early on, Macedonio noted that his ambivalence toward publishing and self-promotion could result in attributing to him ideas and perspectives he never intended to claim. Not only was Macedonio aware of the risks inherent in his status as a "famous unknown author," he was worried about the consequences.

The fact that the preponderance of his work was published posthumously has been the primary evidence of Macedonio's reputed indifference to publishing. Ana Camblong shows us, however, that Macedonio's famous reluctance to take the initiative to publish, especially to publish *Museo de la Novela de la Eterna*, his most read and discussed work, resulted from complex and deeply ambivalent ideas about the nature of authoring, promoting, and publishing one's own writing. While Macedonio indeed published little in his lifetime, he was in fact obsessed with the promotion and eventual dissemination of his supposed masterwork. The perpetual postponement of its culmination was integral to Macedonio's iconoclastic stance toward publication and self-promotion in general. Throughout his writing, both in prose works and in correspondence, Macedonio is obsessed with alternative means of self-promotion in advance of his eventual, constantly deferred, never-accomplished, entry onto the literary scene. Never publishing *Museo* meant never allowing this self-promotion to result in self-realization. Accordingly, Macedonio is always a *recienvenido*, a newcomer to the literary world, and never an established presence in it. And yet, as both Camblong and Bueno have shown, Macedonio very much wanted *Museo* to be read (Bueno 2000, 101–2). Perhaps he hoped someone else would see his major works to publication; references to *Museo* in his letters (*Epistolario*, 25, 37, 51, 53, 55, 61, 90, 153, 189–90, 191) as well as his willingness to share the manuscript, suggest as much. It is equally possible that Macedonio was astute to how a reliance on others could prove compromising.

Macedonio's obsession with creating readership outside the established channels of publication resulted in a lifelong act of pure genius—the campaign in absence: the self-promotion without an identifiable self; the perpetual, as-yet-unpublished newcomer to the literary world; the *autor accidentado*, or accidental author. In 1921, Macedonio launched a farcical run for the Argentine presidency that served as a paradigm for this campaign in absence. This campaign was revisited in 1927, when, according to Carlos García, it became the basis for the campaign to conquer Buenos Aires for beauty invoked in *Museo de la Novela de la Eterna* (C. García 2000, 32–37, 41n, 43–44). The stated objective of the original campaign was the "dissemination of the name" Macedonio Fernández without the presence of any person connected to that name (Borges 1961, 17; Abós 2002, 103). But even this undertaking served, ultimately, as a component for the mythology. Today's store of anecdotes about Macedonio, the peculiar philosophical hermit, routinely include some of his more outlandish campaign tactics (G. García 1996, 71;

1975, 23; Fernández-Latour 1980, 16; Isaacson 1981, 67–68; Abós 2002, 101–5).

Macedonio's characterization as the Socrates of Buenos Aires blossomed and endured well before his death in 1952. It was a legend perpetuated largely through anecdote, much of it apocryphal, and much of it generated by Martinfierrista writers, Borges not the least among them. The legend certainly persists today, its varied episodes having agglomerated into a mythology. Indeed, Macedonio's stature in Argentine letters still seems to rest mainly on this mythology. Even the most tentative of inquiries among Buenos Aires's literary community will yield colorful (and in a brief time, familiar) anecdotes about Macedonio's peculiar lifestyle, his wanderings, his primitive lodgings, his acquaintance with prostitutes, his unsanitary habits, and above all, the superiority of his personal conversation to his written texts. Less easy to find are people who can claim to have read many of Macedonio's writings. Among literary historians, Macedonio's importance still seems to lie primarily in his friendship with and influence on Borges, in his role as a figurehead for the avant-garde movement, and as a foil for Leopoldo Lugones and his *modernistas* (Fernández Moreno 1977, 45).

According to this legend, not only did Macedonio's writing pale compared to his conversation, but he himself considered writing to be secondary. His failure to publish, it is assumed, is a consequence of that deprecation of writing itself. The question at this juncture concerns how the brilliant initial gesture of the campaign in absence led to the creation of a mythological figure: the figure of a Socrates who deprecated his own writing and shunned publication. To understand the evolution of this legend, one must turn to the momentous reencounter between Macedonio and Borges.

Borges's Myth Ready-Made

In 1921, a young Jorge Luis Borges returned to Buenos Aires from Switzerland via Spain, possessed by the new and radical aesthetic sensibilities he had absorbed in Europe and eager to transplant them to his native turf (Borges 1997, 135; Fernández Moreno 1977b, 34–35). Meeting the Borges family at the dock was the family friend and Jorge senior's former law school companion, Macedonio Fernández. Borges was astonished and delighted to encounter in this friend of his father's generation many of the same radical sensibilities he brought with him from Europe. Macedonio, Borges discovered, had been sitting in complete isolation from the cosmopolitan fervor of Europe yet had come up with a startlingly new vision of the world and the means to express that vision. Borges immediately determined that Macedonio's philosophical and aesthetic vision deserved dissemination.

Over the next forty-five years, Borges, along with other avantgarde writers of the Argentine Generación Martinfierrista, made periodic concerted efforts to establish Macedonio's reputation as a founding father of modern Argentine culture, a founder of mythological proportions, simultaneously definitive of Argentine culture and transcendent to its texts. Within ten years after the initial "discovery" of Macedonio—and more than twenty years before his death—this conversion from local character to living mythological figure was established enough to be summarized in an indelible portrait by Raúl Scalabrini Ortiz:

> El primer metafísico de Buenos Aires y el único filósofo auténtico es Macedonio Fernández. Su libro "No toda es vigilia la de los ojos abiertos" es ya una biblia esotérica del espíritu porteño. Todo lo que se pueda decir, ya está en él. Lástima que sólo pocos elegidos pueden salvar el escollo de su idioma enmarañado. Es un alegato pro pasión, un ataque al intelectualismo extenuante. Su filosofía es la filosofía de un porteño: es la quintaesencia, lo más puro, lo más acendrado del espíritu de Buenos Aires. Por eso está sólo y espera; él es también, en gran parte, un eslabón en que el espíritu de la tierra se encarna. Posiblemente seguirá solo y seguirá esperando. Y así por los siglos de los siglos, porque Macedonio ya está para siempre el primero y más grande en la secuela de profetas porteños. Amén. (Scalabrini Ortiz 1931, 123)

> [The first metaphysical thinker of Buenos Aires and its only authentic philosopher is Macedonio Fernández. His book, "No toda es vigilia la de los ojos abiertos," has already become an esoteric bible of the Porteño spirit. Anything that can be said is already in it. It is a pity that only a few chosen can navigate the reefs of its tangled language. It is a plea in favor of passion, an attack on exhausting intellectualism. His philosophy is the philosophy of a Porteño: it is the quintessence, the purest, the most distilled of the spirit of Buenos Aires. This is why he is alone and waits; he is also, in large measure, a link into which the spirit of the land joins. Possibly he shall continue alone and shall continue to wait. And thus it shall be for centuries of centuries, as Macedonio is forever the first and greatest in the line of Porteño prophets. Amen.]

This passage from Scalabrini's best-selling *El hombre que está solo y espera* (The Man Who Stands Alone and Waits, 1931), setting the stage for a virtual apotheosis, served to solidify Macedonio's reputation as a reclusive, Socratic figure, interested in passion and metaphysics as opposed to society, and in conversing as opposed to writing. Reading this tribute, one can see how Macedonio, while still relatively young, should metamorphose from a living cult figure into a veritable mythological one.

Had it not been for Borges's and Scalabrini's efforts, Macedonio might have remained unknown even to Argentines and to the Latin American writers and critics—such as Ricardo Piglia (1988), Alicia Borinsky (1993), Naomi Lindstrom (1981), and Noé Jitrik (1973)—who regard him as fundamental to modern and contemporary literature of the region. Borges and Scalabrini saw to the publication of *No toda es vigilia la de los ojos abiertos* (1928) and *Papeles de Recienvenido* (1929), the only two monographs Macedonio published in Argentina in his lifetime. But these same efforts also contributed to detaching the texts from their author and the author from his context, a situation exacerbated by the fact that most of his work remained unpublished until the 1970s, twenty to thirty years after his death. The severance of texts and context from writer is one reason Macedonio Ferndández's works are almost universally read through a postmodern lens.

Challenging these interrelated traditions—the mythology of Macedonio as a hermitlike philosopher and the practice of postmodern readings of his works—requires examining two interrelated processes. One must examine some of the mechanisms of mythologizing employed by Borges, his generation of writers, and Macedonio himself. It also is important to query Macedonio's motives for collaborating—up to a point—in this process. As part of this examination, it is useful to take a close look at one key text of Macedonio's as a means of deducing how his own self-presentation and self-projection run counter to the mythology and the postmodern readings it has engendered. A reconsideration of Macedonio's writing reveals that the mythological Macedonio in many ways obscures and contradicts Macedonio's own radical notions about the concepts of author, self, and identity.

Confused Oratory

A good starting point for investigating Macedonio's role in cultivating his own mythology is a little-discussed passage found in *Papeles de Recienvenido*, Macedonio Fernández's second published volume (in 1929) and the only work he published twice (again in 1944). *Recienvenido* is really an anthology of passages, many of them first delivered orally, from the ten or so years prior to its first publication. The passage in question is designated by Jo Anne Engelbert as constituting Macedonio's debut on the Buenos Aires literary scene, the first of his famous *brindis*, or oral dedications, delivered to a banquet of literary figures in 1924 (Engelbert 1978, 29–30). "La oratoria del hombre confuso" (The Confused Man's Oratory) was not delivered by Macedonio himself, who had a legendary aversion to public speaking. Instead, it was delivered by Enrique Fernández Latour to an audience gathered to pay tribute to Uruguayan artist Pedro Figari. Macedonio, the author of this speech, it is important to note, was present in that audience.

Also noteworthy is the fact that although it is an important, arguably formative, moment in the development of the mythology of the accidental author, the "Oratoria" is certainly not the moment of its birth. Macedonio's coming out as literary newcomer had been anticipated for at least three years, since his "discovery" by Borges in 1921. In 1923, Macedonio's literary "debut" had also been documented by Borges, in a published review of a book Macedonio never wrote (Borges 1923). Borges initiates his mythology that same year with the publication in Madrid of Macedonio's poem dedicated to Borges, "Al hijo de un amigo" (To a Friend's Son) in an anthology of Argentine poets; significantly, Borges's commentary in this volume already privileges Macedonio's conversation over his writing (Bueno 2000, 92; C. García 2000, 48–51). By 1923, Macedonio was already established in a small literary circle as an absent participant and an unknown, unpublished author.

In his first public presentation, his already anticipated coming-out as a literary recienvenido, or newcomer, to Buenos Aires, Macedonio Fernández turns presentation, presence, and performance upside down. He subverts the terms of author and audience, actor and spectator, for he is absent as author but present as spectator to his own literary tribute. He also subverts the terms of tribute, refusing the authority to pay homage to the guest of honor. The "Oratoria" consists of a long, digressive and frankly weird account of the narrator's troubles caused by "el uso de la palabra" [use of the word] (51). The point of the account, it turns out, is to excuse the narrator's demurral of his very reason for being, that is, to offer a tribute. According to this account, certain "oratory experiments" or "experiences" (*experimentos*) have led Macedonio to shun the role of an author of tributes and to refuse "de dirigiros una sola palabra en el acto de homenaje que os tributamos" [to address a single word to you in the act of homage we are offering you] (53).

The *experimento,* or "use of the word," that launches this bizarre adventure is a very peculiar kind of tribute: a *priropo,* or in Macedonio's words, a *"palabra,"* to a passing lady, while seated at a sidewalk café, resulting in physical violence being done to the narrator. The consequence of his "word" is a blow from a policeman's billy club, which

> hizo dos mitades de mi elocuencia y aun tuve que dividir ésta con un vigilante que se había tenido oculto en mitad de la calzada. (51–52)
>
> [broke my eloquence in two and I yet had to divide this with an officer who had been in hiding in the middle of the road.]

As tempting as it is to conclude that the "Oratoria" is simply a humorous, nonsensical attempt to confound the terms of rendering homage and the social practices allowing that homage, closer examination shows that there is a great deal more going on here. Macedonio accepts an invitation to speak to a public, and to render tribute to an individual. But he uses the opportunity instead to expose the perils inherent in the language of tribute and the dilemma afflicting all public speech in modern society. He aims to reveal the error of performance innate in modern-day use of language.

Utterances, Macedonio suggests, no matter how sincere, heartfelt, and pure (Macedonio Fernández consistently protested his own purity, his own freedom from prurience), are trapped by their subjectivity to our physicality, geometric and clinical as well as sexual. Speech is subject to social, economic, and political structures and the authority they constitute, as well as to place, property, and, as Borges later tells us, to history. Macedonio was acutely aware of these dilemmas.

The "Oratoria," moreover, features a preoccupation characteristic of *Papeles de Recienvenido* and virtually unique to that volume: the violence fostered by this dilemma. The subjectivity constituted in language inevitably leads to violent conflict, and Macedonio seeks an escape:

> El dolor que sentía en aquel de los hombros arriba del cual pende una oreja no era de muelas ni de primera dentición sino del primer uso

de la palabra. A mí me parecía que una vereda completa de las de frente a Plaza Congreso me había acertado en la clavícula. (52)

[The pain I felt in the one shoulder above which hangs an ear was not from wisdom teeth or from first teething but from the first use of the word. It seemed to me as if an entire sidewalk from in front of the Plaza Congreso had struck me on the collarbone.][3]

What is the escape from this dilemma, from this prison house of language, from the physicality, sociality, and historicity it binds us to, and from the violence it fosters? The narrator tells us of a second encounter with authorities threatening his well-being, then provides the solution in a neat verbal trick:

Pero en un movimiento político del cual yo ocupaba la acera—siempre las veredas me han dejado en la calle—pronuncié el siguiente discurso de espectador: "Viva el Presidente Cristóbal Colón Avellaneda". Al instante de terminarlo me vi rodeado de una baratura de bastones como no es de creer dado el alto costo de la mano de obra, los que estaban ya levantados, de modo que hecho el trabajo principal, nada era bajarlos en favor mío y de la ley de la gravitación de las manzanas universales mondada por Newton. Por esta vez me reemplacé yo mismo; con celeridad inapresurable hice ausencia de mi presencia y modestia de mi engreimiento. (52)

[But in a political uprising in which I held the pavement—sidewalks have always left me out in the street—I pronounced the following spectator's speech: "Long live President Christopher Columbus Avellaneda." The instant I finished it I saw myself encircled by so many billy clubs up for a song one wouldn't believe it given the high cost of manpower, already raised so that the main work having been done, it was nothing to lower them in my favor and in favor of the law, picked by Newton, of the gravitation of universal apples. This time I replaced myself; with unhastenable celerity I made absence of my presence and modesty of my self-indulgence.]

To make absence out of presence, submission out of the exercise of authority; refusal, in effect, of that first opportunity to speak: that is Macedonio's solution to this dilemma language has placed him in. In Lacanian terms, it is a rebirth, a return to the moment prior to the one in which language allowed us constitution of ourselves as subjects and led us to the error of performance (Lacan 1968, 60–65, 83–84).[4]

Macedonio himself, in fact, refers to the process in just these terms. In the opening lines of the "Oratoria," the narrator speaks of the "mischief" (*travesura*) caused by the "use of the word." But rather than first recounting his mishap, he begins by remarking on "finding himself at home" after his contretemps, comparing this homecoming to a kind of resurrection. It is perhaps more accurate to call the experience an "undeadness," or a "realization of not being unborn," for the narrator describes it as a "recuerdo de resurrección: un bienestar de sobreviviente tras malestar de persona que está naciendo" [the memory of a resurrection: the well-being of a survivor coming after the discomfort of a person who is being born] (*Recienvenido* 51).

The narrator develops this notion further in the lines that follow. The use of "the word" allows him to soothe the "discomfort" brought on by birth by "certifying" his presence and the "authority" of his voice. He does so by asking his parlormaid for a glass of water, with the "*ánimo*" characteristic of a "muerto interrumpido o un interrumpido de morrer" [a dead man interrupted or a man interrupted in dying]. We, in effect, become subject when our voice allows us to subject another, such as a maid, and, in the process, keep death at bay. But speech, and the consequent ability to account for ourselves that constitutes consciousness, also effects a rebirth, an initial founding of self that follows the initializing birth, a moment that is renewed with each use of speech. Herein is Macedonio's problem. And the solution, also perfectly logical, is to revert the terms of that rebirth, making it a moment of absenting one's self instead of presenting one's self.

For Macedonio, this return or rebirth is the ultimate transgression, for it refuses to accept conflicts, or "difference" in Derrida's terms, as being inherent to language and the human condition. In this sense, Macedonio is completely at odds with Lacan's conclusions regarding this difference. Macedonio proposes, in this rebirth, to escape the sexuality (that is, physical desire, which he often refers to as bestial, animalistic) and the violence or cruelty we are bound to by our language, and which eventually our language in its rawest, least premeditated form always reduces us to.

Reference to falling is also frequent in *Papeles de Recienvenido*. But having acknowledged the inescapability of falling, Macedonio transgresses its accepted principles. Suddenly Newton's "universal" laws are pointedly discarded, and falling takes on a completely new relationship with the human experience, much as it does in Huidobro's

Altazor. Recienvenido's fall is thus not a fall from original grace, not a fall out of pure being, pure innocence in and oneness with the cosmos; it is not a fall into the subjectivity wrought by the knowledge that language constitutes. Macedonio's fall—his rebirth—is a fall out of difference, out of the laws that confirm subjectivity, and into pure being, as Macedonio calls it repeatedly throughout his writings.[5] The very act of writing constitutes the quintessential "productive" fall, the descent out of one's self that leads to a fullness of being (J. Prieto 2002, 158–59).

Thus Macedonio Fernández's public debut as an author, his entry into the literary world, marked by this first public speech at an event in tribute to an artist, serves as the announcement of his rebirth as an author, his arrival as a literary newcomer and public presence. But simultaneously, this same entry and rebirth serve to repudiate the very terms of authorship and presence. On the one hand, the rebirth occurs on his own terms, and completely reconfigures the parameters of author and subject by refusing "el uso de la palabra" and the violent presence it constitutes. On the other hand, it openly and aggressively exploits the tools of self-promotion begun several years earlier with Borges's bogus book review. Macedonio not only agrees to participate in the literary community and the events it organizes to promote itself, he seizes the occasion with extraordinary force. Reading over the "Oratoria," it is easy to believe that his preparations for this moment were both calculated and thorough. For the next twenty years, Macedonio will be exploiting and subverting language, literature, and their various arenas of production and presentation; he will consistently tread the fine line between facilitating a mythology and perpetuating myth.

From Absent Myth to Literary Phantom

Although he never refers to myth, the identity that Macedonio Fernández was elaborating for himself corresponds in many ways to a mythical being. Mythical is the identity without a self, the individual who strives to make himself known yet refuses to appear. Mythical is the personality who is perpetually born and reborn, and whose death is perpetually postponed or interrupted. To this mythical end are the "Oratoria" in absentia, the campaign in absence, and the writer forever preparing to publish but never submitting himself for publication. The outcome of this campaign is an identity constituted entirely by language but refusing to be subjected by it. The myth of the accidental author was no accident.

Macedonio's challenge is to create and perpetuate this elusive, mythlike identity for himself while simultaneously precluding its consolidation into a defined persona with a prior and autonomous self. The predicament is especially complex since Macedonio takes advantage of the avant-garde literary fervor of the moment to foster his efforts. Macedonio's own oblique involvement with, and comments on, this avant-garde activity demonstrate his awareness of the delicacy of his position. On the one hand, his avant-garde comrades help realize the perfusion into the city of the mythical accidental author. On the other hand, this same association with the avant-garde risks reifying that myth into a fixed subject for an Argentine mythology.

If, as this "Oratoria" tells us, Macedonio's resurrection takes place at home, it can only occur as the result of this venture into public. Moreover, the public arena is comprehensive: it comprises the intimate words proffered to a passing lady at a sidewalk café as well as political demonstrations vociferated in a public plaza. It also embraces the various disciplines that shape the culture Macedonio inhabits. The "Oratoria" implicates these disciplines with extraordinary efficiency. Delving into the origins of his troublemaking speech, the narrator explains:

> Tuve siglos antes uno preparado de encargo para recibir a Colón en su segundo viaje que efectuaba bajo instrucciones de hacer cuanto antes el descubrimiento de América, no fuera que los nativos lo verificaran primero que él. Pero como sucede con estos paseos apurados, muchos quedan sin hacer; y los historiadores han establecido que no hubo segundo viaje de Colón sino únicamente primero y tercero. (*Recienvenido* 52)

> [I had centuries earlier prepared one to order to receive Columbus on his second voyage, which he performed under instructions to carry out the discovery of America straight away, lest the natives verify it first. But as happens with these rushed outings, many are left undone; and historians have established that there was no second voyage of Columbus but only a first and a third.]

This short paragraph, together with the previously cited excerpts from the same address, throws into question both the foundational myths defining Spanish America's historical identity (Columbus's nonexistent second voyage) and the scientific method serving as

Western modernity's way of thinking (Newton's contrived falling apples).

But most crucial, the public arena that Macedonio simultaneously courts and eschews is centered on the Buenos Aires aesthetic revolution. In one sense, the standard assessment of Macedonio's "discovery" by Borges and his contemporaries is an accurate representation of the situation. Macedonio's choice of the moment at which to perform his debut as accidental author makes clear his recognition of the vital role this artistic community must play in his identity as an individual revolutionary. Moreover, both the content of this "Oratoria" and its peculiar form of delivery emphasize Macedonio's iconoclastic—and paradoxical—posture with regard to this avant-garde ferment. Macedonio poises just outside of the avant-garde, or above it, always invited but never joining, always revered but never worshipped, wandering omnipresent within the walls of the city but never engaged in its politics. It is also no accident that Macedonio's reputation precedes him wherever and whenever he allows himself to materialize, but especially prior to that moment of his subverted debut as a literary *recienvenido* and a giver of tributes, when he finally refuses the podium and fails to arrive. Macedonio's perpetration as myth is inseparable from his elusive relationship to the Martinfierrista generation.

The legend of the accidental author, on the other hand, requires elaboration by others determined to assign Macedonio his place in a national literature: indeed, an ineffable, founding place. To the Generación Martinfierrista, and to Borges especially, Macedonio is the individual incarnation of a cultural foundation mythology: *mythos* merged with *logos*, archived, institutionalized, and nonevolving. Macedonio wants to inventory history in order to repudiate it as irrelevant and insubstantial. His heirs, in contrast, want to inventory it in order to establish it as irreducible and absolute. To them, Macedonio is the founding father, the mythology behind which to reduce all of modern artistic expression in Argentina. Buenos Aires has gotten its *fantasma*.

But of course, myths and ghosts do not write books, and they certainly do not publish them, any more than Socrates could be the author of a Platonic dialogue or of his own enshrinement in Athenian culture. The Martinfierrista generation indeed loved Macedonio like a father. But in their failure to understand the most fundamental aspects of his writing, they made him a founding father, a mythological father, disconnected from the concerns of publishing and publicity, thus robbing his writing of the power to maintain his absence. David Viñas puts it rather neatly, arguing that Macedonio was the Argentine avant-garde's only bow to the past and to myth: "a un padre nadie lo exhibe; lo reverencia o lo mata" [nobody puts their father on display; they either worship him or kill him] (Viñas 1971, 64). As Horacio González tells us, the Martinfierristas did both. They kept Macedonio Fernández's persona alive, by "convertir la devoción a Macedonio en la epopeya de oralidad" [converting the cult of Macedonio into an epic of orality] (H. González 1995, 173). It is an epic comprising anecdotes and homages and tributes—including a graveside eulogy delivered by Jorge Luis Borges. They preserved Macedonio's authorship of his texts, but at the same time killed the absent Macedonio invested in those texts, burying and refuting "la secreta ambición a seriedad macedoniana" [Macedonio's secret ambition to seriousness] (174). For Macedonio, the obsession with writing, publishing and publicity was essential to staying perpetually a newcomer. Borges cared not for newcomers, he needed ghosts, and Macedonio Fernández was the ideal candidate.

If Scalabrini opened the way for the mythologizing of Macedonio Fernández, Borges is most responsible for completing the process. There is obvious irony in a graveside eulogy, Borges's most famous and widely read commentary on Macedonio, published verbatim in the following issue of *Sur* (Borges 1952). Celebrating the death of a man who devoted a good part of his life to combating the concept of self, Borges chooses the moment of his "eternalization" to represent and archive Macedonio in a portrait that can accurately be called mythological. Moreover, this portrait assertively reinforces the picture of a writer—or rather, a thinker—uninterested in his own identity and unburdened with any investment in his texts.

Borges enhances this portrait eight years later with the forward to his edition of select writings of Macedonio. He begins this portrait with a characterization worthy of Scalabrini's near deification:

> Mi última emoción, en Europa, fue el diálogo con el gran escritor judeo-español Rafael Cansinos Assens, en quien estaban todas las lenguas y todas las literaturas, como si él mismo fuera Europa y todos los ayeres de Europa. En Macedonio hallé otra cosa. Era como si Adán, el primer hombre, pensara y resolviera en el Paraíso los problemas fundamentales. Cansinos era la suma del tiempo y Macedonio, la joven eternidad (Borges 1960, 10).

> [My final emotional moment, in Europe, was my dialogue with the great Judeo-Spanish writer Rafael Cansinos-Assens, in whom were all lan-

guages and all literatures, as if he himself were Europe and all the yesterdays of Europe. In Macedonio I found something else. It was as if Adam, the first man, had thought through and resolved in Paradise the fundamental problems. Cansinos was the sum of time and Macedonio, young eternity.][6]

In addition to reinforcing the transcendence to time and context of Macedonio's thought, Borges simultaneously makes a point of contrasting the ethereal, ahistorical *and foundational* quality of the Argentine Macedonio's words to the encyclopedically historical *European* Cansinos.

In this same portrait, Borges reiterates his assertion of Macedonio as divested of any interest in his own texts. After several pages of now-infamous anecdotes (including a reminiscence on Macedonio's cache of stale *alfajores*—a kind of Argentine pastry—to this day a tired chestnut of Macedoniana in Buenos Aires), Borges informs his readers:

Macedonio no le daba el menor valor a su palabra escrita; al mudarse de alojamiento, no se llevaba los manuscritos de índole metafísica o literaria que se habían acumulado sobre la mesa y que llenaban los cajones y los armarios. Mucho se perdió así, acaso irrevocablemente. Recuerdo haberle reprochado esa distracción; me dijo que suponer que podemos perder algo es una soberbia, ya que la mente humana es tan pobre que está condenada a encontrar, perder y redescubrir siempre las mismas cosas. (15)

[Macedonio gave not the least value to his written word; upon changing lodgings, he did not take with him the literary and metaphysical manuscripts that had piled up on the table and that filled trunks and cabinets. Much was lost that way, perhaps irrevocably. I recall reproaching him for this absentmindedness; he told me that to suppose we can lose anything is arrogance, since the human mind is so poor it is condemned always to keep finding, losing and rediscovering the same things.]

This attribution resounds a bit suspiciously of Borges's own perspective on the nature of knowledge. Although there is no certainty that Borges himself did not first learn such ideas from Macedonio, it is significant that nowhere in his writings does Macedonio voice precisely this sentiment. Others, including Adolfo de Obieta, reiterate Macedonio's lack of initiative to publish and his tendency to lose or discard his own writings (Camblong xlvi-ii). But to dismiss the necessity of publishing one's words is not the same as disdaining one's writing.[7]

Macedonio's self-effacement, however complex and engaged, is also ingenuous and spontaneous. Many of his compatriots, most notably his son Adolfo de Obieta, attest to his shyness, his indifferent health, his peripatetic lifestyle, his disaffection from material comforts or, for that matter, from the material substance of writing. The volume of what Macedonio left unpublished, and arguably unwritten, is probably greater than what is contained in his *Obras completas*. *Museo de la Novela de la Eterna*, eternally promised, continually evolving (Camblong has identified seven manuscript variations), never realized in book form during Macedonio's lifetime, is the masterwork without a master, the ultimate vehicle of self-effacement.

Rather than signaling a disregard for his own writing, it is more likely that Macedonio's reluctance to publish stems from a great preoccupation with the ultimate value of his words. Camblong's research reveals as much, both in Macedonio's own comments about the eventual fate of his manuscripts and in the evidence that Macedonio reworked some of those manuscripts—particularly the manuscript of *Museo*—obsessively. The redundancy of Macedonio's writing, including repeated verbal tricks, metaphors and paradoxes, suggests that Macedonio hoped to disseminate his ideas through sheer volume and frequency—and through the random abandonment of texts—rather than through the established channels of publication.

Borges acknowledges Macedonio's interest in the "mechanism of fame" as opposed to the acquisition of fame itself. In describing Macedonio's campaign for the presidency, however, Borges's error is in assuming that the "diffusion del nombre" (dissemination of name) was, for Macedonio as for other campaigners, preliminary to dissemination of a *persona*. The posthumous anecdotes and the legend they constitute, circulated by Borges, other writers of his generation, and heirs to Argentina's avant-garde legacy, are in effect a means of creating and maintaining such a persona.

This appropriation of Macedonio's words and deeds fails to account for his particular perspective on the nature of names and identity. The perpetual, infinite dissemination of a name is, for Macedonio, the *counteractant* to the establishment of a public persona. Macedonio's persistent, unrestrained and evidently indiscriminate issuing of words is undertaken precisely in order to frustrate the possibility that an abstract identity as "philosopher," "author," or even "citizen" might ever solidify. This motivation is the same one as for Macedonio's absenting himself for the delivery of his first-ever public address, his words of homage to another public self and his supposed debut as an artistic persona. It is also why, as he tells us in that "Oratoria," Macedonio must absent himself from the consequences of using words in any way that allow for such a persona.

Throughout much of Macedonio's writing run obsessions with both the physical body (especially the author's own) and the political city. Even the cursory glance taken here at the "Oratoria" reveals these obsessions and their interrelationship. The "offering of the word" has *corporal* consequences; the pronouncement of a public address engages a *political* discourse. Accordingly, the "Oratoria's" inversion of the acts of tribute and performance respond directly to Porteño social and cultural constructions of the body and the city. It is not the material world that must be rejected, nor the words used to obtain that world. What Macedonio attacks is the use of words to construe an autonomous self for the body, and to contrive a personified political identity for the city.

The anecdotal legends, then, give us a Macedonio Fernández virtually opposite from the one found constituted by Macedonio's own writing. Borges and Scalabrini give us a father, a legend, a mythological figure, a figure who remains unchanged after death, quite severed from the texts he supposedly cared little about. The Macedonio who writes and disseminates his writing exposes himself entirely—and exclusively—in his texts. Exposed are the components of an individual—an aesthetic sensibility, a social and political being, a corporeal entity—but most pointedly not a self. "Self," for Macedonio, is the function of institutions and establishments, and serves largely to legitimize and perpetuate them. He considers self a concept as deleterious to the individual as it is artificial to human nature. A constant in Macedonio's life and works is his refusal to ever impose himself, by means of words, deeds or physical presence. This insistence was clearly a function of always endeavoring to acknowledge a self that might impose. By recapturing the individual, reflected in words that respond to his context, readings of Macedonio's texts can attempt to rescue him from a self that others have imposed on him.

3
An Avant-garde Apart

THE CONTINUED SUCCESS OF THE MYTHOLOGY OF MACEDONIO FERNÁNDEZ depends in large measure on convincingly portraying him as indifferent to, or transcendent to, his literary environment. And there is ample evidence, including repeated statements by Macedonio himself, to support that view. The elusiveness that characterizes his period of greatest literary activity, coinciding with the greatest avant-garde ferment in Buenos Aires, attests to an ambivalence toward the very artistic environment that nourished his reputation as both a great thinker and a radically new kind of author. His much-cited qualities of reclusiveness, hypochondria, asceticism, and shyness reinforce the portrait of an artist-philosopher utterly removed from the influences of his physical, social, and cultural environment.

One reason this view has gone largely unquestioned is because unappreciated differences between Macedonio and the writers of the Martinfierrista generation of the 1920s have obscured and contorted critics' reception of their similarities. Many of these differences reflect Macedonio's recognition of the inadequacies of avant-garde poetics to solve fundamental cultural problems. Always conscious of these inadequacies, Macedonio remained simultaneously apart from and a part of the Argentine avant-garde for consciously aesthetic and ethical reasons.[1] While he seized upon what he saw as the fruitful aspects of avant-garde poetics and practices, he distanced himself from those aspects that—unknown to the Martinfierristas themselves—ran counter to his own poetic and ethical vision.

Macedonio's poetics in many ways coincide much more closely to the principles of the historical avant-garde in Europe, at least when viewed retrospectively. That kinship with European movements is a result of Macedonio's faith in the relationship between art and daily life more than with adherence to aesthetic programs.[2] Much of the difficulty in reconciling Macedonio with his Argentine peers boils down to their different responses to the same problems. Macedonio is in complete accord with the Martinfierristas in their search for a new relationship between aesthetic practice and life experience. But for Macedonio, the reform of that relationship relies largely on a radical reconsideration of subjectivity. Macedonio exploited avant-garde techniques in order to expose the avant-garde movements' inadequate efforts to discard subjectivity.

When speaking of the "historical" avant-garde, we refer to a movement defined in quite narrow terms, both chronologically and canonically. In Argentina, it corresponds to aesthetic movements, from about 1920 to the early 1930s, built largely on, and reacting to, the aestheticism of *modernismo* and sympathetic to contemporaneous avant-garde movements in Europe. In Buenos Aires this includes primarily Argentine Ultraism, and later, the movement anchored by the magazine *Martín Fierro* and the legacy carried forward by the magazine *Sur.* Part of the difficulty in associating Macedonio Fernández with the avant-garde is this definition in terms of concrete literary schools or movements, self-identified by means of declarations or manifestoes, and until recently taken rather at face value by scholars.[3] This essentially European approach has proven inadequate to define an American phenomenon.[4] On the one hand, defining these schools according to European models ignores the specific cultural conditions which one set out to explore in the first place; on the other hand, defining Latin American avant-gardes purely in terms of local phenomena risks ghettoizing these movements, defining them strictly as a non-European cultural "other." As Beret Strong notes, this proceeding also tends to overlook fundamental differences among individual avant-garde poets (Strong 1997, 73).

Vicky Unruh effectively avoids this danger by defining Latin America's early twentieth century avant-gardes:

> not in terms of selected canonical works or individual authors' careers, but rather as a multifaceted cultural activity, manifested in a variety of creative endeavors and events seeking to challenge and redefine the nature and purpose of art. (1994, 2)

For Unruh, the avant-garde seeks "an active reengagement between art and experience" (22); Latin American vanguards feature both this general rearticulation of art with praxis and a more specific engagement with Latin American experience and Latin American contexts (23–26). Accordingly, Latin American avant-gardes maintain a constant tension between "transrational plenitude," or transcendent aesthetics, and cultural or contextual relevance. This tension is analogous to the paradoxical search by Latin American writers for a "linguistically pure space" simultaneous with a culturally and historically specific voice (28).

Typically, commentary on Macedonio Fernández has associated him with only the first half of this equation: aesthetic purity and metaphysical transcendence. The examination undertaken here, by contrast, finds in Macedonio Fernández a kind of "heteroglossia," to use Bakhtin's term, much in keeping with Pérez Firmat's analysis. Accordingly, Unruh's definition of Latin American avant-garde poetics will prove most valuable in assessing Macedonio's relationship to his contemporaries.[5] Like many of his avant-garde counterparts, and like Borges especially, Macedonio imbues his work with historical and literary antecedents in a way that opens those antecedents up to radical new readings. Macedonio's *Museo de la Novela de la Eterna* closely fits Pérez Firmat's description of the vanguard novel, especially in its characterization as leading a "dual existence" and negating "humanity."[6] Macedonio's works take this principle a step further. The negation of "humanity," in *Museo* and other works, is carefully engineered to reflect and refract the personality of its author while simultaneously problematizing the very concept of "author." Macedonio's writing comprises, among other things, a lifelong exercise in cultivating personality as a means of eradicating persona.

The differences in both intent and effect between Macedonio and his Martinfierrista counterparts can be accounted for in part by just this sort of critique, on Macedonio's part, of the institution of art and by his attempt to forge a new kind of integration of art and praxis.[7] Much of Macedonio's peculiar yet intimate relationship with members of the Argentine avant-garde, as well as his resonance with European avant-gardes, is inseparable from his response to his social and cultural context.

Macedonio Apart and a Part

Recognition of Macedonio Fernández as an integral member of the Argentine literary avant-garde has been halting and halfhearted at best. On the one hand, few literary scholars deny his importance to Argentine letters. The strength of his influence on Borges (or of a mutual influence between Borges and Macedonio) is widely acknowledged. On the other hand, no scholar has successfully argued—few have tried—that Macedonio's work is characteristic of the "classical," or historical avant-garde in Argentina.[8] He is not particularly noted as a poet, nor is his poetry typically considered avant-garde in nature, and he wrote no theater, where the preponderance of Argentina's avant-garde production of the 1920s and 1930s has been viewed as poetic and, more recently, theatrical.[9] His only direct association with one of Buenos Aires's many literary magazines was fleeting: he is believed to have served on the editorial board of *Proa*, a principal vehicle for the early Argentine avant-garde, for nine months.[10]

Often Macedonio has been classified as philosopher, or "thinker," a nomenclature he claimed to prefer. Critics who were active during Macedonio's lifetime, such as Guillermo de Torre (1965), and those subsequent, such as José Luis Romero (1965) or Jorge Schwartz (1991), take more or less at face value Macedonio's labeling himself a "metafísico," and mention him in terms of his place among, or response to, modern philosophers. Torre, unable to see much beyond Macedonio's verbal acrobatics, qualifies him as a "humorist," implying that he had only a marginal significance to the avant-garde movement (582–85). This classification is furthered by the emphatic pronouncements of cultural critics of the Martinfierrista generation, such as Borges and Scalabrini Ortiz.

An important exception is César Fernández Moreno, who unequivocally qualifies Macedonio as "a born avant-garde writer." But Fernández Moreno ignores many of the dramatic differences between Macedonio's poetics and those of the Ultraists and the Martinfierristas. He accommodates his omission of these disparities by implying that Macedonio's metaphysical conceits—such as the repudiation of the distinction between dreaming and wakefulness—are solutions to a purely aesthetic problem. He suggests that Macedonio's principal aim is to accomplish the Ultraist goal of "art independent of life." By adhering to the idea of an apolitical, noncontextual avant-garde in Argentina, Fernández-Moreno facilitates Macedonio's inclusion into the movement; but he also perpetuates the image of Macedonio as articulating an "absolute idealism," completely detached from the social and cultural vision that motivated the Martinfierrista generation (Fernández Moreno 1977b, 34–35).

In addition to adumbrating the misconceptions resulting from the mythological treatment of Macedonio Fernández by his Martinfierrista friends, it is important to acknowledge some commonplace truths: the likelihood that Macedonio never published anything purely of his own initiative (Engelbert 1978, 29), that the Argentine avant-garde came to him and not vice-versa (Scrimaglio 1974, 126), and that by the mid-1930s, Macedonio had become distanced from the writers of the Martinfierrista generation, Borges included (Abós 2002, 148, 178–80). Regarding the last point, there are reasons worth considering for this distance. Sources document a brief falling out between Macedonio and Borges in 1928, from which they never fully recovered their former intimacy (Abós 2002, 130). Given that part of Borges's strategy involved obscuring Macedonio's authorial ambitions, Macedonio may have been purposely omitted from Borges's literary vehicle of the 1930s, the *Revista multicolor de los sábados*. He was most certainly not of acceptable social or cultural tenor for Victoria Ocampo's *Sur*, the magazine founded in 1931 that soon become the ascendant Argentine literary journal (Strong 1997, 104). Also, Macedonio's secret relationship with Consuelo Saenz de Valiente, whose family openly opposed the conservative Uriburu government, may have distanced him from his former Martinfierrista companions after 1930.

But a reconsideration of what Macedonio defined as literature, and of his iconoclastic, paradoxical ways of dealing with literature's public functions, demands an equal reexamination of his participation in the public literary movement of the day. Despite his later reputation as a silent recluse, there is ample evidence that the Martinfierristas of the 1920s considered Macedonio one of their number. Macedonio was a regular, enthusiastic participant in the bohemian literary *tertulias* (discussion gatherings) of the decade, most significantly Alberto Hidalgo's *Revista Oral* (Oral Review). Although later accounts, as well as Macedonio's own self-deprecating contribution, refer to his frequent absence, it is clear that he considered himself a leading contributor and that he felt such gatherings to be of great value. A letter to Hidalgo, for example, urges:

> Todo el vanguardismo literario, música, pintura, etc., debiera reunirse y arribar a una reunión mensual en un local subordinado a nuestra tertulia, no nosotros al local. . . . Usted tiene lo que nadie posee y lo que todos le codician: la *Revista Oral*, que espero usted reanimará pronto. . . . El sábado, si no antes, nos veremos en el Royal. (*Epistolario* 88–90)

[All the vanguard—literary, music, painting, etc.—should join together and come to a monthly meeting at a locale subordinate to our gathering, we not at the locale. . . . You have what nobody possesses and what everyone covets: the *Oral Review*, which I hope you will soon revive. . . . Saturday, if not before, we will see each other at the Royal.]

The above citation is also a reminder that absence, to Macedonio, is a weighty and potent phenomenon. The implication in this advice to Hidalgo is that the acknowledged leaders of the Porteño avant-garde exercise their aesthetic influence most effectively by staying away from the "subordinate" happenings they inspire.

Even more intriguing is a letter (undated, probably 1926) to Borges that describes in some detail regular gatherings of bohemian artists at Macedonio's home in Morón, in the countryside outside of Buenos Aires (see C. García 2000, 6–7). The letter describes a shack Macedonio has rented, entirely at his own expense, to accommodate a group of a dozen or so men in a more or less continual nighttime tertulia: guitars, singing, unpretentious food and drink, and above all, the reading and discussion of philosophy. He goes on to tell Borges of his desire to assemble a more seriously artistic "inner circle" to include Borges and several other well known avant-garde writers, including Scalabrini Ortiz and Brandán Carrafa. He presents this scheme as the realization of a longstanding desire of both his and Borges.

These letters suggest that for a brief period at least, Macedonio was fully engaged in the avant-garde artistic community and regarded such gatherings, especially those away from the city, as the ideal environment for artistic invention. For a time, Macedonio enjoyed an active, mutual exchange with the writers of this generation, especially with Borges (Engelbert 1978, 26–44; Lindstrom 1981, 71). This is an essential aspect of Macedonio Fernández's writing that one must never lose sight of: even though he lived and worked in what appear to be hermitlike conditions, collegiality and community remained a constant standard in Macedonio's poetics. This emphasis on congeniality, indeed, makes for a sharp, ironic contrast to *Martín Fierro's* main reasons for being. Masiello and Strong, respectively, identify these reasons as 1) fostering *individual* recognition, for "registration of artistic hierarchy," and 2) empowering individual authors in their efforts to "invade the city" (Masiello 1986, 61–64; Strong 1997, 61).

A summary of the characteristics of the avant-garde shows that, at least in superficial terms, the Martinfierrista generation had much reason to find in the ideas of Macedonio Fernández resonance of their own search for a new poetics. These characteristics, cataloged by scholars from Ortega to Pérez Firmat, are best outlined by Poggioli (1968). They include: a rupture from prior aesthetics, amounting to a rejection of lyricism, realism, and representation generally; a preference for play, humor, irrationality, and irreverence; a favoring of negation, at its most extreme becoming nihilism; an assertion of new art as invention, the mark of a new era or the pioneering of new territory; the eschewing of popular taste; and finally, a sometimes dizzying challenge to received notions on selfhood, authorship, and originality.[11]

Only one primary characteristic attributed to the avant-garde seems not to apply to Macedonio Fernández at all: a highly public combative stance and a determination to establish firmly the "new sensibility" in contemporary society.[12] But even this last quality can be seen to be relevant to Macedonio if we reconsider what it meant to him to battle for radical change. Indeed, the essential differences between the aesthetics of Macedonio and those of the greater avant-garde movement are largely owing to their different conceptions of *how* art was to change the world.

In the case of the Martinfierristas, we have Beatriz Sarlo's definition of the Argentine avant-garde as an effort to establish a new kind of poetic voice in order to integrate modern Argentina, on its own terms, into Western aesthetics. If we accept this definition, Macedonio does remain at odds with the Argentine avant-garde. Much of the contemporary misreading of his works is the fruit of that incompatibility. In contrast, we have Macedonio's basic premise that the only way to reform Western structures of power and culture is to reject the concept of poetic voice and all of its corollary attributes. If we accept these terms, Macedonio's kinship to the avant-garde becomes clearer. On the one hand, his underlying philosophy, which Macedonio repeatedly tells us is indispensable for understanding his conception of aesthetics, differs from that of the classical Argentine avant-garde—the Martinfierristas—as do his ultimate intentions. On the other hand, Macedonio's objectives are more unequivocally coincident with the impulses driving the avant-garde in general.

Accordingly, Macedonio's distance from the Martinfierristas, and his role as spectator and critic of their practices (J. Prieto 2002, 109), coincides with his rejection of those aspects of their poetics he considers pernicious. But many of the devices for realizing those different intentions are in concert with avant-garde poetics. Macedonio shares with his avant-garde counterparts the fundamental conception of radical art as constituting radical change throughout the exercise of culture and power. In effect, by examining the differences between avant-garde aesthetics and Macedonio's "Belarte," one ends up accentuating the similarities. The differences, however, point to ways in which Macedonio grappled with cultural problems that eluded much of the Argentine avant-garde.

RUPTURE AS CONTINUITY

The concept of avant-garde aesthetics as rupture is a commonplace, and there is ample evidence that for the organizers and contributors of *Martín Fierro*, rupture was a primary concern (Sarlo 1983, 129; Collazos 1977, 11). However, just as *declarations* of rupture are universally characteristic of the avant-garde, both in Europe and in Latin America, equally universal is evidence of continuity with prior aesthetic practices.[13] As Sarlo tells us, for this Argentine avant-garde, as for many avant-garde writers and artists throughout Latin America, the self-proclaimed rupture with tradition and convention posed the means to the establishment of a new national culture, freed from subordination to a colonial history and thus freed from a subordinate relationship to Europe. In this sense, avant-garde rupture is a strategy for cultural continuity under a new social-artistic regime. The Argentine literati's attitude toward innovation in Europe reflects this strategy. Even the first Argentines to appreciate Europe's new aesthetics were unreceptive to its stance of destruction of past aesthetics. Both Ricardo Güiraldes and Bartolomé Galíndez, publisher of the pioneering *Los Raros*, repudiated the "excesses" of futurism, cubism, and Ultraism, and rejected their notion that art had to be "useless" (Scrimaglio 1974, 15–23).

The avant-garde sense of rupture was as much a reaction to social and intellectual conditions in interwar Argentina as it was an aesthetic statement. In particular, Argentine avant-garde poets aimed to break the cultural stronghold of *Nosotros* (We), the leading aesthetic journal of the time (Sarlo 1983, 138). One important strategy of this aesthetic conflict was the virtual election of Macedonio Fernández as master, in opposition to *Nosotros*'s Leopoldo Lugones, an arrangement that Macedonio encouraged, although not for the same motivations as his young followers. Another, even more effective strategy was the creation of *Martín Fierro*, purposely given the title of José Hernández's great epic poem as a way of claiming the inheritance of Argentina's autochthonous cultural traditions.

Martín Fierro made use of the same mechanisms of publicity and self-promotion as its rival *Nosotros* (Sarlo 1983, 150). In many ways, the Martinfierristas adapted tactics worthy of Macedonio's own paradoxical rhetoric and behavior, though often in conflict with Macedonio's objectives. In the case of rupture, the Martinfierristas declared themselves as renegades rejecting the past and privileging the marginal in order to appropriate tradition and conquer the center. Their poetics were primarily informed by a concern with "class origins, relation with national tradition, relations with language and disinterest with respect to the literary market" (Sarlo 1983, 152).

Rupture with past aesthetic practice is also fundamental to Macedonio Fernández's poetics. The very premise of *Museo de la Novela de la Eterna* is its ascedency as the "first good novel" in contrast with its companion *Adriana Buenos Aires*, the "last bad novel."[14] Like his Argentine avant-garde companions, aesthetic rupture for Macedonio by no means constitutes a clean break with the past and unproblematic identification with completely new poetics. Macedonio makes this equivocating explicit in one of *Museo*'s fifty-six prologues, "Lo que nace y lo que muere" (What Dies and What is Born). Here, Macedonio asserts that his two novels were meant to be published, sold, and received as an inseparable pair.

> Es cierto que he corrido el riesgo de confundir alguna vez lo malo que debí pensar para *Adriana Buenos Aires* con lo bueno que no acaba de ocurrírseme para *Novela de la Eterna*; pero es cuestión de que el lector colabore y las desconfunda. A veces me encontré perplejo, cuando el viento hizo volar los manuscritos, porque sabréis que escribía por día una página de cada, y no sabía tal página a cuál correspondía . . . ¡Lo que sufrí cuando no sabía si una página brillante pertenecía a la última novela mala o a la primera buena! (*Museo* 267)[15]

> [It is true that I have run the risk of occasionally confusing the bad which I had to have thought up for *Adriana Buenos Aires* with the good that had not yet occurred to me for *A Novel of Eterna*; but it is a matter for the reader to collaborate and disconfuse them. Sometimes, I found myself perplexed, when the wind blew the manuscripts about, because, you must know, each day I wrote a page of each one, and I couldn't tell which page went with which manuscript. . . . What I suffered when I

couldn't figure out if a certain brilliant page belonged to the last bad novel or the first good one!]

While, like the Argentine avant-garde, Macedonio's assertion of rupture with past aesthetics also implies an engagement with prior forms of art, his objectives are rather different. There is no suggestion of a cultural tradition or identity to be appropriated, nor of a contest with a competing aesthetic movement. Although Macedonio does exploit his antecedents, his use of those antecedents is not only subversive, it is explosive. For Macedonio, the aesthetics of realism and modernismo are indispensable precisely because they are methodologically *wrong* responses to the same impulses inspiring "good" writing.

Not interested in Argentine tradition or national culture, Macedonio Fernández is very much interested in the present state of Argentine society. *Adriana Buenos Aires* is the companion and key to *Museo* because it is, in effect, the same novel written according to the wrong rules. Rupture for Macedonio is more radical than for Borges or Oliverio Girondo (whose poetry counts among the more openly transgressive of Martinfierrista production) because it attempts, in Jo Anne Engelbert's words, "nothing less than an alternative to a typical *work* of Western art . . . the antithesis of the typical artifact of Western culture" (Engelbert 1984, 12). Rather than being a merely aesthetic exercise, this revolutionary new genre (the genre "good") is undertaken as a solution to the inadequacies of a bankrupt genre (the genre "bad") in responding to the conditions of humans in a modern world.

Adriana reveals much of what is wrong with the world, or rather with *Buenos Aires*, in terms accessible to people that Macedonio projects as contemporary readers. But it undercuts itself—and provides for the rupture between it and its twin, *Museo*—by revealing also how its own aesthetics are incapable of addressing those ills.[16] *Adriana* makes clear the need for rupture, while both it and *Museo* together painstakingly reveal the nature of aesthetic reform and its relationship to accepted aesthetics. This strategy in *Adriana* and *Museo* is an example of both the complexity of the parody and heteroglossia at work in Macedonio's writing, and of the self-consciousness and openness with which Macedonio pursues these techniques. The rhetoric of the Martinfierristas, in contrast, proclaims rupture while concealing the essential parentage with accepted aesthetics (Strong 1997, 65–69). It is because his interest is in reforming culture and its relationship to the world, not appropriating it, that Macedonio is so much more candid about both his methods and his intentions.

Another proposed effect of this twinning of novels is discussed in *Continuación de la Nada*, written when *Adriana* was already a reality and *Museo* still being developed. The narrative voice presents his revolutionary, but not-to-be-realized scheme of a "double novel." The characters of one narrative gather regularly to read a second narrative . . .

> de tal manera que estas personas que leen la novela se vivifiquen intensamente en la impresión del lector en contraposición con las personas protagonistas de la novela leída. Y nótese que lo que espero de esta constante contraposición paralela . . . es que el lector, usted, viviente, dude por instantes de ser un existente que lee, y se estremezca de creerse por instantes sin más ser que el de personaje leído. (*Recienvenido* 91)

> [in such a way that these people who read the novel are brought intensely to life in the readers' impressions in counterposition to the protagonists of the novel being read. And note that what I expect from this constant parallel counterpositioning . . . is that the reader, you, living, doubts for an instant at a time in his being an existing being who reads, and trembles from believing himself for an instant at a time to be nothing more than a character being read.]

It is easy to surmise that Macedonio may have found inspiration for these tricks in *Don Quijote*. His open admiration of the Cervantes of "Quijote puramente, sin los cuentos" [only the Quijote, without the short stories] (*Museo*, 44) is inspired, at least in part, by Cervantes's manipulation of the phenomena of reader, character and author. His bow to Cervantes includes the naming of characters in *Museo*: "Quizagenio" and "Dulce-Persona" are among the more obvious borrowings. The open appropriation of Cervantine techniques reinforces the observation that rather than a postmodern "pastiche," Macedonio is engaged in complex, heteroglossic parody.

The juggling of rupture and continuity between characters and readers, book and life, that which represents and that which is represented, facilitates Macedonio's questioning of the self. His overt use and updating of Cervantes's tricks illustrates the centrality of his intent on demonstrating the emptiness of the idea of the subject. Don Quijote is a mere representation and has no identity beyond what is written for him. His rules for interpreting the world are the rules given to him by representational art. But Cervantes makes it ironically transparent that the hero behaves according to his belief that he possesses a real, autonomous self and is interpreting the world according to transcendent truths.[17]

Macedonio Fernández's idea is to resolve the ironic tension Cervantes has left us by deciding in favor of literature without representation and characters without selves. His Cervantes-like parody of the novel against itself is heightened toward the end of *Museo*. Characters of the "first good novel"—Quizagenio and Dulce-Persona—read a passage from *Adriana Buenos Aires*. In doing so, they find that the representation of intense passion between *Adriana*'s two principal characters makes them, as readers of the representation, desire real life so deeply, that for a brief moment they experience what it is like to live, rather than to merely be characters. They learn two things from this situation: that it is much preferable to remain characters, and that if they were to become real, their only redemption would be in loving each other intensely (*Museo*, 216–17). At the same time, a "reader" intervenes in the text to declare that he momentarily lost himself to become a character. The "reader" too, then, senses the value of losing certainty in one's autonomy of self. Macedonio's execution of rupture-as-continuity, his creation of tension between representation and transcendence, his scrambling of ironic distance with straightfoward discourse, and his problematizing (or, at least, aggravating) of the relationship between art and life all contribute to the suspension of subjectivity. These techniques, while corresponding to avant-garde spirit in general, highlight Macedonio's apartness from the Martinfierristas, for whom rupture and continuity are principally a matter of appropriating cultural heritage and legitimacy.[18]

The Ludic as Lyrical

This sleight-of-hand approach to narrative leads us to another quality Macedonio shares with avant-garde artists in general. Virtually every assessment of avant-garde art refers to its privileging "play" and its eschewing of the seriousness of art. The recourse to both humor and the irrational are part of that emphasis on play. In Argentina, the ludic aspect of avant-garde art has consistently emphasized the subversion of the *rules* of play. The consummate example of this remastering of the rules is found in Julio Cortázar's *Rayuela* (*Hopscotch*), with its alternative instructions for the order in which to read the scrambled chapters (Cortázar 1985).[19] *Rayuela*'s literary games are strongly reminiscent of *Museo*'s prologues addressed to the "reader who skips" and the "straight-through reader" (119–20). In these two prologues, the author professes his confidence that the reader who skips will afford him the unwonted sensation of being read straight through, then goes on to despair that the straight-through reader will be his undoing.

Many writers contemporary to Macedonio Fernández undertake similar manipulation of the rules of aesthetic play. Implicit in Borges's 1930 *Historia universal de infamia* (*A Universal History of Infamy*) is a redrawing of the rules for writing and reading history, and by extension culture, to suit the perspective of those who receive it.[20] The novels of Roberto Arlt display an obsession with the rules of the cultural game and the power they confer, as well as with methods for frustrating those rules or twisting them to confer power instead on those marginal people the rules are meant to subordinate (Sarlo 1988, 52–56, 61). Even Arlt's peculiar transgressions of accepted grammar and usage are seen as part of his persistent rule-breaking (Leland 1986, 96). In the matter of grammar, Macedonio was fascinated by the "panlingua" of Xul Solar, the twentieth-century Porteño whose radical artwork was complemented by his invention in language and symbols. Xul's panlingua, as Sarlo notes, appropriates rules of play by assuming authority over grammar (Sarlo 1988, 14–15). His incorporation into visual art of graphic signs drained of meaning is symptomatic of his impulse to take charge of the rules and hierarchies of both behavior and communication, turning language into "man's plaything" (Masiello 1986, 150).[21] For Nora Lange, one of only a few women of the Martinfierrista generation, the "cut and paste," in Sylvia Molloy's words, of her autobiographical writing constitutes a strategy for converting writing into play. Here too, however, the objective of this conversion is to assume the authority of self-elaboration by thwarting—and recreating—the rules of authorship and self-accountancy (Molloy 1991, 126–36).

For the Martinfierrista generation and its heirs, as well as its contemporaries, humor and play do not lead to chaos or to nihilism. This is in contrast to most assessments of European avant-garde movements.[22] The ludic dimension of Argentine literature does coincide, however, with a characteristic fundamental to avant-garde art: replacement of synthesis and integrity with chance and fragmentation, and emphasis on the procedure of construction (Bürger 1984, 64–67, 72–79). But in all of the abovementioned cases, Argentine avant-garde writers maintain, to varying degrees, some reliance on subjectivity. In this regard, they are at odds with Macedonio Fernández.

Macedonio's relationship to the avant-garde is evident in his privileging of the ludic, yet as with other aspects of this aesthetics of renovation, his differences from the Martinfierristas, differences they largely failed to grasp, are apparent in the purpose of play. Macedonio's humor, while "eminently personal," rejects the subjective arbitrariness that, as Scrimaglio points out, was so industriously cultivated by his avant-garde colleagues (Scrimaglio 1974, 121). In addition to Xul Solar's linguistic invention, the surrealist muddling of dream and wakefulness especially attracted Macedonio. In both cases, Macedonio makes clear that his intentions have little relation to Argentine avant-garde efforts at forging a renovated national culture. Instead, he turns these ludic devices against the ultimate intentions of his avant-garde compatriots. Macedonio's subversive play with language aims to disrupt and shatter the "grandilocuent fiction" of nation (J. Prieto 2002, 249). While other Argentine radical writers seek to elaborate a new kind of subjectivity, Macedonio aims to create moments of complete nonsubjectivity.[23] In his "Para una teoría de la humorística" (Toward a Theory of the Humoristic), Macedonio is explicit about the purpose of humor in his writing. He lays claim to discovering two "genuinely artistic" moments that can be provoked in a reader's psyche:

> el momento de la nada intelectual por la Humorística Conceptual, mejor llamada Ilógica de Arte, y el momento de la nada del ser conciencial, usando de los personajes (Novelística) no para el hacer creer en un carácter, un relato, sino para hacer al lector por un instante, creer él mismo personaje, arrebatado de la vida. (*Teorías* 260)

> [the moment of intellectual nothingness through Conceptual Humor, better termed the Illogic of Art, and the moment of nothingness of conscious being, through use of characters (Novelistic) not so as to make for the belief in a character, a story, but so that the reader, for an instant, believes himself to be a character, robbed of life.]

While the first of these conceits holds much in common with Dada, the second conceit is original. The connection with some of Borges's best-known puzzles on the nature of consciousness and identity is evident. "Las ruinas circulares" ("The Circular Ruins"), in which the protagonist finds, through the experience of intensive dreaming, that his own reality is uncertain; "El Sur" ("The South"), in which a man's delirium ultimately leads to his absorption into the fictional world of dueling gauchos; "Tlön, Uqbar, Orbis Tertius," in which a fictional world, created collaboratively across generations, seeps surreptitiously into the world of experience to the point of influencing the structures of historical and political discourse—these are just a few of Borges's stories that share a kinship with Macedonio's inventive play between fiction and reality. But Borges's whimsical manipulation of the borders between fiction and lived experience discredits lived reality and recorded history in order to make room for fictional and mythical discourses. These mythical discourses leave intact individual consciousness at their center.

Macedonio's peculiar conception of the purpose of humor and play is integral with his overall campaign for the absence of self and the concomitant reassessment of individual consciousness. The reader projected by this commentary is forced, by questioning the reality of his or her own "self," to reexamine just what individuality consists of. What Macedonio's "teoría" does not mention is the fact that accompanying the disorienting effect of his humor are innumerable passages, like those found in the "Oratoria de un hombre confuso," that not only promote the negation of the concept of self but suggest that the composition of the individual consists of more prosaic material: the sentient body and its relationship to the peopled city. This wholesale reworking of the individual places Macedonio sharply at odds with the surrealist elaboration of self, which according to Bürger reduces society to nature (Bürger 1984, 71). Macedonio is also at odds with Borges's reduction of society to history and myth. It is Borges's elimination of sentient relations that is most responsible for the characterization of his writing as "cold" and "dehumanized." In Borges's stories, intense emotion emerges at crucial moments (Bell-Villada 1999, 46), but always as a function of individual consciousness, not interpersonal connections.

Humor for the Argentine avant-garde is a technique for the rejection of the imposed reality of European culture and, arguably, colonial history. Like surrealism, Argentine avant-garde writers often end up relying ultimately on an autonomous subjectivity to further their goal. This reliance may explain the increasing surrealist tendencies of the immediate heirs to the Argentine avant-garde, such as Cortázar. Macedonio attempts, in a much more systematic and concerted way, to disperse another sort of imposed reality; that of the concept of autonomous self. Like his avant-garde counterparts,

Macedonio finds the source of this imposition in European culture. But he is not concerned directly with the cultural constitution of state, national identity, or even national mythology. The source of delusion that Belarte hopes to remedy lies in a philosophical and ideological legacy of Descartes and Kant, and Macedonio's mission is to undermine the viability of that legacy.

The lyric qualities of Macedonio's prose reflect these same contrasts with the avant-garde generation as do his ludic qualities. Arlt's early novels, Eduardo Mallea's *Cuentos para una inglesa desesperada* (Tales for a Desperate Englishwoman) and Eduardo González Lanuza's 1922 *Aquelarre* (Mire), all characterized by Leland as exemplary works of avant-garde prose, have an entirely different quality from Recienvenido's discourse, Eduardo de Alto's confession in *Adriana Buenos Aires*, or the *Presidente*'s dialogue in *Museo*. In the prose of the three other Argentines, the lyrical voice serves to reinforce the autonomy of individual consciousness—transcendence of self—in the process of putting the self through the test of new aesthetic approaches. Arlt's 1929 *El juguete rabioso* (*Mad Toy*) is essentially a *bildungsroman* (Arlt 1979). *Aquelarre* presents a lyrical voice that renders itself objective by attributing consciousness, motive, and life to the inanimate objects that normally constitute the self's environment. Although González Lanuza makes the self the object, rather than the subject, of lyric prose, in doing so he retains—and emphasizes—the integrity and autonomy of that self and its lyric voice. Similar to *Museo*, Mallea's 1921 *Cuentos para una inglesa desesperada* attempts to express "mental states" in metaphors and to focus almost exclusively on passion and desire as determining those mental states (Mallea 1969). For Macedonio, the sensations and emotions of a lover are not subordinated to a discrete consciousness or a will; rather, the self is persistently subordinated to sensation and emotion. Mallea's prose, by contrast, serves to reinforce the ascendancy of self by defining it in terms of these sensations and desires inspired by various women. The playful lyricism of these authors stands in stark contrast to Macedonio's ludic use of lyric voice to negate, dismantle and erase the self.

Negation as Affect

The rejection of imposed reality is also the motivation behind the Martinfierristas' adoption of avant-garde techniques of negation, which, according to Poggioli, in its most extreme forms in Europe culminates in nihilism (Poggioli 1968, 61–65). For Argentine avant-garde artists, negation, rather than being a purely nihilist impulse, is a means to achieving the "ground zero" that Unruh qualifies as the prerequisite to expressing a distinct national culture. In this regard too, Macedonio applies similar principles toward different aims. Criticism of Macedonio persists in qualifying his rhetoric of negation as a "language of incommunication" and linking it solely to his attack on discourse "for consumption" (J. Prieto 2002, 233–35). But Macedonio's techniques of negation intend to eradicate all possibility of locating or defining individual identity in terms of a self. Accordingly, the negating ploys in Macedonio's prose come much closer to nihilism than in any other Argentine writer of the time. In the above citation concerning Macedonio's "humorística," for example, his valuation of the nihilistic impulse is evident: humor serves to bring about "intellectual nothingness" and "the nothingness of conscious being," so fundamental to his radical aesthetic program. For Borges, Girondo, Scalabrini, or Arlt, the negative only clears the way for the foundations of a new, ostensibly autochthonous cultural edifice. Even if this structure is meant to be more self-doubting than its predecessor, and more liberating for its implied audiences, it remains a cultural structure nonetheless.

Macedonio's interest in cultural structure is limited to the extent that it can be used to demonstrate the emptiness of the concept of self on which contemporary society is built. The foundation he seeks is rather different from the "ground zero" Unruh describes. Macedonio's idea of a valid basis for identity, indeed for existence, is purely affective, as virtually all studies of his work have observed. He repeatedly uses the words "love" and "passion" to refer to this phenomenon. The fact that he devoted a lifetime to writing, to filling hundreds of pages, in an attempting to articulate and achieve such an affective state, suggests the elusiveness of the goal. The characters of *Museo*, for example, function mainly to incarnate, in myriad ways, this seemingly abstract affection-based identity to which negation is a prerequisite:

> Por eso juraría que Deunamor dejó de ser una conciencia personal desde hace muchos años, y yo mismo observo que su conducta en la novela es la de un hombre que nada siente, piensa ni ve, en actitud de espera, pero sin sentir la espera, de volver a reunirse con la amada y ser feliz, o sea que es actualmente una insensibilidad con perspectiva de ser una sensibilidad. (*Museo* 63)

[For this reason I would swear that Deunamor ceased being a personal consciousness many years ago, and I myself observe that his conduct in the novel is that of man who neither feels, thinks nor sees anything, in an attitude of waiting, but without feeling the wait, to be once again reunited with his beloved and to be happy; that is, he is today an insensibility with the perspective of being of a sensibility.]

This affective function of negation extends as well to the novel's "author," "que a veces es y a veces no es el Presidente" [who at times is and at times is not the President] in his relationship with the novel's characters. The author in this respect exists strictly to discharge his "metaphysical" responsibilities to his characters. With Eterna, he must show her that Nothingness and Death are nonexistent "porque para quienes tienen ya el Amor todo su asunto es el porvenir y su posiblidad de cesación." [because for those who already possess Love their only concern is the future and the possibility of its cessation.] With Dulce-Persona, the Presidente must demonstrate the nullity of the past . . .

liberándola de la franja de haber sido real que acompaña a cierta escena de tortura que hay que aniquilar como imagen sida para convertirla en imagen sin esa franja, os sea imagen de fantasía, de mera irrealidad. (287)[24]

[freeing her from the fringe of having been real which accompanies a certain scene of torture and which one must vanquish as a having-been image so as to turn it into an image without this fringe, that is, an image of fantasy, of mere unreality.]

These passages help to illustrate the idiosyncratic—but vital—link in Macedonio's "Belarte" between extreme negation, bordering on nihilism, and the ascendancy of the affective. Deunamor, who is a metaphor, not a person, is reduced to a "perspective of sensitivity" because, not being a person, he cannot be allowed to feel. But even in this most diminished identity—a mere shadow of a single human characteristic, denied all other possibility of being—the one function left him is to wait and hope for his beloved. The "author" is the most powerful figure in the novel and the one closest to life, for he takes on the functions of metaphor and lyric voice (as Presidente) as well as alter ego and invented self for Macedonio, metaphysical philosopher. But even he is limited in his functions to the role of negating: eradicating for Dulce-Persona the hindrance of having been real in the past, and eliminating for Eterna the obstacle of no longer being real in the future.

Macedonio even is more unequivocal about the role of this nihilistic impulse when he addresses in abstract terms the ascendancy of "passion" as the only sure and knowable human phenomenon. He declares that the uniquely "altruistic" state of passion between lovers is the only reality to which individuals should fully commit themselves. In all other cases, he insists . . .

> debiéramos vivir a media luz y media acción, a media vigilia, sin reconocer por entero los sucesos y estados, pues fuera de la pasión la probabilidad es de prevalencia del sufrimiento; el ensueño que rememoro es fórmula del estado de media inadmisión de toda certeza y efectividad. (67)

> [we should live by half light and half action, in half wakefulness, without recognizing entirely occurrences and states, as outside of passion the likelihood is for a prevalence of suffering; the dreaming I recall is a formula of the state of half inadmission of all certainty and effectivity.]

Thus Macedonio sets out a crucial distinction between his vision and absolute nihilism. Macedonio's nihilism serves to set mundane human existence apart from affective phenomena. The negation of objective experience and knowledge is vital because it sets emotion apart from both flesh and intellect. The relationship between two principal figures of *Museo* illustrates this distinction.

> El Presidente y la Eterna no alcanzaron el todoamor porque él no quiere posar su cabeza en el seno de la Eterna, para amparo, y ella no logra (es su única imperfección) liberarse de este declive maternal, que en el amor es el error, y no puede vivir sin esta sensación en su pecho. Por su parte el Presidente tuvo la ineptitud de no poder amar a la Eterna sin pensarla, sin representásela místicamente o sea como imposible en el ser, porque el ser es inintelectualizable. (147)

> [The Presidente and Eterna did not achieve all-love because he does not want to rest his head on Eterna's breast, for shelter, and she cannot manage (it is her only imperfection) to free herself of this maternal proclivity, which in love is an error, and cannot live without this sensation on her chest. For his part the President had the ineptitude of not being able to love Eterna without thinking her, without representing her mystically; that is to say, as an impossibility of being, since being is unintellectualizable.]

A crucial aspect of the relations among these novelistic figures is that the impediments to their unreality are literally flesh, blood, and brain, or at least the manner in which flesh, blood, and brain interpose themselves in human relations. It is not just the idea of or commitment to maternal love that impedes the attainment of "all-love" for Eterna and the President, but the maternal breast and its tactile sensation. Whereas the Presidente can only conceive of Eterna in "mystical" terms, as a pure unintelligible being, Eterna cannot free herself of maternal flesh.[25] These barriers matter to Macedonio because, as he states, an existence weighted in flesh, perceived in sensation and conceived of intellectually, is constantly subject to pain. Like many European expressions of nihilism—with the possible exception of Dada, which serves as a flight into absolute nothingness—Macedonio's nihilism serves to prove the futility of nothingness and to identify knowable alternatives to the perceived, measured, and recorded world.[26] In this respect, Macedonio's poetics of negation implicitly rejects the Martinfierristas' employment of negation as a prelude to cultural appropriation and renewal.

INVENTION AS THE UNINVENTED

One of the more intractable self-contradictions of avant-garde art is, on the one hand, its penchant for negating—and for negating in particular the accepted structures of modern culture and society—and, on the other hand, its claims to invention. The classical European avant-garde undertakes to appropriate for itself the concept of invention and to proclaim its artists as inventors. Outside of Latin America, Gertrude Stein may be the most extreme example of this posture, comparing herself not only to the great inventors of her own era, but to the great innovators in the history of writing: Dante and Shakespeare are her peers. In her 1933 *Autiobiography of Alice B. Toklas,* she unequivocally refers to herself as the first writer of the twentieth century (Stein 1990, 54).

For the avant-garde in Argentina the conceit of invention in new forms of art is applied directly to the "invention" of a nation. At one extreme in this regard is Roberto Arlt, obsessed with the possibilities of invention not only in the world of science and engineering but also in the world of alchemy and the occult. Arlt's mania for invention reflects his fascination with the architecture of power and his desire to find ways to subvert existing power structure in the most fundamental and explosive way possible. Nation, culture, and power are inseparable for Arlt (Sarlo 1992, 15–19, 56–60; Masiello 1986, 214). The goals and the methods of the Martinfierristas, who stand much closer to the center of power in Argentina than does Arlt, are far less revolutionary. Yet virtually all poets of the avant-garde share with Arlt the notion that the reinvention of culture constitutes, ultimately, a reinvention of the nation.

These same poets and writers persistently skirt discussion of a fundamental contradiction in their art: the tension between the privileging of the negative in the avant-garde and the conceit of author as inventor.[27] It is a tension most acute in the works of Macedonio Fernández, commensurate to his more extreme efforts at negation and his more radical claim to invention. Macedonio's claim at having written the "first novel of the genre 'good'" matches Gertrude Stein's self-description as the first writer of the twentieth century. Like Stein, Macedonio revisits this assertion often, tailoring it many different ways; remarkably, he is both less arrogant and more apodictic than Stein in his proclamations.[28] He regards invention as important only for its ethical consequences; accordingly, he considers his innovations in "non-discursive metaphysics" to be the bedrock of his inventiveness (*Museo*, 34, cited by Schiminovich 1986, 75).

The eighteenth "prologue" to *Museo*, for example, called "Prólogo a lo nunca visto" (Prologue to the Never Seen), asserts that *Museo* constitutes the first instance of the "género de lo nunca habido" [the genre of never having been]. More than simply declaring the advent of this invention, Macedonio also touches on its greater implications. He notes that the very act of debuting the "never seen" is unprecedented. That act also renders *Museo* the first truly "futurist" novel, something that it can only call itself so long as the novel remains unrealized. Macedonio's innovation goes well beyond what Julio Prieto calls the "founding of a new discursivity" (J. Prieto 2002, 204); Macedonio claims not only to invent a new aesthetic device, he boasts of the invention of a new conception of "invention:" to remain truly inventive, a thing must be maintained perpetually "potential," and its author perpetually "future." This paradoxical conceit is another wrinkle in the conundrum discussed in our introduction: Macedonio's attempt at a constant tension between the productivity and creativity of the individual and the dissolution of an autonomous biographical and conscious self.

The "Prólogo a lo nunca visto" also elaborates on the suitability, for such an invention, of Buenos Aires:

la primera ciudad del mundo viniendo del campo inmediato, la única ciudad que se presta para conclusión de una vuelta al mundo empezada en ella y lo mismo para concluir las empezadas dondequiera, como lo han descubierto sucesivamente varios inexorables circundantes terráqueos, con vuelta al mundo anunciada partiendo de Berlín o de Río de Janeiro, que se consumó, sin ostentación indiscreta para este tramo, queda y quedamente con desprecio con todo lo demás de andar, en las calles, tranvías y empleos públicos de Buenos Aires, con casita, casamiento, prole, lo que tiene tanta redondez y heroísmo como la ejecución del furioso anuncio de dar toda vuelta. (*Museo* 42)

[the first city in the world to come from the immediate countryside, the only city that lends itself to the conclusion of a trip around the world begun in it and likewise for concluding those begun anywhere, as several successive inexorable earthly circumventors have discovered, with an advertised trip around the world leaving from Berlin or Rio de Janeiro which is consummated, without indiscrete ostentation for this journey, quietly and for good and with disdain for all further wandering, in the streets, streetcars and public offices of Buenos Aires, with a cottage, marriage, a brood, which has as much roundness and heroism as the execution of the fierce announcement of making the whole circuit.]

Buenos Aires is the city of invention because it is itself invented, sprung up from the fields. It is also the site where people reinvent themselves as newcomers, just as Macedonio invents himself as a newcomer to the literary world. But most important, it is where the ideas of invention, discovery and exalted inventor are reinvented as prosaic existence and routine interaction. What is launched from both home and abroad as "execution" and "announcement" is perpetuated in the city as inventive and heroic day-to-day anonymity. Revolution is literally the return to roots and origins (J. Prieto 2002, 104).

Buenos Aires as a site of invention is common to many members of the Martinfierrista generation. Macedonio, however, takes this conceit a step further than his compatriots. For Arlt, the most obvious case, invention is a means to social and cultural revolution, but it is a bellicose and disruptive initiative that exploits, rather than redefines, the accepted terms of invention. Even in his cultural inventions, Arlt exercises a violence on language more analogous to a physical excision, concoction, and reassembly—much like the laboratory inventions attempted in his novels—in comparison to Macedonio's more congenial reorienting of language use. For Borges,

Buenos Aires is a site of cultural invention because it is a cultural void, ripe for acceptance of a mythology and a history hewn by his hand. Borges sees heroism in Buenos Aires, but it is a heroism that must be identified in invented stories and legends—often violent ones, beginning with his first short story, "Hombre de la esquina rosada" ("Streetcorner Man"), which relates the murder of a *compadrito* (neighborhood boss). Macedonio, refusing to work aggression or impose discourse on the city, sees Buenos Aires as possessing the resources to reinvent itself by means of its own momentum. For Macedonio, the city only needs to be awakened to its imaginative potential.

The ethical orientation of Macedonio's invention is reinforced in the next "prologue," where he discusses the effect on his projected reader of "gaining him as a character" and disrupting the reader's belief in being alive. This "impression" created by Macedonio's novel is pronounced to be a first-ever occurrence and an invention of incalculable benefit to humanity. By freeing the human psyche of the dread of "not being," Macedonio's novelistic invention performs a revolutionary liberation (*Museo*, 37).

In making this declaration, Macedonio takes the notion of poetic invention well beyond the confines of avant-garde innovation. Invention, for the avant-garde in general and the Martinfierristas specifically, is an invention of a new aesthetics, announced in manifestoes, attributed to individuals of genius, presented and recorded as any new development to modern society and culture, and valued by virtue of its genius. The literary inventor is a hero, identified and substantiated by his invention; its production is evidence of the genius and consciousness that produces it.[29] For Macedonio, invention is the undoing of just such ideas and institutions.[30] His subversion of the received concept of invention, by means of this innovative articulation of it, implicates both the practices of avant-garde artists and the city they inhabit. Macedonio's disdain for the more routine kind of futurism is explicit here, as he is derisive of routine practices of authorship.

The invention of "bad" writing (J. Prieto 2002, 238–39) is part of Macedonio's challenge to the aestheticist avant-garde concept of originality. It is a concept he finds oxymoronic: originality cannot consist of decorative permutations on an already sanctioned grammatical and artistic edifice. The above-cited passages are followed by a lengthy discussion on the vagaries of self-designated aesthetic inventors (with particular venom reserved for Góngora) and the credulous reading public. Macedonio dwells on the need for reinvented readers to complement (or to complete) this deidentification and deauthorization of the literary process, to undo "good" writing, and concludes: "Efectividad de autor es sólo de Invención" [Author effectiveness is only that of Invention] (*Museo*, 47). There is a distressing irony in the responses of the avant-garde peers with whom Macedonio maintained such a dynamic, yet at times uneasy, relationship. For perhaps their most fundamental and enduring invention has been that of a cultural identity for Macedonio Fernández.

Unpopularity as Celebrity

Macedonio's appropriation and reorientation of the concept of invention also is linked to his attitudes regarding the role of the public as constituting the marketplace for inventions. The kind of ambivalent, evidently paradoxical and tense relationship he maintains with the reading public is, in part at least, common currency among avant-garde writers and artists, both in Europe and the Americas. But Macedonio's particular bent on the relationship between author and public emphasizes important differences from his avant-garde counterparts. The question is further complicated by the fact that "reading public" (like the category "author") can be defined numerous ways. One must consider the public explicitly referred to in Macedonio's prose; the reader implied in both the substance of his writing and in his iconoclastic stance toward publishing; the reading public identified explicitly and implicitly by other avant-garde writers individually and by their collective publications, and finally, the public delineated by historical evidence.

The Argentine avant-garde shares the reliance on unpopularity characteristic, according to Poggioli, of European avant-gardes, but it does so for peculiarly nationalistic reasons. In this regard, the weight of Ortega y Gasset's influence on the Argentine movement is key.[31] Ortega's explicitly elitist approach to culture, and to the avant-garde in particular, stresses the importance of the individual author "acting" on the masses according to the "predetermined mission" of each aesthetic generation, a kind of noblesse oblige of the contemporary artist. (Ortega y Gasset 1938, 14; 1968, 54).[32] Ortega applied these same principles of modern art as an elitist project to his exhortation of Argentine Ultraists towards "true" and "authentic" definition and cultural expression of the Argentine nation (Stabb 1967, 72). There is little doubt that poets of the Martinfierrista generation took up this recommendation. For Borges, Mallea, Girondo, and others, the "unpopularity" of their avant-garde was integral to their determination to exercise an identifiably Argentine aesthetic authority (Scrimaglio 1974, 45).

A primary consequence of the *centenario* project by Argentine writers, just after the turn of the century, was the professionalization of writing and the galvanizing of the relationship between writing and nation-building (Altamirano and Sarlo 1983, 88; Masiello 1986, 31–33). Borges and other modernists of the Martinfierrista generation had a fundamental part in the competition for national cultural legitimacy that grew out of this professionalization (Franco 1967, 92–94). The goals of the Martinfierristas led to a paradoxical, perhaps hypocritical, posture regarding the literary marketplace. On the one hand, they disdained the popular market, and the "mercenary" influences of an immigrant public (Strong 1997, 103). On the other hand, rather than repudiate market forces, these same writers sought to reform literary tastes, creating a public for their works (Sarlo 1983, 142–49; Strong 1997, 62–63).[33]

Macedonio Fernández had a central place in this strategy of altering literary tastes while appearing to eschew popularity. Macedonio served as the personification of an aesthetic principle—a sort of Martinfierrista paragon, to be contrasted with the opponents' figurehead, Leopoldo Lugones—and as a pioneer of radical aesthetic practice (Sarlo 1983, 144). Macedonio unquestionably cooperated in this effort—to a point. But Macedonio's posture toward publishing was hardly uncomplicated. Equally complex was his attitude toward the reading public. He attacked the conventional tastes of the literary market, but his interest in reforming those tastes by infiltrating the market was far stronger than his disdain:

> El horrible arte y las acumulaciones de gloria del pasado, que existirán siempre, se deben: al sonido de los idiomas y a la existencia del público; sin ese sonido quedará el sólo camino de pensar y crear; sin público la calamidad recitadora no ahogará el arte. (*Museo* 44)

> [Horrible art and the accumulations of past glory, which will always exist, are owing to: the sound of languages and the existence of a public; without this sound there would remain only the path of thinking and creating; without a public, recitative calamity would not drown out art.]

3: AN AVANT-GARDE APART

Convendría a una novela que quiera público—la mía se aburre conmigo, quisiera que lleguen visitantes o salir a conversar, le gustaría ser leída—empezar su narrativa por un choque o una buena frenada. El público se junta al punto en tal número que ya quisieran algunos libros tener el de una frenada común. (*Museo* 31)

[It is appropriate for a novel to want a public—mine gets bored with me, would like to receive visitors or to go out and chat, it would like to be read—to begin its narrative with a screeching halt or a crash. The public gathers at the site in such throngs that some books would rather have the public of a single, common crash.]

There is an apparent contradiction in Macedonio's horror of the "recitative calamity" of the reading public and his approval of crashing throngs of readers. He goes on to reveal, moreover, that as an author he dreams of these great collisions of readers going as far as to obstruct the plot, forcing it out from inside the Novel (204). [34]
Implicit in his image of crowds of readers stumbling into each other and into the Novel, impeding the Novel's progress and muddling the author's relationship to both readers and work, is a critique of attempts by other writers to master a reading public and define its relationship to author and work. According to Macedonio, a work not only has its own will to attract a public, but also invariably yearns to draw a crowd by the most natural and efficacious method of causing an accident. Macedonio's sincere desire for a readership finds expression in this reengineering of writer, reader, and work, concomitant with his rejection of authorial control. While not an "accidental author" in the sense that Borges devised—an unwilling and unwitting author, who never desired to be read—Macedonio Fernández insists on the priority of the accidental in the formation of readership and the development of authorship. The invention of the "autor desconocido" [unknown author] serves, among other purposes, to parody the professionalizing, nationalist strategies of the Centenario writers. It also functions as a most fortuitous counterpoint to the self-glorification Lugones engaged in as part of his effort to become "national spokesman" (Masiello 1986, 43). In these respects Macedonio Fernández's humorous prose provokes the admiration of his Martinfierrista colleagues.

The burlesque of the professional author is a repeated theme in *Papeles de Recienvenido*. At one point the narrator compares his "unknown author" to that well-known European civil servant, the "unknown hero," suggesting that the two could almost be hired interchangeably. He elaborates further:

> Nuestro autor es verdaderamente incógnito; si no fuera que Shakespeare tiene ya con quien se le confunda, sería una satisfacción ofrecérselo para ese propósito. (*Recienvenido* 23)
>
> [Our author is truly unidentified; if it weren't for the fact that Shakespeare already has someone to be confused with, it would be gratifying to offer him for the purpose.]

> Surjo únicamente para que no se me confunda con cierto Editor. Soy sólo el autor de un mansucrito encontrado. En tan modesta calidad, no debía deparárseme, no me convenía un inagradecible grandote, de voz resonante, a cuyo lado deba yo pasearme por la publicidad. . . . (*Recienvenido* 25)
>
> [I show up only so as not to be confused with a certain Editor. I am merely the author of a found manuscript. In such a modest capacity, I should not be provided with—it would not be appropriate—a thankless big-shot, with a resounding voice, at whose side I must parade about for the sake of publicity.]

Macedonio implicates literary tradition in this critique of the author-book-public relationship. Literature itself, he suggests, has contributed to the construction of this fictitious edifice, to the point where both the idea and the actuality of author is no less an institution of literary convention than the idea of hero. Contemporary practices of publicity-making—the modern editor and agent—are simply the natural extension of literary convention. Macedonio's parody of these phenomena not only allies him with the Martinfierristas in their reaction to the tactics of the centenary movement, but it also sets him against the avant-garde employment of publicizing tactics. For this reason, Macedonio persists in finding alternative labels for his status among the avant-garde generation. He is the "dead" author "reborn" in the "Oratoria de un hombre confuso," the author other writers confirm as "nonexistent" (J. Prieto 2002, 116–17) or the perpetual newcomer (*recienvenido*).

Macedonio is disparaging as well of the classist motivations that contemporary critics attribute to the Martinfierrista generation. His pointed appropriation for himself—or for his literary alter ego—of the word "*recienvenido*" suggests an unorthodox, rather than xenophobic or classist, attitude toward ethnic and social identity. The deprecating term *recienvenido,* or "newcomer," in the Argentina of the early twentieth century, could not be employed without invoking profound and widespread ethnic, cultural, and social tensions. In Macedonio's case, this ironic self-designation serves to mock those tensions, and arguably to dissolve them, by redefining and defusing a highly charged word.[35] Rather than suggesting an endorsement of the avant-garde classist stance of unpopularity, "recienvenido" refers to Macedonio's refusal to participate in Argentine xenophobia. The human relations explored in literature—seen by the Martinfierristas in the same social and ethnic terms as by their predecessors—are for Macedonio strictly *literary* relations. The "literary world" is the only one in which a person can legitimately be called a newcomer. By applying the term to himself, Macedonio short-circuits both the classist stance and the innate paradox of the Argentine avant-garde's distaste for the market.

Self-Repudiation as Self-Promotion

Macedonio's summary rejection of the autonomous self, and its manifestation in the concept of an artistic persona, is in concert with the questioning, throughout avant-garde movements, of the autonomous individual artist and lyrical voice of prior literary practice. Again, in this respect Macedonio is superficially at one with his avant-garde colleagues. The earliest manifestoes of *Prisma* and *Proa,* the Argentine Ultraists's first attempts at magazines, share Macedonio's rhetoric on the repudiation of self; Borges, in his Ultraist manifesto, borrows Macedonio's very words, referring to the self as a "psychological error," finding in Macedonio's pronouncements resonance with what he had learned in Europe from some of the earliest avant-garde poets there, Rafael Cansinos Assens especially (see Collazos 1977, 133–45). Avant-garde manifestoes almost uniformly perceive and denigrate their predecessors as simplistically accepting the self as an autonomous entity, and Macedonio Fernández shares their distaste.[36]

The problem in identifying Macedonio with the same critical stance of his avant-garde companions is that he does not share their rhetoric beyond the smattering of borrowings from his commentary by Argentine manifesto writers. Pronouncements and manifestoes, by which individual authors identified with a movement or a set of aesthetic principles (however abstract or contradictory), were precisely what Macedonio wished to transcend. His tactic—he is explicit about it—is to forge an aesthetics that renders the autonomous author a gratuitous absurdity. Much of *Papeles de Recienvenido* is just this process of dismantling the modernist concept of author, questioning the concept, twisting it and turning it inside out until the concept is revealed as a hollow convention contrary to Macedonio's "Belarte," the only writing beneficial to humankind. He makes reference to the aesthetics he is writing against, however, in *Adriana Buenos Aires: última novela mala*. The entire novel, the last of the genre "bad," as its title declares, aims at killing off the aesthetics of realism and modernismo.

His technique is as devious as his intentions are forthright. Near the end of *Adriana*, Macedonio includes an attack, standard among his writings, on the autonomous self and the related concepts of attributable authorship and individual originality. Declaring the inexistence of isolated, irreducible selves, he adds that, as a consequence, any writer can be the author of the works of any other writer, despite the objections of purveyors of truth and good taste. He continues:

> La originalidad debe estar a cargo del lector en estas lecturas en que hay que tomarse la fatiga de hacer pensar al autor, perezoso para todo lo que no sea meramente escribir. (*Adriana* 212–13)

> [Originality should be the responsibility of the reader in those readings in which one must take the trouble to make the author think, the author being too lazy for anything that isn't merely writing.]

Fifty years before the diffusion of reader-response theory, Macedonio Fernández displaces the site of meaning from a posited author to a textually evoked reader. The connection to Borges's familiar conceits about the impossibility of authorial and textual originality is obvious. For Macedonio, this proceeding is a direct corollary to the refutation of self. For him, originality is a function of the deception of transcendent selfhood, whereas for Borges, originality is a question of reexamining the nature of individual creative genius, not denying its transcendence.

The foregoing examples are illustrations of how Macedonio routinely upheld the principles announced in avant-garde manifestoes and simultaneously revealed the shortcomings in avant-garde literary practice. Macedonio consistently sustains philosophical and ethical approaches over programmatic ones, and demonstrated principles over declared ones. His playful parody allows him to criticize what he finds false or misleading in the writing of his contemporaries without himself exercising the self-assertion inherent in pronouncements and manifestoes.

Performance as Engagement

Underlying his critique of some of the most basic tenets of avant-garde discourse is Macedonio's refusal to recognize the distinction between narrative and theater, a distinction largely maintained by the Martinfierristas. Opposed as he is to the exercise of representation, it is natural that Macedonio had no interest in theater, for even the most innovative theater is based on the principal of representation. He wrote no theater, never commented on it, and expressed no interest in it. Efforts of Porteño avant-garde playwrights such as Leonidas Barletta, Alvaro Yunque, Elias Castelnuovo or, most significantly, Roberto Arlt, failed to elicit his attention. Both the prescriptive aspects and the forced ironic distance of theater—the effects of making obvious to an audience what is indiscernible to the characters—are inimical to Macedonio's poetics. But as in the case with his relationship to the idea of nation, Macedonio's silence on the merits of theater is indicative of its underlying, fundamental importance to his aesthetic vision. Macedonio presumes all valid art to be essentially performative: to demand if not to enact performance. Accordingly, much of what Unruh specifies as distinctive in avant-garde theater in Latin America is characteristic of Macedonio's literary exercises of the 1920s, both those planned and those executed.[37] The evident contradiction between this presumption and the form of his works lies in Macedonio's understanding of performance and of the purpose of art. To Macedonio, theater is an absurdity precisely because *all* art must be performative, but never representational, to have any real value. Even the legend of Macedonio, when regarded in this light, reveals how integral the notion of performance is to his aesthetics: his famed love of, and reported brilliance in, conversation; his reluctance to "archive" works or fix them by publishing; his love of music. As with the "Oratoria de un hombre confuso," Macedonio's performances consistently focused on remedying the error of performance, an error founded on the reliance on an autonomous self.

The above examples all concern a kind of private, intimate performance, and for the last two decades of his life, Macedonio engaged in little that could be called performance in other than an intimate sense. But the 1920s, Macedonio's most active and productive period, show us a writer engaged in public performance, as in the case of the "Oratorio" and his many "brindis" (J. Prieto 2002, 58–59) and endeavoring to revolutionize the nature of performance. Two important sources inform us of this effort: one source is the anecdotal reports of Macedonio's campaign for the Argentine presidency. The other source is a letter in which Macedonio discusses his concept of a "novela a la calle" or "street novel."

In two undated letters, one to Enrique Fernández Latour and one to Alberto Hidalgo, Macedonio discusses a plan for what he believes to be a completely new idea: an "... acto teatral, teoría de la novela que se vive, presentación de los personajes, etc." [theatrical act, theory of the living novel, presentation of characters, etc.] (*Epistolario* 90).[38] He elaborates the concept:

> mi plan partiendo de su iniciativa es hacer ejecutar en las calles de Buenos Aires, casas y bares, etc., la novela (o sus escenas eminentes, aunque haciendo creer al público que toda la novela se está ejecutando) y anunciándolo así en la Conferencia teatral, y publicar la novela simultáneamente en folletín diario, en *Crítica* preferentemente o *La Nación*. . . . Es necesario un previo período intensivo de hacer sonar mi nombre, para que se espere algo de cualquier actuación en que yo parezca como dirigente. (*Epistolario* 38)

> [my plan departing from your initiative is to have performed in the streets of Buenos Aires, houses and bars, etc., the novel (or its eminent scenes, though making the public believe that the whole novel is being performed) and advertising it thus in the Theatre Conference, and to publish the novel simultaneously in daily installments, in *Crítica* preferably or *La Nación*. . . . We need a prior intensive period of making my name heard, so that something is expected of any staging in which I might appear as director.]

Camblong notes the importance of this idea of public theater as a strategy for action in which the author's identity (as opposed to his name) is established only after the living novel is realized (Camblong, xxxiv). Equally important is the very notion of a "realized" novel, taking the whole concept of theater one step further, akin to the "happenings" of a later era. Macedonio wants the novel to invade the city on the novel's own terms, absent author, absent director, and ultimately, absent the players and audience that give theater its representational—and ironic—aspect.

The overall conceit behind *Museo* is one of a double, or "folded," collaboration. A public of readers, represented and engaged in the novel itself, is gently forced into collaboration in the production of an "open" novel. In this novel characters that have no mimetic value collaborate to "novelize" the real city—that is, to convert the city into an open work of art. In this respect, Macedonio is strides ahead of avant-garde playwrights of the same era, including those active in Buenos Aires's most inventive groups: the Teatro Libre, the Teatro Experimental Argentino and the Teatro del Pueblo. Many features of his prose coincide with those of avant-garde theater. Any number of the prologues to *Museo* for example, as well as virtually the entire text of *Adriana*, emphasize the "disjunctions between represented reality and lived reality," along with the complementary conceit of "continuity between 'real' and 'subjunctive' or make-believe," which Unruh tells us are prominent in the plays of Roberto Arlt (Unruh 1994, 179–80). Similar also to the theater of Vicente Huidobro, *Museo* easily fits the description of a "book of doing, of process, of the *interstices* between art and life" (190).

Even more striking is the similarity between Macedonio's and Huidobro's struggles over the inherent narcissism of their works and the "tyranny" of the author over actors and characters.[39] For Macedonio, the distinction between theater and Belarte is commensurate with the difference in their acquiescence to and exploitation of subjectivity. The ultimate responses of Macedonio and Huidobro to this problem are as different as their personalities: Macedonio Fernández creates the passionate but diffident, impressive but absent Presidente of the *Novela*; Huidobro, ultimately accepting of the existing political process, gives us the self-embattled artistic tyrant. As Julio Prieto remarks, the "novel taken to the streets" is a quintessential example of the tyranny of the work over its intended, or imagined, readers (J. Prieto 2002, 216–17). But the violence Prieto sees, violence akin to Artaud's "theater of cruelty," is counterbalanced by the refusal of Macedonio's absent author to impose himself in a lyrical voice or an alter ego.

Language, History and Myth: Subjectivity Subverted

The avant-garde treatment of subjectivity is never straightforward. There are examples of the questioning of the concept of self throughout the radical poetics of the same period in Latin America. As Unruh suggests, the avant-garde operates in a dynamic tension between self-expansion and self-eradication, precisely the sort of paradoxical challenge to the self in the work of Macedonio Fernández. But among many avant-garde writers in Latin America, this tension is inseparable from the effort to reduce language to "ground zero," prior to its appropriation by the rational discourse of cultural institutions and social norms and simultaneous with a striving to affirm distinctively American national identities constituted in language (Unruh 1994, 210–13). In the case of the Martinfierrista generation, the result is the ostensibly spontaneous generation of culture that discovers in Macedonio precisely the mythical figure it requires: a culturally specific vernacular without reference to historical evolution or institutional legitimation. But both this creation of a mythological subject, and the performance it assigns to the subject, are the exact contrary of what Macedonio Fernández strives to achieve.

Naomi Lindstrom describes Macedonio's relationship with language as a highly subversive one in which language is "being deconstructed and reconstituted in new and ever less communicative ways," asserting the writer's "responsibility to correct readers' culturally-induced trust in language" (1981, 87). Masiello adds that Macedonio's "autonomous words" create their "own language" (1986, 147–48). But Macedonio attacks not so much the communicative function of language as the power assumed by the person who uses it. Macedonio aims to eradicate the sense of self constituted with the performative use of language. By denying human beings the constitution of themselves as subjects in their use of language, he attempts to eliminate the very concept of subject. This is the fundamental impulse behind "La oratoria del hombre confuso." In this respect, Macedonio's subversion of language and its potentiality coincides with the avant-garde assaults in one way, and differs substantially in another way.

The free fall of Huidobro's Altazor is in concert with Recienvenido's, but his apparent affirmation of self, constituted in a poetic voice, is utterly at odds with Recienvenido's refusal of that authoritative and self-constituting performance. In this regard Macedonio is in step with many writers of the avant-garde generation, at least superficially. Several avant-garde manifestoes, Ultraist manifestoes among them, condemn the concepts of originality and of lyricism's "psychologically integrated sense of self" (Unruh 1994, 80). Even the hyperlyrical Altazor, although at times verging on megalomaniacal, inflates lyric presence into a disembodied voice (75–76). To this extent, Altazor participates in the same paradox represented by Macedonio's Recienvenido: Unruh refers to it as Altazor's "tug of war" between the detachment of authorial or lyrical voice of "celestial poetics" and the dispersion of that voice in a fragmented and contingent world (73–74). The difference is that Huidobro consistently returns to the lyrical voice, repeatedly deciding in favor of an observant self.

Unlike such authors as Pablo Rojas Paz, whose 1930 *Hombres grises, montañas azules* (Grey Men, Blue Mountains) is clearly a modernist heir to the gauchesque and to rural *costumbrismo*; or such efforts as Borges's early *costumbrismo urbano*, Macedonio is not seeking to transcribe or document language or usage that is specifically Argentine, or Porteño.[40] His infamous tortured syntax and often peculiar lexicon are more easily seen as unnaturally archaic; even his neologisms have more in common with the Castilian of Cervantes than with the *lunfardo* (patois) of the port or the gauchesque of the Pampas. Rather than violate rules of grammar and usage identified with the Castilian of Europe, Macedonio plays with them and exploits their richness, a function, again, of both the polyglossia and parody at work in his prose. One could argue, however, that this "archaizing" language is Macedonio's version of an attempt to reach the "ground zero," mixing new, invented language with languages from different "realms" as an attack on hierarchies inherent in socially and culturally constructed language (Unruh 1994, 212–13). Certainly Macedonio is fashioning a language suited to a transcendence of cultural nationalism, yet concomitantly responsive to the cultural conditions of his environment.[41]

In keeping with his attack on literature as representation, Macedonio eschews the logical prose of storytelling, the simplified rules of modern, straightforward grammar and syntax, and unambiguous lexicon of representation. His conception of "ground zero" language, however, is designed not to help readers understand and articulate what is specifically Argentine, but to provoke his Argentine readers to question and doubt the foundation of their society. In this respect also, Macedonio's language does not reflect the search for the "primitive" cited by Poggioli as typically avant-garde (1968, 55). He does not, like many of his contemporaries, aim to approach a linguistic "void" (Unruh 1994, 216). Rather than seeking to articulate the "pre-rational," Macedonio is interested in the nonrational. He does not try to dig beneath European or Western culture in search of a language somehow prior to it; he is not trying to elaborate a "home ground" apart from European referents (142–50).

In this vein, it is a mistake to regard Macedonio Fernández in quite the same light as Arlt and Ricardo Güiraldes—author of the 1926 classic, *Don Segundo Sombra*—who Masiello believes form, with Macedonio, a "coherent program which organizes Argentine literature of the twenties," and "place the writer in the role of originating interpreter of national history and the mouthpiece of reform" (Masiello 1986, 168). Arlt exercises an aggression on language that makes language strange by wresting it from the control of the patrician classes. Güiraldes champions rural Argentine society by conferring on it its own mythic dimension, elaborated in its own distinctive language (Güiraldes 1998). Macedonio invents an estrangement of language that doubles hegemonic convention against itself, accomplishing a goal similar to Arlt by different means (J. Prieto 2002, 247–48). Macedonio's linguistic operations are both less violent and less alienating of cultivated urban discourse than either Arlt or Güiraldes.

Macedonio also differs fundamentally from Borges in this respect. Like Borges, Macedonio regards the historical dimension of culture and language as completely irreducible and thus inescapable. Unlike Borges, Macedonio's response is to take history for granted, using for his own purposes the complete historical record of Castilian—thus the archaic aspects of his writing—without worrying about where they come from or what particular bearing they may have on the language and culture of the present. It is this kind of procedure that Macedonio has in mind when he claims to invent the "not yet invented," or to invent a wholly new conception of invention. For the only sort of invention possible in a world without a subject—without autonomous selves to invent new things—is a world in which inventions are either always potential or always repetitions. Macedonio's "Prólogo a la Eternidad" (Prologue to Eternity) resounds of Borges's perspective on the repetition of events and ideas, yet eliminates the role of the lyric self so central to Borges's aesthetic project:

Todo se ha escrito, todo se ha dicho, todo se ha hecho, oyó Dios que le decían y aún no había creado el mundo, todavía no había nada. También eso ya me han dicho, repuso quizá desde la vieja, hendida Nada. Y comenzó.

Una frase de música del pueblo me cantó una rumana y luego la he hallado diez veces en distintas obras y autores de los últimos cuatrocientos años. Es indudable que las cosas no comienzan. O el mundo fue inventado antiguo. (*Museo* 8)[42]

[Everything has been written, everything has been said, everything has been done, God heard what they were saying to him and he had not yet created the world, there was not yet anything. This also they have told me, he replied from the old, cloven nothingness. And he began.

An old Romanian woman sang to me a phrase of folk music and I have since found it ten times in different works and authors from the last four hundred years. Doubtless, things do not begin. Or the world was invented old.]

Whereas Borges, in concert with much of the Argentine avant-garde, wants to integrate a distinctively Argentine voice into the historical flow of Western culture, Macedonio sets out to demonstrate that historical and cultural specificity cannot possibly be superseded and thus simply do not matter. Where other avant-garde writers want to get beneath the skin of the Western culture of logic and representation by rejecting linguistic history, Macedonio wants to show us, by fully exploiting linguistic history, that there is nothing inherently logical and representational about it. In other words, like so many American avant-garde writers, Macedonio wishes to elaborate a world that is simultaneously, and paradoxically, mythical and original. His method, rather than heightening the "tension between language as national myth and language as historically formed" (Unruh 1994, 223), explodes that tension.

At the heart of *Museo* is its ninth chapter, "La conquista de Buenos Aires." (The Conquest of Buenos Aires). The ultimate conquest of the city in favor of "Belleza y Misterio" [Mystery and Beauty] is accomplished, in part, by just that explosion of the tension between history, myth, and language:

A los varios hechos del pasado ocurrido se les fulminó la inexistencia valiéndose del hechizo de la Eterna que desata pasados y ata nuevos pasados sustituyentes. (Por eso veis a veces pálida a la Eterna y notáis que no puede pronunciar las enes de las sílabas finales en "on". Cuando dice "pasiom", "salom", han ocurrido las únicas manifestaciones alteradas que se le conocen, y esa alteración únicamente cuando ha cumplido en la noche la inmensa fatiga mental de nulificar un pasado, y, más aun, la de inventarle otro contentador a algún ser de historia dolorosa). (*Museo* 202)

[Various facts of the past transpired have been struck down by inexistence, which takes advantage of the spell cast by Eterna that unleashes pasts and harnesses new substitute pasts. (This is why you sometimes see Eterna looking pale and you note that she cannot pronounce the final "n" of the syllable "on." When she says "passiom," "salom," you will have heard the only altered declarations that she has been known to make, and this only when she has finished up a night of immense mental exhaustion annulling the past, and, even more, a night of inventing another gladdening one for some creature with a painful history.)]

The elimination of history is an expressly linguistic operation. In the process, Eterna is depleted of the ability to pronounce the syllable most requisite for narrating history in Spanish: the third person plural preterit (*hicier*on, *hablar*on). The passage goes on to describe what past things have been eliminated: the legendary executions of Manuel Dorrego and Camila O'Gorman; the enshrined writing implements of adored authors; homages that failed to address "ninguna magnífica obra de madre, ninguna gracia fantástica de niño"(203) [any magnificent work by a mother, any delightful antic of a child]; all biographical place names, and most especially, all statues. The chapter continues:

En fin, en la ciudad presentista algo hizo al tiempo no transcurrente, como la historia, sino un Presente fluido, con memoria sólo de lo que vuelve cotidianamente a ser, no de lo que no se repite, como los aniversarios. Por eso el almanaque de la ciudad tiene 365 días de un sólo nombre: "Hoy", y la avenida principal se llama también "Hoy".

[Finally, in the presentist city something made time not transpiring, like history, but a fluid Present, with memory only of that which recurs daily, not that which doesn't repeat itself, such as anniversaries. For this reason the city almanac has 365 days with only one name: "Today," and the main avenue is also called "Today."]

For Borges, the city possesses an invented or reinvented past, fashioned from the recomposed fragments of history and language available to the writing subject. For Macedonio, the mythic city—the city that has achieved "mystery"—is the city that, having recognized the speciousness of the autonomous self, eliminates it. The city accomplishes this transformation "por milagro de novela" [by miracle of the novel] (*Museo*, 200), a purely aesthetic—indeed linguistic—operation. This "conquest" reveals the inherent absurdity of written history: that language both constitutes and is constituted by historical occurrences.[43] The revelation in turn exposes the fallacy of the primary source of those historical events: the biographical, subjective self.

Macedonio recognizes what Cascardi later described as the characteristic dilemma of modernity as regards the subject. On the one hand, the ascendancy of reason validates the use of history, or more to the point, the alloying of history and logic, in forging society. On the other hand, Descartes's principles eradicate any essential order governing the reading of history. There can be, according to Cartesian thought, no authority by which to read history except the authority of the self, or of individual will. The abstractions, themselves derived from history by means of reason, prove to be mere conventions of language, and are useless in defining the subject's relation to the world. For the Cartesian self, any representation of the world is tantamount to "a representation of its own formative powers." Representation "reduces nature to *cogito*" (Cascardi 1992, 34), and the subject is reduced to the exercise of will (40). The heart of the dilemma, Cascardi points out, is that reason and passion remain unreconciled (36), and that reason is inadequate to allow the subject to account for its own emergence (57).

Borges, while not entirely discarding passion, opts for the ascendancy of reason. His decision not to attempt to reconcile the intellectual with the irrational, but to leave them in constant play, is the keystone of his fictive world from 1927 onward (the year in which he renounced Ultraism and published the precursor to "Hombre de la esquina rosada"). The fact that the only two vignettes in which Borges openly acknowledges this unresolved tension are two of his most often cited nonfictional pieces suggests the impenetrability of this bedrock. Borges consistently resisted allowing his poetics to be reduced further than the concepts represented in "Borges y yo" ("Borges and I") and "Sentirse en muerte" (Feeling in Death).

For Macedonio, representation, logic, and the structures of subject and object, so fundamental to the language he writes in, are false conceits. He strives to reveal the falsehood in the language purporting to rely on those structures and unchallengeable assumptions. Or in Bakhtin's terms, Macedonio Fernández wallows in heteroglossia rather than shutting it out with the "linguistic control" of poetic language. Not surprising, then, is Macedonio's often-cited assertion that true Belarte can only be elaborated in prose, not in poetry. The point to keep in mind here is that Macedonio's drive to "liberate" the reader by relinquishing control of the text, partly through heteroglossia, stems from similar impulses that lead other avant-garde writers to exercise greater control over the text: what Unruh observes as a desire to challenge the culturally determined structures of language (Unruh 1994, 219–21).[44] Macedonio's technique, however, is in keeping with his repudiation of the very concept of an authorial self (Pagni 1991, 206).

Retrograde as Avant-Garde

Macedonio's attempt at aesthetic rupture is conceptually far more radical than that of the Martinfierristas because his motives are to overturn a basic and highly abstract conceptual assumption rather than to reform aesthetic standards. The Martinfierristas are concerned with appropriating aesthetic tradition and authority for a new, cosmopolitan Argentine voice, or as Masiello states of Borges, creating "a place for word and self in Argentine history" (Masiello 1986, 158). Macedonio aims to completely redefine that voice to better serve the well-being of Argentines. Macedonio's use of the ludic likewise attempts to reduce selfhood to the effects of a make-believe game rather than an unquestioned reality. He uses play to obstruct the rulemaking that constitutes the authority—and legitimacy of this self. The Argentine avant-garde, in contrast, uses play as the means to rewrite the rules for culture and to open up new options for the self to exercise its authority.

Similarly, the avant-garde appropriates the concept of invention, keeping intact its quality as a function of individual genius. In the guise of individual genius, the autonomous self is crucial to the avant-garde endeavor to reinvent culture—and by extension—the nation. This reinvention results in a confirmation and reinforcement of the autonomous self: the self is the constant against which culture is reformed.[45] Macedonio, by contrast, invents—as he puts it—a new form of invention that eliminates the autonomous individual altogether. Inventions are not the product of autonomous authors nor can they be "realized" by the genius of a self.[46] According to Macedonio, there can be only two kinds of inventors. One is perpetually absent and unidentified, such as the eternally "future" author of *Novela de la Eterna*. The other is pervasive and infinitely plural: the city of Buenos Aires. Both entities, as Macedonio presents them, obviate the need for a Cartesian self.

Macedonio's prose has frustrated generations of readers and critics in the past because it breaks from accepted aesthetic form without aggressively contorting either lexical usage or grammatical structure to produce its effect. His operation of language is peculiar, but Macedonio's motivations are philosophical and conceptual rather than primarily aesthetic. Macedonio's chosen medium for effecting radical change, however, is aesthetics—to his mind the most purely aesthetic medium possible—because he believes it to be the medium most able to alter human assumptions and beliefs. As a result, we find these principles in Macedonio's writing analogous to avant-garde poetics, yet we also find differences in form and strategy that reflect these different objectives. Most remarkable about this comparison is the revelation that, among the participants in Argentina's avant-garde revolution, it is Macedonio who most clearly desires to change entirely a way of life—with its social, economic, and material realities as well as cultural and philosophical discourses.

Borges wants to capture a mythical Argentine discourse for use in a cosmopolitan, international literary culture—strange and fast-changing, full of innovation and invention, but anchored by a mythical dimension. Arlt wants to use modernity against itself; to strangle the masters of a new and alienating world with their futuristic inventions. Huidobro wants to fall out of the past into an uncertain, destabilizing future, relying on a tyrannical lyric voice to express and experience the ride. Mallea wants to open up infinite lyrical possibilities for an erotic—and essentially romantic—subject. Girondo surveys the wreckage of modernity, refusing to either make sense of it or transform it. All the avant-garde generation rides a wave of change, trying to capture or conquer the leading edge. Macedonio operates neither in the past nor in the future and regards change as a reprehensible illusion. His dream for the city is unapologetically retrograde: out of time, out of self, ignoring the future, and refusing to either enshrine or reject the past.

The most important constant of this discussion is the one that presents the most controversial aspect of this study: Macedonio's recognition that the radicalization of art is a fundamentally political act. He acknowledges as political the development of a living novel that invades public space. Political too is his absent author who simultaneously leads an aesthetic revolution and completely relinquishes its control; his title is, after all, Presidente. Much of Macedonio's aesthetic strategy of the 1920s—and here we must include his burlesque presidential campaign—coincides with Derrida's assessment of "theater of cruelty, minus the violence": simultaneously prescriptive and nonrepresentative, invasive of both public and subconscious life, eradicating the paternal author, replacing spectacle with festival (Derrida 1978, 232–50). And of this new theater, Derrida insists, "The festival must be a political *act*. And the *act* of political revolution is *theatrical*" (245).

4
The Political Is the Personal

THE EFFORTS TO MAINTAIN A MYTHOLOGICAL MACEDONIO FERNÁNDEZ indifferent to publishing, disengaged from aesthetic movements, and withdrawn from artistic society are echoed by the persistence of his image as apolitical. In the case of politics, even more than in literature, this reputation is perpetuated in the face of manifest textual evidence to the contrary. This insensibility is reinforced by the pronouncements of the same generation of Argentine writers and critics who so persistently argue Macedonio's detachment from aesthetic movements and indifference to the fate of his work. The Socrates of Buenos Aires, immersed as he was in metaphysical abstraction, cared as little for social and political reality as he did for the institutions and dynamics of aesthetic creation.

As in the case of literature, Macedonio's putative political apathy is in keeping with the insistence on postmodern paradox that characterizes so much commentary on his work. His libertarian ideals, his flirtation with anarchism, his quirky commentary on Porteño society and Argentine government, his iconoclastic presidential campaign and other, more subtle employment of political metaphor in *Museo de la Novela de la Eterna*; all of these traces of Macedonio's political engagement are indicated as evidence of his foundation in paradox.

Engelbert, for example, qualifies as "incidental" the social content of even his early, less metaphysically oriented writings (Engelbert 1978, 6–7). Dardo Cúneo selects one of Macedonio's more subtle and dense texts, his early article entitled "La desherencia" (Disinheritance), and misreads it toward his purpose of qualifying Macedonio Fernández as innately "timid," a social and political recluse, a trait which Cúneo furthermore asserts as quintessentially "creole" and "Romantic." Cúneo implies that Macedonio's response to the Positivism predominating centenary-era Argentina is to assert himself as an iconoclastic rebel, setting himself apart from society (Cúneo 1955, 87). More recently, however, Mónica Bueno has identified "La desherencia" as an openly political—and anti-Positivist—commentary (Bueno 2000, 59).

In a 1928 response to Ramón Gómez de la Serna's request for an autobiographical sketch for publication, Macedonio includes a comprehensive self-description, including a summary of his ideas on statecraft and libertarian ideals (M. Fernández 1928). Macedonio not only felt his political views to be integral to his artistic and metaphysical ideas, but saw reason to connect them explicitly in a publicity piece. In the published version of this vignette, Gómez de la Serna (1944) suppresses Macedonio's references to his political convictions as well as references to his own physical appearance—we shall take this second suppression up in the next chapter.[1] While it would be unfair to speculate on Gómez de la Serna's reasons, there is no question that his editing helped perpetuate the image of an apolitical Macedonio Fernández.

Unruh warns against too literal a connection between artistic and political contentions, observing that resonance between the two does not necessarily constitute political engagement (1994, 6–7). She also argues that political engagement, in the avant-garde, can take forms that are not overtly political. Following Unruh's lead, this study regards Macedonio's literary and social-political writings as cut from the same cloth.

Macedonio never makes claims to political apathy. He does persistently challenge the usefulness of government, an altogether different attitude from apathy. Macedonio was a convinced libertarian, but he was neither an anarchist—in the accepted sense—nor a cynic. He was fascinated with the workings of government and political systems, with the problems of modern economics, with the dynamics of labor and other modern organizations, and with the principles of law. He frequently—almost obsessively—discusses politics, but he refuses to discuss politics on its own terms. As with the theory and practice of avant-garde art, Macedonio appropriates many of the techniques, even the rhetoric, of contemporary political discourse, to his own ends. In so doing, he challenges, and reverts, many of the assumptions and beliefs supporting that discourse.

His challenges are compiled most extensively in *Museo de la Novela de la Eterna*. The terms that facilitate his challenges—and the reading of them—are laid out in the works that precede *Museo*, as well as in many of *Museo*'s own prologues. These antecedent texts include *Museo*'s companion, *Adriana Buenos Aires*. But the works in which

Macedonio expresses his political thought most directly are *Papeles de Recienvenido* and other short pieces. These writings elucidate Macedonio's response to his immediate political context—the Radical party government of Hipólito Yrigoyen—and his stance on political systems and organizations in general. Macedonio's letters also are a key to gauging his social and political attitudes, especially regarding the workings of day-to-day life in Buenos Aires of the 1920s and 1930s. In all of these writings, Macedonio's censure of government varies in its specifics according to the salient issues of the moment. Finally, a crucial source is the surprisingly accessible writings now compiled in the *Teorías* (Theories) volume of his complete works.

A persistent, common theme runs through all of these writings: the absolute priority of the individual over any social or political organization—the ascendancy of "Maximum Individual" over "Minimal Government." "El individuo máximo" is also an explicit rejection of "maximalism," which in the first decades of the twentieth century meant Marxism. Macedonio's dislike of leftist ideologies is consistent throughout all but his earliest writings, and it is in keeping with the predominant perspective among the avant-garde. This rejection of Marxism stands despite several peculiar facts. First, the founders of the Socialist movement in Argentina were all friends of the Fernández family during Macedonio's youth and, conceivably, frequent visitors to their household (Abós 2002, 33). Second, Macedonio was a contributor to and supporter of at least one early socialist periodical—Leopoldo Lugones's and José Ingenieros's *La Montaña* (Abós 2002, 34, 36). Macedonio's early flirtation with socialism followed by his absolute rejection of it is typical of many Argentine intellectuals of the time, including Jorge Luis Borges (C. García 2000, 30–31).

It is this theme of opposition to government that leads to the perception of paradox with regard to social and political institutions, for it seems to run counter to Macedonio's insistence on the falsehood of the concept of self. But as with cultural context, Macedonio finds the paradox in modern social institutions themselves. Selfhood, he argues, is a fallacy contrived to maintain institutions detrimental to the individual. Much of the substance of Macedonio's social and political commentary aims to elucidate that distinction between the fictional self and the true individual. He does so partly by attacking the subjectivity that modern political and social institutions rest on. Integral with this effort are passages that rearticulate the individual in highly material terms, but terms still relevant to social and political context.

The following pages will argue that Macedonio's treatment of his specific political context—including his peculiar take on Yrigoyen's personalist politics—is an explicit effort to forge an alternative to the autonomous self, using contemporary political discourse. The analysis will elucidate what aspects of Macedonio's greater social and economic context may have provoked him to this tireless effort, and how, by reading this context, Macedonio laid the conceptual foundation for the replacement of self.

Anarchism Apart

Macedonio Fernández was no anarchist in the conventional sense. He did not take part in organized anarchist activity. According to Adolfo de Obieta (1996), he disapproved of the institutional nature of the anarchist movement. The highly programmatic character of Argentine anarchism, along with the stridency of international anarchism, infamous for its bold acts of violence, makes one hesitate to draw any associations between it and Macedonio's Belarte. But a cautious examination reveals certain striking affinities, and, as with the socialist *La Montaña*, some of Macedonio's earliest published writings first appeared in *Ideas y Figuras*, one of the initial serial publications of anarchist Alberto Ghiraldo, a longtime friend of Macedonio.[2]

One must consider whether the affinities between Macedonio's ideas and those of his anarchist contemporaries are largely the result of independent responses to the same conditions. But there are reasons to believe that above and beyond a reaction to the social and cultural conditions around him, Macedonio's vision for Argentine society draws on the vision, the concepts, and even the rhetoric of Argentine anarchism. Anarchist discourse, and its related utopianism, is an essential element in Macedonio's context, and a critical ingredient in his formation of an alternative to self.

Macedonio Fernández's participation in an 1897 utopian endeavor to found an anarchist community in the jungles of northeastern Argentina has long ago passed into legend (Fernández Moreno 1982, 490–92). This adventure is both more and less than the material for a good story. An unpublished letter from Macedonio Fernández to anarchist Julio Molina y Vedia—said to be the mastermind of this utopian dream—details Macedonio's thoughts concerning the principles that ought to reign in such a community. He speaks of this community in terms of its future realization and adumbrates concepts that are to resonate in his writing for the next fifty years. The letter is dated 1905, six years after the supposed folly in the jungle and four years after Macedonio's marriage to Elena de Obieta. The letter indicates, at the very least, that Macedonio took seriously Molina y Vedia's dream of an anarchist community. It also suggests that if the initial excursion took place—and Molina y Vedia's grandson Juan doubts that it did—that dream was kept alive for at least seven more years, well into Macedonio's adult professional life (Molina y Vedia 1996).

Despite Juan Molina y Vedia's doubts, another unpublished letter—the same partially illegible letter to Ramón Gómez de la Serna cited earlier, affirms that some such excursion took place. Macedonio mentions it as well in a diary (C. García 2000, 50n). Alvaro Abós's credible theory is that Macedonio, Borges senior, and Molina y Vedia traveled together to the Molina y Vedia family estancia in Paraguay in 1897, during which trip they discussed the principles of French-born anarchist Eliseo Reclus, who did attempt to found an anarchist commune in Colombia in 1851 (Abós 2002, 40, 47). Abós also points out that Macedonio never contradicted the improbable legend that grew from that journey—a legend referred to in print in Borges's 1923 "El Recienvenido, inédito aún" (48).

Like Macedonio Fernández, Julio Molina y Vedia had limited ties to the programmatic anarchism of early twentieth-century Buenos Aires. He too was from a wealthy, landowning creole family and had little in common with the immigrant workers who constituted Argentina's greater anarchist movement. Nonetheless, the lack of a social or personal connection does not eliminate the possibility of common ideas. Macedonio Fernández, Julio Molina y Vedia, and their anarchist associates came to anarchism from the perspective of landed families who saw a way of life vanishing. Immigrant workers came to it in their desperation for better material conditions.[3] Despite their different motivation, both intellectual anarchists and their laboring counterparts saw in anarchism the only possible response to a fast-changing, increasingly chaotic urban environment ruled by a conflict-ridden and unresponsive political system. Julio Molina y Vedia's 1929 tract proposing an anarchist revolution for Argentina foretells a harmonious "convergence of popular movements" obviating the need for a state (Abós 2002, 46). Abós even sees a kinship between the fundamental ideas of Pierre Quiroule's 1914 *La ciudad anarquista americana* (The American Anarchist City) and the pyramid structure of Macedonio's word-of-mouth presidential campaign (46).

There are some strong similarities between the utopian visions found in intellectual vehicles—such as Molina y Vedia's writings, or the early anarchist serials of Alberto Ghiraldo—and the programmatic rhetoric of Argentina's primary working class anarchist mouthpiece, *La Protesta* (Protest). Dora Barrancos notes the interrelationship of these different anarchisms and their reliance on numerous common theoretical sources, calling the collective movements "a vast attempt at subversion" (Barrancos 1990, 17).[4] These similar ideas also inform the writings of Macedonio Fernández, lending further evidence to the argument that some of the concepts fundamental to Macedonio's metaphysical vision, and his renovation of the individual, coincide with the principles of a profoundly social movement.

The Error of Government

Macedonio Fernández could reasonably claim to be an anarchist in one sense: his condemnation of all government. In his writings, both democracy as a concept and the actual practice of compulsory suffrage, introduced in Argentina by the 1914 Saenz-Peña law, come under fierce attack (*Teorías*, 163–64). Democracy, Macedonio suggests, is more valuable for its sense of ethical equality than for any inherent justice in government. He denounces universal suffrage as a sham that compromises the individual integrity of citizens. Voting, he insists, constitutes a delegating of individual liberties to institutions—institutions that provoke a further relinquishing of individual freedom.

Macedonio makes his most succinct declarations on forms of government in one of his most remarkable texts. Like the "Oratoria de un hombre confuso," his "Brindis a Marinetti" (Toast to Marinetti) is one of a series of spoken addresses contributing to Hidalgo's *Revista Oral* (Oral Review), given at gatherings in honor of local or visiting artistic personalities. To judge by Macedonio's comments, Marinetti's 1926 visit was a momentous event in Buenos Aires (*Recienvenido*, 44; A. Prieto 1977, 51–52; Abós 2002, 123). Macedonio's address to this visitor reveals some of his most adroit commentary, embracing a fellow poet and his aesthetic accomplishments while rejecting his ideological posture. Macedonio regards Marinetti's ideology-based futurism as inherently paradoxical:

> pues mientras paracéis pasatista en cuanto a teoría del Estado, lo que impresiona contradictorio con vuestra estética, y creéis en el benificio de las dictaduras, provisorias o regulares, yo no conservo de mi media fe en el Estado, más que la mitad, por haberla compartido con nuestro fundador Hidalgo, a quien debemos vuestra presencia aquí. Me quedo una cuarta parte de fe estatal, la indispensable para no confundir dos cosas fiscales: los faroles con los buzones, al confiar a éstos la redacción de mis cartas. (*Recienvenido,* 61)

> [for while you seem to be past-ist with regard to a theory of State, which appears contradictory to your aesthetics, and you believe in the benefit of dictatorships, provisional or regular, I don't retain more than half of my half-faith in the State, having shared it with our founder Hidalgo, to whom we owe your presence here. I'm left with one fourth of state faith, just enough not to confuse two fiscal things: lampposts with postboxes, on trusting to the latter the composition of my letters.]

What Macedonio expresses here as a contradiction, he develops further in this and other "toasts" as paradox. The address to Marinetti contains numerous plays on the concepts of "futurism" and "future;" in his "brindis" to Leopoldo Marechal, another prominent Martinfierrista, Macedonio makes the intent of these word plays clear. He implies that futurism itself embodies a disturbing oxymoron: it treats the future as an artifact, very much the way accepted aesthetics treat the past (*Recienvenido,* 63–4). The enshrinement of government and its ascendancy over individual lives is, to Macedonio, symptomatic of "past-ism." Macedonio identifies worship of the past with the general—arguably Positivist, and ultimately Cartesian—practice of the assertion of self: the subsuming of human interaction to a single, subjective will. This enshrinement of the past, he argues, is ultimately responsible equally for the outbreak of dictatorships in Europe and for the "frenzy" of domestic regulation (specifically, Prohibition) gripping the United States. Macedonio concludes his address to Marinetti:

> hay que confesar, insigne futurista, que el pasado no ha muerto, no le falta un parecido de porvenir. (*Recienvenido,* 62)

[one must confess, renowned futurist, that the past has not died; that it does not lack resemblance to the future.]

The libertarian conceit that democracy is by nature no less obnoxious an institution than dictatorship is a constant in Macedonio's writing. He asserts this conviction in his earlier writings, well before his acquaintance with Marinetti or the surge of interest in fascism corresponding to futurism. Without a doubt, Macedonio's notions on the ills of government were firmly in place by the end of the First World War. A series of writings grouped together by Adolfo de Obieta and entitled "Para una teoría del estado" (Toward a Theory of the State) attests to this fact (*Teorías*, 115–98).

Macedonio Fernández's libertarian commentary at times reads like a hyperbolic paraphrase of Spencerian theory. His most pointed condemnation is reserved for leftist ideology and left-wing movements—he refers to the government of the newly formed Soviet Union as a "grupo ficticio llamándose nación" (*Teorías*, 137). [fictitious group calling itself a nation]. But virtually all forms of government earn his scorn. Macedonio tends to orient these pronouncements to an international perspective, both referring to the principals and practices of government in the broadest possible terms and offering critiques of other national governments, the U.S., U.K., and Spain in particular.

These comments take the classic Spencerian view that most government activity amounts to a limitation of individual potential and initiative, and thus an impoverishment, rather than an enhancement, of civil liberties. Macedonio's political prose often echoes the aggressive, inciting rhetoric of the movements he condemns. Consider a typical excerpt of these remarks, taken from a 1920 essay titled "No existe problema social-económico" (There Is No Socioeconomic Problem):

> Hay que convencer también a obreros, consumidores, pequeños comerciantes y rentistas, es decir el 95% de la humanidad, creyente sin excepción en el Estado providencia. Hay que convencer a todos los militares, a todos los policías, a todos los cleros: todos están con el Estado providencia que comercia y ara, fija precios y salarios, arbitra huelgas como juez forzoso, legisla las ventanas, los muros, las velocidades, las tarifas, las diversiones, los vicios, decreta vacunas, desinfectantes, purgantes, prohibe profesiones, diploma honestidades y sabidurías. (*Teorías*, 127)

> [There also remain to be convinced workers, consumers, small business owners and landlords, in other words, 95% of humanity, believers with-

out exception in the provident State. One has to convince all the military, all the police, all the clergy: all of them are with the provident State that trades and plows, fixes prices and salaries, arbitrates strikes like a binding judge, legislates windows, walls, speeds, tariffs, amusements, vices, decrees vaccinations, disinfectants, enemas, outlaws professions, certifies honesties and wisdoms.]

Macedonio constantly reiterates his opposition to collective industrial action as well as government intervention in relations between labor and capital (for example, *Teorías*, 125–31). This was one of the most explosive issues in Buenos Aires in the years following the First World War, and an issue affecting the population at large.[5] Years of strikes culminated in January 1919 with the eruption of citywide violence in the Semana Trágica (Tragic Week), the result of not only labor unrest, but of inflationary pressures on the working classes, a severe housing shortage, and, not insignificantly, the xenophobic goading of the ultraconservative and paramilitary Liga Patriótica or Patriotic League (Rock 1985, 202).

The beginning of this period of turbulence coincides with the advent of Argentina's "experiment" in democracy brought about by the Saenz-Peña law. Universal and compulsory male suffrage resulted in both Yrigoyen's Radical national government and the strong Socialist presence on the Buenos Aires *consejo deliberante*, or city council (Rock 1975b, 77–80). Macedonio is acutely sensitive to the equivocating government's role in abetting abuses on both sides of the labor conflict. The thrust of his writings responds to what he regards as an explosion of leftist ideology and propaganda in the wake of the Great War (*Teorías*, 162). But these passages also reveal that Macedonio regards "maximalism" as constituting government interference on behalf of capital as well as labor (*Teorías*, 130–31). He is flatly critical of capital's "complacency" in the growth of government, goading government into favorable treatment of capital investors (126). His overall point is the quintessentially libertarian view that government's primary objective is to assert its own authority to resolve social and economic questions.

The evident paradox between Macedonio's championing of the individual over all forms of government and the repudiation of the concept of self is starkest in the light of these early commentaries. One brief clue to understanding his perspective on this paradox is his attempt to explain, in these early writings, how both labor and capital are intrinsic to the human condition:

El trabajo contra el capital es el trabajo actual contra el trabajo anterior, es el trabajo actual contra los ahorros de ese trabajo considerados en el futuro.... El capital es tan biológico como las edades en cada ser vivo. (*Teorías,* 129)

[Work versus capital is current work versus earlier work, is current work versus the savings of that work considered in the future.... Capital is as biological as the stages in each living being.]

The idea that capital is a function of work, and work a biological phenomenon inherent to all human beings, argues, in Macedonio's mind, for the notion that "self" is a fiction serving to obscure the importance of an individual's work in constituting his or her identity. The bearing of this logic on such categories as class, or even "person," and such problems as the relation between physical and spiritual identity, compose much of the substance of Macedonio's prose fiction.

The especially perplexing problem of wealth and inheritance is clarified in these theoretical writings, which express extreme conservatism on economic issues. His repudiation of Marxist arguments that impugn capitalism verge, at moments, on rabid. In that vein are Macedonio's blanket condemnation of collective bargaining of any kind and his rejection of Marxist arguments regarding the inequities of wealth inherent to capitalism. These categorical pronouncements against the validity of the concept of the proletariat seem irreconcilable with Macedonio's sympathy for the dispossessed.[6] His anti-Marxist rhetoric certainly contrasts with his iconoclastic lifestyle, which appeared to reject the most fundamental aspects of bourgeois life.

Fernández Latour argues that Macedonio simply viewed unequal wealth as an immutable feature of human existence (1980, 24–25). José Isaacson reasons that by dubbing them "political," Macedonio was really criticizing the "bad laws" resulting from industrial action (Isaacson 1981, 45).[7] But Macedonio himself tells us that his perspective on wealth is far more radical than such unreflective libertarianism. He is highly sensitive to both poverty and the spreading urban misery around him. His dismissal of Marxism is explained partly by his conviction that material poverty is the worldwide norm. Wealth such as found in modern Argentina, he argues, is scant, fleeting, and insignificant (*Teorías* 132, 147–49). His own lifestyle was a demonstration, although ingenuous, of what he regarded as the insignificance of those small and ephemeral pockets of great wealth exemplified by Argentine society of the time. His defense of the principles of capital, property, and inheritance were based on a genuine desire for the most productive and generally beneficial use of scarce resources. Property, Macedonio adds, along with work, constitutes one of the few irreducible components of "el hombre mismo" (man himself), that is, individual identity (*Teorías,* 140).

The Fallacy of Wealth and Class

The labor conflicts gripping Buenos Aires prior to 1920, not surprisingly, were closely tied to the phenomena of classism and xenophobia. Recent analyses of the failures characterizing the Radical government, and of the economic and civic crises leading to that failure, focus on the rigid social hierarchies of Argentine society and on the economic and political consequences of that hierarchy. Studies of Porteño society prior to 1940 emphasize the physical segregation of the city, still as evident in contemporary Buenos Aires as in any U.S. metropolis: wealthy creoles in the northern neighborhoods of Retiro, la Recoleta, Palermo, and Belgrano; a mixed, middle-class population—including the substantial Jewish community—in the western districts extending out from the Plaza Miserere, and a burgeoning working class of largely immigrant multitudes in the southern districts. The reach of infrastructure and public services to these areas of the city corresponded closely to class and economics. Southern neighborhoods have a long, consistent record of protesting the lack of access to transportation, energy, and hygiene resources amid the rapid growth and modernization of the city (Walter 1993, 53).

Other sources emphasize the extraordinary efforts of lawmakers, administrators, investors, and image-makers to maintain the privileged status of creole families (Yujnovsky 1974, 333; Scobie 1974, 82, 208–14; Ruibal 1993, 33–40; Sebrelli 1964, 34–58). The resistance to such efforts is plain in those political and social movements most intimately tied to the immigrant population: syndicalism, socialism, and anarchism. Creole families, including those outside the ruling oligarchy, felt threatened by the labor and civic unrest resulting from these movements, which in turn responded to the inadequate working and living conditions in the capital for the vast majority of immigrants. The right-wing vigilante Liga Patriótica, whose actions contributed to the violence of the Semana Trágica, was only the most extreme of many efforts to blame these working-class movements on alien influences brought to Argentina by immigrants, particularly Jews (Rock 1985, 202).

As disparaging as Macedonio was of the concept of economic and social disparity, he had manifestly less sympathy for such institutional—and ultimately violent—responses to tensions. He dismisses the Liga Patriótica as perpetuating "maximalism" by promoting an unreformed government inherently disadvantageous to the individual (*Teorías,* 158–59). He rejects institutional anarchism as promoting violence (125), and dismisses socialism as simply another form of "state coercion" (131).

His dislike for political institutions goes much further and is rooted in a reactionary—and at moments almost paranoid—abhorrence of modern commercial culture. In a stunningly foresighted commentary written during the First World War, Macedonio fears that anarchy and dire poverty resulting from the war will engender tyrannical governments oriented exclusively to the production and distribution of wealth (*Teorías,* 156–57). It is this fear that lies at the root of Macedonio's rejection of the concepts of economic and social class, of material progress, and of institutions and governments that, in effect, at once aggravate and legitimize the polemics over the means of the production of goods and wealth. The division between labor and management, and the governments and institutions—including unions—that perpetuate the division, are for Macedonio a fundamental ill.

Concomitant with Macedonio's assault on unions, government intervention, and other institutional incursions in free intercourse between labor and capital is his startling retort to general concerns of the rising cost of living—and deterioration of living standards—for the average working Argentine. Historians demonstrate that this was a serious difficulty in years prior to and during the First World War. The problem was grave enough for the municipal government to experiment with *ferias francas* or open food markets in 1910 (Walter 1993, 35), and for both municipal and federal governments to debate the question repeatedly through the war years, finally resulting in a federally imposed rent freeze in 1921 (72–73). The bearing of the escalating cost of living on labor unrest is universally acknowledged (Skidmore 1989, 81).

Macedonio's response to this crisis is predictably iconoclastic; he denies its existence, or at least, its importance. This denial complements his aforementioned assertion that humans are poor by nature. The world's wealth, equally distributed, Macedonio argues, would amount to no more than forty gold pesos a year:

> Es el costo de un traje con ropa interior, sombrero y calzado, la defensa y sólo por seis meses contra la sola sensación del frío, entre las muchas que tiene el hombre; lo que tiene todo cordero a los tres meses de nacer en capital (¿natural o creado?) para la misma defensa, aproximadamente. (*Teorías,* 147)

> [The cost of a suit with underclothes, hat and footwear, the defense and only for six months against only the sensation of cold, among the many that man has, that which every lamb has three months after birth in capital (natural or created?) for the same defense, approximately.]

This commentary can be interpreted as a rejection of modern consumption and materialism as much as a dismissal of economic ills. Mass-produced fashion, a largely post-World War I development, generalized the equating of attire to the expression of self, especially among the middle class (Jervis 1998, 121). It is not surprising, then, that Macedonio should choose apparel as the best illustration of the vacuity of modern economic activity. It strikes him as perfectly natural that the world should be poor, that goods should be costly, and that providers of capital should profit from their production (*Teorías,* 151, 160). The consequences to the individual, he suggests, are negligible.

Macedonio's solution to the conflicts generated by the misconceptions concerning labor and capital is unapologetically retrograde. Having already condemned the values and consequences of modern industrial culture, he proposes it be substituted with a culture of cottage industries, arguing that to do so would be both more efficient and more salutary for family and neighborhood. This idyllic—and undeniably unrealistic—vision of urban life unspoiled by the institutions of modern commerce and industry hints of a nostalgia for simpler, if arguably imaginary, times. It also has strong resonance of the utopian discourse prevalent during Macedonio's youth and characteristic of Molina y Vedia's aristocratic anarchism.

This sentiment is shared by writers both of Macedonio's generation, including modernistas and naturalists, and by the younger Martinfierristas. Horacio Quiroga's "*cuentos del monte,*" Güiraldes's *Don Segundo Sombra,* Lugones's *El payador,* all reveal the same nostalgic, antibourgois, reaction to urban modernization. Borges, in his early essays and in *Cuaderno San Martín* (1929), opts to "freeze," in a mythical cityscape, the intimate scale of traditional (historical or imagined) neighborhood life. Such a vision is a vital key to a clearer understanding of Macedonio's conception of ideal family and neighborhood dynamics. Family and *barrio* (neighborhood) interdependence, critical as it is to his aspirations for the city, are to be founded on a different sort of individuality than the received notions of self. The institutions of commerce and production, Macedonio implies, by helping to implant this abstract fabrication called "self," hinder the realization of the "maximum individual," and thus the development of authentic, more rewarding interrelationships.

Yrigoyen's Allure

Macedonio's response to the personalist form of liberal democracy of the Yrigoyen and Alvear administrations reflects both his ambivalent view of government and his obsession with the problem of the individual subject. Horacio González in particular has remarked on the paradox of Macedonio Fernández's rejection of government, ideology, and party politics in tandem with his preoccupation with the mechanisms and strategies of disseminating ideology and achieving power (H. González 92–93). Borges, we have already acknowledged, appreciated Macedonio's fascination for the tactics of acquiring power. What Borges and most others are less quick to perceive is that Macedonio's interest in the dynamics of power is immediately responsive to the specific, predominant institutions of politics and self-promotion of the day, to wit, the Unión Cívica Radical and its leader, Hipólito Yrigoyen, who served as president of Argentina from 1916 to 1922 and 1928 to 1930.

A discussion of Macedonio Fernández in terms of Yrigoyen's persona and politics is not meant to suggest a straightforward relationship between them, nor does it mean to limit to Yrigoyenism a consideration of Macedonio's political inspiration. Yrigoyen's personalist tactics belong to a larger, and earlier, tradition of personalist politics in Argentina. But Yrigoyen's influence and administration did coincide with Macedonio's most active creative period. There is no question that regardless of his debt to his predecessors, Yrigoyen constitutes for Macedonio a living paradigm of personalist political strategy.

The identification between the absent writer Macedonio, "who at times is and at times is not the Presidente (of *Museo de la Novela de la Eterna*)," and the elusive president of the Argentine Republic, involves more than the coincidence of their baroque writing styles, noted by one of Ricardo Piglia's fictional characters (1994, 17). It goes further than the "*cotidianeidad elusiva*" (elusive everydayness) observed by David Viñas (1989, 14). Fernández Latour hints at the complexity of this affinity when he notes that Macedonio admires Yrigoyen as a *caudillo* (political boss) but not in his governing role (1980, 17). David Rock summarizes Yrigoyen's political persona thus:

> Yrigoyen made few pronouncements on specific political issues but attacked Roca's system rather by impugning its morality. . . . the historical mission of Radicalism, "the Cause" (*La Causa*), was to overthrow the Regime and implant democracy. Year after year, Yrigoyen sought to publicize this message in long, rambling manifestoes, yet he adopted an air of conspiratorial secrecy, making no public appearances nor ever speaking in public. He also made a cult of personal austerity and lived with deliberate frugality, constantly affecting poverty although he was a landowner of some substance. (Rock 1985, 185).

There is no evidence that Macedonio meant to undertake a wholesale imitation of Yrigoyen's tactics and rhetoric. Adolfo de Obieta affirms that Macedonio's ascetic lifestyle, for one, resulted not from affect, but from real financial limitations as well as from a desire to free himself of the trappings of maintaining a household (Ranieri 1995; de Obieta 1996). Economic circumstances aside, there is ample reason to believe that Macedonio's campaign of absence, both literary and political, both novelized and lived, drew inspiration from Yrigoyen's long public career. As a cautionary note, Horacio González also observes an irony in this influence. González acknowledges the temptation to assert the coincidences in both ideas and style between Macedonio's metaphysics and Yrigoyen's politics as evidence of a mode of thought specific to their "episteme." But he reminds us, as we suggest in our introduction, that neither man would have accepted, had he understood, the concept of episteme. In both cases, their rhetoric constitutes a rejection of the idea of writing as "an anonymous organ of a historical moment" (1995, 210). This caveat, however, leads us to examine these coincidences in the more prosaic terms of influences and inspirations.

It is clear that at the moment of Radicalism's triumph, Macedonio was an open supporter of its leader and recently elected president (Abós 2002, 83). While he regarded the new government as good for the nation, Macedonio's admiration for Yrigoyen had personal significance. Adolfo de Obieta tendered the idea that Macedonio entertained the fantasy of being a sort of advisor to the president without having to exercise command, a role repugnant to him (Fernández-Latour 1980, 18). Both of these observations are crucial to the political implications of Macedonio's renovation of the individual. On the one hand the success of the ubiquitous, yet perpetually absent, larger-than-life caudillo, infiltrating virtually every aspect of modern Argentine life, resonates with Macedonio's desire to revolutionize the very way Argentines see themselves in the world.[8] On the other hand, the epidemic bureaucracy and the seemingly limitless reach of government regulation provoke Macedonio's horror of all aspects of the institutionalizing and imposing of a subjective, governing, self. Macedonio found in Yrigoyen a striking resonance with his own sentiments and ideas on the need to fundamentally reform Argentine society—and by extension all human existence—by modifying individual human behavior and thought. He also perceived a disturbing—to him—faith in systemic political solutions. If contemporary readers find paradox in Macedonio's treatment of the same social concerns addressed by Radicalism, it is because Yrigoyen himself presents to Macedonio such an extreme paradox.

Macedonio Fernández came by his Radical sympathies naturally. Relatively modest creole landowners who lived in an old-fashioned house in Balvanera, the neighborhood of Yrigoyen's birth, Macedonio's family were typical of what historians describe as supporters of the Radical movement (Rock 1975b, 73; Leland 1986, 9; Smith 1974, 9). Middle-class creoles may have desired the wresting of government power from the creole oligarchy, but would not have benefited from the sort of sweeping social and economic revolution promoted by anarchists and socialists (Martínez Díaz 1988, 64).

Macedonio felt a personal affinity for many of Yrigoyen's methods and more than a few of his principles. Radical "intransigence" was instituted and championed by Yrigoyen following Radicalism's repeated failure, around the turn of the century, at revolutionary action. This strategy consisted mainly of Yrigoyen's persistent refusal to participate in either elections or governance until the "movement's" demands of universal suffrage were satisfied.

Yrigoyen's personal habits of austerity and reclusion, whether sincere or calculated, magnified the effect of this intransigent abstention. His startling success at capturing both the imagination and the loyalties of a broad cross section of Argentines lay, in part, in mystery and in the folklore generated by his elusive persona (Cárdenas 1967, 92–93; Rock 1975a, 99–104). This enigmatic demeanor was complemented with another quality attributed as well to Macedonio Fernández: Rock tells us Yrigoyen possessed an exceptional gift for amicable conversation (Rock 1975a, 102). Yrigoyen's most effective tool of self-promotion seems to have been a weighty absence effected by visiting cities around the republic and then refusing to grant interviews or public appearances, limiting his intercourse to private conversations sufficient to "enflame his visitors" (Cárdenas 1967, 98). These sorts of methods were intensified prior to the October 1928 presidential elections, when Yrigoyen was eligible to run for a second term of office after Marcelo Alvear's intervening term. The Radical party postponed its convention, and Yrigoyen was only declared the party's candidate after keeping the public in suspense for over two months (Mayo 1972, 21).

It does not require great imagination to see how impressed Macedonio was with Yrigoyen's technique. Two aspects of Macedonio's burlesque 1921 campaign for the presidency, and its 1927 reiteration as a literary performance, bear emphasizing here. One is that the whole objective was to make the peculiar Christian name ubiquitous while the man in flesh remained unseen: the "difusión del nombre" discussed in chapter 2 of this study. The other was to create such tension and frustration among the populace of the city—where Argentine elections are won and lost—that the physically absent yet renowned Macedonio would be regarded as the "only solution" (G. García 1975, 23).

Macedonio was serious as to the efficacy of this method, whether or not he imagined it would win him the presidency. The Yrigoyenist method extended also to the "intransigent" posture that, prior to the 1914 Saenz-Peña law, was meant to "clear the way" for a completely reformed political process in Argentina (Martínez Díaz 1988, 46). The vague, often abstract principles that both fueled and represented the Radical movement have led numerous analysts to conclude that the Radicals ultimately galvanized into a party without a program (Rock 1985, 186; González Arzac 1970, 28–29). What Yrigoyen realized was that faith in the sweeping change Radicals envisioned could only be inspired by articulating an alternative to programmatic politics. Macedonio understood that Yrigoyen's genius lay in his refusal to play by the same rules and create with the same substance as his forerunners. Macedonio recognized that the epithet of "personalism," inspired by an image of Yrigoyen as charismatic, was a tribute to the president's success at elaborating an alternative to an autonomous self[9].

Like Gertrude Stein, another figure simultaneously integral to and apart from the avant-garde, Macedonio Fernández discovers that the distinction between political message and literary creation has become too blurred to be useful (Garth 1991, 53). H. González dubs Macedonio's presidential campaign "an avant-garde and Dada petition" signaling this crisis in communications (1995, 36). As González notes, one corollary of this conflation of the imaginative and the programmatic is a highlighting of the confusion between purely artistic ingenuity and critique of convention. González also points out that both Borges and Arlt appropriate similar conceits for their fiction (37). This sort of experiment in rhetoric quickly came to be one of the enduring hallmarks of the Martinfierrista generation and of avant-gardes everywhere. Vicente Huidobro's commingling of political grandstanding with literary invention is shared by European surrealists; for the Auden poets, the "fusion of political and literary discourses" was the answer to the salvation of English, and ultimately world, culture (Strong 1997, 123).

Ironically, none of these groups, the Martinfierristas included, learned this lesson well. Political divisiveness was one of the primary forces leading the closure of *Martín Fierro*, and its successors, such as *Síntesis* and *Sur*, were never comfortable with the conflation of the literary and the political (Strong 1997, 104–5). While Borges's claims to being apolitical (and the corresponding criticism of his "aloofness") can be seen as disingenuous, Borges never mastered Macedonio's double-sided exploitation of political strategy and rhetoric.[10] Among the prominent writers of Borges's generation, only Arlt came close to exploring the power inherent in such rhetorical games, reinforcing the illusory distinction between the conservative "Florida" writers as purely aesthetic and the "Boedo" writers as political. Given the discomfort of the Martinfierrista generation, and Borges in particular, with politicized literary production, especially after 1930, one may reasonably ask if Borges's distancing from Macedonio had something to do with Macedonio's persistence in responding to political discourse.

The Novel Solution

Until 1993, the general belief was that *Museo* was written after the 1930 coup that deposed Yrigoyen and ended Radical ascendancy.

Prieto and Camblong argue convincingly, however, that the masterwork was in constant process from at least 1925 onward and pointedly incorporated the 1927 "campaign" into its text (J. Prieto 2002, 79–80).[11] Camblong dates full manuscript versions of *Museo* to 1929 and documents evidence of earlier composition (*Museo*, lx). In any event, it is manifest that *Museo*'s Presidente—who also serves at moments as Macedonio's own alter ego—draws inspiration from Yrigoyen.

This consideration of *Museo*'s Presidente returns us to his campaign to save Buenos Aires from the tragedy of ugliness. The "conquest of the city in favor of beauty and mystery" is the brainchild of the Presidente. While the methods of this campaign constitute a literary version of Macedonio's ludicrous ploys in 1921 (J. Prieto 2002, 67), in "(Que no)," the chapter in *Museo* just prior to the description of the beautification campaign, the Presidente reveals his motives for undertaking the campaign:

Pero un día no fue como todos. Encontraron, volviendo de Buenos Aires, ensimismado al Presidente. Y en la noche avanzada, reunidos todos, díjoles:
"Con mala noticia os hablo.
He prolongado dos años esta prueba de amistad y aunque me dio, por vosotros, una vida que vale más que el no vivir, no ha dado a mi destino conciencia de finalidad, de dignidad. Sólo la Pasión puede darla. Y la curación de mi alma para la pasión que no logré de la amistad, espero, última y nueva esperanza, de la Acción". (*Museo*, 194)

[But one day was not like all the others. Upon returning from Buenos Aires, they found the President lost in thought. And late in the night, as they were gathered together, he said to them:
"I have bad news for you.
I have drawn out this test of friendship for two years, and though it has given me, through you, a life worth more than not living, it has not given to my destiny a consciousness of finality, of dignity. Only Passion can do that. And the healing of my soul for Passion which I haven't accomplished with friendship, I hope to accomplish, new and last hope, with Action."]

The campaign is integral to a perpetual quest for a justification for individual existence; integral to the search for the passion that constitutes a purpose for living. Macedonio's man in charge, intoning with a gravity usually reserved for politicians and clergy, determines that "action" may complete the quest that friendship can only partly accomplish. This fictional determination in favor of action mimics the Radicals' decisive shift, as a result of the Saenz-Peña Law, from "Abstention" to active—indeed highly organized and energetic—political participation. The Presidente's decision echoes Yrigoyen's own sudden change of posture, from elusive and self-effacing to omnipresent and self-promoting, during his first term of 1916 to 1922. The strategy of Macedonio's character, like Macedonio's own parodic political action, is most redolent of Yrigoyen's behavior in that it effects what Rock describes as Yrigoyen's omnipresence in the complete absence of actual public appearances (Rock 1975a, 53, 99–104).

The conditions of the city upon which the campaign in *Museo* is executed also reveal a direct response on Macedonio's part to the Buenos Aires he knew. Striking in this chapter of *Museo* is the description of the circumstance in Buenos Aires that provokes the Presidente's action and determines his tactics. The city finds itself torn apart by two competing "bands:" "*Enternecientes*" and "*Hilarantes*" ("Tenderizers" and "Hilaricizers," though the latter can also suggest "Plotters"). Each tries to dominate the city through a campaign of aesthetic devices conceivably corresponding to popular Romanticism versus avant-garde kitsch. The Hilaricizers, by decree, contort the city's mirrors, resulting in a hysteria that brings business and public affairs in Buenos Aires to a sudden and complete halt (*Museo*, 199).

The Tenderizers, in their turn, seize the city's loudspeakers and force the endless recitation of a preposterous epic poem about literally self-effacing lovers brought to suicide by a series of fears and misunderstandings. The hopelessly ugly heroine incinerates herself when she learns her blind lover has regained his vision; the newly sighted lover kills himself upon learning he will never lay eyes on his beloved. The story is doubly tragic, we are advised, since a man blind from birth would have no innate sense of physical beauty and would not have rejected his homely beloved upon seeing her. We are also told:

> Este relato versificado fue repetido por toda la población como desayuno, almuerzo, merienda y cena, con el resultado de que un niño hubiera podido apoderarse del gobierno de Buenos Aires al finalizar la semana enterneciente. (*Museo*, 199)

> [This story in verse was repeated by the entire population like breakfast, lunch, tea and supper, with the end result that a child could have taken

over the government of Buenos Aires at the end of the Tenderizing week.]

Camblong suggests, reasonably, in her footnote in the critical edition, that this scenario might be allegorical for the Boedo–Florida rivalry among Buenos Aires writers (*Museo,* 108n). J. Prieto expands this idea, suggesting that with this schema Macedonio posits himself as the mediator between avant-garde and traditional poetics (2002, 85–86). The allegory could as easily stand for any number of other aesthetic—and ideological—divisions afflicting Argentine society. Gallo and Segal (1965) emphasize the role of "mounting political intransigence," polarization and divisiveness generally in impeding the development of a viable democracy during this period. And Nicholas Shumway, in his study of their opposing "guiding fictions," elucidates that the various agonizing conflicts between Federalists and Unitarists, traditionalists and cosmopolitans, elitists and populists, have been carried out in poetry and prose as well as in battle.

The practice of "guiding fictions," or of ideology communicated in compelling and enduring stories, is neither specifically modern nor specifically Argentine. It is a phenomenon Macedonio Fernández was acutely sensitive to. Shumway tells us that the twentieth-century political strategies of "intransigence," as well as personalism and the continued manipulation of national mythology, are the legacy of ideological conflicts evolving since prior to Argentine independence (1991, 39–40). If Shumway is right, Macedonio's allegory in his "Conquest of Buenos Aires" implicates the entirety of Argentine cultural and ideological discourse.

What is most striking about the competing gangs in this episode of *Museo* is their manipulation of shared cultural assumptions about individual identity. Both groups act to reinforce and frustrate, simultaneously, the public's faith in identity as equivalent to an autonomous self. Both simultaneously reinforce and frustrate the public's conception of the self as identifiable in *images* of one's own person. Distorted mirrors are cataclysmically disruptive because they focus attention on the frustrated search for the image of the individual that people sense must somehow reveal the true self. The saga of blind love gone awry fixes on the notion that the true self where love resides can be disguised, embellished and contorted but not fundamentally altered; at the same time, it suggests that faith in both this self and the image corresponding to the self is universal, not individual.

The crises resulting from these aesthetic ploys in *Museo* are consummately material, and they are not distant from the realities of Buenos Aires of the 1920s and 1930s. Disruptive strikes, while never reaching the extreme levels of the wartime years, increased steadily throughout the period.[12] More important, the 1929 collapse of financial markets worldwide provoked a crisis in the Argentine economy—and government—that quickly doomed the precarious Yrigoyen administration, disliked among the controlling elites (Rock 1985, 212; 1975b, 85). The quip, that at the end of the "tenderizing week" a child could have taken control of the government, is nearly a paraphrasing of the mood of many Porteños when, after less than two years of a tumultuous second term, Hipólito Yrigoyen was easily deposed in an uncontested military coup in 1930.[13]

Shumway tells us that the political posture of "intransigence," so adeptly used by Yrigoyen, has its antecedent in the work of Mariano Moreno. Moreno's primary contribution to the national mythology is his strategy of defeating "political evil" by "denying it space in the good." Moreno is also largely responsible for the Argentine heroic paradigm: he effectively ties the concept of individual liberty to elitism and, more importantly here, to heroic identity (Shumway 1991, 39–40).

Macedonio's critique of a Buenos Aires under the Yrigoyen he appears to admire and emulate hinges not so much on specific policies and practices of the Radical government or political campaigning, but on the ethical and philosophical assumptions Radicalism adopts wholesale from its predecessors. For all of the inspiration Macedonio may have found in Yrigoyen's demeanor and method, he found both the substance and the underlying tenets of Radicalism to be unredeemable.

The profundity and absoluteness of Macedonio's critique of Radicalism is such that his parody finds resonance at many levels. Rock, for instance, describes the tactics of Radical campaigning during the years between the promulgation of the Saenz-Peña law and Yrigoyen's election; these tactics are a prelude to the actions of Yrigoyen's government. The Radical campaigns established charity centers and entertainment centers, supported holiday celebrations, subsidized public medical and legal services and distributed subsidized food. The campaigns also flooded selected neighborhoods (including Macedonio's own Balvanera Sur) with printed propaganda (Rock 1975a, 57–58).

This was the same Radical organization that, once it occupied the executive branch, engaged in a well-engineered system of political patronage to maintain public support. It was a patronage system inextricable from Radicalism's personalist tactics and partly responsible for the government's vulnerability to the 1930 conservative coup (Rock 1975a, 107–14). Yrigoyen's popularity rested on his success at linking the growth of bureaucratic career opportunities and government services with a faith in the ascendancy of the autonomous self. His individual identity was constituted by his charisma and reputation. He, in turn, anchored a system that tied the realization and validation of self in individual voters to their reliance on government. The underlying tenets of patronage ("it's not what you know but who you know," easily extended to "it's not what you are but who you are") rest on the unquestioned acceptance of a self as prior to and distinct from experience, memory, sensation and even physical traits.

From Macedonio's libertarian point of view, Radical patronage, Radical campaigning and the fantasy contest in *Museo* all have a common fundamental flaw: a reinforcement of the individual's dependency on government, concomitant with a reinforcement of the concept of autonomous self. For Macedonio, the two phenomena are inseparable. The engine of much of his work is this conviction concerning the inextricable *relationship* between the idea of selfhood and the perpetuation of institutions that threaten the individual.

Here is one key to the second paradox adumbrated in our introduction: how Macedonio, so convinced of the libertarian repudiation of all government and the primacy of the individual, could simultaneously refute categorically the concept of self. In Yrigoyen and his Radical "cause," Macedonio sees the same kinds of flaws and contradictions he sees in the avant-garde aesthetic "movement." Macedonio's enthusiasm for the potential of Yrigoyen's novel method, like his enthusiasm for avant-garde aesthetics, is tempered by an analogous criticism of Radicalism's ethics. Just as Macedonio uses the techniques of avant-garde art to expose the error of much avant-garde thought, he seizes upon Radical strategy to critique Radical ideology. If, in the aesthetic avant-garde, Macedonio encounters an inability to make a complete break with subjectivity, despite the avant-garde's myriad innovations for questioning subjectivity, in Radicalism he finds a dogmatic faith in the interdependence of self and instutional governance despite a genuine agenda for change.[14] It is no coincidence that many of those same men who have perpetuated the mythology of Macedonio Fernández,

112   THE SELF OF THE CITY

in detriment to his message, were also adherents to Yrigoyen's Radical Party agenda.[15]

The Truth About Bureaucracy

If Macedonio had cause to identify the obvious flaws of Radicalism in its failure to eliminate crippling strikes or avert a military takeover, he had equal motivation in his observations of the day-to-day workings of its government. Macedonio's parody of Radical campaigning and the government it spawned resonate as well with some of the most pressing and fractious issues of daily life in the capital. While not all of Macedonio's prose fiction, commentary, and humor explicitly attack government's role in creating these problems, criticism of government culture pervades his writing. A representative example is one of his most entertaining lampoons of urban bureaucracy: the Fool of Buenos Aires.

Published in 1944 as part of the second edition of *Papeles de Recienvenido*, but written in part at least eight years earlier, "Del Bobo de Buenos Aires" (From the Fool of Buenos Aires) has been described as a straightforward satire on the vacuous machinations of government functionaries (Lindstrom 1981, 167–68). But the "Bobo" is far more complex than mere parody, for it is more a critique of the *content* of public management than of its execution. For example, the Fool's remarks on streetcars purposely gloss over public outrage concerning fares, frequency, operation, British ownership, and forced government consolidation—all highly volatile issues throughout the 1920s and 1930s in Buenos Aires and one of the most intractable economic problems confronting the Radical government (Potash 1969, 84–85; Walter 1993, 18–20, 69–123, 130–64; Clementi 1982). Instead, Macedonio's "fool" refocuses public discontent on the very logic of organized transport. Having boarded "to aid the cult of the traveler," and having refused to pay the requisite ten centavos for the slip of "obligatory literature" tendered by the fare collector, the narrator relates:[16]

> Lo malo es que el público del tranvía lo había tomado para acercarse a otros puntos de la ciudad en que esperaban encontrarse mejor y no le convino que continuara parado el vehículo a objeto de que la bella cuestión se deliberara. Mis partidarios entre los viajeros armaron zambra y amenazaron con romper los vidrios de las ventanillas (se ve que estaban

en contra de la Compañía) si no me sacaban de allí. Tuve que aprender otra vez a caminar a pie, y por esta rara vez no puedo decir que me haya lucido. (Recuerdo, a propósito, que algunas veces en la Revista Oral ocurrían algazaras análogas, impaciencias del público, que parecía confundir nuestro sótano con un tranvía parado (como si los asistentes lo hubieran subido a él—hablo de subir a la altura intelectual de la Revista—para que los transportaran) por nuestra culpa y en el que hay derecho a amotinarse....)

[The problem is that the public on the streetcar had taken it to reach other parts of the city in which each person hoped to find himself better off and it did not suit them to have the vehicle stopped so that this fine matter could be debated. My supporters among the passengers raised a ruckus and threatened to smash the windowpanes (you see how they are against the Company) if they didn't pull me off. I had to learn once again to walk on foot, and in this one rare instance I can't say I excelled. (I recall, by the way, that sometimes a similar hubbub would occur in the Oral Review, a restiveness of the public, which appeared to confuse our basement with a streetcar stalled (as if the audience had climbed aboard—I speak of climbing to reach the intellectual heights of the Review—to be transported) because of us and in which they had the right to stage a riot....)][17]

Public discontent and violent conflict over the quality and cost of transit could be avoided, Macedonio implies, if the notion that people need to be moved from one place to another were reconsidered. A far more useful form of transit is the "literary streetcar" of the Oral Review, or of the "novelized" city, in which unwitting passersby are transported to "heights" at which their very identities—as passengers versus audience versus participants, as individuals versus a fictional collective "character"—are called into question.

This same observer and rectifier of public discord takes on the task of "classifying (or clarifying) reality" in the style of a government census taker, exposing the fundamental error of accepted inventorying. Rather than assume the usefulness and value of things and facts, the Fool classifies many of the most mundane and unquestioned aspects of urban life according to what they do not contribute to the life of an individual Argentine. In his inventions of new classifications, the Fool labels some of these phenomena "género de la Nada" [a genre of Nothingness] called "aquenó, que estoy formando de objetos, frases, entes a cuyo funcionar o existir precede incrédula expectativa o una incredulidad expectante" [Surelynot, which I'm composing of objects, phrases, beings whose function or existence is preceded by incredulous expectation or an expectant incredulity]. To this series he adds:

> especies inclasificadas de cosas:
> —Especie A: Cosas que nadie cree, universalmente afirmadas: que los japoneses pueden [*sic*] comer arroz con palitos de diente y que los chinos coman nidos de golondrinas; que los romanos se afeitaran pelo por pelo y que comieran acostados. . . .
> —Especie C: La de las insulsas e imbéciles "cosas sin ellas": el vino sin vino o sea alcohol; el café sin cafeína; el tabaco sin nicotina; las papas fritas de nabo; los bollitos de Tarragona; los sombreros de Panamá; los "recuerdos" de Mar del Plata; la plata boliviana. (*Recienvenido*, 114–15)

> [unclassified species of things:
> —Species A: Things that nobody believes, universally affirmed: that the Japanese can eat rice with toothpicks and that the Chinese eat swallows' nests; that the Romans shaved hair by hair and that they ate lying down. . . .
> —Species C: Insipid and idiotic "things without:" wine without wine, that is, alcohol; coffee without caffeine, tobacco without nicotine, fried potatoes from turnips, Tarragon meat balls; Panama hats; "souvenirs" from Mar del Plata; Bolivian silver currency.]

These are more than tongue-in-cheek observations of life's little oxymorons. If this fool does not exactly correspond to the "guardian of truth" noted by Foucault (1988, 14), he does perform a public service invaluable to arriving at truth. This service consists of "classifying and clarifying" everyday experience that reinforces the independence of the sentient individual from convention, accepted knowledge, and unquestioned practice. This inventory is a step in the dissolution of the self in favor of a reconfigured concept of individual. Macedonio's privileging of sensation and experience, evident in the nature of the list of "imbecilities," is the principle of this reformation; this is a commonplace in Macedonio's works (see, for example, *Vigilia*, 33–39). It is not the activity itself of inventorying and classifying, normally undertaken by the functionaries of modern government, that Macedonio disputes, but the orientation and *effects* of the activity. Government census, Macedonio implies, reinforces the illusion of selfhood while simultaneously binding the individual ever closer to the institutions and conventions that stifle the perceptions and sensations of genuine individuality. The invasion of *hronir* or alien objects in Borges's "Tlön, Uqbar, Orbis Tertius" can be regarded as an appropriation of both Macedonio's *aquenó* and his disorienting "campaign" tactics (J. Prieto 2002, 71–72, C. García 2000, 42n). A vital difference is that Borges's hronir are alien, apocryphal, and malignant. The Fool's aquenó are the opposite: prosaic, incontravertible, and salutary. The civic-minded Fool of Buenos Aires, of course, at times is and at times is not Macedonio Fernández himself.

Statues

Macedonio's objection to the concept of public transit is subordinate to his objection to the general concept—and execution—of public works and services. His critique ranges from the virtually transcendent role of railway timetables in the conception and exercise of time (*Recienvenido,* 95–96) to the potential of the civil registry in facilitating forced marriages (71). Most characteristic of Macedonio's derision of government works are his thoughts on statues. He decries the hypocrisy of police officers, who willfully neglect to arrest statues for their flagrant loitering in public plazas:

> y todo para que un hombre esté allí asegurándonos con su mano y su boca que nos va a decir cosas elocuentes y no se le oye en todo el día.
> Si uno fuera hacerles caso, no penetraría en ninguna plaza, pues están en la entrada con el brazo tendido hacia mí (y demás personas). Dicho brazo grita: "Vete, detente". No atienden recomendaciones aunque en vida no hacían otra cosa que pedir o dar empleos. Felizmente la naturaleza los ha dotado de la incapacidad de darse vuelta. (*Recienvenido* 13–14)

> [and all so that some man can stand there assuring us with hand and mouth that he is about to say something eloquent and one hears nothing from him all day long.
> If one were to pay attention to them, one wouldn't venture into any plazas, for there they are at the entrance, their arm stretched out toward me (and others). Said arm screams "go away, stay there!" They don't listen to recommendations though in life they did nothing else but ask for or give out jobs. Fortunately, nature has endowed them with the inability to turn around.]

Statues embody three aspects of modern life and thought that rankle Macedonio Fernández. The first is the devoting of government funds and services to establishing and enshrining selves out of civic figures; the second is the conceit that such embellishment of public spaces is a form of beauty, and the third is the notion that an individual can be represented in an inanimate rendering of his body. Macedonio regards the idea that a physical representation of a person is also the representation of his identity or "self" as among the most troubling of fictions. The body physical is crucial in the constitution of identity in that it is integral with the sensations individual identity comprises. The fiction of plastic representation of the body abets the conflation of identity with an autonomous self—with a transcendent identity that can simply be assigned to the body.

Borges's failure to grasp Macedonio's distaste of statues is manifest in his unsigned announcement in the March 1927 issue of *Martín Fierro* of a committee to honor Porteño poet Evaristo Carriego, a perennial Borges icon. The committee planned to petition to have a block of Honduras Street named after Carriego and to erect a bust of the poet in the adjacent square. Incredibly, Macedonio's name is included on the committee roster; it is extremely unlikely that Macedonio was consulted. In an ironic twist Macedonio would appreciate, that block is now named after Borges and the square is named for Julio Cortázar.

The relationship between this concern and Macedonio's objection to government consecration of civic personalities is obvious. As with the patronage so prevalent in Yrigoyen's administration, public works dedicated to preserving and honoring individuals amount to a government perpetuation of the concept of self. Macedonio designates public statuary as fiction that undermines his vision for a renovated concept of individual identity. He recognizes statuary as an overwhelmingly self-serving practice on the part of government. Such public works—along with the less detrimental naming of streets and buildings after historical personalities—promotes the national and cultural mythology that government rests on.

Against Enforcement

Museo's campaign to beautify the city responds in part to this repudiation of government's role in elaborating the form and organization of the city. His displeasure in government focuses on those institutions, practices, and premises that bind the individual to the state and establish the state's authority over the individual. The institutions that most closely correspond to that function are, of course, law enforcement organizations. As demonstrated by the passage just cited, Macedonio's words regarding the police in particular are pointed yet complex. Judging by the "Oratoria de un hombre confuso," cited in chapter 2 of this study, Macedonio's stance toward police presence in Buenos Aires verges on resentment. It bears emphasizing that his complaint against the offending *vigilantes* of the "Oratoria" is specific to the situation: they have apprehended him for leering at a young woman on the street. Not only have they imposed upon his person, but they have done so in order to limit *his* interaction with another individual. He is more emphatic about it in "Del Bobo de Buenos Aires," grousing that such arrests are "odious . . . stupid" and a bestowal of "humiliation" (*Recienvenido,* 109).

But Macedonio is far from an anarchist condemnation of all police and military restraint of the individual. In one of his cluster of commentaries written in the wake of the First World War, he takes the libertarian stance of unambiguously denigrating all forms of government *except* in their military and police functions of preventing violent aggression by foreign powers or by individual citizens (*Teorías,* 135–36). These words belie a faith that military and police enforcement can be devoted entirely to thwarting aggression and protecting productive individual freedoms. The following page of this commentary argues for the possibility of "just" and "moral" war; a separate essay written during the same period elaborates on this idea. In a commentary written a few years later, Macedonio argues for military and police presences that will neither interfere in labor conflicts nor suppress free expression (*Teorías,* 166–68). This last, incomplete essay concludes with a somewhat cryptic statement, prescribing a police force that lacks the power of "preventive intercession or summary instruction" (168). Employing the legal meanings of *preventiva* and *sumario,* one can argue that Macedonio envisioned a police force with no juridical powers; one that could, of its own authority, neither abridge a person's freedoms nor take steps to punish individuals.

It is not a surprising vision, given the long history of abuses in Argentine law enforcement and Macedonio's views on the individual. It is also a proposition utterly pertinent to the moment. The police in early twentieth-century Buenos Aires retained peculiarly broad powers in cases of arrest for "*contravenciones,*" or infractions against public order (Ruibal 1993, 26–27). The police edicts in these cases are vague as to the definition of *contravención* but clear as to its object: the suppression of socially marginal citizens: drunks, beggars, prostitutes, and especially vagrants, defined by Beatriz Ruibal as individuals "considered capable of work but who lacked a fixed occupation." The police were in conflict with the Judiciary over this area of law throughout the 1920s, claiming exclusive jurisdiction and competence in the enforcement and "immediate repression" in such cases of "offenses against good habits" (Ruibal 1993, 50). It is fitting that Macedonio—who might have fallen under the definition of "vagrant" more than once—suggest the police direct their energies against the vagrancy of statues. But this observation leads to a further question. Other than interference in labor conflicts and the public admiration of women, what specific abuses by law enforcement did Macedonio have in mind? *Adriana Buenos Aires* will give us some clues to a comprehensive answer.

The self, then, is debunked by Macedonio as an invention of contemporary, largely Positivist institutions; it is an invention designed to facilitate the constriction, control, oppression, and abuse of the individual. All of Macedonio Fernández's endeavors to establish the ascendancy of the individual and to expose the falsehood of the self, however, would be inconsequential without a sound conception of what constitutes the individual. We have seen some indications of its makeup, but Macedonio conceived of this phenomenon—the individual—in terms more extensive and concrete than those alluded to in his political and social writings. His impulse to define the individual responded to more than social and political concepts and institutions: his context was material and corporal, not just conceptual. In *Adriana Buenos Aires*, Macedonio shows us just how corporal it is.

5
Minding the Body

Bʏ ᴛʜᴇ ᴇᴀʀʟʏ 1920s, ᴡɪᴛʜ ᴛʜᴇ sᴛʀᴇssᴇs ᴏғ ʙᴏᴛʜ ᴡᴀʀ ᴀɴᴅ ᴡᴀʀᴛɪᴍᴇ labor conflicts abated, Macedonio's fears have metamorphosed into several worries about the state of Argentine society and its bearing on the integrity and freedom of the individual. He returns to his concern over the nature of property—a problem that has preoccupied him from his earliest writings. He critiques the most recent permutation of personalist government, as we have seen in his responses to Yrigoyen's Radicalism. He challenges accepted arguments and complaints about modern urban problems and standards of living. He refuses to deal in received notions of economic and social class. He raises questions about the legitimacy and purpose of civic law enforcement. And he writes *Adriana Buenos Aires*.

Adriana brings these arguably prior concerns to bear on questions that have become increasingly central in his thought. The novel examines the consequences for women, and other marginal people, of modern materialist culture. It explores the possibilities, for such individuals, to reach authentic "plenitude" and to avoid or endure the encumbrances of modern living. And it scrutinizes the consequences of these issues for the relationship between men and women. For *Adriana* is, above all, a novel about how society circumscribes women and their relationships with men. *Adriana Buenos Aires: última novela mala* is a key step in reconstructing the individual in physical terms. The status—or function—of the body in society, in intimate relations and in emotional life, is the centerpiece of the novel.

Adriana Buenos Aires was written in 1921, evidently in a short period with little interruption. In contrast to all of Macedonio Fernández's other works, the handwritten manuscript of *Adriana* is astonishingly tidy: neatly written, consistently and consecutively paginated, almost seamlessly composed, and free of corrections or changes.[1] The manuscript was unearthed and typed for publication by Adolfo de

Obieta in 1938, at which time three important changes were made: the name of the title character was changed from Isolina Buenos Aires, six very brief chapters were added, including the ending—really a sort of afterword (see de Obieta's "Advertencia previa")—and a passage of nearly thirty typed pages was eliminated. Of this suppressed passage we will have something to say presently. None of these changes affect the substance of the novel to be discussed here; the context of the novel's composition is fully 1922.

Adriana's debt to popular romance novels of the time and its burlesque slant are apparent.[2] Adriana is a beautiful, poor, and wayward young woman, in love with Adolfo, a wealthy creole medical student. She is also pregnant with his child. Their marriage is prevented, initially, by Adolfo's betrothal to a woman of his social class; and later, by Adolfo's mental derangement. Their troubled love is observed—and assisted—by the novel's idiosyncratic middle-aged narrator, Eduardo de Alto, who is himself deeply in love with the heroine. Eduardo's service to the struggling couple includes kidnapping Adolfo in an attempt to cure his madness and commandeering the care of Adriana's newborn son. Eduardo also assumes the role of protector to two other, even more destitute young women, fellow boarders in his cheap Buenos Aires pension.

This rather unremarkable plot is interspersed with bizarre coincidences; sophomoric hijinks; extensive colloquies on the nature of love, sanity, and health; reflections on the nature of being and the fallacy of self, and bewildering non sequitur chapters, including a very strange treatise on how to beat the odds at roulette.[3] Joining the assortment of quirky, down-and-out residents of the narrator's boardinghouse are a handful of mischievous medical students and numerous prosperous intellectual men. The inclusion of these men—part of the 1938 revision—is the clearest signal of the novel's autobiographical character. Their descriptions and surnames coincide with Macedonio Fernández's own acquaintances, including Borges.

The exceptional coherence of this manuscript supports de Obieta's spoken assertion that this *última novela mala* is strongly autobiographical (Lindstrom 1981, 86; 81–84, Abós 2002, 143).[4] Its minimal alteration in the typed format, produced sixteen years later, a consistency unique among Macedonio's writings, indicates the persistence of the author's stance on the issues *Adriana* addresses. Its parodic nature, the evidence that Macedonio wrote it in order to nail shut the coffin of the "bad" genre of literature—representation—has led some critics to dismiss *Adriana*, thematics and all, as purely sarcastic and deprecatory (Engelbert 1984, 13). Borinsky reorients this perspective by emphasizing that *Adriana* is intended to be a foil for *Museo*, but she too concludes that as a "bad" or decadent foil, *Adriana*'s lessons, as well as its aesthetics, should be discarded (Borinsky 1993, 432–34).

There are two problems with this conclusion. First, *Adriana* is neither the only nor the last prose work of Macedonio to incorporate realist techniques or a perversion of them. The closure was by no means definitive. Second, the fact that Macedonio felt compelled to expose the errors in the realist, naturalist, and Romantic treatments of certain human problems serves to reinforce the belief that he found the problems themselves to be of vital importance. Macedonio made it clear that *Adriana* was meant to be published in tandem with *Museo de la Novela de la Eterna*. The *primera novela buena*, we are told, was meant to show the world how to deal with the vital human problems of love, passion, beauty, and forgetfulness in an authentic and unaffected way. Its companion, *Adriana*, is meant to reveal to unconverted readers, in the representational terms Macedonio believes they can understand, what the problems are that representation has been mishandling and how representation has mishandled them. The *novela mala* is the key, or even the concordance, to the *novela buena*.[5]

THE ILLS OF HYGIENICISM

Public health and hygienics, a topic of cultural inquiry largely in the wake of Foucault's questioning of the history of sexuality, penal systems, and health care institutions in Europe, has a particular resonance in Argentina. The first half of the twentieth century witnessed an evolving discourse that blended social engineering; classism, racism, and xenophobia; nationalistic mythologizing; Positivist faith in empirical method and progress; and authoritarian repression and sexual paranoia. Amid the almost unchallenged push for a hygienic society, Macedonio Fernández voices protest and subversion; *Adriana* is the vehicle for this challenge.

It is worth reiterating that Macedonio Fernández would not recognize such New-Historicist approaches to culture. He does not, for example, make an overt connection between the social agenda of public health authorities and the fashioning of a national mythology. He does recognize the validity of analogy between medical practice and social institutions, as we shall see presently. More to the point, as a component of his reaction to the general assault on the individual in his society, Macedonio's theories on alternatives to accepted medical care and hygiene bear directly on his efforts to recast the individual without a self.

Macedonio mercilessly attacks hygienicist assumptions. He reveals the contradiction he sees between the hygienicists' concern for healthy, clean, uncomplicated living and their perpetuation of institutional, empirical standards and methods for achieving their goals. One especially memorable character in *Adriana*, Paredes, a fellow resident in the narrator's boardinghouse, makes a career out of being a living subject for the study of disease. He prides himself on his talent for being sick and on his inestimable value to the great clinicians of the day, for whom Paredes provides a kind of public service.[6] The novel elaborates:

> En suma, si la Terapéutica le prolongaba las enfermedades, éstas le prolongaban la vida, y de tan enredada madeja bien podía resultar la eternalización viva de Julio Paredes, porque el contento espiritual es el himno de las células resueltas a vivir, y quien de sus enfermedades se alegre, se cura no sólo de ellas sino de la Terapéutica. (*Adriana*, 44)

> [In sum, if Therapeutics prolonged his illnesses, his illnessed prolonged his life, and from such a tangled web there could well result the live eternalization of Julio Paredes, because spiritual contentedness is the hymn of cells resolved to live, and whoever takes joy from his illnesses is cured not only of them but also of Therapeutics.]

Here we have a classic Macedonian technique: he makes use of the rhetoric of empirical logic (realism), the assumptions of empirical logic (faith in scientific method) and the conditions of a society operating according to empirical principals (physical illnesses require a corresponding clinical cure). By assembling these components in order to relate a perfectly absurd—and completely believable—story (of a man kept alive by the joyful obsession of his hypochondria), Macedonio reveals how utterly contradictory empirical assumptions are to the essence of human survival.

The story of Paredes also reflects an important distinction Macedonio makes regarding modern health care, which roughly is what he means by "Therapeutics." Paredes is kept alive because his identity, his essential interaction with the world, his function, is as a patient. The "complex of cells" that makes up Paredes is sustained by enacting this relationship with his environment. Ironically, Paredes's identity relies on an environment that is fundamentally perverted. "Therapeutics," Macedonio tells us, depends on ministering to—and thus prolonging—illnesses, rather than fostering health. Paredes is a paradox because he has found the key to living in concert with a paradoxical institution.

In fact, Paredes does not survive. He dies a little more than halfway through the novel, of no evident cause, leaving the following note for the narrator in which he quips:

Como agradable, el morirse es algo de lo mejor; haga un ensayo y verá. Lo digo en broma, ¡eh! siento un poquito no vivir varios años más tomando muchos remedios. Así se habrá probado que la Entierrapéutica no sirve para matar. (*Adriana*, 134)

[For pleasure, dying is about the best there is: try it and you'll see. I speak in jest, eh! I feel a bit bad about not living several more years taking lots of medicines; that way there would have been proof that Burialtherapy doesn't work for killing.]

In the end, living as a paradox does not help Paredes, because he still accepts the clinical definitions of health and sickness, life and death. Life, for him, must remain an absurd and bittersweet joke.

In some theoretical writings concerning health care, written in the years just prior to the creation of *Adriana*, Macedonio clarifies his terms and concepts. He redefines "hygiene," appropriating the term to signify something like what today we call "preventive health care." His argument is that one must foster health, itself a positive, progressive phenomenon, and not the mere absence of illness (*Teorías*, 212–19). Macedonio's aim is to redefine the terms of health care, the same tactic he uses regarding politics, economics, and writing itself. "Hygiene," a nomenclature used by Argentine health institutions of the time to include all kinds of regulatory, repressive, and invasive measures, is appropriated by Macedonio as a label for his concept of holistic health care. Standard health care he dubs "Therapeutics."

The question remains as to why health care—both physical and mental—should be central to Macedonio's vision of a society without selves. The answer lies in the specific context of time and place. Interwar Buenos Aires was gripped with an obsession for hygiene, for understandable reasons. Infant mortality was high (Lavrin 1995, 100). The city was plagued with syphilis and tuberculosis and had a fresh collective memory of the devastating 1875 yellow fever epidemic.[7]

A large proportion of the public works Macedonio so disdains in principle were devoted to hygiene and sanitation. In 1890, over 70 percent of Argentina's external debt was accrued in order to finance such projects (Salessi 1995, 21).[8] Of greater concern to Macedonio may have been the progressive centralization, expansion, and enforcement powers of public health officials. Macedonio makes no direct criticism of the growing authority of health institutions per se; he decries certain practices and requirements they imposed on the general public, including mandatory inoculation, quarantine, and forced treatment. But his constant assailing of the assumptions and methods of health professionals, particularly in *Adriana Buenos Aires*, illustrates his sensitivity to the pervasiveness of the profession's influence.

According to Salessi, the importance of hygienicism corresponded to an exaggeration of Positivism, as well as to a twist on social Darwinism, in which populations are regarded as "human capital" of value to the state (1995, 87) and hygiene is conflated with class and respectability (86). This evidence reinforces the suggestion that Macedonio's criticisms of health practices and institutions is inseparable from his critique of Positivist thought.

Beginning in 1892, Argentina's rapidly expanding National Department of Hygiene took on extraordinary enforcement and policing powers, invading many areas of public and private life.[9] The department's enforcement arms worked closely with police; the phrases *policía médica* and *policía sanitaria* represent no exaggeration (Salessi 1995, 102–3). Public health authorities—Emilio Coni and José María Ramos Mejía were the leading figures—were explicit that public health priorities required the abridgment of personal liberties (100).[10] It was the marginal, most fluid, and disenfranchised population of Buenos Aires that was targeted in these efforts: the inhabitants, largely immigrant, of tenements, boardinghouses, inns, pensions, and hotels (102).[11] These are some of people depicted in *Adriana*.[12]

Salessi argues that one primary objective of the hygienicist movement is to counteract the fluctuating "nomadic" aspects of Argentine society resulting from massive immigration, focusing on the unattached, the "vagabond," rather than the specifically delinquent, thus demarcating "the norms of bourgeois respectability" (Salessi 1995, 105–11, 149). Public heath officials were accorded extraordinary powers of arrest; objects of such arrests were systematically and legally denied recourse to habeas corpus, especially after 1889, but such procedures did not apply to people of "social consequence" (150–52).[13]

Although he never makes direct reference to the Policía Médica and its targeting of immigrant and working-class citizens, Macedonio's comments on law enforcement and his extensive writings on health make clear his unwavering opposition to government intervention in questions of both physical and mental health. His occasional jabs at the police (*vigilantes*) voice his objection to the focus on vagabondage. The gratuitous arrest in the "Oratoria de un hombre confuso," for example, illustrates the sort of intervention directed at unattached people—specifically, unattached men—with little regard to their individual freedoms.

Macedonio's letters and theoretical writings demonstrate his awareness of the potential, if not actual, consequences of the galvanizing of medical, police, and penal institutional powers in early twentieth-century Argentina. Comments in his correspondence run from dismissing the medical profession as "meddlesome and salvationist" (*Epistolario* 171), to decrying a government of "specialists in chemistry, hygiene" as opposed to political experts (172). Macedonio's theoretical texts on health and hygiene, some of which are quite early, are even more revealing. An unfinished 1906 treatise on pain and pleasure, called "Crítica del dolor" (A Critique of Pain), insists on the primacy of sensation in gauging health and determining treatment. Sensation is a social and economic equalizer for Macedonio, who observes that there are no "hierarchies" of pain: wealthy and poor, powerful and humble, feel it equally (*Teorías*, 42). Macedonio also explicitly links the ascendancy of sensation to his rejection of the Positivist concept of progress. He argues that although humans evolve, the universal balance of pleasure and pain remains constant; the Positivist notion of an improving, perfectible universe is illusory (53). These comments are remarkably consistent throughout the years, becoming, if anything, increasingly accusatory of the medical professions specifically. Among notes from 1938 through 1940, Macedonio derides the "disgraceful professional intervention" of medical practitioners (*Teorías*, 226), and the immense cost of professional and university "curative" and "preventive" measures that result in relatively little improvement in human health (227).

Specious Heredity

Gabrielle Nouzeilles (1997) has made clear the complex but closely bound relationship, in Argentine culture of the time, between the rationalist self, hygienicism, utopian nationalism and the concept of heredity. Hygienicism was instrumental in delimiting "the imaginary frontiers between a healthy Argentine 'Self' and a sick (interior or exterior) 'Other'" (234). The concept of heredity—its delineation and enforcement—was especially critical to this cultural project. Heredity linked both family structure—and thus marital and sexual relations—and regulatory hygiene to the future prosperity of a rationalist, capitalist Argentina. Mental health was central to hygienicist concerns, as was the notion that both psychological and moral deviations from the norm were inseparable from physiological—and hereditary—flaws. At its worst, hygienicism equated all pathology with "degeneration" (235). The nation's future integrity and prosperity depended on the classification and suppression of all such physiologically evident degradation.

The concept of eugenics especially attracted health and medical practitioners of a libertarian orientation. The international eugenics movement corresponded, logically, to the Positivist faith in the related concepts of progress, the perfectibility of human beings and society, and the methods of quantifiable, experimental science and technology (Kohn Loncarica and Agüero 1985, 120–21). Accordingly, eugenics in Argentina was closely connected to the pursuit of "secure" social conditions for a national progress (Galletti 1985, 103). Race and nationality were strongly tied to eugenics in virtually all of eugenics' permutations worldwide (Stepan 1991, 11). In Argentina eugenics was closely associated with the search for a "national type" in the midst of the cultural and social change brought about, in part, by massive immigration (Stepan 1991, 139–44).

In Latin America, eugenics followed the Lamarckian view that acquired characteristics could be inherited, and, conversely, that heredity was strongly affected by environment. Latin American eugenists were drawn to the theory that environmental amelioration—particularly in hygiene and disease control—could protect and enrich future genetic stock (Stepan 1991, 67–76). This idea followed the growing belief that the "degeneration" associated with modern industrialized life—crime, disease, and perceived moral decay—was connected to biological heredity (24), where the successes enjoyed by privileged sectors of society was a function of a biologically inherited genius not vulnerable to environmental influences. Accordingly, public health and hygiene was increasingly regarded as holding the solutions to both contagions and social problems (81–91). Lamarckian eugenics allowed for the conviction that Argentina could progress toward a more "advanced" European society by more stringent control of environmental and social factors, leading to an "improved," more Anglo-Saxon-like population (Zimmerman 1992, 28–30). "Social action and moral choice" (Stepan 1991, 87), and not strictly physiological natural selection, could contribute to improvement of the national "stock." By the same token, Lamarckian notions reinforced the racist belief in a national degeneracy brought about by the presence of supposedly inferior groups (88). Argentine hygienicists were drawn to the Lamarckian concept of "racial poisons": acquired habits and diseases—often blamed on alien groups—that threatened the future integrity of the Argentine "race" (84–85).

Macedonio Fernández was strongly motivated by the goal of disassociating rationalist modes of thought, and particularly the self as a rational basis for organizing the world, from capitalist praxis. His reaction to the blossoming of a hygienicist culture is integral with that motivation. For Macedonio, hygienic engineering revealed the deplorable effects of modern rationalism on individuals and their interrelations. It is not surprising, then, that Macedonio rejects the related principles of heredity and eugenics:

> ¿Hay herencia de enfermedad? No, ni de predisposición, pero se nace con exigencias de salud diferentes según la salud y estado de salud de los padres. Cumpliendo estas especiales exigencias no hay diferencia de longevidad y exención entre el hijo de enfermos y el hijo de sanos. (*Teorías*, 214)

> [Is there a heredity of sickness? No, nor of a predisposition, but one is born with different health requirements according to the health and state of health of one's parents. These special requirements having been fulfilled, there is no difference in longevity and exemption between the child of sick parents and the child of healthy ones.]

Macedonio Fernández's nearly categorical refutation of the principal of heredity pointedly negates the validity of both the neo-Mendelian concepts of immutable hereditary traits and the neo-Lamarckian belief in the heredity of acquired traits.[14] A child's health requirements must account for the *circumstances* of his or her birth, including the health of the parents, but individuals can never be marked or fated by inheritance of their parents' *attributes*. Acceptance of the ascendancy of heredity in both character and physiology would, for Macedonio, be tantamount to acceptance of government and institutional intervention in the development and free movement of individuals. The implications of this acceptance are, for Macedonio, enormous, and fully apparent in the social context he knew. Not only health and living conditions, but labor laws, law enforcement, education, and immigration policy are implicated by this emphasis on the role of heredity in individual identity.

A pithy illustration of Macedonio's response to these interrelated issues is found in the partly suppressed self-portrait sent to Ramón Gómez de la Serna noted in the previous chapter. In the passage below, the words in standard face type reproduce the portion of Macedonio's original text published in Gómez de la Serna's volume; the words in italics are those Gómez de la Serna left out, and those in brackets (in parentheses in the translation) are his addition:

> *Fui siempre individualista spenceriano en crítica del Estado y en Ciencia Política. Llamo a la Libertad la Beldad Civil, y el aire civil del mundo, considero al Estado pura máquina de empobrecimiento económico y espiritual de la tertulia civil.* Soy, no obstante mi estatura regular y mi edad, sin peso: 53 kilos, sin grasa alguna, piel seca [y fina, lo cual] y *toda de seda más delicada que la de cualquier mujer; esta finura de piel* se debe con certeza a la enormidad de ropas de abrigo que uso, y mi esquema causal en este punto es el siguiente: soy nervioso, o si no, gran activo; por ello soy flaco; por eso friolento en extremo, por eso uso triple y hasta cuadruple ropa interior. *Y por esto mi epidermis no conoce ni el aire ni la luz, merced a lo cual es ella la más tersa, blanca imaginable y sin vello alguno casi. Las mujeres con la práctica creciente de ropa desvestida recobrarán el cuero y la vellosidad de la mujer muy ambigua o salvaje, y el color oscuro.*

> [*I have always been a Spencerian individualist in my critique of the State and Political Science. Liberty I call Civic Beauty and the civic air of the world; I consider the State purely a machine of economic and spiritual impoverishment of civic gathering and conversation.* I am, despite my regular stature and my age, weightless: 53 kilos, with no fat whatsoever, dry (and fine) skin, (which) and *all of the most delicate silkiness like that of any woman; this fineness of skin* is surely owing to the enormity of outer garments I wear, and my causal

scheme on this point is as follows: I am nervous, or if not, highly active; for this reason I am gaunt; for this reason extremely sensitive to cold, for this reason I wear triple and even quadruple undergarments. *And for this reason my epidermis knows neither air nor light, thanks to which it is the firmest, whitest imaginable and almost hairless. Women with the growing practice of undressed clothing will regain the tough and hairy skin of the very ambiguous or savage woman, and her dark coloring.*]

Race, gender, heredity, physiology, psychology, causality, political conviction, and personal identity are all drawn together in a passage Macedonio wrote not only for publication, but for publication in an anthology of contemporary author biographies. Macedonio employs the same technique we have seen used to address other sorts of ostensible paradoxes. He accepts and adopts the principles of heredity in order to reveal their fundamental speciousness. Lamarckian notions are accepted to the extent they show the fallacy of race or of received characteristics of gender.

In exposing what he regards as the paradoxical nature of the faith in a scientific explanation for racial and gender identity, and for the inheritance of an individual's peculiar traits, Macedonio employs the principle of causality, a principle he has frequently lambasted as fallacious. This causal sequence results in a demonstration of arbitrariness: both the end result, Macedonio's own self-described femininity, and the starting point—his supposed agitation—are presented neither as inherent to his gender or his person, nor as inherited traits. They are certainly not given as constitutive of a self. Nor are the qualities of "hairiness" and "darkness" attributed to "savage" women constitutive of a self; such qualities are the mere outcome of circumstance. By linking these unlikely comments to an assertion of his own libertarian political orientation, Macedonio explicitly connects his Spencerian outlook with his rejection of both an empirical approach to selfhood and the relationship between identity and heredity. Implicit in this entire passage is a refusal to admit the possibility of transcribing and presenting, in an autobiographical vignette, a self for public consumption.

The relationship between eugenics, social and political policy, and Macedonio's repudiation of heredity becomes clearer when we consider why racial control became such a prominent question in Argentina, a relatively racially homogeneous country. For social reformers, tying race to evolution and progress meant that state intervention in social questions could be viewed as a matter of science, not ideology; scientific discourse enjoyed greater prestige than ideological discourse (Zimmerman 1992, 45–46). A great range of social legislation, including labor laws, was enacted as a consequence of this "science," and out of "concern for physical degeneration" (41). Macedonio, by appropriating and neutralizing of the concept of degeneration, is also attacking the basis of government intervention in social issues—a practice he explicitly rejects.

We have already suggested that *Papeles de Recienvenido* coopts the concept of "newcomer" so as to purify it of the implications of class so predominant at the time. Accompanying this emphasis on class was the idea of degeneration, so adaptable to eugenist theories. *Adriana* takes to heart the erasure of these beliefs, as one of the novel's main conceits is the spiritual compatibility of a daughter of immigrants with a wealthy creole. Adriana, whose passionate and altruistic nature renders her the heroine of the story, is keenly aware of the tensions occasioned by such a match. Her concern is not for her own material welfare, but for the difficulty her upper-class lover Adolfo has confronting the realities of poverty, which for him amount to a form of "torture" (37).

While Adriana's affection—aided by Eduardo's own altruistic attendance—results in the desired outcome (though not, strictly speaking, a happy ending—Adriana and Adolfo's marriage is not a success), Macedonio creates a twist on the moralistic outcomes characteristic of the "novela mala" he is satirizing. Popular romance novels of the day emphasize the possibility of salvation and success for those dispossessed women who conform to the demands of a Positivist society (Guy 1991, 161). Success, of course, means marriage, a sanctified relationship with a man that complies with the boundaries of the Positivist vision. The myth of integration is held out as the motivation for conformity. The possibility of integration, and the consequent guarantee of success and fulfillment—economic, social, physical, sexual, and spiritual—is put forward as reason for condemnation of those "bad" immigrants who fail to conform (Guy 1991, 168–70). Macedonio overtly flaunts that myth by presenting a scandalous alternative: a conjugal partnership between two individuals in love, regardless of the social impediments and regardless of the pressures to conform.

The "Science" of Healthy Offspring

Within the Argentine medical community, eugenics and hygiene were also linked to views on sex, marriage, pregnancy, and child care. The formation of the Sociedad Eugénica Argentina (Argentine Eugenics Society) and pronouncement of its efforts to promote the principles of eugenics within the Argentine medical community surface repeatedly and persistently in *Semana Médica* (Medical Week), Argentina's professional medical journal, in the years immediately following the First World War. Although their proponents were few, the eugenists' prolonged, regular, and vocal presence in so prominent a mainstream professional journal suggests the seriousness and strength of their voice. The primary advocate of "eugenic matrimony" in Argentina was none other than the nation's most influential hygienicist, Emilio Coni, who figures prominently in the journal.[15]

The concern for "future generations" of healthy children, and the converse problem of "degeneration" among the mores and habits of the masses, pervades the eugenicist and sexologist commentary in *Semana Médica*.[16] Given the association between the hygienics movement in Argentina, its flirtation with eugenics, and its preoccupation with future generation versus degeneration, the concomitant emphasis on childbearing and child care is not surprising. The obsession with the production of healthy children to populate a new and growing nation is universal, from the anarchists to the hygienicists, to the government and to the most conservative of institutions. Macedonio Fernández is not an exception, but unlike so many of the people addressing these issues at the time, he does not present the production of children as the central issue to which all other issues are subordinate.

Macedonio is not so naive as to believe that the most pressing social problems of the day can be solved by focusing on their repercussions for the raising of healthy Argentine children. Nor is he so calculating that he recognizes the effects on children as a way to provoke discussion of other social issues. *Adriana Buenos Aires* is the only one of his works in which children and childbearing have any importance, and in *Adriana* there is no question that this is an issue subordinate to one of Macedonio's central preoccupations: the nature of love between men and women. Love unfettered by social convention, *Adriana* suggests, would result in healthier offspring.

About two thirds of the way into the novel, Adriana gives birth to a son, Sergio. The immediate care and the future prospects for Sergio are complicated by the fact that Adriana is unmarried and that her lover, Sergio's father, Adolfo, is prevented from marrying her by his periodic bouts of madness. The situation is further complicated for both Adriana and the first-person narrator, Eduardo, by the fact that Eduardo loves and desires Adriana deeply. Eduardo's role with respect to the newborn is extraordinary: he takes over the child's care completely. This decision is remarkable in part because Adriana has a sister who is as attached to the child as anyone, and in part because it is the only instance in any of Macedonio's works where a first-person narrator asserts his authority (189).

The passage includes a two-page diatribe against "scientific" child rearing, including rejection of "medicine cabinetry." Eduardo deplores a long list of clinical and hygienic interventions to a child's health, from purgatives to sterilization, ending with a direct attack on vaccination:

¡el niño de un día suporta con perfecta tolerancia la vacuna, acrobatismo formidable para su organismo, que en cambio carece de tolerancia para la leche de su madre! (*Adriana*, 190)

[a day-old infant tolerates the vaccine perfectly, formidable acrobatics for its organism, which in contrast cannot tolerate his mother's milk!]

Immediately following this passage, there is an entire page devoted to the virtues of breast-feeding.

Macedonio's *antiboticario* (anti-medicine-cabinet) ideas on child rearing, which might now be regarded as far from either radical or reactionary (except for his rejection of vaccination), are a characteristic synthesis of a hygienicist concern for a very real social problem, on the one hand, and anarchist views on personal health, on the other hand. The hygienicists' push for "scientific" baby care, eventually taken up by Socialist institutions, included a campaign to promote breast-feeding that reached near obsessive proportions before 1920 (Lavrin 1995, 98–115).

The anarchist perspective on child rearing, in contrast, focuses on its objection to hygienicist and child-care practices that deprive family members of individual liberties and individual dignity. Issues of *La Protesta*, the anarchist daily, from the period, feature regular articles and commentary of this nature.[17] Most noteworthy is a regular *La Protesta* column by Lelio Zeno called "Medicina Social e Individual" (Social and Individual Medicine), which, in spite of its broad rubric, focuses primarily on questions of child care. Like Macedonio Fernández, Zeno assails the mainstream practices of "*médicos diplomados*" (physicians with diplomas) rejecting standard, blanket treatments and prophylaxes such as commercial drugs and vaccines. Stressing the individual variations in the manifestations of illnesses, he concludes, "There are no sicknesses, only sick people" (December 9, 1919). Zeno encourages eating habits gauged to "bodily necessity," linking extremely logical and empirical analysis of the human digestive system with a faith in the accuracy of sensations (October 28, 1919).[18] Macedonio joins the ascendancy of sensation to the efficacy of nutrition in exactly the same way throughout his writings on pain and health (*Teorías*, 22, 27–28, 69–70, 207–8; *Epistolario*, 34–35, 40–41, 200–210, 220–22).

Zeno also exemplifies both the complexity of the hygienicist movement and the kinds of contradictions Macedonio was so acutely aware of. Along with his exhortation to gauge sensation as a guide to health, Zeno propounds basic eugenic ideas. He urges a "humanistic eugenics" in which "weak" women are "persuaded" not to bear children (November 12, 1919). These are precisely the sort of ideas Macedonio finds so disturbing in all institutional movements, anarchism and hygienics included. It is why he goes to such lengths to expose these contradictions as constitutive of fundamental paradoxes and to urge a complete rethinking of the terms of health care, including child care. At points, *Adriana* reads like a retort to the articles and editorials of the professional journal, *La Semana Médica,* and the anarchist daily, *La Protesta*. The women of *Adriana* are Macedonio's answer to Zenos's "weak" women: single, dispossessed, sexually active. Adriana, the dressmaker daughter of Eastern European immigrants, pregnant out of wedlock, is a direct challenge to the prejudice that such women should not have babies.

What is Family?

These challenges—to family structure, institutional medicine, to standard child care procedures and to the failings of institutionalized alternatives—are openly presented in *Adriana*, though not always in the form of parody. These concerns are subsumed to the overarching concern of the novel: the troublesome relationship between an unlikely pair, the beautiful, young, dispossessed single mother Adriana, and the aging bachelor Eduardo. Culminating the passages describing the care of the baby and Eduardo's related theories comes this startling paragraph describing Eduardo's feelings upon watching Adriana nurse her baby:

> Muy leve incitación terrenal diré, denominado así al apetito que se promueven entre sí las fisiologías de distinto sexo y de la misma familia zoológica concurra o no a ello el amor eterno, experimentaba yo debido ante todo al sentimiento general de precariedad en lo terrenal que dominaba nuestro enlace con Adriana; y luego a la presencia del niño que estaba conmigo largo rato. La puer-presencia, digamos, y la función de nutrición en que estaba el niño y en que estaba el mismo seno, que visto durante la danza o en otra situación habla únicamente como forma sexual, son ambas: la puericia y la nutrición, antagónicas con el deseo de la fusión corporal. (191–92)

> [I experienced, owing above all to the general feeling of precariousness in the earthliness that dominated our connection to Adriana, and then to the presence of the infant who was with me a long time, a very slight earthly incitement, thus denominated the appetite promoted between themselves by physiologies of the same sex and of the same zoological family concomitant or not to eternal love. The child-presence, shall we say, and the function of nutrition of the child and of the same breast which, seen during the dance or in another situation speaks only as a sexual form; they are both, childhood and nutrition, antagonistic to the desire of corporal fusion.]

This passage reflects the complexity and the profundity of Macedonio's ideas on the relationship between family interdependence and individual identity, linking that relationship to the phenomena of corporal sensation and attraction. Families, along with the obligations and dependencies they entail, are for Macedonio the function of the needs and pleasures dictated by those sensations. The reliance on sensations, in turn, liberates the family from the artificial concept of self. Macedonio's vision of the family negates its constitution as a nucleus of autonomous selves. By disallowing for an identity of self confirmed by pure reason, and thus subject to intellectual definition, Macedonio invalidates the concept of intellectually determined roles and relationships for family members.

On several occasions, Macedonio reiterated the daring statement that it was impossible to love one's children. Children, he states, compel a parent's unconditional support and affection rather than the sharing of two "selfless" souls that defines love. In this respect, Macedonio defines families just as he defines community: in terms of the mutual functions constituted by its individuals, functions in turn determined by concrete, physical demands and sensations. *Adriana Buenos Aires* materially resists the contemporary norms circumscribing the family—norms upheld by Positivist and some anarchist ideology (Zeno, December 30, 1919) as well as traditional Catholicism. Baby Sergio is cradled by a caring, nurturing family consisting of his unwed mother, her married sister and brother-in-law, and an unrelated, but passionately engaged, older bachelor.

It is significant that the novel's main locus is a boardinghouse. Macedonio was fascinated with the relationships that emerge in the sort of alternative to family found in boardinghouse life. The potential in such settings for the lives of otherwise displaced, dispossessed, or marginal individuals is implicit throughout *Adriana*. The boardinghouse, more than any other setting, embodies Macedonio's conceit that family relationships must be based on individual desires, the sensations they derive from and the bonds they induce. Interestingly, this alternative conceptualization of family is also reflected in anarchist debate (see, for example, "El secular prejuicio," 1919). If *Adriana* depicts this conceit in terms accessible to readers of representational literature, *Museo de la Novela de la Eterna*'s cast of unreal, immaterial characters—whose identity is pure sensation and pure affection—gathered together on the metaphorical estancia, is Macedonio's attempt to render the idea in a form truer to his vision.

The Trouble with Fathers

Macedonio's anxiety about the authority of government and social organizations over both the physically and emotionally defined individual shape his treatment of physical and emotional relations, including family relations. The culmination of his anxiety, however, is found in his explorations of the dynamics of *individual* authority: the imposition of the will of one individual over others. If Macedonio's attitudes toward Yrigoyen's personalism, toward the dynamics of law enforcement, or toward the failings of hygienicist culture reflect his anxiety, his comments on the nature of parent-and-child relationships suggest the crux of the matter. Individuals are, according to Macedonio's vision, identified in large part by their symbiosis with those they love, by their altruistic participation in a society without selves imposing their will on others. If this is to be the case, how can one account for parental authority? How does one escape the obvious paradox that in an altruistic society, parents must exercise their will over both the minds and bodies of their children?

Macedonio carried this problem to its greatest possible extreme.

His musings on the subject are scandalous enough to have never been put into print. In an undated, scrawled and partly illegible letter to Ramón Gómez de la Serna, Macedonio unfolds a scenario that seems almost calculated to shock:

> En la Novela figura la más intensa concepción y elección de asunto que creo se le haya ocurrido a nadie. ¿Y se me ocurre a mí que niego los asuntos? Es el pensamiento y principio de imposible ejecución de violar por castigo sin deseo en repugnancia un padre a su hija que lo llevaba a la desesperación de la miseria por sus destrozos, desórdenes y que él creía viciosa sexual, lo que no era sino muy pura pero histérica.[19]

> [In the Novel there figures the most intense choice and conception of subject that I think has ever occurred to anyone. And it occurs to me; I who deny subjects? It is the idea and principle impossible of execution of a father raping his daughter as a punishment without desire, in repugnance, the daughter driving him to the desperation of abject poverty through her destructiveness, misbehavior and who he believed to be addicted to sex, which she was not, rather quite pure but hysterical.]

The above-mentioned observation that "child-presence" is "antagonistic to the desire for corporal fusion" only intensifies the dilemma represented by parental authority. Fatherhood is delimited both by the needs of a child for material and emotional sustenance and by the responsibility of a parent for moral and practical guidance. The taboos pertaining to this relationship, Macedonio implies, are also a function of that relation, and therefore not absolute, at least not conceptually; taken to its extreme, a father's authority can suggest the possibility of the most barbarous crime.

This idea, "impossible of execution," turns up as a critical moment in *Museo* when Dulce-Persona, one of two primary female characters, crosses paths with a minor character simply named "Padre" (Father). She confronts him with her awareness of some unspeakable act he considered perpetrating on her as a girl. Padre's planned punishment, she acknowledges, was conceived out of a desperate need to stem the ruinous "carelessness" caused by her incapacity to remember, and not out of desire on his part. Silently contrite, Padre reflects on his relief that the unnamed act "could not be consummated" (*Museo* 131–32, 134). It is this silenced, "unexecuted" act, evidently, that necessitates the eradication of the past from Dulce-Persona's consciousness.

The incorporation of this profound absence—of Macedonio's unnamed, impossible "idea"—into *Museo* indicates how his worries over the dilemma of parental authority galavanize with two other fundamental impulses: 1) the desire to cleanse human identity and consciousness of its burdens of heredity, and 2) distress over the vulnerability of young women. In effect, Macedonio grapples with awareness of the same dynamics of identity in the modern family that Lacan later described (Lee 1990, 14–17). This encounter with the authority of the father, moreover, is the same fictional encounter Robert Con Davis argues is always explored in terms of absence (1981, 2–8). The disruption of these relations—Padre bids farewell to Dulce-Persona convinced that she will completely forget him—is tantamount to a young woman's reconciliation with and liberation from the tyranny of her father (Con Davis 1981, 136).[20]

Macedonio's easy declaration, in his letter to Gómez de la Serna, that the scenario is "impossible of execution," and has never occurred to any previous writer, belies his intense anxiety over the nature of individual authority and its immense repercussions. The declaration suggests that only a radically original thinker—one able to invent the category of the uninvented and interpolate absences—can effectively question the boundaries of individual authority. It is, Macedonio implies, his responsibility to do so.

Adriana Buenos Aires attempts to refine further that anxiety and to suggest the entree to resolving it, in anticipation of more abstract explorations in *Museo*. In both novels, the central male character (Eduardo de Alto, the narrator, in *Adriana*, and the Presidente in *Museo*) is undeniably a father figure. This older father must devise a way to reach a oneness with the younger female characters he deeply loves while simultaneously respecting—and protecting—their individual integrity. *Museo*'s solution to this challenge lies partly in its refusal of representation and its insistence on characters that have no physical dimension and no past. *Adriana Buenos Aires*, in resolving to render representation obsolete, tackles head-on the problem of physicality.

The Selfless Margin of Society

We have noted that Positivist Argentina's eugenic theories and hygienic policies of identifying and suppressing abnormal individuals and practices—particularly sexual practices—that threatened the hereditary future of the nation, were directed at socially marginal people: immigrants, Jews, homosexuals, prostitutes, and disinherited, unattached, or antisocial individuals. Outside the pages of Roberto Arlt's portrayals of Buenos Aires's underworld and underclass, few representations of such marginal characters can best *Adriana Buenos Aires*.

Adriana is a woman literally on the edge. She represents the large number of such women in interwar Buenos Aires and illustrates the gravity of their situation. The plight of dispossessed women was related to a web of social problems plaguing the city during this period, all of which hinged on the issue of legal prostitution. An overarching question, during the first three or four decades of the century, was how to prevent a new class of working mothers—disinherited, disenfranchised, and unmarried—from resorting to prostitution in order to survive.

Adriana is undeniably such a woman. Her condition as an unmarried mother, with no male legally obligated to protect her, makes her predicament obvious enough. In addition, she is a seamstress. Scobie and Guy both indicate that seamstresses were one very shaky rung above prostitutes on the economic scale (Scobie 1974, 143, 204, 216).[21] Adriana is not the only such character in the novel; in fact, there are three, Adriana, Estela, and Susanita, each coping in her own inadequate way with a different variation of the impossible situation of a single woman with no material resources.

Adriana and Estela each spend a night, consecutively, in the bed of narrator Eduardo de Alto when they are at their most alone, disoriented, and dispossessed. Of this intimacy between narrator and dispossessed young women there will be more to say presently. But in addition to portraying a peculiar kind of intimacy, this sequence affords speculation on the material condition of these women. While caught in the middle of this bizarre pair of encounters, the narrator muses of Adriana:

> Con su amador en demencia, perdido quizá, viuda a los diecinueve años, en una viudez sin nombre civil, más dolorosa, más sobresaltante que si la debiera a la muerte; madre, además, sin calidad de esposa, sin sostén para ella y para su hijo, con tales lutos en su alma de niña, con cuán afanoso apego tenía que haberse asido a la fe en mí. (142)

> [With her lover in dementia, perhaps lost, a widow at nineteen, in a widowhood lacking civil name, more painful, more frightening than if it were caused by death; a mother, moreover, lacking the status of wife,

lacking support for herself and her son, with such grief in her child soul, with what anxious attachment must she have grabbed hold of her faith in me.]

This is the figure of the woman who must live on the margins of society, virtually without means, always at the precipice of a fall into utter degradation. Eduardo de Alto is presented, not as her savior, but as the necessary ingredient in a viable life. Implicit in Eduardo's role as both narrator and protector is, of course, a rejection of government solutions to the dilemmas suffered by many thousands of such women.

Today's social historians are neither the first nor the only people to have recognized her existence, nor is Macedonio. The fate of the disenfranchised and marginal was a central issue in libertarian debate in the 1920s (Barrancos 1990, 30–31). The margins of society are also very much present in a handful of efforts, during the same period, to capture in essays and evocations the essence of Porteño life and culture.[22] A small volume published in 1927 by Julio Aramburu, titled *Buenos Aires: Ciudad, mujeres, hombres, muestrario urbano* (Buenos Aires: Women, Men, an Urban Sampler), offers an evocation of what the author presents as quintessential, irreducible Porteño types, including vignettes entitled "Las mujeres humildes" (Humble Women) and "La modistilla" (The Little Dressmaker). These women, invariably young and "bewitching" (*hechicera*), have absolutely no means nor useful family, but are "ennobled" by work; they are unfazed by hunger and drudgery. They are simultaneously blessed and cursed by their innocent loveliness, which enables them either to "conquer" men or to be ruined by them. Indeed, their vulnerability is integral to their charm (79–80).

Macedonio is not interested in such women as types. He is interested in their souls. To be more accurate, he is drawn to women like his fictional Adriana in the belief that in this "mother-child," who finds that "the true life is in love," may lie the solution to those problems that plague the world she lives in. Both Adriana and Estela are saved by yielding to their impulse to love, and by placing their trust in the instincts of their passion and of the man, or men, who most love them. Macedonio's ideas about women are hardly visionary or liberating by today's standards, and it is evident that he did not subscribe to Argentina's nascent feminist movement (though Alicia Moreau de Justo, one of Argentine feminism's earliest and most successful leaders, was a personal friend). But Macedonio's overall goal is to explore and promote ethical alternatives to institutional solutions for an evidently intractable social problem. Macedonio's perennial reliance on passion and sensation as near panaceas sometimes obscures a remarkably progressive viewpoint on numerous women's issues.

The instinct for passion is most sharply presented in two scenes of intimacy between the narrator and these disenfranchised women. On the two successive occasions in which Eduardo finds himself alone in his boardinghouse room with one of these women—first with Adriana, then with Estela—the episode results in great sexual tension, culminating in a single kiss through which that tension is resolved. In the first case, Eduardo finds Adriana in his bed, asleep but desirous, and upon kissing her receives confirmation of her undying love for Adolfo and, by logical association, reciprocation of his own passionate obligation to her: "Ella me nombraba: porque Adolfo era el nombre de su amor y yo la amaba" (*Adriana*, 129). [She was calling my name: because Adolfo was her love's name and I loved her.]

In the second encounter, Estela allows Eduardo to view her naked body. He then "satisfies her need" by lulling her to sleep with his conversation. The single kiss that follows this scene is: "No por deseo, no por amistad, no por avaricia de aprovechamiento. Por saber si en ella se sabía de amor. Lo conocía: respondió apenas y prosiguió su sagrado sueño" (139). [Not out of desire, not out of friendship, not out of a greed to take advantage. Out of a need to know if she knew about love. She did: she barely responded and continued her sacred sleep.] Eduardo then leaves Estela and goes to another room in his boardinghouse to visit the corpse of the recently deceased Paredes, the same character whose enthusiastic submission to clinical medicine could not save him from death. In a coincidence truly worthy of the "bad" genre, Eduardo is ignorant that Estela is Paredes's dispossessed—and now orphaned—daughter, for whom he, Eduardo, will henceforth be responsible.

Macedonio makes a point of highlighting, in both scenes, the single, chaste kiss. The kiss, rather than excite, augment, or test sexual impulses, functions to diffuse them in favor of a purely emotional, altruistic affection. It must be a kiss, rather than a word, a look, or even a caress, that assumes this function. The kiss pinpoints and heightens the fact that the ascendancy of emotion over sex is itself a function of sensation. The kiss also delineates neatly, more than any other act, the participation of sentient individuals—rather than egos, wills, or selves—in constituting this shared affection.

On a more prosaic level, both of these scenes also serve to emphasize that love, for Macedonio Fernández, does not mean sex. In Macedonio Fernández's schema the two are largely in opposition. Where the issue of sex does enter the novel, it is inexorably linked to prostitution. The third "woman-child" of this novel is the most emphatically bereft, and she is unequivocally regarded as a prostitute. "Susanita" is only fifteen; lacks beauty; has a lover three times her age to whom, it is pointed out, she is unwaveringly faithful; and has a past, however brief, that strongly suggests liaisons with multiple men. She is also the underdog of the novel, suffering the disdain of even her fellow boarders, and thus is the most dependent of all on the narrator's kindnesses.

The question of prostitution has a relevance to interwar Buenos Aires that is difficult to recapture. Prostitution's legal status—bordellos were permitted by law from 1875 until 1934—was the subject of a pitched and protracted battle that engaged feminists, socialists, and anarchists; hygienicists and the medical community; religious organizations, including the Catholic Church and Jewish organizations; municipal and federal governments; foreign delegations; and, of course, law enforcement and organized crime. The irony of this debate is that it focused largely on the existence, location, size, and operating conditions of bordellos, whereas a great proportion of prostitution was in fact individual and clandestine. The debate also focused on the women themselves and on the nature of healthy and adequate, versus perverted or excessive, sexuality, rather than the social and economic conditions that perpetuated prostitution.

Interested groups manipulated, for various political and social purposes, the issue of prostitution, or more specifically of "white slavery" and the impressing of white immigrant women into prostitution. Donna Guy observes that the definitions of family and nation used by these groups made it impossible for women to be regarded as independent or as potential victims of men. The abridgment of individual liberties in the campaign against prostitution was seen simply as a function of community well-being (Guy 1991, 35). Control of prostitution in Buenos Aires served as an instrument for the control of women, and for the contesting of power among numerous authorities (39). The controversies over prostitution and the enforcement of its controls were focused on the women rather than their clients. The legalization and regulation of prostitution resulted from government's concern over public health, especially venereal disease (48).[23]

Like the other two disenfranchised women of *Adriana Buenos Aires*, Susanita sleeps in the narrator's bed. In a twist characteristic of Macedonio, Susanita is the only character described as "without any sexual impulse" (161). She demonstrates this trait by being the only character in the novel to actually share a bed, innocently, with Eduardo while he is—what else?—nursing her through an illness. Macedonio makes several important points here. First, he notes that prostitution has nothing to do with sexuality. Second, he emphasizes the utter dependency, and the consequent resourcefulness, of such dispossessed girls who, like Estela and Susanita, have no family. Finally, he recalls repeatedly that these women are able resolve their dilemma and find happiness only to the extent that they are able to identify, and learn to rely on, the genuine form of love that the narrator equates with altruism and—literally—selflessness: "Sigo a la virtud, no a sus equipajes: *impedimenta of virtue*, de Bacon, y la única virtud, la única belleza, el único asunto ético-estético de las cosas es el altruismo, el amor, la ruptura del yo" [I subscribe to virtue, not its baggage: Bacon's "*impedimenta* of virtue," and the only virtue, the only beauty, the only ethical-aesthetic subject of things is altruism, love, the breaking of the self] (*Adriana*, 153–54). Macedonio explicitly defuses the moral arguments surrounding prostitution by tying them to the dissolution of self. While keeping the focus of the discussion on women—it would have been practically impossible to do otherwise—he refuses to pass moral judgment on their lot in life, shifting the emphasis to their emotional capacities.

Susanita gives us a hint of the personal perspective Macedonio Fernández had on prostitution-related issues. Although prostitution was the only alternative for Buenos Aires's legions of undercompensated and unemployed women, women known or suspected to have earned a living this way were treated badly by authorities and neighbors alike (Guy 1991, 45–46). Susanita is ill regarded in her boardinghouse, disdained by men and women, and rendered all the more dependent on the narrator's attentions.[24] By 1921, the year Macedonio wrote *Adriana*, Socialist-inspired reforms had closed all bordellos, effectively forcing women to either work alone, at great financial loss, or to rely on clandestine operations and police corruption (Guy 1991, 108–9). Independent prostitutes experienced increased—and disproportionate—police harassment, as well as the kind of increased financial stress and social isolation *Adriana*'s Susanita suffers.

In *Adriana*, characters allude to Eduardo's various "infatuations" with female pensionmates, and to his various "conquests." The narrator makes clear the error of attributing any prurient aspect to his genuine attraction to these unattached women. His attraction to them is invested entirely in their happiness, including their physical good health; they are beloved by Eduardo *because* they are his daughters and his patients: recipients of his naturalistic and passionate form of child care.

To emphasize his point, Macedonio creates an original twist in the fate of these women. Susanita, by virtue of her goodness and faith in Eduardo's altruism, has graduated from prostitute to faithful "*cortesana*." Having done so, she is impeded from greater happiness by her youthful inability to identify and respond to adult love. Her only hope for happiness is an adolescent affection corresponding to her age (*Adriana*, 217). Estela, by contrast, has the advantage of understanding the nature of altruistic love. Rather than save her from men, Macedonio launches (he uses this word: *lanzamiento*) his character into a life as a kept woman. He "saves" her by means of promoting her investment in passion—not sexual interest—for one man alone. The idea of becoming a kept woman is Estela's. Having quit a respectable secretarial job Eduardo has arranged, she observes that her character is such that she cannot tolerate an environment of indifference. She prefers being despised to working among people who ignore that she is "una vida, que está en mí como en ellos un destino, una felicidad o una tragedia en obra" [a life, that there is a destiny in me as there is in them, a happiness or a tragedy in the making] (206).

In each of these women's cases, Eduardo can only hope to rescue them from prostitution by availing them of opportunities for a love that is *both* altruistic *and* adequate to their physical and sexual makeup. Macedonio emphasizes their physical stature as an indication of their particular needs: Estela is "tall," which indicates her inability to suffer being loved more than she loves (214). Susana has a distinctive defect of stature, an asymmetry indicative of her "malformed," premature femininity (225). Even allowing for the satirical nature of these observations, these passages affirm that the inventory of their corporal features is prerequisite to an *escape* from the sexual exploitation threatening displaced women. Integral to this exploitation is the identity imposed upon them by means of the creation of a self that can be categorized, segregated, controlled and suppressed by other selves. Such accounting of the body helps define their individuality, their appropriateness for a match in which their identity can be shared, not subsumed.

We can see clearly from *Adriana Buenos Aires*, particularly in the light of Macedonio's other work, that Macedonio objected not only to the conditions afflicting the lives of young women either forced into prostitution or in danger of so becoming. He objected even more strenuously to the terms of the debate over prostitution and its control. Testifying to this stance is *Adriana*'s simultaneous attack on the culture and enforcement of hygienicism, on the legitimacy of discussing the conditions and behavior of such women in terms of their sexuality, and on the general treatment in society—particularly by men—of dispossessed women.

Macedonio's displeasure with the institutions of law enforcement and public hygiene can be understood even more clearly in light of his treatment of the afflictions of disenfranchised young Porteñas. For Macedonio, the restriction of individual liberties is never justified by concerns for public health, nor is the law an acceptable forum for the discussion of female sexuality. The dilemma of young women forced to survive by becoming sexual objects can be resolved only under the terms of Belarte, terms to be explored in the *primera novela buena*. These are questions of love and passion, not of physiology and sociology. They are also questions with implications for the economic and legal status of women in modern Argentina, another issue that concerned Macedonio.

Women on the Edge

In 1897, Macedonio Fernández wrote a brief but carefully researched and reasoned thesis for the degree of *Juris Doctor*. Titled "De las personas" (On Persons), the thesis has as one of its most remarkable features the observation of the imperfect legal status of women, condemned to something less than personhood.[25] Of particular concern is the deprivation of women of the right of guardianship (*la tutela*) and of parental authority (*patria potestad*). Macedonio refutes the allegation of women's inferior intelligence and morality (arguing, among other things, the dependency of intelligence on emotion) and deplores both the historical and the contemporary lesser status of women before civil law resulting from the belief in their lesser intelligence. While the conclusion in his thesis suggests that women deserve the equal exercise of parental authority and guardianship, his later writings imply a more radical solution: to change the nature of law altogether.

A year prior to the composition of his thesis, Macedonio published in *El Tiempo* thoughts on the relationship between morals and social science. He argues that the problems of governance boil down to the question of goodwill, and that the understanding of goodwill is dependent on the exploration of metaphysics. He suggests that the whole point of the examination of morals is to elucidate social problems, including the forces of socialism and anarchism, to guide education to "the application of true scientific principles," and to inject "goodwill and beauty" into the consideration of these problems (*Papeles Antiguos*, 53).

To bring this discussion full circle: if beauty and metaphysics are to be the guides in forging a better society, and if that better society is to benefit the dispossessed, bereft women illustrated in *Adriana Buenos Aires*, how are the advocates of these women to proceed? Appreciating their beauty—both physical and abstract—respecting their integrity, perpetuating and learning from their loyalty, and protecting their material welfare, all figure naturally, almost casually, into Macedonio's treatment of these women. But there is something more, an attendance upon these women that conflates material well-being with what one might call spiritual respect. This attendance also demands a delicate suppression of subjectivity and identity, in constant balance with the paternalism of a dedicated protector.

In *Adriana Buenos Aires*, the best example of this form of attendance upon dispossessed women is the narrator's handling of Estela's inheritance. Paredes has posthumously commended to Eduardo a substantial sum of money to be given to Paredes's daughter, whom he identifies as Estela Paredes of Santiago, Chile. Upon deducing the bizarre coincidence that Paredes's daughter has been assigned her deceased father's lodgings, in Eduardo's boardinghouse, the day after Paredes's death, Eduardo attempts to press Estela's inheritance upon her without revealing its origins. He invokes his paternalistic authority as her protector, urging her not to question him in this matter. Estela objects:

> yo sin nada, me encuentro en usted con un dueño obligado cuya alma, quizá la de un tirano, cuyos fines me son desconocidos, que dispone de

mis secretos, me llena de tinieblas y quizá contempla complacido la obra de desmoralización que emprende en mí con este obsequio cubierto de mentiras e historias enredadas que quiere imponer a mi aceptación. (*Adriana* 175)

[I, with nothing, find myself with an obligatory master in you, whose soul, maybe that of a tyrant, whose intentions, are unknown to me, who is privy to my secrets, fills me with darkness and perhaps complacently ponders the work of demoralization he attempts with this gift covered by lies and tangled stories which he wishes to impose upon my acceptance.]

Macedonio manifestly believed in the rights of property inheritance (Fernández Latour 1980, 25). The question explored here is not whether Estela deserves to inherit. The issues at stake are her right to know whom she inherits from and the legitimacy of any authority attempting to determine or control her right to know. The issues are extremely pertinent to the time, as Asunción Lavrin attests. Both anarchists and socialists of the period persistently called for laws permitting the investigation of the paternity of illegitimate children and for laws giving equal status to natural children (Lavrin 1995, 108–10, 150–53).[26] This issue was doubly important to women, since not only did illegitimate daughters have no rights of inheritance or recognition, but mothers of illegitimate children had limited power to pursue those rights for their children or to exercise parental authority (Lavrin 1995, 151). Illegitimate births, moreover, continued to be common—over 10 percent of live births—throughout the first decades of the century (148).

Macedonio's ethical stand on these questions seems clear enough according to prevailing logic. Just as he would favor Adriana's meriting *patria potestad* over her illegitimate son, he would argue Estela's interests in knowing her father's identity and in receiving his legacy. But by the time he writes *Adriana Buenos Aires*, Macedonio has long maintained his silence on actual legal questions. There is no extant text, for example, acknowledging the controversy over legal paternity investigation, nor does he ever again mention patria potestad after writing his university thesis.

The key to this silence can be found in the call for "goodwill and beauty." His libertarian stance does not tolerate government arrogation of the issue of paternity rights and responsibilities. For disenfranchised women such as Estela, Adriana, and Susanita, the hope to enjoy the benefits one expects from a father, a husband, and a lover does not lie in government intervention. Their restitution is brought about by another disenfranchised character, a substitute father, living in the boardinghouse margins of society, who, like the Presidente of *Museo*, takes action based on the will of a passionate heart and the search for beauty. These women, like the city of Buenos Aires, are saved "by miracle of the novel."

Macedonio's insistence on regarding people as interdependent individuals, defined in part by their circumstances and in part by their interrelationships, is central to this salvation. The government and its laws would regard these women much the way Aramburu does: as "types," as classifiable selves, deemed autonomous by the prevailing ideas of the day, but effectively enslaved and abject by virtue of the very social institutions claiming to promote the women's autonomy. For Macedonio, an acknowledgement of their dependency on the kindness of strangers, as it were, is a fundamental step toward liberation.

Sex

A similar approach to liberation concerns debates over women's sexuality. Of the various resonances between Macedonio's prose and Argentine anarchist tracts, the most striking is the call for eradication of the conventions placed on love and sex. The contrast between libertarian-inspired calls for a reevaluation of sex and healthy human physiological impulses and the emphasis on spiritual, not carnal, love resulted in inconsistencies and tensions reflected in Macedonio Fernández's work. On the one hand, the consensus among anarchists seems to be that normal and healthy sexuality is determined by nature, thus should be free of the strictures of social institutions. On the other hand, the same consensus would impose constraints on "unbalanced persons," including anyone whose sexuality is viewed as excessive or perverted (Barrancos 1990, 20). A similar contradiction arises concerning the definition of healthy sexual activity. On the one hand, it is agreed that the ultimate end of sex is procreation; on the other hand, prescribed conditions for healthy sex include intellectual and sentimental compatibility and, ultimately, a "pure spiritual life" (21). This ideal love constitutes an important component of the anarchist utopian dream (22). These contradictions are in keeping with Foucault's assessment of the conventions governing sex in modern discourse. Scientific and medical authorities are called upon to pronounce what is natural and normal, thereby opening public dialog on a previously proscribed topic, yet simultaneously establishing the conventions for what is permissible (Foucault 1990, especially 54–55).

The coincidence of these preoccupations between the anarchist press and the writings of Macedonio Fernández is even more striking when one considers that through the 1920s, the public discussion of sex in Argentina was limited almost exclusively to the libertarian press. There were only two exceptions to this limitation. One was the Catholic Church, which acted to curb any legitimation of sexual pleasure and to promote sexual productivity. The other was the hygienicist discourse exercised in conjunction with the Policía Médica (Barrancos 1990, 22–23). These are the two forums that played the most crucial roles in the appropriation of sexual discourse into the contention for social and political power.

What is more, the medical-hygienicist forum was by no means exclusive of the anarchist movement. Two of the most vocal and prolific contributors on sexual topics to *La Semana Médica* were regular contributors to the anarchist press. While the social and political oligarchy, and its most powerful ally, the church, initially resisted all dialog on the nature of sexuality and its relationship to mental and physical health, the anarchists embraced it. Highly relevant to our study is the fact that Macedonio Fernández engaged in both the discussion on health and hygiene and the discussion of sexuality— often associating the two, while maintaining in many respects the church's censure of sexual pleasure. His peculiar yet consistent treatment of these issues suggests that he is responding directly to many of the same conflicts inciting anarchist, hygienicist, and Catholic pronouncements on the subject.

Relevant here is the anarchist condemnation of marriage. From Spencer comes the notion of the institution of marriage as being "in decadence," of favoring pleasure over the social pragmatism of childbearing. From Tolstoy comes the condemnation of the modern conventions of marriage as a legitimized form of prostitution, undertaken for economic and sensual gain as opposed to spiritual fulfillment (Barrancos 1990, 25–27).[27] Anarchist rhetoric often represented "free love" as a natural step in the progressive evolution of human relations, in which sexual relations embody "the supreme enjoyment of free choice" (Bianchi 1904). The argument against institutional matrimony was routinely incorporated in this sort of argument (F.M. Fernández 1917). Anarchist debate, however, also incorporated the advocacy of such values as the "*pudor*" (modesty) and natural passivity of women (Aracemi 1908) and the suppression of animal "desires" (Barberena 1902). Macedonio Fernández's approach to relations between the sexes clearly echoes this debate, despite its rejection of evolutionary dogma.

CRIME

Early twentieth-century Argentina's obsession with public hygiene and the efforts to control prostitutes under the gaze and machinery of government institutions was integral with the evolution of criminology, and it was partly xenophobia that bound these phenomena together. One of the salient preoccupations of anti-immigrant sentiment in Buenos Aires was the growing crime rate (Solberg 1970, 96). As with hygienicist and eugenicist concepts of disease and degeneration, developments in criminology and penology during the period were tied directly both to Positivist thought and to the predominant, immigrant-fearing attitudes about race and class (Salvatore 1992, 279). Argentine criminology was oriented toward comprehending, classifying, and ordering the working class, an objective made conspicuous by arrest statistics (280, 293–94)[28] This evidence underscores a redefinition of crime in the early twentieth century along the Positivist lines of Italian theorist Lombroso, who conceives of crime as a social disease (Ruibal 1993, 9–10). On the one hand, the delinquent personality can be diagnosed and treated according to empirical means; on the other hand, crime itself is defined relative to social norms. Empirical evidence was interpreted to affirm that immigrants were more inclined to crime because of a natural, physiological disposition.

Macedonio Fernández seizes upon this contradiction. At first glance, he seems not to have concerned himself much with the issue of crime. Crime in *Adriana Buenos Aires* appears as an almost incidental occurrence, when Adolfo, Adriana's beloved, is given a gunshot wound by his jilted fiancée. Crime is absent altogether from *Museo*. But there is one important indication that Macedonio categorically discounted Positivist ideas on crime and the resultant enforcement policies. A 1902 letter to José Ingenieros, in his capacity as director of the National Penitentiary and editor of the *Archivos de criminología, medicina legal y psiquiatría* (Archives of Criminology, Legal Medicine and Psychiatry), urges criminologists to consider the importance of "genius," rather than physiology, in criminal behavior (*Epistolario*, 98). This letter is noteworthy in that Macedonio saw to its publication twice, first in 1902 and again in 1940 in the journal *Argentina Libre* (A Free Argentina), suggesting the he regarded midcentury criminology attitudes and procedures as little changed from the 1920s, when xenophobia was at its peak.

Macedonio follows his own recommendation and in 1940 pens several "*esquemas*" (schemas or vignettes) pursuing this line of thought. The most extraordinary is "El asesino anual," (The Annual Assassin) which features an assassin who finds one person each year to "annihilate" after having brought him to the pinnacle of happiness (*Relato,* 71–72). A second, perhaps more pertinent, is "La Santa Cleptomanía," (Holy Kleptomania) which, Macedonio notes, he has written as a legal proof of insanity (*Relato,* 82–83). In this sketch the narrator speaks of his sister, who is kleptomaniac not by virtue of a criminal nature, but by virtue of living in and conforming to a materialist, commercial society that accords women none of their own resources of productivity. He describes his sister's habit as "Egoísomo sin Maldad, y Robar para Dar, de un régimen aleatorio de Propiedad y Poder" [An egotism without Ill-will, and Stealing for Giving, in an aleatory system of Property and Power] (82).

Again, in both of these schemas Macedonio takes the contradictions inherent in contemporary social practice to their maximum logical extreme. The condition of womanhood is, by definition, constitutive of a criminal personality. Crimes are defined in quintessentially Positivist terms of quantified and logically reasonable deviations from social norms. The social norms themselves are revealed as unreasonable. And none of these logical analyses, in the end, sufficiently explain the criminal impulse. In both cases, the criminal behavior can be explicated in terms of altruism and selflessness. The annual assassin possesses a perverted sense of altruism; the blessed kleptomaniac an extreme egotism that is perfectly natural given her context. The proof of the narrator's insanity, according to Positivist method, is his very questioning of the terms of criminality.

Adriana to Zunz: The Female Abject

Macedonio was not the only writer of the Martinfierrista movement to address all of these issues—public hygiene, prostitution, sexism, criminology, and mental health—as a single, systemic set of interrelated phenomena. He was surely the first, however, to regard these social problems as not only interconnected, but as all resting on related fundamental metaphysical errors. If Macedonio, in some respects, anticipated Foucault in this regard by sixty years, it is worth looking to Borges to speculate on continuity. Borges's most noteworthy reflection on these problems is his short story "Emma Zunz," written in the early 1940s and set in 1922 Buenos Aires. While Borges's story is not normally regarded as a commentary on social issues, the interconnections between it and *Adriana* are most provocative.

Emma is very nearly an anti-Adriana, or at least an abject version of a composite of the women featured in Macedonio's novel.[29] Like Adriana, she is an adolescent, cut loose from her Eastern European immigrant parents, living in a boardinghouse, single, poor, and a laborer. Above all, Emma—a virgin, repulsed by men, who prostitutes herself in order to fulfill a plan to murder the man she believes ruined her father—operates outside legitimate sexual boundaries for women in 1922 Argentina. But while Macedonio's women find salvation in their sexual marginalization, Emma Zunz finds an unnamable horror and an a source of motivation and power for violent revenge (Bell-Villada 1999, 191). Macedonio's Estela escapes the indifference of the world to the fulfillment of unconventional love; Borges's Emma wraps herself in the indifference of the world in order to accomplish her unstoppable goal (192). Where Adriana, Susanita, and Estela forge a link, through unconsummated intimacy with the father-narrator, Eduardo, to a community and to emotional fulfillment, Emma Zunz finds in anonymous sex a wall that isolates her from the world, from her past and from the father who, she determines, has performed a sadistic act upon her mother. Emma's realization in sex means she is compelled to kill; her crime means that the truth is trapped inside her head forever (Sarlo 1999, 235, 238).

Borges's tale is also the inverse of Macedonio's with respect to the role of sensation and consciousness. In *Adriana Buenos Aires*, sensation and the link between sensation and passion are the only reliable guides to physical and emotion health. Adriana, Estela, and Susanita must turn to their physical impulses—impulses that respond to "pure love"—to achieve functioning, balanced lives. It is specifically the separateness of body from consciousness that must be overcome. Beatriz Sarlo demonstrates how in "Emma Zunz," sensation is patently unreliable; Emma's unverifiable interpretation of facts—her father's suicide, Aaron Loewenthal's guilt, her mother's suffering—are all based on the *sensations* she feels upon being confronted with the evidence (Sarlo 1999, 234). The supposedly unimpeachable justice of which she feels herself to be the vehicle ends up being completely uncommunicated and incommunicable. Emma's entire procedure is made possible, and ultimately inexorable, by her sensation of being apart, in a dimension separate from those who surround her, and by her converting her body into a "a passive object, governed by her conscience" (239). Moreover, it is the clinical gaze—of paying sailors, of the crowds in the *arrabal* (outlying district), and most notably of the health inspectors at the women's club she joins—that supports this sense of corporal objectification and apartness.

The remarkable thing about "Emma Zunz" is that, like *Adriana Buenos Aires*, it is one of its author's few tales that represent the city in a realistic way: Emma lives in a historically recognizable 1922 Buenos Aires, walking its streets, riding its trams, wandering its port, suffering under the gaze of its working-class multitudes (Bell-Villada 1999, 192). But by cutting her off from her historical environment, rendering her as separate from time and space as the characters in *Museo de la Novela de la Eterna*, Borges accomplishes his goal of creating a mythic figure of the immigrant-class girl—practically the same girl Aramburu identifies as a "type" only twenty years earlier. This mythic figure personifies the morally ambiguous valor and violence Borges admires in all of his Argentine myths, from the *compadrito* to the gaucho to the creole warrior. In Emma Zunz, Borges accomplishes an inversion of the principles of Macedonio's Belarte, more complete and more diametrical than any of his generation. For Arlt or Girondo, in different ways, the Buenos Aires seamstress, prostitute, or factory girl would be the means of illustrating the alienation inherent in the modern urban wasteland. For Mallea or González Lanuza she might be the female object against which the male subject, adrift in the urban maelstrom, anchors and measures himself. But for Macedonio, the "types" of Buenos Aires are those who best possess the potential to populate the "novelized" city, a city in which the problems of a dispossessed and deprecated underclass are transcended through the affective capacities of sentient individuals.

Madness

Perhaps it is madness, more than any other phenomenon, which motivates Macedonio's efforts to reconfigure individual identity and eradicate the self. The engine of the conflict in *Adriana Buenos Aires* is Adolfo's insanity, which impedes his marriage to Adriana. Their marriage ultimately does not end in fulfillment. We are told in the final chapters that Adolfo is not cured of his dementia, and that his madness acts as a corrosive both against the love between him and Adriana and against the love between Adriana and Eduardo. The last bad novel proves to be a tragedy—the only possible tragedy, according to Macedonio—as love is defeated by a force external to it.

Adolfo's insanity is the product of his sense of self and his inability to abandon self in favor of affection and sensation: "La locura única es la ilusión del yo, tan fuerte que en la locura práctica o terrenal el yo es lo último que naufraga, si acaso naufraga" (*Adriana* 119). [The only madness is the illusion of the self, so strong that in practical or earthly madness the self is the last thing to founder, if it does founder.] Neither the distraction of a costume party, nor the passion of gambling, nor the salubriousness of isolation and contemplation succeed in animating Adolfo to devote himself with complete abandon and altruism to his beloved.

In early twentieth-century Buenos Aires, the marginal and nomadic populations marked for observation, isolation, control, and reduction by government authorities are not limited to immigrants, women, and social misfits. The insane prove to be a crucial target for hygienicist programs of social engineering. Hugo Vezzetti argues, following Foucault's line of thought, that the very category of insanity, formulated by the same authorities that masterminded the implementation of both Positivist criminology and hygienics, is constituted as a counterweight to the Positivist vision (Vezzetti 1985, 363). As with criminology and hygienics, Macedonio finds ideas of merit in the modern treatment of insanity, but bridles at its institutional nature as well as its clinical, diagnostic approach. To Macedonio, the concept of behavior modification, itself valid, is in contradiction to empirical study and treatment. The cure for insanity outlined in *Adriana* simultaneously underscores the paradoxical nature of modern methods while elaborating Macedonio's own brand of holistic mental health care. A dialogue between the narrator, Eduardo, and César, a character referring to Macedonio's physician friend César Dabove, discusses how to treat Adolfo's recurring madness:

> —En éste, como en la mayor parte de los casos, habría cura, y firme, si se hiciera todo lo que debe hacerse: gran higiene de espíritu y cuerpo.

Pero la gente no tiene fe: cree más en los destructores bromuros y clorales. (Hay más de treinta específicos para el hígado.) El campo, cultivar el jardín o un sembradito: nada de visitas de las personas queridas o que le traen recuerdos, y en un año está perfectamente sano. Vos que creés que la Higiene lo cura todo y que la Terapéutica es una desastrosa ilusión.
—La terapéutica indicada por la sensación no la niego, y la llamo Higiene. Lo que niego es que debamos seguir la sensación en la salud y prescindir de ella, eludirla y contrariarla, en la enfermedad. (87)

["In this, as in the majority of cases, there would be a cure, for good, if one did everything that should be done: an overall hygiene of spirit and body. But people have no faith; they believe in destructive bromides and chlorals. (There are more than thirty specified for the liver.) Countryside, cultivating a garden or a patch; no visits from loved ones or anyone who provokes memories, and in one year the patient is perfectly healthy. You who believe that Hygiene cures everything and that Therapeutics is a disastrous illusion."
"I don't deny therapeutics indicated by sensation; I call it Hygiene. What I deny is that we should follow sensation in heath and disregard it, avoid it and interfere with it, in sickness."]

Eduardo de Alto's prescription for curing madness serves several purposes. First, by entering into a dialogue with a sympathetic physician, he can reinforce his—rather, Macedonio's—appropriation of medical concepts for his own means: "hygiene" is explicitly redefined to conform to Macedonio's particular take on health care. Macedonio also reveals what he regards as the paradoxical nature of modern medicine. He acknowledges, and approves of, the emphasis on the environmental conditions and habits that promote and preserve health—called hygiene. He exposes and attacks the concomitant focus on diagnosing and treating specific diseases—"therapeutics"—as if they were completely disassociated from environment.[30] Macedonio also addresses the contradiction inherent in what Foucault terms the "clinical gaze" and the gaze's relationship to its primary facilitating space, the asylum. The clinical gaze's uses of the asylum dehumanize, objectify, and isolate patients in order to study them, on the one hand, and to exercise control over them, on the other hand.[31]

Macedonio's treatment of madness reinforces his insistence on the indivisibility of the physical from the psychological, or emotive. Positivist psychology focuses on the symptoms of madness, orienting the study and treatment of insanity as a nervous, not physiological, disorder (Vezzetti 1983, 52–54). This same practice applies the Positivists' empirical method to the observation and control of symptoms, treating them in the same manner as clinicians treat physiological disease. Macedonio's "hygiene of sensation" relies on the conceit that physical and mental distress are essentially indistinguishable, both being purely a function of "sensation." While critics have regarded this approach to health as a function of Macedonio's peculiar metaphysics, one can as easily argue that his metaphysical vision serves to solve what he regards as the intractable contradictions of medical theory and practice. These contradictions are twofold. First, the medical system of examination, diagnosis, isolation, control, and medication are carried out simultaneously with a campaign of public hygiene; the result is authoritarian control of individuals' environment and behavior. Second, medicine applies this same process to behavioral pathology, conflating a process of objectification with a problem that is essentially—to Macedonio's thinking—subjective. Macedonio's insistence on the ascendancy of subjectivity solves both of these paradoxes.

Even Macedonio's singular ideas on the nature of family and generations resonate with contemporary assessments of the psychiatric movement he so disliked. Positivist psychological practice, and the environment of the asylum especially, usurped the "degenerate" or "inadequate" family structure of the patient, with the alienist serving as surrogate father (Vezetti 1985, 371). Disproportionately, the family usurped was an immigrant family. The "hygienic" treatment undertaken by Eduardo de Alto can almost be read as *Adriana*'s retort to the alienists' efforts to impose a highly regimented, institutionalized alternative "family" on the most marginal individuals; and *Museo* presents this same retort in the terms of Belarte. Against the asylum, *Adriana* proffers the boardinghouse; against the psychiatrist, the passionate, altruistic bachelor. *Museo* substitutes these entities with the estancia La Novela and the Presidente.

Cure

There is substantive evidence attesting to how integral were Macedonio's metaphysical vision, aesthetic renovation, social dissent, and corporal focus. This evidence is found in several pages of the 1938 typed manuscript of *Adriana* that either Macedonio or his son—de Obieta could not recall who—chose to omit from the published version (de Obieta 1996).[32] These paragraphs explicitly associate Macedonio's approach to mental illness with his ideas on the priority of sensation. When Adolfo objects that he can't follow Eduardo's discussion of the nature of identity "en la parcialidad de la noche para el misterio" [within the night's inclination for mystery], Eduardo defers his explanation to the following day. The scene of the following day is described:

> Acostado en la pendiente leve de las arenas de la orilla del mar, desnudos del todo, bajo cálida siesta cubierto por las sombras de un árbol solitario, en paraje salvaje de la costa, distante y olvidado de ciudades y hombres, contemplo, miro, escucho, con completo sentimiento y soledad y pensando con intensidad y placer grande.
>
> [Lying on the gentle slope of the sandy seaside beach, completely naked, beneath the warm siesta protected by the shade of a lone tree, in a primitive coastal spot, forgotten and far from cities and men, I ponder, I watch, I listen, with full feeling and solitude and thinking with intensity and pleasure.]

Following this introduction is a rendering of Macedonio's ideas on the denial of death, the speciousness of self and an evocation of those moments of transcendent "plenitude" in which genuine selflessness is achieved. At one point in this lengthy excerpt, Eduardo pronounces to his "patient," Adolfo, that "a personality change like dementia is nothing more than a thematic lettering of the soul, but not of affection."

Numerous aspects of these pages resonate surprisingly with Plato's *Phaedrus*, a concurrence of themes and metaphors that may not indicate outright influence. The relationship between an individual's physical and spiritual being, between affection and *eros*, between love and a sense of personal fulfillment, and between this sort of spiritual exploration and reclusion from the city, all figure as fundamental tensions in the *Phaedrus*. For Macedonio Fernández, these associations are important not only as a means to arrive at an alternative to the self, but also as a cure for madness. "*Afección*" is the constant that anchors and circumscribes the individual. It is an arrival at pure "afección"—by means of isolation, liberation of one's body, and contemplation—that returns us to sanity. Where the prevailing psychiatric method attributes a self to a madman that allows observation and control of the patient as a subject, Macedonio's cure entails the *shedding* of self through the focus on sensation and affection.

For others of the Argentine avant-garde, madness is a touchstone of the modern experience, with the exception of Borges. Borges prefers to explore the compulsion to recreate mythic archetypes rather than the anguish of mental dysfunction. In this respect, too, Borges inverts Macedonio, for he uses the relativism of Schopenhauer to build a mythical universe in which the link between evidence and belief, between sensation and knowledge, is eternally slippery and indeterminate. For Macedonio, Schopenhauer's principles are the key to bridging the gap between function and compulsion; making reality subjective and affective is the only means of synchronizing forces such as desire and aggression with environment.

For avant-garde writers such as Girondo and, especially, Arlt, madness is the means to explore the dysfunction, alienation, and anxiety of the modern experience. In many respects Arlt and Macedonio resonate with each other, despite the fact the Arlt's cynicism and belligerence was anathema to Macedonio. In Arlt's 1929 *Los siete locos* (*The Seven Madmen*), madness is frequently ironic, equated by the desperate and self-loathing Erdosain with his perverse sexual fantasies (Arlt 1958, 11), his attraction to the abject (14), others' faith in goodwill (17), and the consequence of crime (64). Ultimately, it is the environment that pushes Arlt's characters over the edge, and the deadened, unproductive relations between people, relations short-circuited by a maddening city. At moments, *Los siete locos* appears to be the dark side of *Museo de la Novela de la Eterna*. Where Macedonio's Presidente resolves on action as a culminating effort to liberate the populace from their selves, Arlt's Erdosain concludes that murder is a necessary prerequisite to proving the existence of self and to discover the god hidden within the man (Arlt 1958, 72, 86).

Pain

According to Macedonio's vision, the individual is to be reconstituted by means of sensation. All institutions, political, economic, and ethical, as well as health related, are to be subsumed by the dynamics of individual sensation and the "affective" interrelationships integral to those sensations, the only allowable resource for determining and protecting the integrity of the individual. Given this remarkably comprehensive—and systemic—conceptualization of a new kind of civilization for modernity, one would expect all aspects of physical sensation, as well as emotional sensation, to be comprised in its elaboration. In particular, the phenomenon of pain must be addressed, and Macedonio Fernández was acutely alert to the problem of pain as well as pleasure, and the need to account for both in his discourse on the sentient individual.

Elaine Scarry tells us that physical pain is a unique and potent instrument of power precisely because it cannot be accurately represented in language nor appreciably shared between individuals (Scarry 1985, 4–14). Pain shatters or "unmakes" the world and the images we obtain of it; the creative imagination, the "making" capacity of the mind, therefore, has a role in retaining the power of pain inflicted by, or on, the body (22).

Macedonio concerns himself with this problem as early as 1906. His frame of reference for elaborating an alternative theory of pain is largely philosophical; his motivation for articulating this theory in such minute and concrete detail lies in the context we have been exploring. He maintained both his interest in this problem and his confidence in the accuracy of his "Eudemonología," as he terms his theory on pain and pleasure. In 1938, he returned to these writings, making some clarifications and additions without substantively altering them. Just as he regarded *Adriana Buenos Aires* as an essential chapter in his endeavor for a new kind of society, he continued to view his theory of pain as a valid foundation for reform.

Much of his "Eudemonology" argues for the stability of the ratio of pleasure to pain in the world. Macedonio rejects the "pessimist" attitude he attributes to Schopenhauer; more pertinently, he also rejects the Positivist idea of the infinite improvability of life and society (*Teorías*, 17, 53). He denies the existence of differing "natures" that predetermine individuals' degree of enjoyment of life regardless of circumstances. This repudiation of nature is consistent with the rejection of self, or with the notion of a transcendent phenomenon that shapes an individual's personality.

Despite this rejection of nature, Macedonio affirms that the constant relativism, or balance, of pleasure and pain in life is not absolute. His whole objective in a detailed "eudemonology" is to facilitate the individual's maximum possible management of these sensations, for the maximum individual benefit (*Teorías*, 34). Under the subtitle "Arte de vivir" (Art of Living), Macedonio adds that the dynamics of altruism are not an exception to this relativist theory of pain. A person whose happiness is entirely invested in the well-being of another suffers, by virtue of that association, the same sort of interplay of pleasure and pain as a purely self-interested individual:

> Y, por tanto, la madre, el héroe, el santo, el asceta, actúan con respecto al Placer y Dolor exactamente como el más simple individuo humano o animal, y cuando el dolor invade sus existencias caen en las mismas supersticiones y temores, buscando amuletas y refugios ya en las religiones, ya en los moralismos, ya en tal o cual sistema higiénico, sociológico, psicológico, cultura de la voluntad, "conciencia tranquila", etcétera. (*Teorías* 42–43)

> [And therefore the mother, the hero, the saint, the ascetic, all act with respect to Pleasure and Pain exactly as does the simplest individual human or animal, and when pain invades their existence they fall back on the same superstitions and fears, seeking amulets and refuges, be it in religions, be it in moralisms, be it in this or that system of hygiene, sociology, psychology, culture of goodwill, "soothed consciousness," etcetera.]

This passage illustrates the connection in Macedonio's vision between the dynamics of individual pleasure and pain—corporal as well as emotional—the rejection of selfhood, and the critique of the innumerable systems of thought and behavioral control permeating modernity. The reliance on the dynamics of sensation is key to the individual's liberation from both self and the institutions that perpetuate it.

In several lengthy sections, the text discusses, in concrete and practical terms, the balanced management of the sources of pleasure and pain and also discusses distinctions in the nature of those different sources. Finally, in the section subtitled "¿Cuál es mi estado total actual?" (What is my total current state?), Macedonio addresses coping with pain that is imposed upon the individual, as opposed to pain that results from deferred pleasure or from the conscious management of stimuli. He dwells in particular on physical pain, taking as his example the extraction of a tooth. Arguing that the overcoming of fear is a prerequisite to this process, Macedonio recommends a daily regimen of preparing one's self for the pain in advance by "a psychological effort to represent the sensation that awaits." He describes this "psychological effort" (which he also terms "psychological courage") as "la máxima concentración *muscular* y atencional (la atención es una especie de contracción)" [the maximum *muscular* and attentional concentration (attention is a kind of contraction)] (*Adriana*, 63, emphasis added). He discourses on the advisability of building "reserves of energy" for the tolerance of any future voluntary or involuntary pain (65).

This exegesis on pain is hardly in keeping with the legendary Macedonio Fernández, elaborated by others, whose obsession with his own physical sensations—heat and cold and light especially—resulted from his fundamental *fear* of pain and disease and thus represented a paradoxical transcendence of physical and corporal existence (Borges 1961, 113). Many critics share the perspective of Juan Carlos Foix, who interprets Macedonio's fascination with the body as an engagement with the greatest of obstacles to an authentic life. For Foix, Macedonio's body is his primary hindrance; Foix designates it as chief among Macedonio's aquenó, like those adumbrated by the Bobo of Buenos Aires.[33] Abós's biography makes clear the error of this interpretation. Macedonio's obsessive monitoring of his own body was the means to practice his alternative "hygiene" and "eudemonology" as he elaborated them in his writings; he was, in effect, his own laboratory (Abós 2002, 186). In fact, Macedonio's Eudemonology resounds much more closely of Scarry's observations on the implications of pain for the nature of individual power. He certainly never includes the human body, or any part of it, among the Bobo's litany of aquenó.

The body and its sensation are necessarily the primary ground for delineating, defining, and identifying the individual. It is also the focal point for Macedonio's resistance against the institutions of Positivist society, ranging from democracy, to law enforcement, to health care. Acceptance of Macedonio's steadfast equating of physical being with sensation is prerequisite to reconciling his exploration of corporal phenomena with this resistance to institutions. The ascendancy of sensation is the key to the evident paradoxes of championing the individual while denigrating the self, and of endlessly inventorying physical experience while privileging the phenomena of absence and nothingness.

Sensation is the key as well to Macedonio's relationship to the city. More to the point, sensation is the key to accepting the possibility that an individual can save the city, can transform it miraculously into the city of his vision, while simultaneously absenting himself from it. Just as the body physical must be the ground on which the erasure of self takes place, the city physical must be the space in which society is transformed. Streets and buildings, commerce and trade, property and assets are the means for uncovering new dimensions, relations, and energies.

6
The Self of the City

IN THE BUENOS AIRES OF THE 1920s AND 1930s, MACEDONIO FINDS, WHERever he turns, paradox; and it is a paradox ultimately attributable to the modern concept of self. More recent—and more methodical—examinations of modern urban life reveal the same kinds of contradictions that troubled Macedonio, placing them in cultural and historical context. Angel Rama's 1996 landmark *Lettered City* (*La ciudad letrada*) identifies dissonance and contradiction as not only endemic but also a priori characteristics of Latin American cities. Rama reveals how this dissonance corresponds to the disjuncture between the material world and the world of signs, owing to the fact that Latin American cities were "imagined before they were built," and imagined, moreover, in "inalterable rational principles" (1996, 6).

Two basic aspects of Rama's analysis make it especially pertinent to discussing Macedonio Fernández's response to the modern city. The first is the conception of these new, imagined, rational cities as sites for the advent of capitalism (2), itself integral with both the rational imagination and the exploitation of newly conquered land and people. The second aspect is the observation that the founding and development of these cities are inseparable—yet also discrete—from the practice and culture of writing (25). The result is two interdependent sets of urban entities, one concrete, the other one textual (27). The textual city, moreover, is composed by a virtually autonomous class of men charged with "managing a system of signs for ordering" this civic and administrative city of letters (16). This fusion of civic order with written expression determines not only the structure of urban life in Latin America, but also predetermines the nature of any response to that structure. Opposition to the discourse and its authors requires writers to "present an alternative dream of the future" for the city (8).

Rama's theories may fail to explain fully contemporary urban phenomena in Latin America, but they find a stunning resonance in Macedonio Fernández's critique of and "dream" for the city. Macedonio might not have recognized Rama's elaboration of this peculiar phenomenon galvanizing literary praxis and urban experience, but his own writing shows us that he understood fully what he was up against. The myriad assaults of modern urban life on the integrity of individuals and their possibilities for fulfilling interrelationships were inseparable from the ideological order ascendant in modern-day Buenos Aires. The ideological order, in turn, was inextricable from the conventions and assumptions governing writing. Those assumptions brought Macedonio full circle to the problem of the individual, governed so absolutely by the Cartesian conception of authorship and its foundation in consciousness.

Macedonio's ambivalence over Buenos Aires permeates his writing. The city is the site of all of his fiction—sometimes explicitly, other times implicitly—and many of his theoretical texts. Yet direct representation of Buenos Aires is rare and, when it does appear, is always equivocal. In both *Adriana Buenos Aires* and *Museo de la Novela de la Eterna*, Macedonio's ambivalence is reflected in alternate praise and condemnation of the city and in the vacillation of characters between urban and rural environments. In both novels, characters committed to the health and lifeblood of the city are also in perpetual retreat from Buenos Aires, an ambivalence of posture and movement that is evident in Macedonio's biography as well. Macedonio's attacks on the city are usually abstract and conceptual, yet leave little doubt as to the palpable, tangible qualities of the city being assaulted.

Streets

For Rama the most basic evidence of the galvanizing of textual and concrete city is found in the naming of streets. The rational systematizing of street addresses in Latin American cities, contrary to historical common and practical usage, demonstrates how utterly the rational lettered city determines the structures of the material city (1996, 26–27). In Macedonio's writing, names of Buenos Aires's streets, plazas, and public sites are woven into the text with little apparent self-consciousness; it would be easy to conclude he intended his works to be read only by Porteños. *Adriana Buenos Aires* cites specific addresses and even phone numbers, an incongruity in a book mainly about feelings, sensations and ideas, even given its "bad" aesthetics. But in *Museo*, Macedonio anchors his "alternative dream" for Buenos Aires on just such specifics. For Macedonio, the problem of street names involves not only social structure but also moral terrain, and, therefore, human self-conception. As part of his campaign to beautify the city, the Presidente propounds in *Museo* that streets and monuments ought to be named for virtues rather than people; doing so would greatly reduce the common impulse of men toward shameful behavior in their pursuit of fame:

> sobresalta notar tanto trabajo de los hombres para parecer buenos, en una civilización tan enamorada de las cerraduras Yale y de los buenos modales, trampa de adormecer víctimas.
> Ciudades de mejor gusto tendrían calles llamadas de la Lluvia, del Despertar, la Madre, el Hermano, el Llamado, Vive sin Nunca, Volverás, Despedida, Espérame Siempre, Retorno, Familia Amorosa, Beso, Amigo, Saludo, Sueño, Otra Vez, Desvelo, Quizá, Rehácete, Olvido, Emprende, Vuelve a Mí, Tertulia, Vive en Fantasía, Dolor Fantasía, Cerco Florido, el Camino Rocío, la Risa, Mesa de Hogar, Sonríe, Llama a Mí, y la gran avenida El Después Sueña con el Hoy Cruzada por la avenida del Hombre No Idéntico.
> Darle a la vida luz y no cenizas. (*Museo*, 195)

> [it is astonishing to observe all the work men do to appear good in a civilization so enamored of Yale locks and of good manners, a trap for lulling victims to sleep.
> Cities with better taste would have streets called Rain, Awakening, Mother, Brother, The Call, Live Without Never, You Shall Return, Farewell, Wait for Me Always, Homecoming, Loving Family, Kiss, Friend, Greeting, Dream, Yet Again, Insomnia, Perhaps, Makeover, Forgetfulness, Endeavor, Come Back to Me, Gathering, Live in Fantasy, Fantasy Pain, Flowering Hedge, Dewpath, Laughter, Home Table, Smile, Call Me, and the great Avenue Dream After with the Today Crossing at the Avenue of the Not Identical Man.
> Give light to life and not ashes.]

Street names not only constitute, for Macedonio, a rationalist discourse completely unrelated to the real life of the city's inhabitants, they also betray the moral bankruptcy of that discourse. It is, not surprisingly, the same bankruptcy revealed by the enshrinement of selves: dead historical fables, or "ashes," imposed on the city as "lives," or immutable truths, in the form of statues. This discourse of selves infects the day-to-day living of the city's inhabitants, encouraging them to strive for notoriety rather than passion.

Macedonio also objects to the streets themselves, or, to be more specific, to the way streets, sidewalks, plazas, parks, and arcades, are conceived of, defined, set down, and used—the rational "ordering" for the very fabric of the material city. Richard Sennett, analyzing the development of Edwardian London and Second-Empire Paris, associates the development of efficient avenues, grand boulevards, sweeping parks, and, later, underground transit, to the analogous development of Enlightenment and Positivist perspectives on the body. The park, the boulevard, and the subway perform two critical functions. The first is the segregation of bodies that must cohabitate the city: the elite from the masses. The second is the efficient movement and circulation of those bodies in a way that maintains that separation while enabling maximum comfort and rest (Sennett 1994, 323–53).

The principal of segregation applies both to the Buenos Aires of today and to the city of the early twentieth century, whose design was directly inspired by the nineteenth-century development of London and Paris. A vibrant urban core, dedicated for the creole elite, insulates that elite from outlying dependencies housing the darker-skinned, poorer, less privileged subordinate classes (Yujnovsky 1975; Morse 1992, 6–8). Equally characteristic of Buenos Aires of the 1920s is the ubiquitous objective of protecting the body, cushioning it from sensation and promoting its rest, as well as safeguarding it from the alien threats of disease and degeneration.[1] This objective is in concert with Positivist Argentina's efforts at isolating, organizing, and controlling bodies in health and criminology.

To Macedonio, neither the process of organizing the city's streets nor the fabric the process renders make sense. The results are manifestly detrimental to healthy interaction. In the opening vignettes of *Papeles de Recienvenido*, Recienvenido's misfortunes seem to hinge entirely on being made a public spectacle in the street. His troubles range from being the object of great curiosity and journalistic interest upon taking a bad fall (16–19), to being forced into the role of inventor of "removable lapels" by a singular encounter with an irritable passerby (25–26). Not only does much of the action of *Recienvenido* take place in the streets of Buenos Aires, but also Recienvenido's very identity is constituted in those streets. It is an identity plainly fragmented, confused, and paradoxical, because the identity is imposed on him by those who confront and observe him, manifestly in conflict with his own sensations and sentiments. Recienvenido is made an "*accidentado*" subject, just as Macedonio is made an "author," by virtue of the public self the streets and the city's lettered institutions impose on him.

Adriana Buenos Aires contrasts noticeably with *Recienvenido* in this respect. Despite the frequent references to thoroughfares and squares in *Adriana*, very little happens in them. When scenes do occur in public venues, the streets and plazas of Buenos Aires are usually either places of friction or of almost unbearable solitude, and, in either case, of impersonal specularity. A crowded street scene is described thus:

> Estamos llegando, después de haber codeado sin mirarlos—Adriana no mira sino a su interlocutor cuando está fuera de casa—a los grupos que acuden al Colón, al Cervantes, ante la puerta de un buen edificio de altos. (*Adriana*, 30)

> [We are arriving, after having elbowed without looking—Adriana looks only at her interlocutor when she is outside the house—the groups gathered by the Colón and Cervantes Theatres, before the door of a fine apartment building.]

A contrasting scene occurs when Adolfo parts from Adriana and Eduardo sometime before dawn, leaving them in a deserted street:

> Cuando volviendo una esquina, con un saludo cariñoso y animoso Adolfo nos dejó solos en la acera, parados de frente uno al otro mirando hacia él, sin atinar Adriana, abatida, a contestar aquella a mano que se agitó en el aire, sentimos recién que entraba en realidad el múltiple diálogo ilusionador de aquella larga noche. (*Adriana*, 42)

> [When Adolfo, turning a corner, with a fond and cheerful wave left us alone on the sidewalk, standing opposite each other looking toward him, Adriana downcast, unable to bring herself to answer the wave, we sensed that just then the hopeful multiple dialogue of that long night was awakening to reality.]

In both these cases, Macedonio contrasts the fellowship and communication achieved in domestics settings with the alienation felt on the streets. This is a constant in Macedonio's work: one either escapes the hubbub and impersonal gaze of public spaces to find intimate connection at home, or one leaves the joy of domestic sharing to be broken by the cold solitude of the streets.

Balconies

But ambivalence persists: street scenes can occasionally be poetic and inspiring, for the movement of Buenos Aires "una ciudad de gran alma tonifica y descansa por alternación" (*Adriana*, 127) [a city of great spirit, alternately acts as tonic and calmant]. The city only inspires from the protected vantage point of home—of a balcony—or the window of a café. At such moments in *Adriana* there are glimpses of the "*querido*" Buenos Aires that Borges attempts to capture in his myth-making poetry:

> La puerta del balcón a la calle también está abierta y tengo un buen cuarto de hora de gozar la soledad de la calle, algún transeúnte que pasa frente a una luz, puertas que se cierran, vidrieras que se bajan, el vigilante muy contento golpeándose la bota con el blanco palo de señales. (*Adriana*, 135)

> [The door to the streetside balcony is also open and I have a good quarter hour to savor the solitude of the street, a passerby crossing in front of a light, doors being closed, shop windows being lowered, the watchman, content, striking his boot with his white signal stick.]

This vigil is distinctly different from the nostalgic evocations of Borges's early poetry or from the haunting, frenetic kaleidoscope of Girondo. Macedonio finds poetry in common city sights that involve everyday people going about their business. But these same sights—the same people on the same street viewed from the same balcony—are also the locus of violent confrontation, when, earlier in the novel, an impromptu musical performance from the balcony raises the ire of both passersby and policeman (*Adriana*, 78–79).

This specularity is regularly troubling to Macedonio, as we have seen in the "Oratorio de un hombre confuso." Balconies present the problematic issue of distinguishing performers from spectators; as often as they figure in both *Adriana* and *Papeles de Recienvenido*, balconies on city houses emphasize the bankruptcy, or irrelevancy, of the division between subject and object, between self and other. In *Museo*, the ubiquitous Buenos Aires balconies have vanished. Macedonio discards, with "bad" aesthetics, all representation of subject-object specularity. Only in a single passage found in two of the manuscript variations to *Museo* does Macedonio present the problem of specularity directly, when the "author" asks the "reader" how, at the scene of a car accident, one can know "if the one feeling such pain, struck down by a car in the street is another person and not you?" (197n)

Houses

Street balconies were an advent of modernity in early twentieth-century Buenos Aires, along with apartment buildings and other multistory buildings. One palpable change from the nineteenth-century city was the disappearance of the traditional creole house, most often a single story laid out around three successive patios.[2] By the 1920s, the fashion for Parisian architecture was echoed by the beaux-arts apartment building. Macedonio experienced this change firsthand, being raised to adulthood in a traditional house and continuing to visit his mother and daughter in an elegant apartment building in the same neighborhood.[3] These sorts of changes in residential space reflected analogous changes in the family life of the upper classes; the intensely private and self-contained domesticity of the traditional colonial patio was rapidly supplanted by the more outward and accessible habits of the modern metropolis. Houses opening inward onto a secluded patio were replaced by houses with balconies opening outward conspicuously to the street.

The Beaux-arts style was echoed in middle-class dwellings. By the turn of the century, small single-level houses in the urban center were replaced by two-story, two- and four-family houses (with a separate entrance for each dwelling) along urban European lines (Scobie 1974, 129); these same houses later were converted into the boardinghouses Macedonio inhabited and featured in his writings after 1920.[4] By then, small, rudimentary single-family dwellings, destined for the working classes, began to spring up in great numbers on the outskirts of the city (Liernur 1984).

Changes in architectural style did not seem to bother Macedonio; unlike Borges, Macedonio made no effort to capture the vanishing iron window grates and dusty patios of the previous era. The buildings themselves troubled Macedonio far less than their effects on personal relations. While urban structures are rarely represented in *Recienvenido* and *Adriana*, and not at all in *Museo*, the connection between modern buildings and personal alienation is explored. In addition to the troubling specularity of street balconies, apartment buildings in *Adriana* contrast sharply with houses with regard to the personal relations they frame. Eduardo de Alto meets Adriana in his boardinghouse, where the two immediately come to trust and understand each other completely. Adriana takes Eduardo to meet her lover, Adolfo, at a modern, spacious apartment. In the large drawing room of the apartment, talk is stilted and awkward until after dark, when the three friends prepare *mate* and are able to enter into confidences.

Adriana's move to an apartment building is soon followed by her lover's abandonment. The narrator, Eduardo, persuades Adriana to stay in his boardinghouse room, where, in a parodically idyllic nighttime scene, he confirms both his Platonic commitment to Adriana and her absolute love for Adolfo. When the pregnant Adriana, desperate to track down Adolfo, returns to the apartment building, Eduardo follows her and finds her late at night, absurdly, asleep on the cold marble steps leading from the street (167). Consistently, the intimacy of the plain boardinghouse is the setting for the blossoming and consolidation of passion and friendship. The apartment building, instead of shelter, offers a limbo between the indifference of the streets and the hopelessness of empty rooms, a limbo broken only occasionally by introducing intense, passionate companionship into the vast spaces of modern apartments.

Cafés

Public gathering places are problematic in a similar way. The setting for many of the characters' most important revelations in *Adriana Buenos Aires* alternates between the domestic intimacy of Eduardo's boardinghouse room and the public conspicuity of the Bar Ideal. Eduardo de Alto spends a great deal of time at the Ideal, taking breakfast there, drinking coffee, meeting with his friends, and watching the city hurry by. In his words, "Yo viviría en los bares, pero el 'Ideal' se cierra después de la una" (208). [I could live in bars, but the Ideal closes after one o'clock.] The Ideal was a real café, one in which members of the avant-garde, including Borges, often gathered just as they are represented in the later chapters of *Adriana*. Café society was an important component of 1920s Buenos Aires, much as it is today, both for the artistic avant-garde and for social and political groups.

Commercial public spaces such as cafés fall into the realm Sharon Zukin calls the "symbolic economy" of cultural institutions. A primary function of cultural institutions is in inventing and controlling "symbolic languages of exclusion and entitlement" (Zukin 1995, 7). Public cultural spaces are both territories to be claimed by communities and zones in which groups and communities take stock of their own cultural behavior and identity (11). Although primarily interested in museums and parks, Zukin also points to the modern shopping district, which increasingly, throughout the twentieth century, has emphasized display and segregation (of discretionary consumers of fashion and luxury goods, say, from the purchasers of basic goods) over neighborhood belonging and interaction (60–75). By means of designated shopping districts, urban planners have delegated areas of the city into "consumer playgrounds" for urban "delectation" (19, 14).

In Macedonio's Buenos Aires, the dynamics of urban "delectation" were most evident on calle Florida. In one of his earliest published pieces, an 1892 vignette entitled "La calle Florida," Macedonio makes an acerbic commentary on window shopping. His target is the "see and be seen" ostentation of Florida along with the obsession with consumer goods. Rather than regard such behavior as the fruits of democracy, Macedonio labels it "burrocracía o aburrocracia" [burrocracy or bore-ocracy] (*Papeles antiguos*, 26). He also explicitly links the physical form of the street, "the "horizontal column . . . stretching interminably northward," to the perverse relations it fosters.[5] Macedonio continued to harbor this distaste for modern consumer delectation and its related social interactions. His critique of delectation is elaborated at length in "Una novela que comienza" (A Novel that Begins), composed and amended at the same time as *Adriana* and containing many of the same characters as the novel. As with "La calle Florida," the fascination with shop windows impedes authentic affection between men and women (*Relato*, 11–28). The spaces as well as the institutions of urban consumer culture figure in Macedonio's writing as tandem to the pernicious institutions of heath and hygiene, and to the degradation of women.

Public eating and drinking establishments add another layer to this problem. Richard Sennett identifies the café as a symptom of the increasing specularity of urban life. City thoroughfares are no longer places of encounter and exchange; they become sites of passive observation and individual, but public, isolation (Sennett 1994, 345). In this vein, the bar presents Macedonio with a far more complex and equivocal set of problems than the street because it is the perpetual scene of confidences and revelations as well as observation and display.

When Eduardo and Estela need to broach the delicate question of Estela's future—essentially, how to find a man who will maintain her—he takes her from the boardinghouse to the Ideal. The outing proves to be a test; Eduardo wants Estela, who has been in Buenos Aires less than two days, to see how men at the Ideal will react to her. Her entrance provokes a stir; a nervous Estela pretends not to notice as men gaze at her slowly making her way among the tables in the bar (*Adriana*, 209). Eduardo proves his point: Estela will have no trouble attracting a man. But the act of putting her on display disturbs them both. In addition to allowing them to gauge the reaction of the public, Estela's display permits the public to examine her. She finds the experience so unnerving that she asks Eduardo not to look about him; she doesn't want him to "study their thoughts" (210). Eduardo discovers that he is so unsettled by the gaze of other men viewing him in the company of a beautiful woman that he can't concentrate on the purpose at hand. Eduardo and Estela return to the boardinghouse, where the real confidences, the heartfelt discussion of Estela's prospects as a "courtesan," ensue.

The bar is a place where Macedonio finds both fellowship and provocative discussion; where the truths concerning individual and society can be revealed and examined. At times in *Adriana* it is a place of calming encounters and lyrical, picturesque observations; at other times it is enervating and intimidating. At the height of his avant-garde collaboration and companionship, Macedonio is ambivalent about the dynamics of avant-garde café society. In *Museo*, for the most part, Macedonio opts decidedly against the café. Although the residents of the estancia La Novela enjoy the fellowship of relaxing together in the bar of Constitution train station at the end of a hard day's work (*Museo*, 144), bars, like balconies, are ubiquitous in the "bad" novel and nearly absent in the "good" novel. When they are mentioned, it is in order to completely invert their dynamics of exhibition and performance. The Novel, Macedonio states in one of *Museo*'s fifty-six prologues, plans to send rafts of guitarists to several bars (including the Ideal) to perform "polyphonies" for the bars' orchestras to hear:

> El Polígrafo de Silencio con eruditos gestos explicará el propósito, y circulará entre el personal de las orquestas escuchantes la bandejita sin fondo de la gratitud, haciendo sonar las moneditas del agradecimiento. El público funcionará también en armonía de contento, como orquesta de escuchar, trocando luego por un momento sus instrumentos de llamar al mozo por instrumentos de aplaudir, palmotear (43).

[The Polygraph of Silence, with learned gestures, will explain the purpose and circulate among the members of the listening orchestras with the bottomless little tray of gratitude, jingling the coins of thanks. The public will also function in a harmony of contentment, like a listening orchestra, changing for a moment its instruments for calling the waiter into instruments for applauding, clapping.]

Invading the café, the Novel manipulates the café's specularity to recuperate the affective function of music. Performers confer happiness, not spectacle; the public applauds rather than demands service for payment. Later in *Museo*, when the Novel actually conquers the city, part of the consternation it provokes is by carrying kettles of homemade stew through the city's bars, "que despamarra el perfume hogareño, enternecedor, de sus vapores, operando el desmontamiento del humor de orgía" [wafting the homely, touching fragrance of its vapors, effectively clearing away the humors of orgy] (200).

Given the constant return to the domestic nest in *Adriana* and the role of "homeliness" in conquering the city in *Museo*, it is not surprising that one of the first prologues in *Museo* is titled "Hogar de la no existencia" (A Home of Nonexistence) and begins with the words, "El anhelo que me animó en la construcción de mi novela fue crear un hogar, hacerla un hogar para lo no-existencia" [The desire that pressed me in the construction of my novel was to create a home, to make it a home for nonexistence] (22). Modern urban dwellings, together with urban public venues, prove so ill adapted to the fostering of human relations that the only solution is to invent and build a new dimension of home, a dimension realized only in the novel. The novelization of Buenos Aires means also the salvation of its domestic and public spaces.

Streetcars

As Sennett suggests, urban transit is an integral part of the ordering, insulating, and segregating characteristic of Positivist urban planning. Since the late nineteenth century, Buenos Aires has been one of the world's most transit intensive cities.[6] Trains and streetcars were principal players in the spatial expansion, mobile acceleration, and overall organization of Buenos Aires and its environs for the entire first half of the century. An important part of the urban landscape, streetcars also receive an ambivalent treatment by Macedonio Fernández, though as with balconies, bars, and other accoutrements of modernity, he ultimately rejects them. In *Papeles de Recienvenido*, Macedonio negates the principal of efficiency behind urban transport:

> una brusca interrupción en el servicio de no haber tranvías en Buenos Aires—la acumulación de muchos en una cuadra los hace no haber, y da gran prestigio y velocidad a las veredas—nos [ha] llenado de preferencias por la abundancia de no haber tranvías en La Plata. (*Recienvenido* 43)

> [a sudden interruption of the service of not having streetcars in Buenos Aires—the accumulation of many in one city block renders them not there, and gives the sidewalks great prestige and velocity—has filled us with preference for the abundance of not having streetcars in La Plata.]

The more streetcars accumulate, the more useless they are. Meant to resolve the problems of time and distance created by the expanse and density of the city, streetcars end up exacerbating those problems. One's sense of velocity, frequency, and extension are contorted by their existence, and they take on dynamics of their own that are at odds with their supposed purpose. In the same vein, sidewalks are perfectly suited to velocity when one measures speed according to the duration and frequency of human intercourse. Sensation is the crux of these concepts; Macedonio requires that his readers know Buenos Aires in terms of the sensation and the relationships sensation affords.

Manfred Max-Neef's arguments on "subjective" time and space echo Macedonio's objections to urban transport. The intensity of urban space is so great, "the amount of spatial information is so great"(Max-Neef 1992, 91), that the subject is much more remote than in a small community. Similarly, the intensity of events is so much greater in an urban environment that their repeated processing by the brain greatly magnifies the time they occupy (92).[7] For Macedonio, both the objectivity of dimensions and the subjectivity of humans are implicated in the crisis of urban time and space. The need to overcome the difficulties of urban dimensions is obviated by the denial of autonomous subjectivity—of the self.

In *Adriana Buenos Aires*, trains and streetcars are granted two beneficial functions that have nothing to do with mastering distances. At one point in the novel, Eduardo de Alto meets Estela on a train; a poem he leaves on her seat convinces her he must be kind, and she follows him to his boardinghouse, unwittingly renting the room her long-lost father died in the day before. At another point, weeks after Adriana has disappeared from Eduardo's life without a trace, a young friend of Eduardo's follows a young woman onto a streetcar and is led unwittingly to Adriana, who is caring for an Adolfo lost in delirium. The strange woman, it turns out, is Adolfo's fiancée. Public transport, in which strangers, from disparate parts of the city and walks of life, are drawn together and thrown apart, is instrumental in enabling lost, wandering souls to find their helpmates. At another juncture, Eduardo takes a ninety-minute streetcar ride with Adriana, concluding:

> Me placía mucho estar a su lado en el tranvía: es más franco, menos oculto, más de personas que se entienden bien y serenamente, que se poseen en el afecto sin ocultaciones ni apuros, que las disparadas en auto. (147)

> [It pleased me a great deal to be by her side in the streetcar; it is more frank, less secret, more for people who understand each other well and serenely, who possess each other in affection without dissimulation or embarrassment, than racing off in a car.]

The mastery of speed and distance judged irrelevant, streetcars remain interesting as environments for human interaction. At one moment, Eduardo de Alto also judges streetcars, watched through the window from inside the Bar Ideal, to be picturesque. His description of one, "detenida temblando de motricidad suspensa" [still, trembling with suspended motoricity] (*Adriana*, 221), verges on the Martinfierristas' more precious renderings of urban scenes.

But as with bars and cafés, Macedonio is ambivalent about public conveyances, always aware of their pernicious aspects. Throughout *Museo de la Novela de la Eterna*, Macedonio devotes the novel to correcting the errors that streetcars perpetuate. The Novel, he promises in a prologue, will not dissemble its pauses and accidents the way transport companies try to cover up service interruptions with a frenzy of activity (31). One of the tactics of the conquest of Buenos Aires by the Novel involves decreeing free bus passage for anyone exceeding ninety kilos, causing endless disputes (201). In a passage from two manuscript variations, Nicolasa, the fat cook who is barred from the Novel for being too substantial and too carnal, opens an empanada stand at the train station nearest the estancia La Novela, causing the trains to delay, "bewitched" by the smell of her empanadas (285).

The most fundamental challenge to accepting the underlying logic of urban transport, however, is the novel itself. Julio Prieto points to Macedonio's metaphor of the "*novela-tranvía*" (streetcar-novel) to argue that in *Museo*, the novel is meant to become both a text and a character; things happen *to* and *in* it concomitantly (J. Prieto 2002, 220). The novel *is* the streetcar (Bueno 2001, 54). Like the streetcar, the "first good" novel contains accidents and suffers them. Its passengers are contained within but also enter and leave at will. It is in motion even when stalled and often stalled in motion. The "good" novel is porous, transitory, ubiquitous, and constant.

These qualities are achieved by the novel's conquest of the modern city's components. Streetcars, trains, and buses are boarded or detained and converted from vehicles that travel distances to spaces that bring together wandering souls. Bars and cafés are invaded and changed from establishments of consumption and ostentation to places of passionate exchange and discovery. Cold, impersonal apartment houses are penetrated and turned into sites of heartfelt confidence. And the streets themselves become the locus of the novel. The "novel taken to the streets" makes characters, readers, and authors of mere types, consumers, and crowds.

Neighborhood

Behind Macedonio's attacks on the modern city and his proposal to save the city "by miracle of the novel" lies a nostalgia, rarely explicit, for simpler—if arguably imaginary—times. It is a yearning for an environment less corporate, less materialistic, and less structured by bureaucratic, centralized powers. Like Borges, Macedonio turns to *barrio*, or neighborhood, to find in the city vestiges of the affective community he longs for in the modern metropolis. Unlike Borges, Macedonio has no interest in representing "timeless" elements of the *arrabal*, or outlying neighborhood, that Borges regarded as uniquely and elementally Porteño. Nor does Macedonio attempt to portray mythical types, such as the valiant, amoral *compadrito*, or neighborhood boss, made famous by Borges's very first short story, "Hombre de la esquina rosada" ("Streetcorner Man"). Borges's persistent return to this story, and to the nostalgic aspects of his early poetry, suggest that he retained his attachment to the arrabal throughout his life.

Macedonio Fernández may have shared Borges's yearning for a nineteenth-century way of life, but his aesthetic response was simultaneously more personal and less mimetic. Biographical sources, including comments by Adolfo de Obieta (1996), suggest that Macedonio never took part in the barrio life of union meetings, neighborhood political caucuses, and demonstrations. Such institutional activities have no place in Macedonio's Belarte.

Macedonio's commitment to the idea of neighborhood is most evident in *No toda es vigilia la de los ojos abiertos*. This philosophical treatise that challenges the underpinnings of modern Western thought features an almost fanciful beginning. Thomas Hobbes arrives in 1920s Buenos Aires from seventeenth-century England and settles down in a hotel like an ordinary traveler. Presently, Hobbes relates to an Argentine friend an utterly innocuous event, transpired in his Buenos Aires hotel room, which has prompted him to a total reconsideration of the distinction between dreaming and wakefulness. This illumination leads Hobbes to question whether or not he is dreaming his presence, four hundred years after his birth, in this very concrete city, consisting of "compras, museos, bibliotecas, y monumentos (polillas del placer de viajar), placeres, negocios e instrucciones" [shopping, museums, libraries and monuments (the moths of traveling pleasure), pleasures, business and instruction] (*Vigilia*, 249). The friend then commends Hobbes to Buenos Aires's own metaphysicist, one Macedonio Fernández. He adds that Macedonio has proven so successful at resolving all metaphysical difficulties that his entire urban neighborhood, while benefiting from metaphysics, has come to rely on him completely and has left off concerning itself with the subject altogether:

> el barrio, fiado en él, ha llegado a una perfección tan extraordinaria de no saber nada de metafísica que es cosa de no creer que haya alguna vez sabido alquien algo, una pizca de ello. Muchos no quieren creer que el barrio haya estado anoticiado alguna vez del misterio metafísico. (*Vigilia*, 253)

> [the district, trusting him, has achieved such an extraordinary perfection of not knowing anything about metaphysics that it is hard to believe that at one time anyone knew anything, even a little bit, about it. Many people don't want to believe that the district has ever been made aware of metaphysical mysteries.]

Macedonio anchors the most fundamental principles of his philosophical thought not only to the city, but to the neighborhood he inhabits. Despite, or perhaps as a result of, the manifest absence from the institutions of neighborhood life of the biographical Macedonio Fernández, the fictionalized Macedonio has made himself so indispensable to his neighborhood that they are able to ignore him thoroughly, or at least to ignore his concerns. This little tale serves almost as a precis of Macedonio's conundrum regarding his relationship to the city: how to repudiate the assumptions the city is founded on without abandoning the city; how to resolve the city's metaphysical crisis without ending up with the city's abandonment of him.

Macedonio's implication is that a radical change in the assumptions, beliefs, and interrelations of city life must start with the neighborhood; the "novelization" of the city must begin at the grass roots. His call for mass industry to be replaced by neighborhood cottage industries is integral with that focus. *Adriana Buenos Aires* is faithful to this approach in that most of its events—except the various excursions associated with attempts to cure Adolfo's madness—take place in a compact and fairly defined area around the Plaza Lavalle. Part of the effect of naming specific streets, addresses, intersections, and establishments is to render *Adriana* a neighborhood melodrama—a kind of 1920s Argentine *East Enders*.

During the decade or so prior to the First World War, dramatic changes in neighborhood patterns, concomitant to the changes in living spaces, swept greater Buenos Aires. As immigration, eased credit terms, and streetcar expansion created sprawl and pushed the working classes toward the suburbs, the pull of the increasingly cosmopolitan center drew trade and intercourse out of the neighborhoods. The result was an urban core ever more dynamic in commerce and culture, but more markedly exclusive and homogeneous in residents. The modest neighborhoods outside the core became simultaneously less economically and socially cohesive but more ethnically ghettoized (Scobie 1974, 176–93; 201–7).

Francis Korn illustrates how the area around the Plaza Miserere and Once Station suffered all of these phenomena of increased commercialization, decreased coherence, intensified ghettoization, and segregation. The neighborhood's location at the convergence of the downtown core to the east, the elite barrio Norte to the north, and the working and middle class districts of Boedo and San Cristóbal to the south make it a near microcosm of many of the changes undergone by the city as a whole. The district's changes are illustrative of both the integration of immigrants into neighborhood life and their integration in the commercial life of the city (Korn 1974, 179–81).[8] This is the neighborhood Macedonio Fernández grew up in and remained in throughout the 1920s, where he lived in a succession of small residential hotels close to his mother's apartment on Rivadavia, and not far from his sister and three sons at Otamendi 622.

Macedonio Fernández witnessed these dramatic changes in the texture of his Buenos Aires and of his district, and *Adriana* reflects that experience. But Macedonio was not so bothered by the phenomenon of growth itself, the means by which growth occurred, nor even the actual material conditions resulting from growth. He was repelled by the effects of growth on individuals and on the interactions and relationships among individuals inhabiting the city. The city, he concluded, impeded all possibility of true beauty. Macedonio also asserted that the modern city was economically untenable. His letters to his cousin Gabriel del Mazo, vice-president of the University La Plata, and a civil engineer partly responsible for the organization of mass transit in interwar Buenos Aires, are nearly vitriolic on this point. In 1939, Macedonio writes:

> El más sesudo dictamen y triunfo de la ciencia del Urbanismo decretará la Incineración de las Ciudades. En esto la Urbanística se dotará de su axioma. Y no tan imprevisto, pues las ciudades han vivido del ingrave, molesto y caro Remiendo, el trabajo más irritante y frustráneo antieconómico que toca a los hombres. Se concibió genialmente la Gran Ciudad, pero no se logró nunca del todo y debe morir el Urbanismo y la super-comerciación que ella implica. Se inventó la casa no-propia, el campo no-propio, un monstruo de costoso sustamiento. (*Epsitolario*, 153–54)

> [The most intelligent dictum and triumph of the science of urbanism will decree the Incineration of Cities. In this Urban Studies will endow itself with its axiom. And not so unforeseeable, for cities have lived off of unserious, bothersome and expensive Mending, the most irritating and frustrating antieconomic work known to men. The Great City was conceived of genially, but it was never completely achieved and Urbanism, and the super-commerce that it implies, should die. The unowned house, unowned land have been invented, a monster of costly maintenance.]

Museo de la Novela de la Eterna reiterates this summary rejection of modern urbanism when the Presidente declares that the conquest of Buenos Aires for Beauty has proven insufficient. Cities are "irremediably ugly" for the reason that living without access to nature makes beauty and cordiality impossible to sustain (*Museo*, 229). In the end, Macedonio has decided in favor of the country over the city.

COUNTRYSIDE

Macedonio's preference for a rural environment, and the countryside's vital importance for mental and spiritual health as well as for the elaboration of beauty, is sustained in both his writing and his life. The constant movement from city to country and back again constitutes one of the basic structures of the narrative components of *Museo* and plays an important part in *Adriana*. Macedonio champions the rural both as an antidote to the effects of the urban complex on the individual and as model for reconsideration of the idea of the city. An isolated beach beyond the reaches of the metropolis, in *Adriana Buenos Aires*, is the place of cure and restoration for the insane individual, where the claims of class, intellect, and money are displaced by the bonds of genuine personal affection. In *Museo*, an estancia in the nearby Pampa is the incubator for the campaign to transform the alienating city into an environment of beauty, cordiality, and compassion.

Macedonio's biography is marked by his impulse to escape the oppressiveness of Buenos Aires. His removal to a rustic shack in Morón in 1926, from which he ventured into the city periodically, was meant not only to satisfy his yearning for a green environment but also to create an environment conducive to the prolonged "conversation" of music, reading, refreshment, and discussion that must replace professionalized literary relations (Abós 2002, 108–11). Macedonio's stays at La Verde, the country estate of the Saenz Valiente family, from 1929 onward, were the result of his romance with Consuelo Bosch Saenz Valiente, a relationship that lasted until his death. But Macedonio clearly felt that in order to continue thinking and writing he needed the rural setting that Consuelo was able to provide (Abós 2002, 146).

The context for similar critiques of urban life in favor of rural environments is rich and extensive. Thinkers as diverse as Thomas Jefferson, Max Weber, Oswald Spengler, and Georg Simmel all observed the contradictions, paradoxes, and dangers in the city and its relations with the countryside. Weber equates the city with marketplace, distinguishing "semi-rural" cities as those communities where agricultural needs are satisfied with locally grown foods (28). Spengler, qualifying the city as inherently cut off from the land, criticizes it for its subjection both to money and to the abstract phenomenon of "culture," which he views as a poor substitute for a community's soul (1969, 76–79). Simmel (1968) argues urban environments promote a modern "calculating intellect," dulling individual emotional and spiritual personality, while at the same time requiring heightened intellectualism and materialism in order for people to defend their individuality (49–51). Simmel's analysis in particular articulates the sort of paradox Macedonio finds in modern Buenos Aires. In this most individualistic of cultures, "authentic" individual personality is supplanted by a self made up of entirely artificial relations: intellectual culture and material wealth.[9] Macedonio's and Simmel's sources are partly the same: eighteenth-century transcendentalism and nineteenth-century German philosophical ideas on the relationship between self and society; and, more importantly, the disorienting surge of urban modernity to which those ideas often respond. Unlike Simmel, however, Macedonio Fernández's objective is to articulate a solution to the paradox.

Other nineteenth- and twentieth-century critics of the urban emphasize the peril to the physical as well as psychological and moral well being of individuals (Lees 1985, 152–87). As Andrew Lees tells us, such commentators were especially concerned with the degenerative effects on women of city life, manifest in the recourse to prostitution of many female newcomers (Lees 1985, 161). This was not a small preoccupation in Macedonio's Buenos Aires. Among Latin American critics, the call was often for *moral* regeneration in contrast to the technological and institutional responses of North America (Morse 1992, 13). The German alarm regarding socialism, as well as American apprehensions over urban bossism (Lees 1985, 169–77), have a vivid reflection in Macedonio's writing. Equally pertinent, many antiurban commentaries are routinely laced with nostalgia for a vanishing, or vanished, or partly imaginary, rural idyll (179–84). From the swallowing up of green spaces to the disfiguring of the traditional villages, European cries over the loss of rural paradise resonate loudly in Macedonio's Argentina as well.[10]

None of these sentiments were lost on Argentine thinkers of the time. Nostalgia for traditional rural culture is evident in Sarmiento's Positivist vision for a modern, urbanized Argentina (Morse 1992,

14), and endures—along with that vision—in apologies for cosmopolitanism, right up to the present. The Argentine debate between rural *barbarie* and urban *civilización* has so permeated national discourse that it remains a driving force in national culture and politics, according to Nicholas Shumway. Throughout his writings, Sarmiento's plan for the prosperity of the nation depends heavily on a utopian rural vision (Morse 1992, 13). Similar voices are heard in the twentieth century. As early as 1917, in an untitled commentary in the journal *Nosotros*, Ezequiel Martínez Estrada attacks urban development and culture. Like his German counterparts, he links urbanism with excessive rationalism. In *La cabeza de Goliat* (Goliath's Head), first published in 1943, Martínez Estrada contrasts the "Goliath's head" of the all-consuming urbanism of Buenos Aires to the irrational culture of rural life and to the emotional and spiritual bonds among country people (Martínez Estrada 1956). He associates these bonds with a virtually mystical relationship with the land.

In 1933, Martínez Estrada still had hopes that the city might be infused with the "mystery" of traditional creole culture. His *Radiografía de la Pampa* (*X-Ray of the Pampa*) shares many of Macedonio Fernández's assessments of Buenos Aires: a great city generated spontaneously by the pampas, imprisoned and cut off from its origins by its own rigid grid of boulevards and skyscrapers and by the artificiality, flimsiness, and fetishism of commercial urban culture (Martínez Estrada 1985, 193–206). His dream for the city resuscitates—or reinvents—the traditional relations of the "gran aldea" ("great village") and the structures or institutions that accommodate them: the inward yet fervent family life of the creole house; the energetic union with the land experienced in horsemanship (228–37).

Peruvian Luis Alberto Sánchez criticized the city to similar effect. Sánchez's thoughts require our attention because of Macedonio Fernández's express affinity for them. The two men, who had met in the late 1930s, read each other's works (*Epistolario*, 339) and enjoyed a correspondence during the 1930s and 1940s (M. Fernández 1938).[11] Sánchez argues that Latin American civilization, from its precolumbian origins, is essentially rural in nature. The imposition, by colonial culture, of planned, ordered cities, has created a disjuncture between city and land that continues to plague Latin American societies. Cities control commerce and economy while land provides the means for it (Sánchez 1967).[12]

Macedonio's critique of the urban is not purely negative; he does offer a hypothetical solution for the city. The *ciudad-campo* (country-city), which Macedonio claimed to have invented, is conceived as "un millón de chacras y diez mil fábricas, exenta totalmente del horror de la palabra alquiler" [a million small farms and ten thousand factories, totally exempt from the horror of the word rent] (*Epistolario*, 160). Among the advantages he imagines for this vision, Macedonio includes the country-city's immunity from attack, freedom from disease, reduction in "unproductive" commerce, and reduction in the presence of a disruptive proletariat. In material composed for the journal *Papeles de Buenos Aires* around the same time as the above letter, Macedonio details this utopian vision further. Emphasizing that household family life (what today is called "quality time") is the foundation of both morality and prosperity, he quips, "mínimo de Calle, máximo de Casa" [minimum of Street, maximum of House] (*Teorías*, 183). He describes an idyllic small-scale community maintaining immediate contact with nature, especially water, and demarcating separate zones for industry and public works.

Macedonio flatters himself by crediting himself with the invention of this concept. The context for similar critiques is rich indeed, embracing philosophical, socioeconomic, cultural, and political perspectives. In Britain and the U.S. especially, idealization of rural life was a strong component in the "garden city" movement, which has had such an enduring impact on twentieth-century urban and suburban development. Similar to Macedonio's thinking, the championing of the individual was at the core of the garden city.[13] Macedonio's "ciudad-campo" also bears a close resemblance to the utopian anarchist city of Joaquín Falconnet, whose *La ciudad anarquista americana* (The American Anarchist City) circulated widely under the pseudonym Pierre Quiroule early in this century (Weinberg 1976, 23). Macedonio was impressed by this almost Emersonian vision of a self-sufficient, minimally governed community of independent freeholders. Falconnet's utopian city was intimate of scale, sensitive to the landscape, and thoughtfully zoned. Juan de Molina y Vedia (1996) has pointed out that this blueprint was particularly dear to anarchists like his grandfather Julio, companion to Macedonio and Jorge Borges senior in their youthful dream of utopia. The visions of such men from families of landowning gentry was closely linked to a nostalgia for the lost "rural golden age," an Argentina in which social distinctions were—from their perspective—minimized by a mutual close relationship to the land.[14] Macedonio's critique of modern Buenos Aires hinges on this point. If the "ciudad-campo" is celebrated for its healthy closeness to nature, the modern city stands to be criticized for its relentless efforts to segregate humans from the elements (*Teorías*, 119–20).

The dearth of Macedonio's comments on parks, in a city with a notable number of public squares and parks, may reflect his dissatisfaction with the concept of urban greenery. The artificially set aside, government-managed urban park, province of the privileged classes in Buenos Aires, is an unworthy alternative to his "cuidad-campo." Two allusions to urban greenery support this speculation. In "Los amigos de la ciudad" (Friends of the City), published in 1925, Macedonio recalls the private gift to the city of a wood (*un bosque*), which the municipality immediately endows with trees:

> pues nuestra comuna no aprobaba otro decorado, con fondos oficiales, que el constituido por plantas y no era congruente que el bosque, nuevo bien municipal gratuito y valioso, careciera de este ornato invariable de calles, plazas y jardines. (*Recienvenido*, 33)

> [for our commune approved of no other décor, paid for with official funds, than one composed of plants and it was not fitting that the park, a new, free and valuable municipal property, lacked this invariable ornament to streets, plazas and gardens.]

It is the convention of the public park that irks Macedonio—spaces such as Palermo park, managed by the government according to unquestioned, uniform, and consummately artificial standards of adornment. The idea that a tree can be regarded as a decoration is revealed here as an obvious paradox.

The other reference to green spaces is more poignant. In a letter to his cousin Jorge del Mazo, who, like his brother Gabriel del Mazo was a prominent urban planner, Macedonio congratulates him on the inauguration of the avenida General Paz, a greenbelt parkway circumscribing the city. Macedonio praises the project, "un Palacio de la Ambulación" [A Palace of Perambulation], as a space for all, "taller-paseo del viandante obligado" [studio-way for the man of the road by necessity]. Macedonio is impressed by the realization of a space designed both to simplify mobility and to facilitate genuine encounter and intercourse for the entire spectrum of Porteños (*Epistolario*, 242). The sad irony here is that the present-day General Paz is a nightmare of urban planning: a superhighway belt literally constricting the City of Buenos Aires and cutting it off from the suburbs.

Property

The anarchist roots of his antipathy for the city help explain Macedonio Fernández's seemingly self-contradictory pronouncements on capitalism. Urbanization, to Macedonio, figures as one of the most damaging of artificial *economic* structures imposed on the individual by institutions—government most of all. A truly capitalistic city would not be urban, modern, organized, or oriented toward the increase of material accoutrements. "Capitalismo Vocacional, no de Apropiación o de Consumo" [Vocational Capitalism, not Capitalism of Appropriation or Consumption], as he calls it in a letter to Gabriel del Mazo (*Epistolario*, 157). Macedonio's utopia would be the realization of a utopian existence for individuals, and that existence would be founded on a metaphysical, affect-centered identity and on relationships that have nothing to do with material commerce.

Macedonio believed his "vocational capitalism" was a prerequisite to such an ethical society. Much of his commentary regarding the state of the world, particularly during both world wars, did not imply optimism that such changes would ever materialize. He acknowledges that the realization of such a utopian society would require radical change. Among his theoretical writings, Macedonio speculates on how a libertarian utopia might develop on a deserted island (*Teorías*, 167). At another point, he speaks of unfettered economic development occurring after "Un momento de nuevo arreglo del capital natural" [A moment of rearrangement of natural capital] that might correspond to his hypothetical "incineration of cities."

When discussing economics, Macedonio frequently uses the term "capital natural" to refer to resources from which humans derive material wealth. He censures categorically the individual "appropriation" or inheritance of these resources (*Vigilia*, 219). While his comments on "natural capital" seem to contradict his rejection of Marxist tenets (*Teorías*, 123, 150–51), if one squares this concept with Macedonio's vision of a "ciudad-campo" and his championing of personal, small-scale production over modern industry, this approach to capital accords perfectly with the concerns presented in his fiction. The fate of Argentina's wealth—which for Macedonio comprises mainly its cultural and natural endowment—in an era of convulsive change, is never far from Macedonio's mind. His dream for the city incorporates his desire to prevent the squandering of those resources by self-interested, commercial capitalism.

It is no minor detail that the monumental *Museo de la Novela de la Eterna*, eternally evolving and perpetually archived, is set on an *estancia*, called La Novela, located within a train commute to Buenos Aires. Consider the significance of the passage describing this "property:"

> Era la Estancia un campo de unas cien hectáreas, en litigio eterno, al cual tenía derecho prominente el Presidente, existiendo otros interesados por él reconocidos y de quienes había obtenido dos años antes adquiescencia para domiciliarse en dicho fundo, a cambio de vigilar la propiedad y solventar sus cargas. Congregados así al azar como personajes puestos juntos a arbitrio del artista en páginas de fantasía, acompañaban al Presidente desde casi dos años en aquella estanzuela vieja, tierra a espera de frecuentes decisiones judiciales. (*Museo*, 140)

> [The estancia was a property of some one hundred hectares, in eternal litigation, to which the President had prominent right, there existing other interests recognized by him and from whom he had obtained, two years earlier, acquiescence to dwell on said property, in exchange for watching over the property and settling its taxes. Gathered this way at random, like characters thrown together at the whim of the artist in pages of fantasy, they had been accompanying the President for nearly two years on that old bit of a ranch, land in wait of frequent judicial decisions.][15]

In this one brilliant paragraph, Macedonio has conflated his concerns for the disposition of property or "natural capital," the fate of an obsolescent way of life, the stewardship of a political leader, the economic and social health of the nation, and the ethical dilemma of an artist commanding subjects in a work of art. The paragraph also serves as an autobiographical paraphrase for Macedonio's frequent periodic residency at Consuelo Saenz-Valiente's Estancia La Verde, in Pilar.[16] Macedonio's conflation of all these concerns into a single metaphor is so perfectly natural to him because, in his singular vision of the world, they *are* the same thing.[17] The fate of the nation, its culture and its resources, the legitimacy of leaders, and the future of art all hinge on a radical reconception of self. Dissolve our selves into this novel, says Macedonio, and Argentina will be a livable place.

The Miracle of the Novel

This observation returns us to the campaign of the residents of La Novela, under the direction of the Presidente, to beautify Buenos Aires, which in turn has been linked to Macedonio's campaign-in-absence for the presidency of the Republic. With *Museo*, Macedonio demonstrates that a novel can constitute a kind of campaign, and the museum of a novel is an archival record of that campaign. Any possible realization of Macedonio's dream for the city hinged in large measure on his success at disseminating his ideas outside the channels of authorship and publishing. If the social, political, and medical institutions of Buenos Aires and the city's very fabric and form rest on the faith in subjectivity, the campaign to reform the city "por milagro de novela" takes place perforce outside the boundaries of that faith. For this reason, the "first good novel" must invade the city on the novel's own terms, not those of its subjective author, editor, publisher, or readers. It is also why the concept of "novel taken to the streets" so appealed to Macedonio. He reiterates this idea in the first pages of *Museo*:

> Habríamos menudeado imposibles por la ciudad.
> El público miraría nuestros "jirones de arte", escenas de novela ejecutándose en las calles, entreverándose a "jirones de vida", en veredas, puertas, domicilios, bares, y creería ver "vida"; el público soñaría al par que la novela pero al revés: para ésta su vigilia es su fantasía; su ensueño la ejecución externa de sus escenas. (*Museo*, 14)

> [We would have rained impossibles on the city.
> The public would watch our "art strips," scenes of the novel performed in the streets, intermingling with "life strips," on sidewalks, in doorways, houses, bars, and they would think they were seeing "life;" the public would dream just like the novel but backward; for the novel, its wakefulness is its fantasy; its dream is the external performance of its scenes.]

The idea of the "novel taken to the streets" is key to understanding the relationship between two apparently unrelated concepts central to *Museo*. On the one hand, this novel dwells almost interminably on the process of "desidentificación del autor" [de-identification of the author] or of "el trabajo de quitar el yo, de desacomodar interiores, identidades" [the work of getting rid of the self, of dispensing with interiors, identities] (*Museo*, 33). On the other hand, the point of the novel is the beautification of the city. For Macedonio, these two fundamental objectives are inextricably linked.

In his "Prólogo a lo nunca visto," Macedonio suggests that the novel and the city are destined to be one and the same: both are completely unprecedented, having been invented from nothingness, having drawn the world irresistibly to them as a new-world Utopia. Ultimately, they are, or will be, indistinguishable:

> Tal colección de sucesos se encerrará dentro de (la novela de lo nunca habido) que no dejará casi nada para el suceder en las calles, domicilios y plazas, y los diarios faltos de acontecimientos tendrán que conformarse con citarla: "en la novela de la Eterna ayer a media tarde se produjo el siguiente coloquio"; "se encuentra esta mañana sonriente la Dulce-Persona"; "el Presidente de la Novela, reporteando en vista de los rumores circulantes entre sus numerosos lectores, se sirvió manifestarnos que positivamente lanzará hoy su plan de histerización de Buenos Aires y conquista humorística de nuestra población para su salvación estética". (*Museo*, 43)

> [Such a collection of events will be enclosed inside (the novel of never having been) which will leave almost nothing for events in the streets, homes, and plazas, and the newspapers void of occurrences will have to resort to citing it: "in the novel of Eterna yesterday at midafternoon the following conversation took place;" "this morning Dulce-Persona finds herself smiling;" "the President of the Novel, reporting in view of the rumors circulating among its many readers, is pleased to reveal that today positively he will launch his plan for the histericization of Buenos Aires and humoristic conquest of our populace for its aesthetic salvation."]

The pages following this passage dwell on various aspects of the suppression of the self, of demonstrating its falseness or effecting its undoing. Constantly interspersed with these discussions on the self are discussions on the nature of the absent or unknown author, the promised-but-unexecuted novel, the speciousness of subjectivity and the ascendancy of dreams. The sum effect of these passages is to persistently reinforce, prior to the actual "novel," Macedonio's peculiar vision.

His author so successfully suppresses subjectivity so as to make his person intangible and his affection ubiquitous. His novel so effectively suppresses representation as to absorb the city into itself without ever taking a definitive archival form; rather it is an archive that evolves perpetually. The city, in being so absorbed, is transformed into a utopia of affection.

A corollary of this project focuses on the Presidente (who, it is useful to recall, "sometimes is and sometimes is not" the Author), and his relationship with one of the two female residents of the estancia, and the Novel: La Eterna. The Presidente's task regarding Eterna is analogous to the job he has given the other residents of beautifying the city. He must convince Eterna of the "nihilidad," or nonexistence, of death and of the past "para quienes tienen ya el amor" [for those who already have love]. His goal in convincing her of this power of love to eliminate death and the past is to liberate her "de la franja de haber sido real" [of the fringes of having been real] (Fernández 1982, 261).[18] The analogy in question is clarified in a separate passage. A reflection on the novel's other female character, the visitor Dulce-Persona, provokes a meditation on the nature of passion and—most significant here—on the appropriateness of Buenos Aires as a city defined by passion:

> En las formas tan sensuales e inocentes de Dulce-Persona se miraba el resplandor de Buenos Aires, suprema ciudad merodeada por las sombras de campos sin límites, viviendo a oscuras de su destino, como el transatlántico, iluminado, en la vasta oscuridad del mar en cuyo seno se avanza; en ambos se vive sin noción de rumbo, por lo tanto con entero sentido del presente; en cambio, cuando se vive históricamente, no hay más parte adonde ir la Pasión. (*Museo*, 135)

> [In Dulce-Persona's form, so sensual and innocent, one saw the glow of Buenos Aires, city supreme prowling with the shadows of the limitless fields, living hidden from its destiny, like the transatlantic steamer, brilliantly lit, in the vast darkness of the sea in whose breast it moves forward; in both, one lives without a sense of direction, therefore with a complete feel of the present; in contrast, when one lives historically, there is no longer a place for Passion to go.]

This project—to rid Buenos Aires of its history and objectivity and return it to its passionate essence—is in keeping with the utopian vision of Macedonio's anarchist origins, with his desire to reconstitute the very fabric of the city, and with his efforts to write an alternative to the lettered city. Macedonio's conceit linking this vision to the eradication of subjectivity in individuals, and especially in affective relations between individuals, is consonant with other contemporary visions for urban culture.

The eradication of subjectivity through passion is a component, for example, of the positive potential Bonnie Menes Kahn speaks of in her meditation on urban cultures (1987). Great cities, she argues, are characterized by diversity, cosmopolitanism, and, above all, a tolerance that transcends bricks and mortar and yet is inseparable from them. To express it in only slightly more prosaic terms, great cities are enhanced by a mythical life binding their citizens with their environment and with one another. This is the mythical foundation lacking, according to Lawrence and Raffestin (1994), in modern, rationally planned cities. In their view, the myths and rituals binding people to the origins of their cities also imbue their daily lives with shared ideals and beliefs about the universe and the cosmos. These same myths generate shared ethical and moral values and an identifiable community voice.

When Macedonio refers to Argentines as uniquely gifted to "denationalize humanity" by virtue of their "enactment of cordiality" (*Teorías*, 95), he is also referring to the potential of Porteños to dissolve barriers of all kinds and effect the "miracle of the novel." The streets of Buenos Aires can become places of affectionate relations; its plazas and marketplaces, sites of passionate exchange; its neighborhoods, communities of metaphysical discourse; its homes, centers of emotional health; its individuals, sentient beings freed of the artificial constraints of the self. Buenos Aires can be a city endowed with a "mystery" that it never had (Fernández 1982, 311).[19]

This is the challenge that faces Recienvenido in his peregrinations about the city—both the concrete Buenos Aires and the lettered city of the "mundo literario"—to which he is a newcomer. It is what motivates Eduardo de Alto in his efforts to rescue, protect, reconcile, and promote the Porteña women so bereft of resources and advantages, yet so innately capable of making the city love them. It is the goal of the Presidente, who, ensconced in his estancia, simultaneously campaigns for the miraculous dissolution of the polis of Buenos Aires and the self of Dulce-Persona in the eternal dynamics of love. It is also the objective of Jorge Luis Borges and others of his generation, who recognize the mythologizing of Buenos Aires to be a prerequisite to its greatness.

The ultimate difference between Jorge Luis Borges and Macedonio Fernández is that Borges appropriates the lettered city, whereas Macedonio abandons it.[20] If the Presidente must declare the incineration of cities, it is because his project to beautify the city still relies on *the Novel,* whose place and characters still bear the vestiges of the lettered republic and its falsehood of self. The Novel is still a Museum: its value lies in its capacity to inspire radical change, but it alone cannot effect that change. In this respect, *Museo* criticizes *all* novels, "good" and "bad" (J. Prieto 2002, 92, 178–79). For Macedonio, the miracle of mythification occurs in the streets of Buenos Aires *outside* the pages of the printed archive.

The miracle relies on people, not characters. The city can't invade the Novel, but the Novel needs the city to realize its vision. Macedonio tells us this in the contrast between two characters barred from the Novel. Frederico, "El chico del palo largo" (the Boy with the Big Stick), is banned because he is the epitome of "bad" discursivity: mimetic, literary, and traditional, an icon of the picaresque. Desperate to gain admission, Frederico attempts to ingratiate himself to the Novel by producing an invention: he sets up a "noise factory." The plan backfires, filling Buenos Aires with a racket coming from everywhere at once. Fathers all over the city, reacting immediately, pack their sons, presumably the hired noisemakers of the factory, home and into bed. Frederico is left perplexed in his failure, not knowing whether to blame it on strikes, oil trusts, German hyperinflation, or Wilson's Fourteen Points (*Museo,* 72–74). Macedonio implies that mere avant-garde literary invention, while trying to pass itself off as worthy of the Novel, does not help save the city. It merely fills Buenos Aires with static, failing to affect the cultural, economic, and social structures responsible for the city's woes.

By contrast, Nicolasa the cook (all one hundred forty kilos of her), barred from the Novel because of her devotion to the reality of nourishment, does not try to worm her way in—her bulk makes that impossible. Instead, Nicolasa makes herself useful in Buenos Aires's grand avenues by sheltering pedestrians from the fierce wind with her corpulence (*Museo,* 284–85).[21] Her marvelous empanadas manage to disrupt one line of urban reality—the rail line linking the Novel to Constitution station—not from within the Novel, but adjacent to it. Fleshy Nicolasa, although barred from the Novel, is useful toward the novelization of the city. Literary Frederico is of no use whatsoever. As Julio Prieto argues, Macedonio's Novel does not open itself to readers; it tyrannically makes performers and *authors* of the citizens who come in contact with it. This new kind of discursivity—this new way of inventing things—is a political as well as aesthetic act (J. Prieto 2002, 200–212).

It is also a civic act. In this respect, Macedonio Fernández, in his treatment of the city, is actually closer to social realist Robert Arlt than to Borges, Girondo or the other Martinfierristas. For Arlt, Buenos Aires consists of "tumultos monstruosos de las ciudades de Portland y de hierro, cruzando diagonales oscuros a la oblicua sombra de los rascacielos bajo una amenazadora red de negros cables de alta tensión" [the monstrous tumult of iron and concrete cities, crossing dark diagonals under the oblique shade of the skyscrapers beneath a menacing net of black high-tension wires] (1958, 55). The only solution Arlt's characters see is to turn the structures, institutions and assumptions of the city upon itself; they try to use the city against itself. Marrying a blind prostitute is a mark of sainthood; legalized prostitution is the means to building a perverse secret society that will control the world; conceiving of useless inventions is proof of genius. Arlt's service to the city is not *in* the novel, but *by means* of the novelized city.

Macedonio's mission, while far less pessimistic than Arlts's, similarly relies on the city and similarly is hampered by the city's shortcomings. The neighborhood philosopher requires this city's compliance, but his efficacy confirms the city's ignorance. His only hope is to seduce Porteños into enacting the novelization of the metropolis themselves. Macedonio is not just the Socrates of Buenos Aires, he is the philosopher whose very existence means to remake the city—remake the *idea* of city—entirely.

7
Continuities

ABANDONING THE LETTERED CITY DOES NOT MEAN ABANDONING WRITing, and it is not accurate to accuse Macedonio of having done so. The problem he grappled with was how to save the city, through literature, without endowing himself with the self of authorship. To write within the parameters of the "literary world," as he called it, would risk endowing the Presidente with the weighty self of an Yrigoyen, or Eduardo de Alto with the authority of a father and husband. Macedonio must invent a new poetics for the city much as Socrates creates a new philosophy for the polis.

Macedonio did elaborate an aesthetic system, but its entire objective is to reveal *systematically* the fallacy of objective reality as conceived of in modernity, and of the subjectivity supporting it. The lettered city serves, in part, to perpetuate the institutions that pose as reality. Macedonio's aesthetics must elaborate an alternative to the lettered city and those institutions it maintains.

It is his need to invent something completely new, to invent the very genre of "never having been," an entirely new discourse for the city, which compels Macedonio into the realm of philosophy and metaphysics and leads him to his novelistic "home for nonexistence." This is not to say that Macedonio's response to the city, its institutions and relations, are chronologically prior to his pursuit of metaphysics. Rather, his continual probing of metaphysical problems and his evolving poetics are simultaneous with and inseparable from his unwavering commitment to saving the city. City and metaphysics exist for each other. Aesthetics exists for metaphysics and for the city.

This symbiosis is overlooked partly because Macedonio's philosophical enquiry is usually regarded as purely intuitive and therefore haphazard (Lindstrom 1981, 18, 72–73). This view is abetted by the general belief that Macedonio shunned the philosophical discussions of his day. Rather than engage in the current debates over the validity of existentialism versus Positivism, Macedonio persists in engaging the ideas of Kant, Schopenhauer, Spencer, and Hobbes.[1] But as philosopher Sonia Vicente de Alvarez (1996) has so astutely asked, *why* does Macedonio persist, anachronistically, in querying Kant? Assuming he recognized existentialism's threat to metaphysics, why turn to nineteenth-century German nominalism to formulate his defense?

We can reiterate Vicente de Alvarez's conclusion that Macedonio's thought is systematic. His refutation of Kant's *noumena*, the a priori reality that gives rise to all sensation and perception, is fundamental to this system (Engelbert 1978, 69; Lindstrom 1981, 76). All other assertions of Macedonio's metaphysics—the repudiation of time, space and causality; the conflation of dreaming and wakefulness; and the elaboration of an alternative to self—all depend on his challenge to Kant's principals (Vicente de Alvarez 1982, 193–216). Schopenhauer attracts Macedonio for similar reasons. Schopenhauer's metaphysics falls short of Macedonio's ideal in its maintenance of the dichotomy of subject and object (Engelbert 1978, 87; Fernández-Latour 1980, 27). Because Schopenhauers's philosophy asserts the irreducibility of affection, it allows for the rigorous analysis of human emotion and sensation while dismissing their reification in institutions and rituals (Vicente de Alvarez 1982, 225–28).

The point of this cursory reference to Macedonio's philosophical antecedents is to restate one fundamental argument: that every aspect of Macedonio's vision—from metaphysics to aesthetics—is part of an integral response to his environment (Vicente de Alvarez 1982, 234). Macedonio endeavors to disprove Kant's noumena because he regards it as an elemental buttress to modernity's Cartesian conception of the world; it is the same motivation he has for disproving the self.

Cascardi's extensive study on the history of subjectivity supports this view as well. He presents the subject as an invention that aids Western societies in their adjustment of values to "a series of destabilizing historical conditions" (Cascardi 1992, 35, 67). This invented entity functions in tandem with representation, which "frames" social and historical conditions so as to be "grasped" by the individual, now conceived as a subject autonomous from those conditions (70). Given this interdependency between subjectivity and representation, Macedonio's admiration of *Don Quijote* is not surprising. Nor is the obvious nostalgia, as implicit in Macedonio's works as in Cervantes's. Cervantes exposes the irony—thus the falseness—inherent in the relationship between self and representation: the self, while presented as belonging to the realm of essences, can only be obtained as a subject in the realm of representation (Cascardi 1992, 76–77). Macedonio goes further. He attempts to replace the realm of representation with the realm of essences by refusing the validity of everything that is represented: self, city and the institutions that bind them together.

Another way of regarding this process is as the conversion of the polis of institutions into the city of essences. Macedonio's dream for the city may resemble Socrates's vision for the polis in its goal of always seeking out the "soul" or "truth" of things and relations, rather than appearances or reputation. But the Platonic concept of "forms," or essential given reality, and of laws that derive from those forms, is anathema to Macedonio (*Vigilia*, 243–48; 317–20; 402–4). Given forms or essences still permit the institutionalization of relations and the reification of sensations into objects and subjects. The Platonic polis is, ultimately, an institution comprising "functionally integrated groups" (Morse 1992, 3). Macedonio's city is pure affection and sensation. This is the aspect of Macedonio's poetics that Borges cannot accept. Although Borges obsessively challenges the existence of noumena, he is in constant search of Platonic forms. For Borges, myths, whether time honored or newly invented, reflect ethical and affective *forms*.

Subjectivity also means that the thinking subject regards the human body as an object. The self is a spectator to that object, and society is an "atomistic" gathering of selves (Cascardi 1992, 61). A large part of Macedonio's brilliance lies in his recognition of the devastating consequences of this conception. Restoration of power to the individual means restitution of the power of the body over itself. Liberating the body from subjectivity and submitting it to sensation also means liberating individual relations—especially the relations between men and women—from the panoply of institutions imposed on them, all of which depend on the acceptance of subjectivity.

The alternative to self that Macedonio spent a lifetime elaborating is thus revealed through the affective relations among his novelistic characters and the corporal sensations that help sustain those relations. The miraculous city of "maximum individuals" is the city comprising these relations and sensations. It is identifiable as a physical city, just as the individual is identifiable as a body. But Macedonio's radically redefined person is an absence, not a presence, of self. In contrast to the individual of the Western literary and philosophical tradition, which exists to take stock of its presence, recognize its subjectivity, and literally assert its self, Macedonio's individuals exist to eschew subjectivity and abandon self. The physicality of the individual is acknowledged and explored as a means to the abandonment of the constructed self. The repudiation of authorship and authority are an ongoing exercise in the displacement of self. The refusal of government and institutions of all kinds is prerequisite to the ascendancy of the affective, sentient individual that replaces the self. The "home for nonexistence" that Macedonio strives to create by "novelizing" the city is the only home where such individuals can thrive. The polis of corporal functions supporting a society of selves is transformed into the city of felt and dreamed relations.

Macedonio permits absolutely nothing to subordinate these relations, least of all his own authorial voice. His motivations for absenting the author—for fragmenting, subverting, impeding a unitary, autonomous authorial identity—throughout his works and his life, are analogous to his Presidential campaign in absence. If Macedonio refuses to speak at the lectern, to emerge into the "literary world" of publishing and promotion, or to cast his ballot in elections, it is because he must remain the perpetual Newcomer, and never establish himself. The establishment of his presence—and his voice, even in the form of a book—would hopelessly compromise his dream for the city. The dream, much of it in the form of remarkable prose, remains his single investment in the city, and it must be kept perpetually alive. For this reason, Macedonio worked steadily against the Argentine avant-garde generation at the same time as he collaborated with them. The Martinfierristas, even in their most sincere attempts at aesthetic reform, self-consciously wanted to constitute a new *literary* generation. Macedonio would have none of it.[2]

For this reason, the legacy spun by Borges is so problematic. When Borges alters the title of his early poem from "Fundación mitológica de Buenos Aires" to "Fundación mítica de Buenos Aires," he is attempting to keep the city open and alive, perpetually and mythically evolving (Madrid 1992, 348–50). This "absence of foundation," given Borges's unwillingness to archive history into a national mythology, necessarily relies on a personal mythology, the *patria chica* of the lyric voice (348). Borges's poetic voice may be dissolved in the text, thus situated nowhere; the text, in turn, may be dissolved in endlessly repeating history and memory.

The problem arises because Borges's Buenos Aires still must stake out its place in this infinite flow. Borges's solution constitutes a paradox: by rejecting the transcendence of historical origins, he achieves a transcendence of ahistoricity (350). The poem also, therefore, constitutes a paradox of the subject: a self that is transcendent by virtue of refusing transcendence of voice. Borges spends much of his energy in the mid-1920s inventing that paradoxical voice. Having achieved this goal, Borges suppresses everything he wrote previously except the few pieces that constitute the underpinnings of that voice. If the city and the voice evoking it are to have any identity, the city and the voice must have mythological figures to shape, or delineate, or articulate that identity. Borges's negation of origins for the city also amounts to a displacement of the father, of the genesis of language itself (351). But Borges has a father, progenitor of his poetic paradoxes, and the father's name is Macedonio Fernández. Macedonio is the perfect father for Borges's poetics because he can assign him a paradox as well: he is father by virtue of his refusal to sire a literary offspring and found a literary mythology. Borges's Buenos Aires is still a polis, an entity of functionally integrated figures, if not precisely groups; and Borges's Macedonio remains a central figure, a mythological father figure, at the service of that polis.

For Macedonio, being a father means absenting his self—abdicating the authority of fatherhood, whether biological or literary—for the benefit of the city. Macedonio Fernández does not abandon his family when, in 1920, he dismantles his household and places the children with relatives. By relinquishing his paternal authority, he draws himself into an even closer affectionate relationship with his children. His physical presence is equivocal: constantly moving, never imposing, but always lingering nearby and perpetually engaged with his loved ones.[3] Likewise is Macedonio's relationship with the city. The peripatetic philosopher renounces his authority within his own barrio. He is rarely seen there and often hovers outside; yet his involvement with the city is as constant as his affection for it.

The peripatetic Macedonio, in his dissolution or fragmentation of self in the city, and in his emphasis on physical sensation as fundamental to his relationship with the city, resembles the urban vagabond that Unruh tells us is characteristic of avant-garde literature (Unruh 1994, 105–9). He corresponds to the avant-garde's attraction to the suburban margins—hovering just outside the city—as "undefined cites of transformation" (112). Whether in conversation or on paper, the dialogues of literature and philosophy are also dialogues between the city and its surrounding countryside, between the barrio and the *chacra* (farm). But Macedonio pointedly repudiates the same avant-garde wanderer in its capacities that Unruh classifies as spectator and contender (89). Rather than confronting the city, for confrontation is his nemesis, Macedonio burrows into it and lingers outside it. Rather than managing its aesthetic possibilities, for he abhors management, he promotes the beauty of Buenos Aires by revealing its soul to itself. Macedonio Fernández finds the self of the city in its men and women without selves; and in the self of the city, he finds its salvation.

Notes

Chapter 1. Departures

1. The literary avant-garde in Buenos Aires first crystallized around Borges, who in 1921 promoted the ideals and aesthetics of Spanish Ultraism among young poets looking to "renovate" Argentine letters. These writers saw themselves in opposition to *modernistas* (analogous to European symbolists and Parnassianists), headed by the venerable Leopoldo Lugones. This generation also saw itself divided into opposing groups, termed "Florida," which favored "pure" aesthetics, and "Boedo," which propounded social commitment. Later commentary determined this division to be largely artificial and specious, the most explicit critics insisting it was a public relations sham from the beginning. Spearheaded by Borges, the avant-garde founded several literary magazines in quick succession, culminating in *Martín Fierro*, whose sixteen issues ran from 1924 to 1927. Directed by Evar Méndez, the magazine served as a nucleus for Argentine avant-garde writers and artists. In 1927, simultaneous with the demise of *Martín Fierro*, Borges vocally repudiated Ultraism and its poetics. His attention shifted to other publications, including his own *Revista multicolor de los sábados*. From 1930 onward, Victoria Ocampo's journal *Sur* was the main vehicle for many of these writers (absent Macedonio, among others). As a more or less coherent group, however, this generation is best identified as the Martinfierristas, after the most successful of their collaborative ventures.

2. The constant references among critics and commentators of Macedonio's correspondence with William James are based solely on Macedonio's own accounts of these "several" letters (*Vigilia* 39, 237–38). In fact, Macedonio cites only two such letters; the existence of a more extensive correspondence is apocryphal, no evidence of it having been found among James's papers. On James's influence, see also Biagini, 1981.

Chapter 2. The Myth of the Accidental Author

1. Lindstrom (1981) and Rodríguez Monegal (1952) cite this passage in slightly different form.

2. All translations of Macedonio Fernández's text in this study are mine.

3. The Plaza Congreso remains today an important site of political protest.

4. Engelbert points to a passage in *Vigilia* that describes the "mystic state" Macedonio seeks in almost exactly these terms (Engelbert 1978, 80–83).

5. This "pure being" resembles Kristeva's "plenitude," but it pointedly transcends rather than exploits sexual difference.

6. Borges reiterates this sentiment, along numerous other aspects of Macedonio's legend, in an autobiographical essay he wrote with Norman Thomas di Giovanni for *The New Yorker* in 1970.

7. Julio Prieto goes so far as to suggest that Borges's strategy of self-promotion in the 1960s and 1970s included an explicit appropriation of Macedonio's poetics, in tandem with an obdurate devaluation of Macedonio's writing—a strategy that Borges made transparent attempts to obfuscate (2002, 122–24). Ana Camblong even asserts that as early as the 1930s, Borges's essays relied on Macedonio's basic concepts on paradox, unreality, and eternity without ever citing or acknowledging his mentor (Bueno 2001, 19).

CHAPTER 3. AN AVANT-GARDE APART

1. J. Prieto describes this relationship as a dialogue, Macedonio's works constituting "a system of affinities and rejections regarding avant-garde propositions" (2002, 57).

2. Naomi Lindstrom observes similarities between Macedonio's poetics and German expressionism (1981, 69); Flora Schiminovitch (1986) reads Macedonio's work in terms of French surrealism. J. Prieto points out Macedonio's explicit "dialogue" with European "isms" (2002, 57). These studies, rather than document direct influences, suggest that Macedonio drew inspiration from many of the same literary and philosophical antecedents as did these European movements.

3. There is great value in studies such as Jorge Schwartz's 1991 exhaustive chronicle of these publications and their defining texts, or Collazos's 1977 landmark compendium of Latin American avant-garde manifestoes and discussion of the movements they represent. Similarly useful are such overviews of the Argentine avant-garde as Scrimaglio (1974) and Salvador (1962).

4. Osorio (1982) points out that European models of avant-garde art and criticism ignore fundamental differences in both the conditions and the motivations of Latin American writers from their European counterparts. Initial Latin American reception of European avant-garde schools such as futurism and surrealism was quite critical (8–11, 39–41). Schulman (1986) warns that the literary chronology formed in Europe and North America leaves "gaps and misapprehensions" with regard to assessments of Latin American avant-gardes. Fábio Lucas (1975) and José Ferreira Gular (1974) argue that adaptations of European models of avant-garde art are loaded with the problems of cultural dependency. Despite their socialist and nationalist agendas, these critics make valid arguments.

5. Part of Unruh's conclusions is based on Pérez-Firmat's observation that Latin American avant-garde prose is particularly intent on exploiting and manipulating its "ancestors" (Pérez-Firmat 1982, 33). Unruh also takes cues from Peter Bürger, who asserts: 1) that the avant-garde challenges, rather than exploits, the autonomy of art, and aims "to integrate art into the praxis of life, (revealing) the nexus between autonomy and the absence of any consequences," and 2) that the avant-garde criticizes art as an institution rather than merely criticizing the schools that preceded it (Bürger 1984, 48–49).

6. "Outwardly they look like novels . . . but . . . have no plot, little or no characterization, little or no humanity. They are lyrical, do not copy life, do not efface the

personality of their authors" (Pérez-Firmat 1982, 31–32). While detractors might argue that these remarks are not very different from prior descriptions of avant-garde poetics (such as Poggioli's or even Ortega's), Pérez-Firmat's comments do reinforce the aesthetic kinship between Latin American avant-gardes and their European counterparts; they also help highlight Macedonio Fernández's kinship to both. In that vein, it is equally worth noting the importance, documented by Pérez-Firmat, of Ramón Gómez de la Serna as initiator and champion of the avant-garde novel (1982, 19, 31). That Macedonio and Gómez de la Serna shared a great deal—aesthetic principals, a deep friendship, an extensive correspondence—is another indication of how engaged Macedonio was in the overall aesthetic movement of the time.

7. Julio Prieto suggests that Argentine vanguardists admired Macedonio specifically for his resistance to the institutions of literature (2002, 55). My argument is that no evidence indicates that the Martinfierristas appreciated the profundity and complexity of Macedonio's resistance at the time.

8. José Isaacson insists on Macedonio's classification as avant-garde, but in order to do so redefines the term "avant-garde" so broadly as to completely disassociate it from any specific context (Isaacson 1981, 22–23). Masiello regards Macedonio as integral to the Argentine avant-garde, but her reasoning relies on the demonstration of a poetic self in his works, contrary to most other assessments, including the present one. "Historical" avant-garde is Germán Gullón's term for a specific group of writers during a specific period labeled "avant-garde," referred to as "classical" avant-garde by other critics (Gullón 1996). These divergent perspectives makes Unruh's definition all the more valuable.

9. To date the only monograph devoted to Macedonio's poetry is E. McVicker's 1987 unpublished dissertation.

10. Carlos García points out that there is no hard evidence that any such collaboration—with *Proa* or any other publication—ever took place (C. García 2000, 57–58).

11. Justifiable are objections to Poggioli's definitions as too reliant on description of aesthetic procedure, too broad and thus effectively conflated with a more general description of all modernism (Schulte-Sasse 1984, vii–ix; Strong 1997, 20). These objections, however, do not invalidate Poggioli's study as a useful guideline to the "external" or technical characteristics of avant-garde art.

12. This aspect coincides with Bürger's and Calinescu's assertions, inspired by Adorno (Bürger 1984, 85), that an underlying drive of avant-garde art is "the need to disrupt and completely overthrow the whole bourgeois system of values" (Calinescu 1987, 119).

13. Where Poggioli aims to demonstrate the avant-gardes' continuity with Romanticism, Bürger argues that only aestheticism's emphasis on the autonomy of art could have made the avant-garde possible (Bürger 1984, 17–19).

14. *Museo de la Novela de la Eterna* consists of fifty-six prologues (more or less, depending on the manuscript version), and eighteen chapters. At its center is the *Presidente* who serves simultaneously as a character, a metaphor for author and Macedonio's alter ego. He presides over a small group of similarly nonmimetic characters on an *estancia* (ranch) called *La Novela*, from which he directs the characters in a campaign to convert the city of Buenos Aires into a place of "civic beauty." Much of the book deals with the nature of the characters and their rela-

tions, the nature of this *primera novela buena* (first good novel), and the relationship of the Novel to author, characters and readers. For a synopsis of *Adriana Buenos Aires,* see the beginning of chapter 5.

15. Constituting the third prologue of the Ayacucho edition (M. Fernández 1982, 190–91) and other posthumous editions, this passage is found in the appendix of the critical edition.

16. J. Prieto argues that Macedonio invented Adriana's "bad" status, and its tension with *Museo*, retrospectively, only after contact with the avant-garde propelled him to begin writing *Museo* (2002, 82); part of *Adriana*'s "badness" is its heterogeneity—its incorporation of "good" characteristics (89).

17. According to Anthony Cascardi, *Don Quijote* epitomizes the paradox of modernity by simultaneously relying on and compromising the effectiveness of the subject in representational art. Since "Don Quijote can't successfully imitate heroic values in the real world . . . the novelistic hero poses as *self*-made, its *own* model . . . faithful first to its own heart" (Cascardi 1992, 96–97).

18. These techniques correspond to Bürger's theory of avant-garde art. Avant-garde works draw attention to their nature as both fragmentary and manufactured, first killing the life of the artistic material, "tearing it out of its functional context," then joining "fragments with the intent of positing meaning" (Bürger 1984, 70). This technique intends to "revolutionize life by returning art to its praxis," in its refusal to grant art autonomy, and thus value as representative or symbolic.

19. See *Lo lúdico y lo fantástico en la obra de Cortázar,* 1986.

20. For Borges, history possesses, in Balderston's words, "fascinating possibilities for narrative fiction" (Balderston 1990, 11) if historical record is regarded as a text that can be assembled, shuffled and reassembled.

21. Xul Solar's motivations, moreover, are overtly related to the "creolizing" of these hierarchies and systems—an explicitly nationalistic project (Sarlo 1988, 118).

22. Calinescu insists nihilism is a determining characteristic of avant-gardes (1987, 96). The extreme irrationalism of Dada did not make much of an impression in the Argentine avant-garde, nor did the classical surrealism of France find much resonance in Argentina until the mid-1930s (Scrimaglio 1974, 33–37).

23. Typical of Argentine avant-garde poets is Oliverio Girondo, whose "ludic relations" serve to displace rational order in the search for "new sites of signification perceived by a unified subject" (Masiello 1986, 73).

24. This passage figures as the first paragraph of a separate prologue in the Ayacucho edition (Fernández 1982, 260–61) and other posthumous editions, but is placed in the appendix to the critical edition.

25. Macedonio follows the predictable pattern of assigning flesh and instinct to women while reserving intellect and prowess for men. But while he accepts this dichotomy as the rule, it is a rule he often transgresses. For Macedonio, the common ground for men and women is outside the boundaries of these assumed and accepted spheres.

26. Macedonio's amalgam of the nihilistic and the affective exemplifies numerous dominant theories on the avant-garde. The priority of passion and its relationship to the problematizing of self coincides with Poggioli's (arguably simplistic) thesis on the Romantic origins of the avant-garde. Octavio Paz (1974) links Romanticism's ambivalence toward religion to the avant-garde's appropriation of the philosophy of irrationality as the means to revealing and transforming "marvelous

reality" (72–74, 77–83). Calinescu associates the avant-garde's nihilism with its "originating from romantic utopianism with its messianic fervor" (1987, 96). Bürger asserts that the avant-garde's nihilist impulse always aims to revive and preserve "[V]alues such as humanity, joy, truth, solidarity." (1984, 50).

27. Unruh elucidates the reasons for that tension, pointing to the paradox of the search for a cultural "ground zero" simultaneous to the attempt to forge distinctive national poetic voices.

28. Reichardt (1991) is even more categorical, proclaiming Macedonio as the only writer of his times to truly "cuestionar los presupuestos de la literatura" (219).

29. For the Argentine avant-garde, the conceit of inventor as hero is an essential component to their own self-invention, self-promotion and, accordingly, self-empowerment (Masiello 1986, 194–95, 214).

30. Curiously, Bürger regards the conflation of art with invention to be a primary explanation for what he sees as the avant-garde's ultimate failure. As each violation of the bounds of autonomous art eventually becomes recognized as an invention, a "work," it joins the institution of art. Its very reliance on the market for the dismantling of art as institution makes the avant-garde vulnerable to faddism (Bürger 1984, 35, 57–60).

31. Ortega made two successful visits to Argentina during the height of historical avant-garde activity, and his German-influenced philosophical perspective met with eager welcome. In some respects, Latin America, and Argentina in particular, served as an object of Ortega's ideas about culture and society (Stabb 1976, 67–72). Anderson (1996) and Gullón (1996) have questioned the influence of Ortega's pronouncements on both writers and readers of avant-garde poetry, but while his influence in Europe may be arguable, the alacrity of the reception of his ideas in Argentina (even as much as twenty years later) reinforces Sarlo's assertions about the classist nature of avant-garde polemics there.

32. Calinescu's assessment includes many of these qualities as characteristic of the self-perceived role of the avant-garde artist: an elite leader in a revolutionary aesthetic endeavor to achieve a kind of utopian anarchy, overthrowing the traditions of art and the "stylistic expectations of the general public" (Calinescu 1987, 102–5, 112).

33. The equivocating stance of Latin American writers with respect to a middle-class market has its origins in late nineteenth-century chroniclers of modern urban life, particularly José Martí (Ramos 2002, 221–28).

34. "The Novel," in *Museo*'s scheme, serves as text and vehicle but also as a character or actor, along with author, editor and reader. This is in contrast to "the novel," which in our study, unavoidably, regards the text as an artifact.

35. Sarlo notes that in one passage of *Recienvenido* Macedonio makes a point of his pure creole and Spanish roots (1988, 44). But the evidence here suggests that Macedonio dismissed the importance of creole "identity" rather than attach special pride to it.

36. The posture of the poets of Romanticism and modernismo regarding self-hood is not so unequivocal and uncomplicated as their detractors believed. Lugones was far from straightforward and decisive in his ideas about the genius of creation and its implications for self (Kirkpatrick 1989, 74–80, 147–50), and while Modernistas consciously struggled against the erosion of the autonomy of self and author brought about by the rise of journalism, their efforts reveal their acute awareness that these concepts were highly problematic (A. González 1993, 88–98).

37. Much of Unruh's study is devoted to Latin American avant-garde theater, partly because it has been so neglected and partly because theater embodies much of what the avant-garde movement tried to accomplish. The theater's ability to incarnate concepts, its interactive nature, its capacity to both prescribe and discuss aesthetic solutions, and its "transformative powers" (Unruh 1994, 174) all contribute to its importance as an avant-garde medium.

38. See also Fernández Latour's reminiscences on this subject (1980, 22).

39. On Huidobro's "tyranny," see Unruh 1994, 194.

40. Rojas Paz, according to Masiello (1986), qualifies as avant-garde, for his assault on urban, literary language is tantamount to a "gratuitous act of rebellion" (87).

41. It may be for this reason that José Isaacson refers to Macedonio's writing as nationalistic, or "the only true Argentine nationalism; a nationalism of universalist cloth" (1981, 18, 31–37, 122).

42. The title is used in the Ayacucho edition of *Museo* (M. Fernández 1982, 191); the prologue is untitled in the critical edition.

43. Accordingly, as J. Prieto points out (2002, 179), Macedonio also proposes to write a novel that can be "undone" or stripped down to mere history.

44. Prieto argues that the "tyranny" of Macedonio's text, rather than "inviting" the reader to collaborate, "traps" the reader, "enslaving" him to the author; the text then resolves itself in "liberation" by forcing the reader into the role of writer, for only the textually defined reader is empowered to continue the text (J. Prieto 2002, 197–212). I regard Macedonio's texts as more seductive than tyrannical.

45. As Masiello describes the process, Argentine avant-garde poetics intertwines self and the authority exterior to the self, so that fragmentary life is united, publicly, by a myth of totality. The avant-garde is a public movement professing originality, but the movement emphasizes the personality of the artist and supports each artist's invention of a persona (1986, 82–88).

46. Masiello's argument that "Macedonio alternately affirms and negates the self as an organizing principle of reality" (1986, 97) is in keeping with most other assessments. What critics so often perceive as a "literary self" (98) is rather an utterly contingent and self-erasing—thus evidently paradoxical—device for achieving "states of consciousness" that serve as a satisfying alternative to self. The fact that other Argentine avant-garde writers have no transcendent solution to the problem of subjectivity, and end up with various ways to ally the self with the objective world (107–8, 122, 153–55), motivates Macedonio in his endeavors to create such a transcendent alternative.

Chapter 4. The Political Is the Personal

1. The passages in question remain unpublished; the complete letter is in the University of Pittsburgh's Gómez de la Serna Collection. The *Epistolario*, unfortunately, transcribes Gómez de la Serna's published version rather than Macedonio's original; it also erroneously divides the text into two separate letters (49–50, 45).

2. Both Bueno and Horacio González describe *La Montaña* as an amalgam of socialist and anarchist ideology, a description which perhaps also applies to the rad-

ical political thought of the youth of Macedonio's generation (including Lugones, Ingenieros, and Ghiraldo) in general (H. González 1995, 163; Bueno 2000, 54).

3. For a brief summary of anarchism and labor in Argentina, see Skidmore 1989, 79–85; Oved (1978) is the standard comprehensive study on this subject.

4. Delfín Garasa's 1968 summary of anarchist literary expression suggests as well the existence of a good deal of mutual influences between the different "anarchisms" of the period.

5. Labor strikes accelerated virtually consistently from the onset of the war, including a general strike in 1917, and peaking in 1919, when 367 strikes involved over 300,000 workers (Walter 1993, 49).

6. The denial of the existence of classes in Argentina was also, at points, a stance of Radicalism (Rock 1975b, 78).

7. Sonia Vicente de Alvarez (1996) has pointed out that Isaacson's 1981 study was constrained by fear of the far-right military junta; her thinking allows one to see in Isaacson a between-the-lines portrait of Macedonio as antiauthoritarian.

8. The ascendancy of absence in Macedonio's elaboration of individual identity is a commonplace in studies of his writing (Goloboff 1983; Garth 1996, 95).

9. For a discussion of the definitions of the terms "charisma," "personalism," and "populism," see Calvert and Calvert 1989, 80–82, 106.

10. Borges insisted that his anti-Peronist efforts of the 1940s and 1950s were "ethical" rather than political (Strong 1997, 108–9). Some of his anti-Peronist writings took the form of histories "à clef" and thinly veiled allegories. See, for example, "La apostasía de Coifi," published only in Uruguay in 1953.

11. Carlos García argues that *Museo*, along with all of Macedonio's major works, was begun in 1921 (C. García 2000, 53).

12. Korn (1974) documents 1,029 strikes involving from 4,700 to 277,000 workers; 72 percent of those strikes were resolved to the detriment of the strikers (148).

13. Significantly, Camblong has determined that this chapter of *Museo* figures only in manuscript variations dating after 1929 (see *Museo*, lxv–lxvii).

14. For related comments, see J. Prieto's analysis of Macedonio's project as a critique of the "contradictions inherent to the democratic system in a mass society" (2002, 67).

15. Borges was the president of the 1927 "Comité Yrigoyenista de Jóvenes Intelectuales" (Yrigoyenist Committee of Intellectual Youth); Macedonio's name appears as a member, but Abós suggests his name was included without his consent (Abós 2002, 135–36).

16. The reference to streetcar tickets as "obligatory literature" is based on reality. Every tram passenger was required to retain a ticket; these "legendary bits of paper" carried designs and typeface that varied from line to line and year to year, and which read (among variants): "Sírvase conservar este boleto para entregarlo al inspector o al guarda cada vez que le sea exigido. En su defecto el viaje se pagará nuevamente." [Please retain this ticket, to be surrendered to the conductor or guard upon request. Failure to produce a ticket will result in payment of another fare.] Men often secured these bits of "obligatory literature" in their hatbands (González Podestá 2002a; 2002b).

17. "La Compañía" is the Anglo-American Tramway Company, the British firm that ran the majority of the city's streetcars throughout the 1920s. This reference dates the passage prior to 1936, when forced government consolidation created the

Corporación de Transportes de Buenos Aires (González Podestá 1986, 38). References to the *Revista Oral* indicate that this passage alludes to the mid-1920s. This allusion also is based on reality; Abós suggests that attendance at the *Revista Oral* was in fact swelled by bystanders waiting for the opening of a nearby cabaret (2002, 121).

Chapter 5. Minding the Body

1. Only one handwritten alteration is noteworthy: the change of the male protagonist's name from Sergio to Adolfo.

2. J. Prieto asserts that Macedonio's ironic conception of *Adriana* as a "bad" novel came only with the 1938 revisions, as a result of his interactions with the Martinfierristas (2002, 81–82). A more tenable thesis is that Macedonio used the revisions to make more explicit this irony, to emphasize the complexity of the relationship between "bad" and "good" aesthetics, and to incorporate into his critique of modern society an implicit questioning of avant-garde sincerity.

3. This passage was substantially—and mercifully—reduced in the published version.

4. Abós declares *Adriana* to be a "thinly veiled diary," noting the character of Adriana was based on a real person, of Italian extraction, named Cavendra Lamac (2002, 143). C. García has closely documented the autobiographical nature of both *Adriana* and the related *Una novela que comienza* (C. García 2000, 53–54).

5. J. Prieto observes that *Adriana* and *Museo* are structurally inverse to each other and thematically analogous (2002, 82).

6. In telling Paredes's story, Macedonio lists the names of actual clinicians; Macedonio, in lampooning their culture and their beliefs, meant to preserve respect for their intelligence and integrity (see, for example, *Recienvenido*, 49). In Paredes there is a good dose of Macedonio's own obsession with his bodily functions.

7. See Scobie 1974, 121–26.

8. The aesthetics of the projects themselves reveal the mentality behind them; the Buenos Aires waterworks (Aguas Argentinas), which dates from this period, can only be described as monumental.

9. Just one example of the pervasive influence of hygienicist control: the ticket-roll dispensers on streetcars, for decades unique to Buenos Aires, were mandated in 1906 as an antituberculosis measure; conductors were regarded as a likely source of contagion (González Podestá 2002a, 51).

10. The campaign against tuberculosis, spearheaded by Coni, resulted in the highly invasive practices codified into law in 1902: obligatory denouncement, forced decontamination, quarantine, and institutionalization, and numerous preventive measures such as public spittoons. The laws allowed ample opportunity for police abuse, and were directed primarily at the poor, the dispossessed, and at immigrants (Recalde 1994, 19–23, 40–43).

11. The discourses described by Salessi owe much to the xenophobic tendencies of such officials. Public policy of all kinds can be traced to the analogy between the hygienicist terror of the invasive germ and the concept of immigrants as an invading foreign pestilence. Legislation of the period leading up to the 1920s reflects

this discourse in laws such as the 1908 Ley de Residencia (Residence Law) and the Ley de Defesa Social (Law of Social Defense) of 1910 (Solberg 1970, 117–27).

12. Coni, for example, among his many contributions to *Semana Médica*, recommends strict control of sanitary and working conditions among at-home seamstresses (Sept. 5, 1918); *Adriana*'s title character is a dressmaker.

13. Hygienicists also envisioned coopting trade unions and other proletarian organizations into a State-organized enforcement program (Delfino 1919); Macedonio's mistrust of the relationship between government and unions, then, is in keeping with his dislike of institutional hygienicism.

14. It was Mendel's observations on the immutability of genetic traits that led to Darwin's theory of natural selection. German and North American eugenists favored these theories, leading to the social Darwinism most characteristic of American and German eugenics.

15. A sampling of *Semana Médica* articles on these topics reveals how interrelated they were. Emilio Coni's frequent articles focus primarily on hygiene and disease prophylaxis, but also refer to eugenics, especially "matrimonio eugénico" (Sept. 11, 1919); Víctor Delfino (who served as president of the Sociedad Eugénica Argentina) and Lázaro Sirlín are largely concerned with sex education and healthy sexual behavior and its social repercussions, but both men also promote eugenics, often with, in the case of Sirlín, an overtly racist objective (Sirlín 1920, Jul. 6, 1922, Apr. 13, 1922, May 12, 1921; Delfino, Oct. 19, 1922, Mar. 22, 1923).

16. In addition to the above-mentioned articles by Coni, Delfino and Sirlín, see, for example, "Profilaxis de suicidio," Mar. 25, 1920; Secame, Sept. 21, 1922; Garrahan, Dec. 22, 1921.

17. Such articles include rejection of the conventions of the nuclear family as hypocritical and oppressive (Nov. 13, 1919; Dec. 30, 1919), and of the status of women as "baby factories" (Nov. 15, 1919). Also attacked is the institution of the orphanage, especially with regard to the internment in orphanages of illegitimate children (Monart 1919).

18. Similarly, see Cardi (1917).

19. This unpublished letter is among the Gómez de la Serna papers at the University of Pittsburgh library.

20. Also significant is the fact that Dulce-Persona's father contemplated exercising violence on her in order to stop her forgetting, that Dulce-Persona learned of her father's transgression by reading the Presidente's diary, and that the Presidente regards Dulce-Persona's memory as her one obstacle to freedom from selfhood. As with the "Oratoria de un hombre confuso" examined in chapter two, memory, constituted in language, is the foundation of selfhood; and this process is inexorably tied to violence.

21. See Guy 1981, 65–76. Many women resorted to home piecework because of concerted union and government efforts to exclude them from factory work (69–70). Guy elaborates: "women who sewed piecework could barely afford to pay for one-room flats, let alone feed themselves and their families" (70). "No matter what type of work, women received miserable wages and labored under deplorable conditions. If factory work was unacceptable, then prostitution, legal or clandestine, rather than staying at home, was the only alternative for the woman who had to work" (71). To be fair, Adriana is actually a *modista*, or dressmaker. Scobie indicates that dressmakers were the least desperate subset among seamstresses, and the most likely to make a secure living by their trade (1974, 204).

22. The best known of these is Raúl Scabrini Ortiz's first book, which includes the vexatious portrait of Macedonio mentioned in chapter two. Such mythologizing projects are in contrast to social realist portraits of Porteño life, the most noteworthy of which are Roberto Mariani's 1925 *Cuentos de la oficina* (Office Tales, Mariani 1956) and his 1926 *El amor agresivo* (Tough Love), which deals with prostitution.

23. For a detailed account of the legal role of public health authorities in monitoring and restricting prostitution, see also Domínguez 1946, 167–84.

24. Even the specific setting of *Adriana* suggests the relevance of the prostitution question. *Casas de inquilinato*, or "family-dwelling tenements," on Libertad Street were "considered foci of clandestine prostitution" (Guy 1991, 45). Eduardo and Susana's boardinghouse is in the 400 block of Libertad, where Macedonio in fact lived for a time (*Adriana*, 43).

25. This thesis is unpublished. Missing for many years from the archives of the University of Buenos Aires law school, the manuscript is now in private hands.

26. The issue was also raised among hygienicists as pertinent to the war against venereal disease (Giménez 1918).

27. Tolstoy's discussion of love, sexuality, and marriage appears under the title "El amor sexual" in the anarchist periodical *Los Intelectuales*, in 1922.

28. In 1915, arrests were heavily skewed to minor and day laborers of immigrant appearance, and were usually incurred for public behavior rather than criminal activity; 29 percent of all prisoners were detained without cause (Salvatore 1992, 293–94).

29. While it is impossible to affirm that Borges was inspired directly by *Adriana Buenos Aires*, it is certain that he knew the novel well, having cowritten the prologue to the 1938 manuscript.

30. Macedonio would also agree with Vezzetti that a prevailing belief of Positivist psychiatry rests on a contradiction: that the city, the great civilizing organism, is also the "generator of conflict and crime" (Vezzetti, 1985, 368).

31. Vezzetti is quick to associate the clinical gaze with the Positivist alienist (1983, 62).

32. A similar passage is found in the opening paragraphs of the essay "Bases en metafísica" (Bases in Metaphysics), dated 1908 (*Vigilia*, 43).

33. In Foix's interpretation, the body, as with all aquenó (such as coffee without caffeine or wine without alcohol), is understood by convention to be something highly efficacious and utilitarian, but for Macedonio its defining attribute is that it serves only to frustrate all usefulness (Foix 1974, 16–21, 32).

CHAPTER 6. The Self of the City

1. Hardoy (1992) specifies the creation of Palermo Park as a particular consequence of Haussman's Parisian influence in the development of Buenos Aires (32), an observation in keeping with Sennett's critique of Regent's Park in London (1994).

2. A few such houses (most modified to two story residences prior to the turn of the century) are still evident in San Telmo, the only extant cluster of traditional upper-class dwellings in Buenos Aires. The gradual conversion of these houses to *conventillos*, or tenements, accompanied the growing preference among moneyed

families for Italianate or Beaux-arts mansions openly imitative of current Parisian styles (Scobie 1974, 129–32).

3. The building is still standing, at Rivadavia 2625, little changed; its large apartments and generous rooms are vast, far from intimate by today's standards.

4. Of the numerous pensions Macedonio inhabited, only half a dozen or so addresses are mentioned in his correspondence. Of that handful, only one, at Misiones 139–145, is still standing. Macedonio lived briefly at number 143. Number 145 (a different entrance to the same building) is still a residential hotel today. At one time, this entire neighborhood consisted largely of this type of modest but decorative dwelling.

5. M. Bueno regards "La calle Florida" as an attack on the conception of the urban center as the site of the possibility of "social betterment" for the masses (2000, 66–67).

6. By 1877, Buenos Aires had one of the world's densest horse-car networks; by the 1930s, the world's largest privately held streetcar system (González Podestá 1986, 14, 28).

7. Max-Neef's solution to these problems seems to lie in his preference for cities that retain the intimacy of neighborhoods; curiously, he proffers Buenos Aires as an example (1992, 97).

8. Apart from these generalizations, historical evidence on the nature of residential development in the Buenos Aires of Macedonio's youth is muddled and tends to follow diverging ideological lines. Scobie (1978) presents census data that argues convincingly against Korn's thesis regarding the Once district. Yujnovsky argues that unfettered private development led to increased housing density and worsened living conditions for the great majority (1974, 336–37). Korn and de la Torre (1989) demonstrate that home ownership increased dramatically between 1887 and 1914 (95–97), that tenement conditions were not as bad as often portrayed (93–95), and that working-class Porteños generally improved their living standards. J. F. Liernur insists that the Buenos Aires of 1890 was hardly the endangered "gran aldea" depicted by historians, but rather an urban "encampment," chaotic, expanding voraciously, self-consciously marked with the accoutrements of modernity and home to large numbers of temporary structures and displaced "urban nomads" (1993, 183).

9. In Simmel's words, "the metropolis is the genuine arena of this culture which outgrows all personal life. Here in buildings and educational institutions, in the wonders and comforts of space-conquering technology, in the formations of community life, and in the visible institutions of the state, is offered such an overwhelming fullness of crystalized and impersonal spirit that the personality, so to speak, cannot maintain itself under its impact" (1968, 59).

10. In Argentina, this rural paradise was, to a point, real. Morse signals the period from independence to 1875 as Argentina's "golden age for rural elites," when the centers of its confederated political and economic power lay outside its cities (Morse 1992, 9).

11. Sánchez saw to the 1941 publication of "Una novela que comienza," to which he wrote the prologue. Not coincidentally, the two men were introduced by Macedonio's cousin Gabriel Del Mazo, the same engineer (and later Minister of Defense) whose correspondence engaged Macedonio in discussions on the nature of the city.

12. These tensions are still evident today. In August 2003, Argentine president Néstor Kirchner was roundly criticized for failing to preside over the opening ceremonies of La Rural, Buenos Aires's annual rural fair and exhibition. La Rural is still widely considered a vital expression of traditional rural creole culture and thus essential to Argentina's identity as well as to its economy (see Editorial, "El presidente y La Rural," *La Nación*, August 1, 2003, Opinión 18. http://www.lanacion.com.ar/03/08/01/do_515666.asp).

13. Robert Owen's garden city projects echo the idealization by Jefferson, Thoreau, and, later, Lewis Mumford, of the "'American Dream' of rural independent living" (Thorns 1976, 30). Ebenezer Howard's garden city contribution to the residential landscape of the U.K. and the U.S. arises directly from the widespread faith in a "community life" based on a consensus of individuals (31).

14. Utopian discourse was itself ideologically contested territory. Numerous visions for the city competed for legitimacy; among these was the hygienicist vision, whose claim on utopian discourse is evident in a published exchange of "letters" between Coni and Delfino in *Semana Médica* (April 13, 1919). In this context, Macedonio had good motivation to lay claim to "invention" of his utopian "ciudad-campo."

15. Camblong notes one interpretation to this passage as connecting the Presidente to the "patriarchal families" of Argentina who were "progressively losing their possessions" (*Museo*, 140n), a situation characteristic of the Fernández family (G. García 1996, 25).

16. It is noteworthy that Pilar lies northwest of Buenos Aires, on rail lines to Lacroze and Retiro terminals, whereas La Novela lies along the River Plate, near a rail line to Constitución station. The river and the "constitution" are also, arguably, components of the "national patrimony."

17. For Macedonio, says Alicia Allievi, *estancia* means "*estar en el mundo*" [to be in the world] (Bueno 200, 41–42).

18. This passage is found in all three posthumous editions of *Museo*, including the Ayacucho edition, from which it is cited here. It is not included in the critical edition, having been considered spurious by Camblong (*Museo*, 115n). There is little question, however, that Macedonio wrote this passage, whether or not he intended it for inclusion in *Museo*.

19. This phrase occurs in a paragraph included in posthumous editions, including the Ayacucho edition cited here, but omitted from the critical edition.

20. Mattalía (1992) argues a similar point, insisting that Borges's "distance" from Macedonio is ultimately because of his "ironic affirmation—resigned and destructive at the same time—of the symbolic order" (504).

21. This passage constitutes a prologue in the Ayacucho edition (Fernández 1982, 245) and other posthumous editions; it is included in the appendix of the critical edition.

Chapter 7. Continuities

1. In fact, Macedonio read the works of several of Argentina's more forward-thinking philosophers. He corresponded with both Miguel Angel Virasoro and Carlos Astrada (*Epistolario* 135–40, 173, 313–14, 344). Astrada's 1933 *El juego existencial*

(The Existential Game) interested Macedonio enough for him to own a copy of it (although the book, while it was still in Adolfo de Obieta's library, had numerous pages uncut), and Astrada read and commented on *Vigilia*. Macedonio also owned a copy of Angel Vasallo's 1929 very thinly veiled retort to *Vigilia*, entitled *Elogio de la vigilia* (In Praise of Wakefulness), taking the trouble to read it and scrawl deprecating remarks in its pages. (This book was also in de Obieta's library.) Macedonio's taste in philosophical readings, moreover, was catholic enough to include Heidigger, whom he learned of through his correspondence with Astrada (Ranieri 1995, 43).

2. It is entirely appropriate, furthermore, that Camblong's herculean critical edition of *Museo*, rather than result in a definitive version of Macedonio's masterwork, ends up confirming the impossibility of archival closure (see *Museo*, lxxvii).

3. De Obieta confirmed that one of Macedonio's main criteria for his choice of boardinghouse was proximity to his family.

Works Cited

Abós, Alvaro. 2002. *Macedonio Fernández: La biografía imposible*. Buenos Aires: Plaza Janés.

Altamirano, Carlos, and Beatriz Sarlo. 1983. La Argentina del Centenario: Campo intelectual, vida literaria y temas ideológicos. In *Ensayos argentinos: De Sarmiento a la vanguardia*. Edited by B. Sarlo and C. Altamirano. Buenos Aires: Centro Editor de América Latina.

Anderson, Andrew. 1996. Remarks. Hilton Hotel, Washington, DC, 29 December.

Aracemi, Máximo. 1908. El amor libre. *Suplemento de La Protesta* 4.

Aramburu, Julio. 1927. *Buenos Aires: Cuidad, mujeres, hombres, muestrario urbano*. Buenos Aires: El Ateneo.

Arlt, Roberto. 1958. *Los siete locos*. Buenos Aires: Losada.

———. 1979. *El juguete rabioso*. Barcelona: Bruguera Alfaguara.

Astrada, Carlos. 1933. *El juego existencial*. Buenos Aires: Biblioteca Babel.

Balderston, Daniel. 1990. Historical situations in Borges. *MLN* 105 (2): 331–50.

———. 1993. *Out of context: Historical reference and representation of reality in Borges*. Durham: Duke University Press.

Barberena, Joaquín D. 1902. Carta abierto a Roberto de las Carreras. *La Rebelión* 9.

Barrancos, Dora. 1990. Anarquismo y sexualidad. In *Mundo urbano y cultura popular: Estudio de historia social argentina*. Edited by D. Armus. Buenos Aires: Editorial Sudamericana.

Bell-Villada, Gene H. 1999. *Borges and his fiction*. Revised ed. Austin: University of Texas Press.

Biagini, Hugo E. 1981. William James y otras presencias norteamericanas en Macedonio Fernández. *Hispanic Journal* 2 (2): 103–9.

Bianchi, Edumundo. 1904. Hacia el amor libre. *Futuro* 3.

Borges, Jorge Luis. 1923. Macedonio Fernández: "El Recienvenido", inédito aún. *Proa (1a época)*: July, 2.

———. 1927. Homenaje a Carriego. *Martín Fierro* 4 (39): 8.

———. 1952. Macedonio Fernández. *Sur* (March–April) 209–10.

———. 1953. La apostasía de Coifi. *Entregas de La Licorne* (1–2): 45–48.

———, ed. 1961. *Macedonio Fernández*. By M. Fernandez. Buenos Aires: Ediciones Culturales Argentinas.

———. 1977. Ultraísmo. In *Los vanguardismos en la América Latina*. Edited by O. Collazos. Barcelona: Península.

———. 1991. *Historia universal de la infamia*. Madrid: Alianza.

Borges, Jorge Luis, and Norman Thomas Di Giovanni. 1970. Autobiographical Notes. *The New Yorker*, 19 September, 40–99.

Borges, Jorge Luis, and Carlos V. Frias. 1989. *Obras completas*. Barcelona, Spain: Emece.

Borinsky, Alicia. 1978. *Macedonio Fernández y la teoría crítica: una evaluación*. Buenos Aires: Corregidor.

———. 1993. An Apprenticeship in reading: Macedonio Fernández. In *Theoretical fables: The pedagogical dream in contemporary Latin American fiction*, by Borinsky. Philadelphia: University of Pennsylvania Press.

Bueno, Monica. 2000. *Macedonio Fernández, un escritor de fin de siglo: Geneología de un vanguardista*. Buenos Aires: Corregidor.

———, ed. 2001. *Conversaciones imposibles con Macedonio Fernández*. Buenos Aires: Corregidor.

Bürger, Peter. 1984. *Theory of the avant-garde*. Translated by M. Shaw. Edited by W. Godzich and J. Schulte-Sasse. 4 vols. Vol. 4, *Theory and history of literature*. Minneapolis: University of Minnesota Press.

Calinescu, Matei. 1987. *Five faces of modernity: Modernism, avant-garde, decadence, kitsch, postmodernism*. Durham, N.C.: Duke University Press.

Calvert, Susan, and Peter Calvert. 1989. *Argentina: Political culture and instability*. Pittsburgh: University of Pittsburgh Press.

Camblong, Ana. 2003. *Macedonio: Retórica y política de los discursos paradójicos*. Buenos Aires: Eudeba.

Cárdenas, Felipe. 1967. Ese enigmático conductor. *Todo Es Historia* 2 (1): 89–99.

Cardi, Marconi. 1917. La medicina futurista. *La Protesta*, 10 Feb.

Cascardi, Anthony. 1992. *The subject of modernity*. New York: Cambridge University Press.

Clementi, Hebe. 1982. *El radicalismo: Nudos gordianos de la economía*. Buenos Aires: Ediciones Siglo Veinte.

Collazos, Oscar, ed. 1977. *Los vanguardismos en América Latina*. Barcelona: Península.

Con Davis, Robert. 1981. Introduction. In *The fictional father: Lacanian readings of the text*. Edited by R. Con Davis. Amherst: University of Massachusetts Press.

Coni, Emilio. 1918. Reglamentación del trabajo a domicilio. *Semana Médica*, 5 Sept.

Coni, Emilio, and Víctor Delfino. 1919. La ciudad argentina ideal o la del porvenir. *Semana Médica*, 13 Apr., 342.

Cortázar, Julio. 1985. *Rayuela*. Barcelona: Planeta-De Agostini.

Cúneo, Dardo. 1955. *El romanticismo político*. Buenos Aires: Ediciones Transición.

Delfino, Víctor. 1919. Higiene y proletariado. *Semana Médica*, 17 April, 407–9.

———. 1922. Medicina Social. *Semana Médica*, 19 Oct., 829.

———. 1923. Medicina Social. *Semana Médica*, 22 Mar., 559.

Derrida, Jacques. 1978. *Writing and difference*. Translated by A. Bass. Chicago: University of Chicago Press.

Díaz, Lidia. 1990. La estética de Macedonio Fernández y la vanguardia argentina. *Revista Iberoamericana* 56 (151): 497–511.

Domínguez, Alberto. 1946. *Policía sanitaria: Doctrina, legislación nacional y provincial.* Buenos Aires: Editorial DePalma.

Dreyfus, Hubert L., and Paul Rabinow. 1983. *Michel Foucault: Beyond structuralism and hermeneutics.* 2nd ed. Chicago: University of Chicago Press.

Engelbert, Jo Anne. 1978. *Macedonio Fernández and the Spanish American new novel.* New York: NYU Press.

———. 1984. Introduction. In *Macedonio: Selected writings in translation*, by Macedonio Fernández. Edited by Engelbert. Fort Worth, Tex.: Latitudes.

Fernández, F. M. 1917. *La Protesta*, 18 Feb.

Fernández, Macedonio. 1897. De las personas: tesis. Buenos Aires: Personal collection of Alejandro Vaccaro.

———. 1905. Letter to Julio Molina y Vedia. Buenos Aires: Personal collection of Juan Molina y Vedia.

———. 1928. Letters to Ramón Gómez de la Serna. Ramón Gómez de la Serna Collection. Pittsburgh: University of Pittsburgh Libraries.

———. 1938a. Adriana Buenos Aires (TS). Buenos Aires: Fundación Palermo.

———. 1938b. Letters to Luis Alberto Sánchez. Luis Alberto Sánchez Collection. University Park: Pennsylvania State University Archives.

———. 1981. *Papeles antiguos; Escritos, 1892–1907.* Edited by A. de Obieta. Buenos Aires: Corregidor.

———. 1982. *Museo de la novela de la eterna.* Edited by C. F. Moreno. Caracas: Ayacucho.

———. 1987. *Relato: Cuentos, poemas y misceláneas.* Edited by A. de Obieta. Buenos Aires: Corregidor.

———. 1988. *Adriana Buenos Aires: Ultima novela mala.* 2nd ed. Buenos Aires: Corregidor.

———. 1989. *Papeles de Recienvenido y continuación de la nada.* Edited by A. de Obieta. Buenos Aires: Corregidor.

———. 1990. *Teorías.* Edited by A. de Obieta. Buenos Aires: Corregidor.

———. 1991. *Epistolario.* Edited by A. Borinsky. 2nd ed. Buenos Aires: Corregidor.

———. 1996. *Museo de la Novela de la Eterna.* Edited by A. M. Camblong. 2nd Critical ed. Paris: ALLCA XX/Colección Archivos.

Fernández Moreno, César. 1977a. Distinguir para entender: Entrevista con Leopoldo Marechal. In *Los vanguardismos en la América Latina.* Edited by O. Collazos. Barcelona: Península.

———. 1977b. El ultraísmo. In *Los vanguardismos en América Latina.* Edited by O. Collazos. Barcelona: Península.

———. 1982. Cronología. In *Museo de la Novela de la Eterna*, by Macedonio Fernández. Caracas: Biblioteca Ayacucho.

Fernández-Latour, Enrique. 1980. *Macedonio Fernández, candidato a presidente y otros escritos.* Buenos Aires: Aragón.

Ferreira Gular, José. 1974. Arte o Alienação na Cultura de Massa. In *Formalismo e tradição moderna: O problema da arte na crise de cultura.* Edited by J. G. Melquior. Rio de Janeiro: Editor Forense-Universitária.

Foix, Juan Carlos. 1974. *Macedonio Fernández*. Buenos Aires: Editorial Bonum.
Foucault, Michel. 1972. *The archaeology of knowledge*. Translated by A. M. S. Smith. New York: Harper Colophon.
———. 1983. The Subject and Power. In *Michel Foucault: Beyond structuralism and hermeneutics*. Edited by H. L. Dreyfus and P. Rabinow. Chicago: University of Chicago Press.
———. 1988. *Madness and civilization: A history of madness in the age of reason*. Translated by R. Howard. New York: Vintage Books.
———. 1990. *The history of sexuality: Volume I, an introduction*. Translated by R. Hurley. New York: Vintage Books.
———. 1994. *The birth of the clinic: An archaeology of medical perception*. Translated by A. M. S. Smith. New York: Vintage Books.
Franco, Jean. 1967. *The modern culture of Latin America: Society and the artist*. London: Frederick Praeger.
Galletti, Alfredo. 1985. Ideas políticas y sociales. In *El movimiento positivista argentino*. Edited by H. E. Biagini. Buenos Aires: Belgrano.
Gallo, Ezequiel, and Silvia Segal. 1965. La formación de los partidos políticos contemporáneos: la Unión Radical Cívica, 1890–1916. In *Argentina: Sociedad de masas*. Edited by T. Di Tella. Buenos Aires: Editorial Universitaria.
Garasa, Delfín Leocadio. 1968. Repercusión literaria del anarquismo. In *Actas de las terceras jornadas de investigación de la historia y literatura rioplatense en los Estados Unidos*. Mendoza: Universidad Nacional de Cuyo.
García, Carlos, ed. 2000. *Correspondencia, 1922–1939: Crónica de una amistad*. By M. Fernandez and J. L. Borges. Buenos Aires: Corregidor.
García, Germán Leopoldo. 1975. *Macedonio Fernández: La escritura en objeto*. Buenos Aires: Siglo Veintiuno.
———, ed. 1996. *Hablan de Macedonio Fernández*. 2nd ed. Buenos Aires: Atuel.
———. 2000. *Macedonio Fernández: La escritura en objeto*. Buenos Aires: Adriana Hidalgo.
Garrahan, Juan P. 1921. Higiene escolar. *Semana Médica*, 22 Dec., 874–77.
Garth, Todd S. 1991. Identity for Gertrude Stein and Macedonio Fernández: I know; no I. Master's Thesis, University of Maryland, College Park.
———. 1996. Politicizing myth and absence: From Macedonio Fernández to Augusto Roa Bastos. In *Structures of power: Essays on twentieth-century Spanish-American fiction*. Edited by T. J. Peavler and P. Standish. Albany: State University of New York Press.
———. 2001. Confused oratory: Borges, Macedonio and the creation of the mythological author. *MLN* 116 (2): 350–70.
Giménez, Angel. 1918. La lucha antivenérea. *Semana Médica*, 11 July.
Goloboff, Gerardo Mario. 1983. El uso sabio de la ausencia en la aventura de Macedonio Fernández. *Revista Iberoamericana* 51 (103–31): 167–75.
Gómez de la Serna, Ramón. 1944. *Retratos contemporáneos*. Buenos Aires: Editorial Sudamericana.
González, Aníbal. 1993. *Journalism and the development of Spanish American narrative*. Cambridge: Cambridge University Press.

González Arzac, T. 1970. Hipólito Yrigoyen, Doctor. *Todo Es Historia* 35.

González, Horacio. 1995. *El filósofo cesante: gracia y desdicha en Macedonio Fernández.* Buenos Aires: Atuel.

González Podestá, Aquilino. 1986. *Los tranvías de Buenos Aires.* Buenos Aires: Asociación Amigos del Tranvía.

———. 2002a. Sobre vías con troley: Boletos, primera parte. *Historias de la Ciudad: Una revista de Buenos Aires* 3 (16): 50–54.

———. 2002b. Sobre vías con troley: Boletos, segunda parte. *Historias de la Ciudad: Una revista de Buenos Aires* 4 (17): 52–54.

González-Lanuza, Eduardo. 1922. *Aquelarre.* Buenos Aires: J. Samet.

Güiraldes, Ricardo. 1998. *Don Segundo Sombra.* Edited by S. Parkinson. Critical ed. Madrid: Cátedra.

Gullón, Germán. 1996. Remarks. Hilton Hotel, Washington, DC, 29 December.

Guy, Donna J. 1981. Women, Peonage, and Industrialization: Argentina, 1810–1914. *Latin American Research Review* 16 (3): 65–89.

———. 1991. *Sex and danger in Buenos Aires.* Lincoln: University of Nebraska Press.

Hardoy, Jorge. 1992. Theory and practice of urban planning in Europe, 1850–1930. In *Rethinking the Latin American city.* Edited by R. M. Morse and J. Hardoy. Washington, DC: Woodrow Wilson Center Press.

Holloway Jr., James E. 1988. Borges' early mythicization of Buenos Aires. *Symposium* 62 (1): 18–36.

Huidobro, Vicente. 1988. *Altazor, or voyage in a parachute: A poem in VII cantos.* Translated by E. Weinberger. St. Paul, Minn.: Greywolf Press.

Isaacson, José. 1981. *Macedonio Fernández, sus ideas políticas y estéticas.* Buenos Aires: Belgrano.

Jameson, Frederic. 1991. *Postmodern, or the cultural logic of late capitalism.* Durham, N.C.: Duke University Press.

Jervis, John. 1998. *Exploring the modern: Patterns of western culture and civilization.* Oxford: Blackwell.

Jitrik, Noé. 1973. *La novela futura de Macedonio Fernández.* Caracas: Universidad Central de Venezuela.

Kahn, Bonnie Menes. 1987. *Cosmopolitan culture: The guilt-edged dream of a tolerant city.* New York: Atheneum.

Kerr, Lucille. 1992. *Reclaiming the author: Figures and fictions from Spanish America.* Durham, N.C.: Duke University Press.

Kirkpatrick, Gwen. 1989. *The dissonant legacy of modernism.* Berkeley: University of California Press.

Kohn Loncarica, Alfredo G., and Abel L. Agüero. 1985. El contexto médico. In *El movimiento positivista argentina.* Edited by H. E. Biagini. Buenos Aires: Belgrano.

Korn, Francis, and Lidia de la Torre. 1989. Housing in Buenos Aires, 1887–1914. In *Social welfare, 1850–1950: Australia, Argentina and Canada compared.* Edited by D. C. M. Platt. London: MacMillan Press.

Korn, Francis, et al. 1974. *Buenos Aires: los huéspedes del 20.* Buenos Aires: Sudamericana.

Lacan, Jacques. 1968. *The language of the self: The function of language in psychoanalysis.* Translated by A. Wilden. Baltimore: Johns Hopkins University Press.

Lavrin, Asunción. 1995. *Women, feminism and social change in Argentina, Uruguay and Chile: 1895–1940.* Lincoln: University of Nebraska Press.

Lawrence, Roderick, and Claude Raffestin. 1994. Mythical and ritual constituents of the city. In *The urban experience: A people-environment perspective.* Edited by A. J. Neary, M. A. Symes and J. E. Brown. London: E. and F. N. Spon.

Lee, Jonathan Scott. 1990. *Lacan.* Boston: Twayne.

Lees, Andrew. 1985. *Cities perceived: Urban societies in European and American thought, 1820–1940.* New York: Columbia University Press.

Leland, Christopher Towne. 1986. *The last happy men: The generation of 1922, fiction, and the Argentine reality.* Syracuse, N.Y.: Syracuse University Press.

Liernur, José Francisco. 1993. La ciudad efímera: consideraciones sobre el aspecto material de Buenos Aires, 1890–1910. In *El umbral de la metrópolis: Transformaciones técnicas y cultura en la modernización de Buenos Aires, 1870–1930.* Edited by J. F. Liernur and G. Silvestri. Buenos Aires: Editorial Sudamericana.

Liernur, Pancho. 1984. Buenos Aires: la estrategia de la casa autoconstruida. In *Sectores populares y vida urbana.* Edited by D. Armus. Buenos Aires: Consejo Latinoamericano de Ciencias Sociales.

Lindstrom, Naomi. 1981. *Macedonio Fernández.* Lincoln, Neb.: Society of Spanish and Spanish American Poets.

Lo lúdico y lo fantástico en la obra de Cortázar. 1986. In *Coloquio internacional: Lo lúdico y lo fantástico en la obra de Cortázar.* Madrid: Editorial Fundamentos.

Lucas, Fábio. 1975. Dependência ideológica e vanguarda. *Hispamérica* año IV, anejo 1:33–56.

Madrid, Lelia. 1992. "Fundación mítica de Buenos Aires" o la utopía de la historia. *Bulletin of Hispanic Studies* 69:347–56.

Mallea, Eduardo. 1969. *Cuentos para una inglesa desesperada.* 4th ed. Madrid: Espasa-Calpe.

Mariani, Roberto. 1926. *El amor agresivo.* Buenos Aires: Gleizer.

———. 1956. *Cuentos de la oficina.* Buenos Aires: Editorial Deucalión.

Martínez Díaz, Nelson. 1988. *Hipólito Yrigoyen: El radicalismo argentino.* Buenos Aires: Biblioteca Iberoamericana.

Martínez Estrada, Ezequiel. 1917. Untitled article. *Nosotros* 11.

———. 1956. *La cabeza de Goliat: Microscopia de Buenos Aires.* 3rd ed. Buenos Aires: Editorial Novo.

———. 1985. *Radiografía de la Pampa.* 11th ed. Buenos Aires: Editorial Losada.

Masiello, Francine. 1986. *Lenguaje e ideología: Las escuelas argentinas de vanguardia.* Buenos Aires: Hachette.

Mattalía, Sonia. 1992. Macedonio Fernández/Jorge Luis Borges: La superstición de las genealogías. *Cuadernos Hispanoamericanos* 505–7:497–505.

Max-Neef, Manfred A. 1992. The city: Its size and rhythm. In *Rethinking the Latin American city.* Edited by R. Morse and J. Hardoy. Washington, DC: Woodrow Wilson Center Press.

Mayo, Carlos Alberto, and Fernándo García Molina. 1972. Yrigoyen, 1928: Top Secret. *Todo Es Historia* 83.

McVicker, Elizabeth Ruth. 1987. The poetry and poetic theory of Macedonio Fernández. Ph.D. Diss., New York University.

Molina y Vedia, Juan. 1996. Personal conversation. 27 May.

Molloy, Sylvia. 1991. *At face value: Autobiographical writing in Spanish America.* Cambridge: Cambridge University Press.

Monart, Luis. 1919. Untitled article. *La Protesta*, Nov. 21.

Morse, Richard. 1992. Cities as People. In *Rethinking the Latin American city.* Edited by R. M. Morse and J. Hardoy. Washington, DC: Woodrow Wilson Center Press.

Nouzeilles, Gabriela. 1997. Ficciones paranoicas de fin de siglo: Naturalismo y policía médica. *MLN* 112 (2): 232–52.

Obieta, Adolfo de. 1996. Conversations. May 10–26.

Ortega y Gasset, José. 1938. *El tema de nuestro tiempo.* Buenos Aires: Espasa-Calpe.

———. 1968. *The dehumanization of art and other essays on art, culture, and literature.* Translated by H. Weyl. First Princeton Paperback ed. Princeton, N.J.: Princeton University Press.

Osorio, Nelson. 1982. *Futurismo y vanguardia literaria en América Latina.* Caracas: Centro de Estudios Latinamericanos Rómulo Gallegos.

Oved, Isaac. 1978. *El anarquismo y el movimiento obrero en Argentina.* Buenos Aires: Siglo XXI.

Pagni, Andrea. 1991. Macedonio Fernández o la escritura del lector. In *Europaïsche avantgarde im Lateinamerikanschen kontext: Akten des Interntionalen Berliner Kolloquiums, 1989.* Edited by H. Wentzlaff-Eggebert. Frankfurt Am Main: Vervuert Verlag.

Paz, Octavio. 1974. *Los hijos del limo.* Barcelona: Seix Barral.

Pérez-Firmat, Gustavo. 1982. *Idle fictions: The Hispanic vanguard novel, 1926–1934.* Durham, N.C.: Duke University Press.

Piglia, Ricardo. 1988. Notas sobre Macedonio en un diario. In *Prisión perpetua.* Buenos Aires: Sudamericana.

———. 1994. *Respiración artificial.* Buenos Aires: Seix Barral.

Plato. 1956. *Phaedrus.* Translated by W. C. Helmbold and W. G. Rabinowitz. Indianapolis: Liberal Arts Press.

Poggioli, Renato. 1968. *The theory of the avant-garde.* Translated by G. Fitzgerald. Cambridge, Mass.: Belknap Press.

Potash, Robert. 1969. *The army and politics in Argentina, 1928–1945: Yrigoyen to Perón.* Stanford, Calif.: Stanford University Press.

Prieto, Adolfo. 1977. Una curiosa revista de orientación futurista. In *Los vanguardismos en América Latina.* Edited by O. Collazos. Barcelona: Ediciones Península.

Prieto, Julio. 2002. *Desencuadernados: Vanguardias ex-céntricas en el Río de la Plata, Macedonio Fernández y Felisberto Hernández.* Buenos Aires: Beatriz Viterbo.

Profilaxis de suicidio. 1920. *Semana Médica*, 25 Mar., 431–32.

Quiroule, Pierre [Joaquín A. Falconnet]. 1914. *La ciudad anarquista americana.* Buenos Aires: Editorial La Protesta.

Rama, Angel. 1996. *The Lettered City*. Translated by J. C. Chasteen. Durham, N.C.: Duke University Press.

Ramos, Julio. 2002. *Divergent modernities: Culture and politics in nineteenth-century Latin America*. Translated by J. D. Blanco. Durham, N.C.: Duke University Press.

Ranieri, Sergio. 1995. Macedonio tenía una certeza absoluta de la eternidad. *La Maga* Dec. 30, 1995, 42–45.

Recalde, Héctor. 1994. *Vida popular y salud en Buenos Aires, 1900–1930*. Vol I. 2 vols. Buenos Aires: Centro Editor de América Latina.

Reichardt, Dieter. 1991. Macedonio Fernández y Omar Viñole: Dos caras del vanguardismo en Argentina. In *Europaïsche avantgarde im Lateinamerikanischen kontext: Akten des Internationalen Berliner Kolloquiums, 1989*. Edited by H. Wentzlaff-Eggebert. Frankfurt Am Main: Vervuert Verlag.

Rock, David. 1975a. *Politics in Argentina, 1890–1930: The rise and fall of Radicalism*. Cambridge: Cambridge University Press.

———. 1975b. Radical populism and conservative elite, 1912–1930. In *Argentina in the twentieth century*. Edited by Rock. Pittsburgh: University of Pittsburgh Press.

———. 1985. *Argentina, 1516–1982: From Spanish colonization to the Falklands War*. Berkeley: University of California Press.

Rodríguez Monegal, Emir. 1952. Borges, Macedonio y el ultraísmo. *Número* 4 (19): 171–83.

Rojas Paz, Pablo. 1930. *Hombres grises, montañas azules*. Buenos Aires: Gleizer.

Romero, José Luís. 1965. *El desarrollo de las ideas en la sociedad argentina del siglo XX*. Buenos Aires: Fondo de Cultura Económica.

Ruibal, Beatriz Celina. 1993. *Ideología del control social*. Buenos Aires: Centro Editor de América Latina.

Salessi, Jorge. 1995. *Médicos maleantes y maricas: Higiene, criminología y homosexualidad en la construcción de la nación argentina: Buenos Aires, 1871–1914*. Buenos Aires: Beatriz Viterbo.

Salvador, Nélida. 1962. *Revistas argentinas de vanguardia, 1920–1930*. Buenos Aires: Ediciones Culturales Argentinas.

———. 1986. *Macedonio Fernández: Precursor de la antinovela*. Buenos Aires: Editorial Plus Ultra.

———. 2003. *Macedonio Fernández: Creador de lo insólito*. Buenos Aires: Corregidor.

Salvatore, Ricardo. 1992. Criminology, prison reform, and the Buenos Aires working class. *Journal of Interdisciplinary History* 23 (2): 279–99.

Sánchez, Luis Alberto. 1941. Prólogo. In *Una novela que comienza*, by Macedonio Fernández. Santiago de Chile: Ercilla.

———. 1967. Urban growth and Latin American heritage. In *The urban explosion in Latin America*. Edited by G. Beyer. Ithaca: Cornell University Press.

Sarlo, Beatriz. 1983. Vanguardia y vida literaria. In *Ensayos argentinos: De Sarmiento a la vanguardia*. Edited by B. Sarlo and C. Altamirano. Buenos Aires: Centro Editor de América Latina.

———. 1988. *Una modernidad periférica: Buenos Aires 1920 y 1930*. Buenos Aires: Nueva Visión.

———. 1992. *La imaginación técnica: Sueños modernos de la cultura argentina*. Buenos Aires: Nueva Visión.

———. 1999. El saber del cuerpo. A propósito de "Emma Zunz." *Variaciones Borges* 7:231–47.

Scalabrini-Ortiz, Raúl. 1931. *El hombre que está solo y espera*. Buenos Aires: Gleizer.

Scarry, Elaine. 1985. *The body in pain: The making and unmaking of the world*. Oxford: Oxford University Press.

Schiminovich, Flora H. 1986. *La obra de Macedonio Fernández: Una lectura surrealista*. Madrid: Editorial Pliegos.

Schulman, Ivan. 1986. Las genealogías secretas de la narrativa: Del modernismo a la vanguardia. In *Prosa hispánica de vanguardia*. Edited by F. Burgos. Madrid: Editorial Orígenes.

Schulte-Sasse, Jochen. 1984. Forward. In *Theory of the avant-garde*. Edited by P. Bürger. Minneapolis: University of Minnesota Press.

Schwartz, Jorge. 1991. *Las vanguardias latinoamericanas: Textos programáticos críticos*. Madrid: Cátedra.

Scobie, James R. 1974. *Buenos Aires: Plaza to suburb, 1870–1910*. New York: Oxford University Press.

———. 1978. Changing urban patterns: The Porteño case. In *Urbanization in the Americas from its beginnings to the present*. Edited by R. P. Schaedel, J. E. Hardoy and N. S. Kinzer. The Hague: Mouton Publishers.

Scrimaglio, Marta. 1974. *Literatura argentina de vanguardia, 1920–1939*. Rosario: Editorial Biblioteca.

Sebrelli, Juan José. 1964. *Buenos Aires: Vida cotidiana y alienación*. Buenos Aires: Ediciones Siglo Veinte.

Secame, Ernesto. 1922. Sexología. *Semana Médica*, 21 Sept.

El secular prejuicio de la familia. 1919. *La Protesta*, 13 Nov.

Sennett, Richard. 1994. *Flesh and stone: The body and the city in Western civilization*. New York: W. W. Norton.

Shumway, Nicolas. 1991. *The invention of Argentina*. Berkeley: University of California Press.

Simmel, Georg. 1968. The Metropolis and Mental Life. In *Classic essays on the culture of cities*, by Kurt Wolff. Edited by R. Sennett. New York: Appleton-Century-Croft.

Sirlín, Lázaro. 1920. Algo sobre eugenía y educación. *Semana Médica*, 23 Dec., 875.

———. 1921. Prostitución y enfermedades venéreas. *Semana Médica*, 12 May, 692.

———. 1922a. La perversión de la sensualidad: Inferiorización de la especie humana. *Semana Médica*, 13 Apr., 609.

———. 1922b. Sexualidad, sensualidad y sensualismo. *Semana Médica*, 6 Jul., 47–9.

Skidmore, Thomas, and Peter Smith. 1989. *Modern Latin America*. New York: Oxford University Press.

Smith, Peter H. 1974. *Argentina and the failure of democracy: Conflict among the political elites, 1904–1955*. Madison: University of Wisconsin Press.

Solberg, Carl. 1970. *Immigration and Nationalism: Chile and Argentina, 1890–1914*. Austin: University of Texas Press.

Spengler, Oswald. 1969. The soul of the city. In *Classic essays on the culture of cities.* Edited by R. Sennett. New York: Appleton-Century-Croft.

Stabb, Martin S. 1967. *In quest of identity: Patterns in the Spanish American essay of ideas, 1890–1960.* Chapel Hill: University of North Carolina Press.

Stein, Gertrude. 1990. *The autobiography of Alice B. Toklas.* New York: Vintage.

Stepan, Nancy Leys. 1991. *The hour of eugenics: Race, gender and nation in Latin America.* Ithaca: Cornell University Press.

Strong, Beret E. 1997. *The poetic avant-garde: The groups of Borges, Auden and Breton.* Evanston, Ill.: Northwestern University Press.

Thorns, David C. 1976. *The quest for community: Social aspects of residential growth.* New York: John Wiley and Sons.

Tolstoy, Leo. 1922. El amor sexual. *Los Intelectuales* 100.

Torre, Guillermo de. 1965. *Historia de las literaturas de vanguardia.* Madrid: Editorial Guadarrama.

Unruh, Vicky. 1994. *Latin American vanguards: Arts of contention.* Berkeley: University of California Press.

Vasallo, Angel. 1929. *Elogio de la Vigilia.* Buenos Aires: n.p.

Vecchio, Diego. 2003. *Egocidios: Macedonio Fernández y la liquidación del yo.* Buenos Aires: Beatriz Viterbo.

Vezzetti, Hugo. 1983. *La locura en la Argentina.* Buenos Aires: Folio Ediciones.

———. 1985. El discurso psiquiátrico. In *El movimiento positivista argentino.* Edited by H. E. Biagini. Buenos Aires: Belgrano.

Vicente de Alvarez, Sonia. 1982. El pensamiento metafísico de Macedonio Fernández. *Cuyo: Anuario de la historia de pensamiento argentino* 15:183–236.

———. 1996. Personal conversation. June 8.

Viñas, David. 1971. *De Sarmiento a Cortázar.* 3 vols. Vol. 1, *Literatura argentina y realidad política.* Buenos Aires: Siglo XX.

———. 1989. Algunas protagonistas, nudos y crispaciones. In *Historia social de la literatura argentina.* Edited by D. Viñas. Buenos Aires: Editorial Contrapunto.

Walter, Richard J. 1993. *Politics and urban growth in Buenos Aires, 1910–1942.* Cambridge: Cambridge University Press.

Weber, Max. 1969. The nature of the city. In *Classic essays on the culture of cities.* Edited by R. Sennett. New York: Appleton-Century-Croft.

Weinberg, Felix. 1976. *Dos utopías argentinas a principios de siglo.* Buenos Aires: Editorial Solar.

Yujnovsky, Oscar. 1974. Políticas de vivienda en la ciudad de Buenos Aires, 1880–1914. *Desarrollo Económico* 14 (54): 327–72.

———. 1975. Urban spatial structures in Latin America. In *Urbanization in Latin America: Approaches and issues.* Edited by J. E. Hardoy. New York: Anchor Press.

Zeno, Lelio. 1919. Medicina social e individual. *La Protesta,* 28 Oct., 13 Nov., 15 Nov., 9 Dec., 30 Dec.

Zimmerman, Eduardo A. 1992. Racial ideas and social reform: Argentina, 1890–1906. *Hispanic American Historical Review* 72 (1): 23–46.

Zukin, Sharon. 1995. *The cultures of cities.* Cambridge, Mass.: Blackwell Publishers.

Index

abjection, 151–52, 157
Abós, Alvaro, 13, 19, 93–94, 160, 204 n. 15, 204 n. 17, 205 n. 4
accidental author, 32–47, 73
Adorno, Theodor, 200 n. 12
Adriana Buenos Aires: altruistic love in, 130, 140, 142, 155; autobiographical elements in, 120, 205 n. 4; Buenos Aires in, 163, 167; child care and childrearing in, 131–33; compared with "Emma Zunz," 151–52; compared with *Museo de la Novela de la Eterna*, 121, 163, 205 n. 5; compared with *Papeles de Recienvenido*, 166; countryside in, 179; crime in, 149; demographic change in, 178; domesticity in, 172; family in, 133–35; fatherhood in, 137, 138–39; as last "bad" novel, 120–21, 130, 140, 201 n. 16, 205 n. 2; madness in, 153–55; medical practice in, 122–24, 131, 133, 205 n. 6; neighborhoods in, 177; physicality of individual in, 119–24; prostitution in, 138–44, 207 n. 24; public spaces in, 169–72; public transit in, 173–74; and romance novels, 130; seamstresses in, 206 n. 12, 206 n. 21; specularity in, 171; women in, 138–44, 145–47, 206 n. 21; writing of, 119–20, 205 n. 1, 205 n. 2, 205 n. 3, 207 n. 29
aesthetics: avant-garde, 49–50, 54–55, 70, 200 n. 13; "bad" versus "good," 167, 205 n. 2; and the city, 192 (*see also* Buenos Aires: beauty of; Buenos Aires: campaign to beautify; city: campaign to beautify the); Macedonio's pronouncements on, 18; Macedonio's use of, 87. *See also* beauty
affection, 179, 193; affective interrelationships, 157, 189, 194; altruistic or selfless, 140, 153; as cure for madness, 156–57; and negation or nihilism, 64–67, 201 n. 26
alienation, 168, 179
Allievi, Alicia, 209 n. 17
altruism, 135, 142, 150, 159. *See also* selflessness
Alvear, Marcelo, 102, 105
anarchism, 90, 92–94, 99, 101, 203 n. 2, 204 n. 4; alternative conception of family in, 135; anarchist community, Macedonio's participation in, 92–93; Argentine, 92; institutional, 92, 100; international, 92; and labor, 204 n. 3; treatment of love and sexuality, 147–48; treatment of women, 148–49. *See also* utopianism
Anderson, Andrew, 202 n. 31
antiboticario, 132
apartment buildings, 168–69, 175
apparel, 101
aquenó, 113–15, 160, 207 n. 33
Aramburu, Julio, 139, 147, 152; *Buenos Aires: Ciudad, mujeres, hombres, muestrario urbano*, 139
archeology, 29–30. *See also* Foucault, Michel
architecture, 167–69, 172, 207 n. 2, 208 n. 3; Beaux-arts style, 168, 207–8 n. 2; Parisian, 168
Argentina: culture of, 126; economic conditions of, 98; foundational myth of, 22, 23, 35; law enforcement in, 125; living standards in, 100; penal institutions in, 125; public health and hygiene in, 123–26; society in, 57, 104, 119
Argentina Libre, 150

221

Argentine identity: heroic identity, 110; Macedonio's renovation of, 104
Argentine mythology, 42, 82, 152, 195; *compadrito*, 152, 175; creole warrior, 152; gaucho, 152; use by Borges, 152
Arlt, Roberto, 60, 63, 82, 87; as avant-garde playwright, 77, 79; comparison with Macedonio, 25, 63, 106, 157, 191; *El juguete rabioso*, 63; and invention, 67–68, 69; *Los siete locos*, 157; and negation, 64; portrayal of Buenos Aires by, 138, 152; treatment of madness by, 157
arrabal: Borges's representation of, 175–76. *See also* suburbs
art: autonomy of, 199 n. 5, 200 n. 13, 201 n. 18, 202 n. 30; avant-garde, 200 n. 12, 201 n. 18; as institution, 199 n. 5; as invention, 54, 202 n. 30; and life, 48–49, 51, 79; as political act, 87; and praxis, 50, 199 n. 5, 201 n. 18; radical, 55. *See also* aesthetics
Artaud, Antonin: "theater of cruelty," 79, 88
artist: artistic persona, 75; avant-garde, 202 n. 32, 203 n. 45. *See also* author
Astrada, Carlos: *El juego existencial*, 209–10 n. 1
asylums, 154–55
Auden poets, 106
author, 22, 28, 31, 36, 41, 50; absenting of, 37, 46, 71, 79, 87, 187, 195; accidental, 32–47, 73; burlesque of, 73; deidentification of, 186; eradication of, 88; as inventor, 68; Macedonio as, 32, 41, 44; in Macedonio's texts, 203 n. 44; *modernista* treatment of, 202 n. 36; modernist concept of, 76; as reader, 31; relationship to reader, 73; relationship to work, 73; status of, 25, 65, 71; "tyranny" of, 79; unknown, 73–74. *See also* authorship
authority, 39, 135, 192; avant-garde treatment of, 203 n. 45; law enforcement, 116–18; Macedonio's critique of, 86, 195; parental, 135–37, 196
authorship, 25, 32, 33, 41; avant-garde treatment of, 70; Cartesian concept of, 163; Macedonio's critique of, 74, 76, 86, 195; of *Museo*, 65; repudiation of, 54, 60, 73; without a self, 192; without selfhood, 31. *See also* author
autor accidentado. *See* accidental author
avant-garde, 34, 48–88, 91; Argentine, 35, 44, 46–47, 48–88, 157, 169, 171, 195, 198 n. 1, 200 n. 7, 200 n. 8, 201 n. 22, 201 n. 23, 202 n. 29, 202 n. 31, 203 n. 45, 203 n. 46 (*see also* Martinfierrista generation); art, 200 n. 12, 201 n. 18; artist, 202 n. 32; characteristics of, 22, 53, 54, 201 n. 18, 201 n. 22; classism of, 202 n. 31; comparison with Macedonio, 27, 74–77, 80–83, 86–87, 199 n. 1, 199 n. 6; European (historical or classical), 48–50, 51, 55, 59, 60, 63–64, 67, 70, 71, 75, 199 n. 4, 199 n. 6, 200 n. 8; failure of, 202 n. 30; Latin American, 49–50, 55, 71, 83, 87, 199 n. 3, 199 n. 4, 199 n. 5, 199 n. 6 (*see also* avant-garde: Argentine); Macedonio's classification as, 200 n. 8; Macedonio's critique of the, 111, 190, 205 n. 2; Macedonio's relationship with the, 13–14, 42–43, 49–50, 53–54, 106, 195, 201 n. 16; misreading of Macedonio by the, 20; nihilistic impulse of the, 201–2 n. 26; novel, 199 n. 6; poetics, 199 n. 6; poetry, 202 n. 31; political engagement of the, 90; privileging of the ludic by the, 59; Rojas Paz as, 203 n. 40; Romantic origins of the, 200 n. 13, 201 n. 26; theater, 77, 79, 203 n. 37; theories of the, 201 n. 26; treatment of madness by the, 157; treatment of vagabond by the, 196; "unpopularity" of the, 71–72. *See also* Martinfierrista generation

Bacon, Francis, 142
Bakhtin, Mikhail, 50, 86
balconies, 167–68
Balderston, Daniel, 22, 201 n. 20
barbarie y civilización, 180–81
Barletta, Leonidas, 77
Barrancos, Dora, 94
barrio, 102, 175–79, 196–97. *See also* neighborhood

INDEX

bars, 169, 170–71, 175
beauty, 121, 145, 147, 178, 186–88. *See also* aesthetics
Beaux-arts style, 168, 207–8 n. 2
being. *See* "pure being"
Belarte, 55, 63, 65, 144, 155, 176; Borges's inversion of, 152; compared with anarchism, 92; compared with theater, 79; as contrary to modernist concept of the author, 76; prose versus poetry in, 86
Biagini, Hugo E., 198 n. 2
boardinghouses, 135, 155, 168
body, 19, 26, 119–61; integrity of the, 26; liberation from subjectivity of, 194; power of the, 26, 27; regarded as object, 194; relationship to city, 62; segregation of bodies, 165; and self, 30, 47; separateness from consciousness of the, 151; status or function in society of the, 119. *See also* corporality
Boedo-Florida rivalry, 109. See also *grupo Boedo*; *grupo Florida*
Boom literature, 18
bordellos, 141, 142
Borges, Jorge Luis, 13–14, 41; anti-Peronism of, 204 n. 10; appropriation of Macedonio's poetics by, 199 n. 7; and the avant-garde, 53, 86, 198 n. 1; comparison with Macedonio, 25, 57, 61–62, 64, 73, 82–85, 106, 168, 191, 209 n. 20; discovery of Macedonio by, 23, 32, 34–36, 43; knowledge of *Adriana Buenos Aires*, 207 n. 29; Macedonio's falling out with (1928), 52; Macedonio's influence upon, 32, 50–51; misunderstanding of Macedonio by, 20, 116; mythicization of Argentina by, 87; mythicization of Buenos Aires by, 101–2, 167, 189, 196; mythicization of Macedonio by, 34–37, 44–47, 52, 93, 102, 116, 195, 199 n. 6; named in *Adriana Buenos Aires*, 120; as part of Martinfierrista generation, 72, 83; political activity of, 204 n. 15; promotion of Macedonio by, 36; rejection of Macedonio's poetics by, 194; rejection of socialism by, 91; self-promotion by, 199 n. 7; treatment of authorship, 76; treatment of Buenos Aires, 69, 70; treatment of history by, 82, 201 n. 20; treatment of madness by, 157; treatment of originality by, 76; treatment of poetic voice by, 22–23; treatment of social issues by, 151–52; and Ultraism, 75, 85, 198 n. 1; use of *costumbrismo* by, 81. *See also* Borges, Jorge Luis, works of
Borges, Jorge Luis, works of: "Borges y yo," 22, 85; *Cuaderno San Martín*, 101–2; "El Recienvenido, inédito aún," 93; "El Sur," 62; "Emma Zunz," 151–52; *Historia universal de infamia*, 60; "Hombre de la esquina rosada," 70, 85, 175; "La apostasía de Coifi," 204 n. 10; "Las ruinas circulares," 61; *Revista multicolor de los sábados*, 52; "Sentirse en muerte," 85; "Tlön, Uqbar, Orbis Tertius," 62, 115
Borges, Jorge (senior), 13, 34, 93, 182
Borinsky, Alicia, 18, 36, 121
breast-feeding, 132, 133–34
brindis, 37, 95
Bueno, Monica, 19, 33, 90, 203 n. 2, 208 n. 5
Buenos Aires, 13, 26–27, 87, 207 n. 1, 208 n. 5; architecture of, 167–69, 207 n. 2; beauty of, 197; body in, 165; of Borges, 196; bureaucracy in, 112–15; café society in, 169; call for moral regeneration in, 180; campaign to beautify, 33, 83, 107–8, 116, 178–79, 186–90, 200 n. 14 (*see also* city: campaign to beautify the); changing demographics in, 178; class conflict in, 99, 110; conditions for women in, 137–44; conquest of, 174–75, 178–79; as defined by passion, 188; economic conditions of, 97, 99; ghettoization in, 177; housing in, 208 n. 8; ideological order in, 163; living conditions in, 91, 93; Macedonio's views of, 163, 179, 182–83, 186; Macedonio's vision for, 189; modernity in, 168; mythicization of, 23,

101–2, 167, 189, 196; neighborhoods in, 175–79, 208 n. 7; "novelization" of, 79, 85, 152, 172, 175, 177, 191, 195; organization of, 166, 172; poetry of, 167; police presence in, 117; prostitution in, 138, 139, 141–43; public health and hygiene in, 123–26; public transit in, 172–73, 208 n. 6; realistic representation of in "Emma Zunz" and *Adriana Buenos Aires*, 152; segregation in, 165; as site of cultural reinvention, 68–70; social conditions in, 137–44; treatment of mentally ill in, 153; under the Yrigoyen government, 110. *See also* city
bureaucracy, 104, 112–15
Bürger, Peter, 62, 199 n. 5, 200 n. 12, 200 n. 13, 201 n. 18, 202 n. 30

cafés, 169–72, 175
Calinescu, Matei, 200 n. 12, 201–2 n. 26, 201 n. 22, 202 n. 32
Camblong, Ana, 19, 20, 33, 46, 78, 107, 109, 199 n. 7, 204 n. 13, 209 n. 15, 209 n. 18, 210 n. 2
campaign in absence, 33, 41, 103. *See also* presidential campaign
Cansinos Assens, Rafael, 44–45, 75
capital, 97–99, 100, 101
capitalism, 98, 126, 127, 162, 184–85
Carrafa, Brandán, 53
Carriego, Evaristo, 116
Cartesian philosophy, 85, 95, 193. *See also* Descartes, René
Cascardi, Anthony, 85, 193–94, 201 n. 17
Castelnuovo, Elias, 77
Catholic Church, 141, 148. *See also* Catholicism
Catholicism, 135. *See also* Catholic Church
caudillo, 103, 104
causality, 129; Macedonio's repudiation of, 193
celebrity, 46, 71–75, 165
centenary movement, 72, 73, 74, 89
Cervantes, Miguel de, 21, 58–59, 193–94; *Don Quijote*, 58–59, 193
character, 24
characters, 79, 113; Aaron Loewenthal, 152; Adolfo, 120, 130, 131–32, 140, 149, 153, 156, 166, 169, 173–74, 177; Adriana, 120, 130, 131–32, 133–34, 137–44, 146, 149, 151–52, 153, 166, 168–69, 173–74, 205 n. 4, 206 n. 12, 206 n. 21; Deunamor, 64, 65; Dulce-Persona, 58–59, 65, 136–37, 188, 189, 206 n. 20; Eduardo de Alto, 63, 120, 130, 132, 133, 137, 138–40, 142, 143, 145–47, 151, 153–55, 156, 168–69, 171, 173–74, 189, 192; Emma Zunz, 151–52; Estela Paredes, 138–40, 143, 145–47, 151, 171, 173; La Eterna, 65, 66–67, 83, 84, 188; the Fool of Buenos Aires, 112–13, 115, 117, 160; Frederico, 190; Julio Paredes, 122, 140, 145, 205 n. 6; of *Museo*, 64, 66, 137, 200 n. 14; Nicolasa, 174–75, 190; Padre, 136–37; Presidente, el, 63, 65, 66–67, 79, 88, 103, 107–8, 137, 178–79, 186, 188, 189, 192, 200 n. 14; Quizagenio, 58–59; as readers, 58–59; Recienvenido, 63, 80, 81, 165, 189; Sergio, 131, 135; Susanita, 138, 141, 142, 143, 146, 151; without selves, 59, 137
childbearing, 130–33, 146
child rearing, 130, 132, 133–35
children, 130–35, 144–47; illegitimate, 146
citizenship, 27, 46, 94
city, 27, 28, 161, 162–91, 196, 207 n. 30; beauty of the, 128; Borges's treatment of the, 196; campaign to beautify the, 33, 83, 107–8, 116, 164, 186–88; critiques of the, 179–80; identity of the, 47; Latin American, 162; lettered, 162, 163, 189–90, 192 (*see also* city: textual); Macedonio's approach to the, 87, 162–91, 192–95; Macedonio's repulsion against urban growth, 178; and metaphysics, 177, 192; mythic, 84–85; mythical foundation of the, 189; and neighborhood, 102, 175–79, 196–97; and novel, 186–91; "novelization" of the, 79, 85, 152, 175, 177,

191, 195; organization of the, 163–66; paradox of the, 26; relationship to the body, 62; relationship to the individual, 160; and self, 162–91, 196; textual, 162, 163; urban development, 182; urban life, 119, 162–91, 202 n. 33; urban planning, 172, 207 n. 1; urban space, 173; urban time, 173; as work of art, 79. *See also* Buenos Aires; polis

ciudad-campo. See country-city
civil liberties, 96, 144
class, 98, 99–102, 119, 124, 130, 149, 204 n. 6
classification, 113–14
classism, 74–75, 99, 121, 202 n. 31
Collazos, Oscar, 199 n. 3
colonialism, 55, 62, 181
Columbus, Christopher, 42
community, 134
Con Davis, Robert, 137
Coni, Emilio, 124, 131, 205 n. 10, 206 n. 12, 206 n. 15, 209 n. 14
consciousness, 151, 163; comparison between Macedonio's and Borges's treatment of, 62; individual, 61–62, 63; separateness of body from, 151
consumer culture, 101, 170
contexts of Macedonio's work, 18–21, 25, 29, 31
continuity: of avant-garde with Romanticism, 200 n. 13; and rupture, 55, 59
contravenciones, 117–18
corporality, 26, 118, 119–61, 134. *See also* body; physicality
Cortázar, Julio, 62, 116; *Rayuela*, 59, 60
cosmopolitanism, 86, 109, 181
costumbrismo, 81
country-city, 181–82, 184, 209 n. 14. *See also* countryside
countryside, 179–83, 197, 208 n. 10. *See also* country-city
creoles, 99, 104, 165, 168, 209 n. 12
crime, 127, 149–50, 157; and immigrants, 207 n. 28; organized, 141; and prostitution, 149. *See also* criminology
criminology, 149–50, 151, 153, 154, 165. *See also* crime

critical readings of Macedonio's work, 17–23; contextual vs. noncontextual, 18–21, 29; historical and biographical, 19–20; Lacanian, 30; political, 19; postmodern, 17, 18, 20, 36; psychoanalytic, 18, 19, 20
cubism, 55
culture, 68; cultural institutions, 169–70; cultural mythology, 116; reinvention of, 86
Cúneo, Dardo, 89

Dabove, César, 153
Dada, 61, 67, 106, 201 n. 22
Dante, 67
Darwin, Charles, 206 n. 14
death, 65, 123; negation of, 26, 40, 156, 188
"degeneration," 126–27, 130, 131, 149, 155, 165, 180
de la Torre, Lidia, 208 n. 8
Delfino, Víctor, 206 n. 15, 209 n. 14
del Mazo, Gabriel, 178, 183, 184, 208 n. 11
del Mazo, Jorge, 183
democracy, 94, 96, 97, 204 n. 14
Derrida, Jacques, 40, 88
Descartes, René, 24, 63, 85. *See also* Cartesian philosophy; self: Cartesian
Díaz, Lydia, 19
dictatorship, 95–96
difference, 40, 41
disease, 127, 149. *See also* health; illness; madness; public health
domesticity, 168–69
Don Quijote, 58, 193, 201 n. 17
Dorrego, Manuel, 84
dreaming and wakefulness, 51, 61–62, 176, 193
dreams, 187

economics, 90, 97–102, 119, 138, 184–85
Ediciones Corregidor, 14
Eliade, Mircea, 23
elitism, 71, 109
"Emma Zunz," compared with *Adriana Buenos Aires*, 151–52

emotion, 63, 140, 154, 193. *See also* affection
empiricism, 19, 30, 121, 122, 149, 155
Engelbert, Jo Anne, 13, 18, 37, 57, 89, 198 n. 4
Enlightenment, the, 165
"Enternecientes" and *"Hilarantes,"* 108–9
episteme, 28; epistemic rupture, 30; Foucault's concept of, 28; Macedonio's understanding of the term, 103
eternity, 199 n. 7
eudemonology, 158–60
eugenics, 126–30, 130–33, 137, 149, 206 n. 14, 206 n. 15. *See also* heredity
Europe: European culture, 63, 82; Latin American subordination to, 55; rejection of European culture, 62. *See also* colonialism
evolution, 129. *See also* eugenics; progress
existentialism, 193
expressionism, German, 199 n. 2

Falconnet, Joaquín, 182. *See also* Quiroule, Pierre
falling, 40, 41
fame. *See* celebrity
family, 133–35, 135–37, 155, 206 n. 17; as autonomous selves, 134; and heredity, 126; and neighborhood, 102. *See also* childbearing; children; heredity
fascism, 96
fatherhood, 135–37, 155; Macedonio's relinquishing of, 196. *See also* paternity laws
Federalists, 109
female abject, the, 151–52
feminism, 139, 141
ferias francas, 100
Fernández, Macedonio: as absent author, 102; as accidental author, 32–47; ascetic lifestyle of, 103; biography of, 13–14, 19, 179; critical readings of, 17–23, 48; critical reception of, 87; as *fantasma*, 43; as humorist, 51, 61, 64; individual identity of, 32; as literary father figure, 13, 72, 196; as mediator between avant-garde and traditional poetics, 109; myth of, 17, 21–23, 27, 29, 34–37, 41, 48, 89, 111, 160; as newcomer, 37, 69, 74, 75, 195; as philosopher, 51, 65; physical appearance of, 90; physical presence of, 196; political convictions of, 89, 89–118; as President, 103; public reception of, 87; public self of, 46, 166; relationship to his own texts, 32; relationship to the city, 196; relationship with his children, 196; self-description by, 90; self-effacement of, 46; as Socratic figure, 34, 36, 43, 89, 191
Fernández, Macedonio, works of: *Adriana Buenos Aires*, 13–14, 56–59, 76, 79, 90, 119–61, 163, 166, 167, 178, 179, 201 n. 16, 205 n. 2, 205 n. 4, 205 n. 5, 205 n. 6, 206 n. 20, 206 n. 21; "Al hijo de un amigo," 37; "Brindis a Marinetti," 94; *Continuación de la Nada*, 14, 58; "Crítica del dolor," 125; "De las personas" (doctoral thesis), 144, 207 n. 25; "Del Bobo de Buenos Aires," 112–13, 115, 117, 160; "El asesino anual," 150; "La calle Florida," 170, 208 n. 5; "La conquista de Buenos Aires," 83, 109; "La desherencia," 89–90; "La oratoria del hombre confuso," 37–43, 47, 62, 74, 77–78, 80, 94, 117, 125, 167, 206 n. 20; "La Santa Cleptomanía," 150; "Lo que nace y lo que muere," 56; "Los amigos de la ciudad," 183; *Museo de la Novela de la Eterna*, 14, 20, 28, 33, 46, 50, 56–57, 60, 63, 66, 68–69, 79, 83, 87, 89, 90, 106–12, 116, 121, 135, 136–37, 155, 157, 163, 167–68, 171–72, 174–75, 178, 179, 186–90, 200 n. 14, 201 n. 15, 201 n. 16, 201 n. 24, 202 n. 34, 203 n. 42, 204 n. 11, 204 n. 13, 205 n. 5, 206 n. 20; "No existe problema social-económico," 96; *No toda es vigilia la de los ojos abiertos*, 14, 35–36, 176, 198 n. 4; *Novela de la Eterna*, (see *Museo de la Novela de la Eterna*); *Papeles de Buenos Aires*, 182; *Papeles de Recienvenido*, 14, 36–38, 40,

73–74, 76, 91, 112, 130, 165–66, 167, 173, 202n. 35; "Para una teoría de la humorística," 61; "Para una teoría del estado," 96; "Prólogo a la Eternidad," 82; "Prólogo a lo nunca visto," 68, 187; "(Que no)," 107; *Una novela que comienza*, 14, 170, 205n. 4, 208n. 11
Fernández Latour, Enrique, 37, 78, 98, 103, 203n. 38
Fernández Moreno, César, 51
Ferreira Gular, José, 199n. 4
fiction and reality, 62
Figari, Pedro, 37
Foix, Juan Carlos, 18–19, 160, 207n. 33
forgetfulness, 121
Foucault, Michel, 20, 23, 27–29, 114, 121; "clinical gaze," 154; Foucauldian analysis, 27–29; Macedonio's anticipation of, 28–29, 151; treatment of insanity, 153–54; treatment of sexuality, 147–48
foundational myths, 42, 45, 81, 195
Fundación Palermo, 14
future, 95
futurism, 55, 68, 70, 95, 96, 199n. 4

Galindez, Bartolomé, 55
Gallo, Ezequiel, 109
Garasa, Delfín, 204n. 4
García, Carlos, 33, 200n. 10, 204n. 11, 205n. 4
García, Germán Leopoldo, 18, 19, 30
"garden city" movement, 182, 209n. 13
gauchesque, the, 81. *See also* Argentine mythology: gaucho
gaze, 166, 171. *See also* specularity
gender: Macedonio's treatment of, 201n. 25; relationship to self, 129
German expressionism, 199n. 2
Ghiraldo, Alberto, 92, 94, 203–4n. 2
Giovanni, Norman Thomas di, 199n. 6
Girondo, Oliverio, 57, 64, 72, 87, 152, 157, 167, 191, 201n. 23
Gómez de la Serna, Ramón, 90, 93, 128, 136, 137, 199–200n. 6
Góngora, Luis de, 70
González, Horacio, 19, 44, 102, 103, 106, 203n. 2

González Lanuza, Eduardo, 63, 152; *Aquelarre*, 63
goodwill, 145, 157. *See also* altruism
government: government census, 113–14; Macedonio's critique of, 90, 91, 102, 104, 111, 112–15, 116, 135, 195; treatment of paternity, 146–47; treatment of prostitution, 141–43; treatment of women, 139, 141–43, 146–47; and unions, 206n. 13
grupo Boedo, 106, 198n. 1. *See also* Boedo-Florida rivalry
grupo Florida, 25, 106, 198n. 1. *See also* Boedo-Florida rivalry
guardianship, women's right to, 144–47
Güiraldes, Ricardo, 55; *Don Segundo Sombra*, 82, 101
Gullón, Germán, 200n. 8, 202n. 31
Guy, Donna J., 138, 141, 206n. 21

Hardoy, Jorge, 207n. 1
Haussman, Georges-Eugène, 207n. 1
health, 26, 121–26, 170, 179. *See also* disease; health care; hygiene; illness; public health
health care, 121–26, 133, 154. *See also* medical practice
Heidegger, Martin, 210n. 1
heredity, 126–30, 137, 206n. 14. *See also* eugenics
Hernández, José, 56
heroic identity, 110
Hidalgo, Alberto, 52–53, 78, 94
"Hilarantes" and *"Enternecientes"*, 108–9
history, 22–24, 29, 80–86, 195–96, 203n. 43
Hobbes, Thomas, 176, 193
Holloway, James, Jr., 23
homosexuality, 138
houses, 168–69, 207n. 2
Howard, Ebenezer, 209n. 13
hronir, 115
Huidobro, Vicente, 79, 80–81, 87, 106, 203n. 39; *Altazor*, 40–41
humor, 54, 61–62, 64
hygiene, 26, 121–27, 154–55, 160, 170
hygienicism, 121–26, 133, 137, 205n. 9, 206n. 13, 207n. 26, 209n. 14; and

crime, 149; and eugenics, 131–32; and heredity, 126–27; and immigrants, 124–25, 205 n. 11; and law enforcement, 124, 125, 205 n. 10; madness, 153; and prostitution, 141, 144; and sexuality, 148. *See also* public health

Ideas y Figuras, 92
identity, 22, 36, 64, 116, 144, 156; creole, 202 n. 35; ethnic, 75; and family, 134; and heredity, 128–29, 137; heroic, 110; individual, 24–26, 109, 116, 204 n. 8; Latin American, 80; and madness, 152–53; modern, 24; relationship to authorship, 46; representation of, 116; social, 75; spiritual, 98; without a self, 41, 64; of women, 145
illness, 122–23, 127, 133. *See also* disease; madness
immigrants, 72, 93, 99, 138, 155; and crime, 207 n. 28; and hygienicism, 124–25, 205 n. 11; integration of, 178; and prostitution, 141; and reproduction, 133. *See also* immigration
immigration, 75, 177, 205–6 n. 11; and crime, 149; and eugenics, 126; and hygienicism, 124; and public health, 205 n. 11. *See also* immigrants
individual, 31, 98, 119, 163; and authority, 135; economic conditions of the, 101; effects of city upon the, 179; and family, 134–35; fragmented, 24; and government, 95–96, 100, 111, 116, 128, 147; individual existence, 107; integrity of the, 158; liberation of the, 27, 159, 195; Macedonio's championing of the, 97, 111, 117–18, 158, 160; "maximum individual," 24–25, 27, 91, 102, 194; and physicality, 119, 195; priority of the, 91; relationship to environment, 122–23; relationship to others, 135, 147; renovation of the, 25, 27–28, 91–92, 102, 104, 114, 188; selfless, 27, 30, 47; social and political components of the, 26; without a self, 30, 68, 122. *See also* self; subject
individuality, 114, 144

individuation, 28, 29
industry, 101; cottage industry, 101, 177, 184; industrialization, 127; mass industry, 177
Ingenieros, José, 91, 203–4 n. 2; *Archivos de criminología, medicina legal y psiquiatría*, 149–50
inheritance, 98, 99, 146. *See also* property
insanity. *See* madness
institutions, 26, 29, 91, 192, 193; literary, 29; Macedonio's critique of, 195; medical, 29; political, 29, 100; relationship to individual, 91; social, 29, 121–22
"intransigence" as political strategy, 104–5, 109, 110
invention, 24, 54, 67–71, 82, 86, 192; avant-garde concept of, 202 n. 29; conflation with art, 202 n. 30; of self, 202 n. 29
inventor, 68, 87; as hero, 202 n. 29
irrationality, 54, 201 n. 22, 201 n. 26
Isaacson, José, 19, 98, 200 n. 8, 203 n. 41, 204 n. 7

James, William, 30, 198 n. 2
Jameson, Frederic, 20–21
Jefferson, Thomas, 179, 209 n. 13
Jewish community, 99, 138, 141
Jitrik, Noé, 18, 36
jouissance, 30
journalism, 202 n. 36
judiciary, 118

Kant, Immanuel, 63, 193. See also *noumena*
Kerr, Lucille, 22
Kirchner, Néstor, 209 n. 12
kitsch, 108
Korn, Francis, 177, 204 n. 12, 208 n. 8
Kristeva, Julia, 31, 198 n. 5

labor, 90, 97–101, 204 n. 3, 204 n. 5; labor laws, 130
Lacan, Jacques, 137
Lacanianism, 30, 137; Lacanian approach to self and identity, 31, 39, 40;

Lacanian readings of Macedonio, 18–19
Lamac, Cavendra, 205 n. 4
Lamarckianism, 126–29. *See also* eugenics
Lange, Nora, 60
language, 30, 38–41, 80–86, 206 n. 20; Castilian, 81–82; constitution of subjectivity in, 38–39, 80; Macedonio's subversion of, 61, 69, 80–84, 87; of negation, 64; performative use of, 80; violence against, 69, 82
Lavrin, Asunción, 146
law, 90, 144–47; labor laws, 130
law enforcement, 115, 116–18, 119, 207 n. 28; and hygienicism, 124, 125, 205 n. 10; and libertarianism, 117; and public health, 205 n. 10; relating to prostitution, 141–43
Lawrence, Roderick, 189
Lees, Andrew, 180
leftism, 91, 96, 97
Leland, Christopher Towne, 63
libertarianism, 13, 26, 89–90, 96–98; debate on women, 139; and eugenics, 126; and law enforcement, 117; and paternity laws, 146; treatment of love and sexuality, 147–48; and utopianism, 184
Liernur, José Francisco, 208 n. 8
life and art, 48–49, 51, 79
Liga Patriótica, 97, 99–100
Lindstrom, Naomi, 18, 21, 36, 80, 198 n. 2, 199 n. 2
linguistic history, 83
literary marketplace, 72, 75
"literary streetcar," 113
literary tradition, 74. *See also* tradition
Lombroso, Cesare, 149
London, 165, 207 n. 1
love, 64–67, 109; altruistic, 141, 143; and family, 134–35; between men and women, 131; and negation of death, 188; and selflessness, 139–44; and sex, 147–48; spiritual, 147. *See also* altruism; relationships
Lucas, Fábio, 199 n. 4
ludic, the: avant-garde preference for, 54, 59–63; Macedonio's privileging of, 61; Macedonio's use of, 24, 86
Lugones, Leopoldo, 34, 55, 72, 73, 91, 198 n. 1, 202 n. 36, 203–4 n. 2; *El payador*, 101
lunfardo, 81
lyricism, 54, 59–63, 81
lyric voice. *See* poetic voice

Macedonio. *See* Fernández, Macedonio
madness, 152–55, 156
Mallea, Eduardo, 72, 87, 152; *Cuentos para una inglesa desesperada*, 63
Marechal, Leopoldo, 95
Mariani, Roberto: *Cuentos de la oficina*, 207 n. 22; *El amor agresivo*, 207 n. 22
Marinetti, Filippo Tommaso, 94–96
marriage, 126, 130–31, 206 n. 15; anarchist condemnation of, 148; "eugenic matrimony," 131; and prostitution, 148
Martí, José, 202 n. 33
Martínez Estrada, Ezequiel: *La cabeza de Goliat*, 181; *Radiografía de la Pampa*, 181
Martinfierrista generation, 51, 54, 70, 75, 198 n. 1; adoption of Macedonio as literary father figure, 13–14, 43, 44, 54, 55, 72; appreciation of Macedonio, 200 n. 7; comparison with Macedonio, 48–88, 106, 151, 191, 195; contribution to myth of Macedonio, 23–24, 32, 34–36, 43, 52, 80, 89; distinction between narrative and theater, 77; foundation of Argentine myth, 22, 72, 189; and invention, 68; and the ludic, 60–63; Macedonio's relationship with, 20, 43, 48–49, 52, 71, 73, 205 n. 2; mythicization of Buenos Aires by, 189; and negation or nihilism, 63–64; reaction to modernization by, 101; treatment of social issues, 150–51
Martín Fierro (literary journal), 14, 49, 53, 55–56, 106, 116, 198 n. 1
Marxism, 91, 98, 184
Masiello, Francine, 53, 80, 82, 86, 200 n. 8, 203 n. 40, 203 n. 45, 203 n. 46

materialism, 101, 119
materiality, 26, 32
Mattalía, Sonia, 19, 209 n. 20
"maximalism," 27, 91, 97, 100
"maximum individual," 24–25, 27, 91, 102, 194
Max-Neef, Manfred, 173, 208 n. 7
McVicker, Elizabeth Ruth, 200 n. 9
medical practice, 26, 122, 125, 132–33, 141. *See also* health care
memory, 206 n. 20
men: association with intellect and prowess, 201 n. 25; relationships between women and, 139, 194. *See also* gender; women
Mendel, Gregor, 206 n. 14
Mendelianism, 127–28
Méndez, Evar, 198 n. 1
Menes Kahn, Bonnie, 189
mental health, 125, 126, 151, 153, 179
mental illness. *See* madness
metaphysics, 25–27, 68, 145, 155, 176, 192–94; and city, 192; essences, 193–94; of Macedonio, 103; metaphysical inquiry, 19; metaphysical transcendence, 50; "metaphysical vision," 27, 94; non-discursive, 68; *noumena*, 193, 194; Platonic forms, 194
military, 117. *See also* law enforcement
modernism, 17–18, 72, 81
modernismo, 49, 57, 76, 198 n. 1, 202 n. 36
modernistas, 34, 101
modernity, 20, 22–23, 158, 180, 192–93, 208 n. 8; avant-garde treatment of, 87; in Buenos Aires, 168; dilemma of the subject in, 85; Macedonio's rejection of, 172–73; paradox of, 201 n. 17
modernization, 99, 101
Molina y Vedia, Juan, 93, 182
Molina y Vedia, Julio, 92–93, 94, 101, 182
Molloy, Sylvia, 60
Montaña, La, 91, 92, 203 n. 2
morality, 145
Moreau de Justo, Alicia, 139
Moreno, Mariano, 110
Morón, 179

motherhood, 138. *See also* women
Mumford, Lewis, 209 n. 13
Museo de la Novela de la Eterna, 135, 155, 163, 164, 167–68, 206 n. 20; bars and cafés in, 171; beautification of Buenos Aires in, 186–90; compared with *Adriana Buenos Aires*, 121, 163, 201 n. 16, 205 n. 5; compared with Arlt's *Los siete locos*, 157; domesticity in, 172; editions of, 201 n. 15, 201 n. 24, 203 n. 42, 209 n. 18, 209 n. 21, 210 n. 2; fatherhood in, 206 n. 20; as first "good" novel, 121; the Novel in, 202 n. 34; portrayal of countryside in, 179; portrayal of fatherhood in, 136–37; public transit in, 174–75; rejection of urbanism in, 178; structure of, 200 n. 14; treatment of specularity in, 167–68; writing of, 204 n. 11, 204 n. 13
myth, 32, 41, 80, 83, 85, 194; Argentine, 23–24, 195; mythic archetypes, 157; national, 195; personal, 195

narrative, 77, 81
nation, 68, 72, 131, 137, 141; fiction of, 61; invention of, 67, 68, 86; national culture, 55, 61, 64; national history, 82; national mythology, 83, 109, 110, 116, 121–22, 195 (*see also* Argentine mythology); nation-building, relationship to writing, 72. *See also* nationalism
National Department of Hygiene, 124
nationalism, 22, 81, 126, 199 n. 4, 201 n. 21; Argentine, 203 n. 41; in Macedonio's writing, 203 n. 41
nationality, 23, 126
naturalism, 101, 121
negation, 54, 63–68; affective function of, 65; poetics of, 67
neighborhood, 175–79, 208 n. 7. See also *barrio*
newcomer, 37, 75, 130, 195; Macedonio as, 37, 69, 74, 75, 195. *See also* characters: Recienvenido
New Historicism, 121
Newton, Sir Isaac, 39, 40
nihilism, 54, 64–67, 201 n. 22; and the

affective, 201 n. 26; of the avant-garde, 201–2 n. 26
nominalism, 193
nonbeing, 70, 194, 195
nonrational, the, 82
Nosotros, 55, 56, 181
nostalgia, 175–76, 180
nothingness, 64, 65, 67, 113
noumena, 193, 194. *See also* Kant, Immanuel
Nouzeilles, Gabrielle, 126
novel, 73, 79, 202 n. 34, 203 n. 43; avant-garde, 199–200 n. 6; "bad" novel, 56, 76, 120, 121, 130, 190; and city, 186–91; "double novel," 58; futurist, 68; "good" novel, 56, 121, 175, 186, 190; invention of the, 28; "living novel," 78, 87, 88; as miracle, 85, 185, 186–91, 190; *"novela a la calle,"* 78, 79, 175, 186; *"novela-tranvía,"* 175; "novelized" city, 113, 191; "open" novel, 79; parody of, 58, 59; as theater, 78; vanguard, 50
Novela de la Eterna. *See Museo de la Novela de la Eterna*
nutrition, 133, 134

Obieta, Adolfo de, 14, 17, 45–46, 92, 96, 103–4, 119–20, 156, 176
Obieta, Elena de, 13, 93
Ocampo, Victoria, 52, 198 n. 1
offspring. *See* children
O'Gorman, Camila, 84
originality: avant-garde repudiation of, 81; Macedonio's critique of, 70, 76; repudiation of, 54
Ortega y Gasset, José, 54, 71, 202 n. 31
Osorio, Nelson, 199 n. 4
Oved, Isaac, 204 n. 3
Owen, Robert, 209 n. 13

Pagni, Andrea, 19
pain, 67, 125, 133, 157–61
pampas, 181
"panlingua," 60. *See also* Solar, Xul
Papeles de Recienvenido, 165, 167; compared with *Adriana Buenos Aires*, 166; concept of "newcomer" in, 130; streetcars in, 173; treatment of creole identity in, 202 n. 35
parental authority, women's right to, 144–47
parent-child relationships, 135–37. *See also* family
Paris, 165, 207 n. 1
parks, 165, 183
Parnassianism, 198 n. 1
parody, 57, 58, 73, 74, 77, 81, 112
passion, 24, 26, 27, 107, 121, 140, 144, 147, 165, 188, 189; altruistic, 64, 143, 155; ascendancy of, 66, 201 n. 26; and reason, 85
past, 95; enshrinement of, 95; negation of, 188; "past-ism," 95. *See also* history
pastiche, 21, 58
paternity. *See* fatherhood
paternity laws, 146
patria potestad. *See* parental authority
Paz, Octavio, 22, 201 n. 26
penal institutions, 125. *See also* penology
penology, 149. *See also* crime; criminology; penal institutions
Pérez Firmat, Gustavo, 50, 54, 199 n. 5, 199 n. 6
performance, 39, 77–81, 190
persona: artistic, 47, 203 n. 45; eradication of, 50; Macedonio's creation of, 46
personalism, 92, 102, 106, 109, 111, 119, 204 n. 9
personality, 158, 180
philosophy, Argentine, 209–10 n. 1
physicality, 38, 134, 137, 143, 154. *See also* body; corporality
Piglia, Ricardo, 36, 103
Plato: *Phaedrus*, 156. *See also* Platonism
Platonism, 194
pleasure, 125, 158, 159
plenitude, 156, 198 n. 5
poetics, 19, 21–22; avant-garde, 48, 55, 87, 199–200 n. 6, 203 n. 45; of Borges, 22; of Macedonio, 19, 21, 25, 56, 192; systematic, 21
poetic voice, 22–23, 63, 65, 79, 80, 195, 196; Argentine, 23, 83; avant-garde establishment of, 54; Borges's idea of,

23; Macedonio's idea of, 23; Macedonio's rejection of, 54; national, 202 n. 27
Poggioli, Renato, 54, 64, 71, 82, 199–200 n. 6, 200 n. 11, 200 n. 13
police, 115, 117, 124–25, 142; harrassment by, 142, 205 n. 10; *policía médica*, 124, 125, 148; *policía sanitaria*, 124. *See also* law enforcement
polis, 24, 26–28, 192. *See also* city
political campaigning, 110, 112. *See also* presidential campaign
populism, 109, 204 n. 9
Positivism, 121, 130, 135, 165, 172; creation of the self by Positivist institutions, 118; and crime, 149–50; and eugenics, 126, 137; and hygienicism, 124–26, 137; Macedonio's critique of, 89–90, 95, 124–25, 149–50, 158, 160, 193; and madness, 153–55, 207 n. 30–31; of Sarmiento, 180–81
postmodernism, 58, 89; postmodern readings of Macedonio's work, 17–18, 20–22; postmodern theory, 20
postmodernity, 17–18
poverty, 98, 100–101. *See also* class; wealth
power: aesthetic, 27; Arlt's fascination with, 67–68; corporal, 26, 27; economic, 27; Foucauldian analysis of, 27–28; individual, 25, 26, 194; Macedonio's fascination with, 102; pain as instrument of, 158; resistance to, 28–29, 54, 80
pregnancy. *See* childbearing
presidential campaign, 33, 46, 78, 88, 89, 94, 103, 105–7, 115, 195
Prieto, Julio, 19–20, 68, 79, 107, 109, 190, 199 n. 1, 199 n. 7, 200 n. 7, 201 n. 16, 203 n. 43, 203 n. 44, 204 n. 14, 205 n. 2, 205 n. 5
Prisma, 75
Proa, 51, 75, 200 n. 10
progress, 121, 125, 126, 129
Prohibition, 95
proletariat. *See* labor
property, 99, 119, 184–85; women's property rights, 146

prostitution, 137–44, 206 n. 21, 207 n. 23, 207 n. 24; and crime, 149; in "Emma Zunz," 151; and immigrants, 141; legalization of, 138, 141–42; and marriage, 148; and public health, 142, 144, 207 n. 23; and sexuality, 142; and urbanization, 180
Protesta, La, 94, 132, 133
psychiatry, 155, 207 n. 30
psychoanalytic approach, 18–19. *See also* Lacanianism
psychology, Positivist, 154. *See also* Positivism
public, 71, 78, 109, 112, 186. *See also* reading public
publication, Macedonio's ambivalence toward, 25, 32–33, 43–46, 71–72, 89, 195
public health, 121–26, 127, 165, 170, 206 n. 12; and criminology, 149; and immigration, 205 n. 11; and law enforcement, 124, 125, 205 n. 10; and madness, 155; and prostitution, 142, 144, 207 n. 23; and public transit, 205 n. 9. *See also* hygienicism
publicity, 71, 74, 90. *See also* celebrity
public spaces, 87, 207 n. 1; cafés, 169–72; parks, 183; public transit, 173–75; statuary in, 115–16; streets, 163–66
public transit, 112–13, 115, 172–75, 204 n. 16, 204 n. 17; in Buenos Aires, 208 n. 6; Macedonio's ambivalence toward, 173–74; and public health, 205 n. 9. *See also* streetcars; trains
public works, 99, 112–16, 124, 163–66, 172–75, 205 n. 8
publishing. *See* publication
"pure being," 41, 198 n. 5

Quiroga, Horacio: "*cuentos del monte*", 101
Quiroule, Pierre: *La ciudad anarquista americana*, 94, 182

race, 126, 129, 149
racism, 121, 127, 206 n. 15
Radical government. *See* Yrigoyen government

Radicalism, 105, 110–12, 119, 204n. 6; Macedonio's critique of, 111; Radical party, 91, 97, 99, 102–5, 108, 112, 204n. 15. *See also* Yrigoyen government; Yrigoyen, Hipólito
Raffestin, Claude, 189
Rama, Angel: *La ciudad letrada*, 162–63
Ramos Mejía, José María, 124
Raros, Los, 55
rationalism, 85, 126, 127, 164
reader, 73, 76, 121; as character, 58, 59, 60, 61, 62, 70; Macedonio's attempt to liberate, 86; in Macedonio's texts, 203n. 44. *See also* reading public
reader-response theory, 76
reading public, 33, 71–73, 79, 135
realism, 57, 76, 121; avant-garde rejection of, 54; Macedonio's appropriation of, 122
reality, 21, 26, 63, 79, 203n. 46; fallacy of, 192; unreality, 199n. 7
reason, 85; Borges's privileging of, 85. *See also* rationalism
rebirth, 39–41
Reclus, Eliseo, 93
Reichardt, Dieter, 202n. 28
relationships, 26, 27; among individuals, 28; institutionalization of, 194; between men and women, 119, 131, 137, 139, 144, 146, 152, 194; parent-child, 135–37
relativism, 157, 158
religion, 201n. 26
repetition, 82
representation, 59, 79, 81, 85, 116, 167; avant-garde rejection of, 54; literary, 120; mishandling of human problems through, 121; of pain, 158; physical, 116; refusal of, 137; and self, 194; and subject, 194; suppression of, 187; theatrical, 77
reproduction, 130–33
Revista multicolor de los sábados, 52, 198n. 1
Revista Oral, 52, 113, 204–5n. 17
Rock, David, 103, 105, 108, 110–11
Rodríguez Monegal, Emir, 198n. 2
Rojas Paz, Pablo, 203n. 40; *Hombres grises, montañas azules*, 81
romance novels, 120, 130
Romanticism, 108, 121, 200n. 13, 201n. 26, 202n. 36
Romero, José Luis, 51
Ruibal, Beatriz, 118
rupture: aesthetic, 54–58, 86; avant-garde break with tradition, 30, 56–57; and continuity, 55–59; epistemic, 30

Saenz-Peña law, 94, 97, 105, 108, 110
Saenz Valiente, Consuelo Bosch, 52, 179, 185
Saenz Valiente family, 179
Salessi, Jorge, 124, 205n. 11
Salvador, Nélida, 18, 199n. 3
Sánchez, Luis Alberto, 14, 208n. 11; critique of the city, 181
Sarlo, Beatriz, 22, 54, 55, 60, 151, 202n. 31, 202n. 35
Sarmiento, Domingo Faustino, 180–81
Scalabrini Ortiz, Raul, 14, 35–36, 44, 47, 51, 53, 64, 207n. 22; *El hombre que está sola y espera*, 36
Scarry, Elaine, 158, 160
Schiminovich, Flora, 18, 21, 22, 199n. 2
Schopenhauer, Arthur, 157, 158, 193
Schulman, Ivan, 199n. 4
Schwartz, Jorge, 51, 199n. 3
Scobie, James R., 138, 206n. 21, 208n. 8
Scrimaglio, Marta, 61, 199n. 3
seamstresses, 138, 206n. 12, 206n. 21. *See also* prostitution
Segal, Silvia, 109
self, 21–22, 27, 36, 91, 97, 134; Argentine, 126; authorial, 31, 32–47; and authority, 203n. 45; avant-garde treatment of, 54, 63, 80, 86, 203n. 45; and body, 30, 47; Borges's treatment of, 22, 23, 24, 76, 82; Cartesian, 24, 85, 87; Cervantes's treatment of, 58–59; and character, 24; and city, 162–91, 196; definition of, 25; eradication or negation of, 40, 62, 64, 68, 80, 82, 85–87, 97, 114, 186–87, 195–96, 203n. 46; fiction of, 91, 98, 102, 113–14, 153, 156, 190; Huidobro's affirmation of, 80, 81; as institutionally constituted, 27, 47, 104, 111, 116, 118; La-

canian approach to, 30; and language, 30, 47, 80, 82, 206n. 20; literary, 203n. 46; Macedonio's critique of the, 19, 22, 30, 62, 86, 95, 97, 109, 111, 116, 158–59, 185, 193–94, 203n. 46; and madness, 153, 156–57; *modernista* treatment of, 202n. 36; and other, 167–68; and performance, 77–78; physical components of, 30; poetic, 200n. 8; rationalist, 126, 127, 129; relation to gender, 129; replacement with individual, 25, 27, 92, 114; and representation, 116, 194; Romantic treatment of, 202n. 36; self-effacement, 46; self-image, 109; self-promotion, 32–33, 41, 75–77, 102, 105, 195, 199n. 7, 202n. 29; self-repudiation, 75–77; and sensation, 159; social components of, 30; social construction of, 47, 143–44, 180; as spectator, 194; transcendent, 63, 76, 196, 203n. 46; Ultraist negation of, 22
selfhood. *See* self
selflessness, 137, 142, 150, 156. *See also* altruism
Semana Médica, La, 131, 133, 148, 206n. 12, 206n. 15, 209n. 14
Semana Trágica, 97, 99
Sennett, Richard, 165, 170, 172, 207n. 1
sensation, 26, 63, 67, 133, 140, 153–57, 165; and affection, 193–94; and consciousness, 151–52; and family, 134–35; and nutrition, 133; and pain, 125, 157–61; primacy of, 114, 125, 173
sexism, 151. *See also* women
sexuality, 40, 121, 130, 134, 136, 137–44, 206n. 15; feminine, 141, 142, 144, 147–50; homosexuality, 138; and prostitution, 142
Shakespeare, William, 67, 74
shopping, 170
Shumway, Nicholas, 109, 110, 181
Simmel, Georg, 179–80, 208n. 9
Síntesis, 106
Sirlín, Lázaro, 206n. 15
Skidmore, Thomas, 204n. 3
social, the, 26, 27

social Darwinism, 124, 206n. 14
social engineering, 121
socialism, 99–100, 104, 145, 180, 203n. 2; Argentine socialist movement, 91, 97; and child rearing, 132; and prostitution, 141–42
social realism, 207n. 22
social science, 145
Sociedad Eugénica Argentina, 131
society: Macedonio's critique of, 205n. 2; without selves, 123
Socrates, 192, 194
Solar, Xul, 60, 61, 201n. 21
Soviet Union, 96
Spain, 96
spectator, 37; self as, 194
specularity, 167–68, 170–72, 194
speech, 38, 39
Spencer, Herbert, 148, 193; Spencerian theory, 96, 128, 148
Spengler, Oswald, 179–80
spiritual health, 179
state, 93, 96–97, 116, 124, 128; intervention of, 129; theory of, 95. *See also* government
statuary, 115–16, 118, 164
Stein, Gertrude, 30, 67–68, 106; *The Autobiography of Alice B. Toklas*, 67
Sterne, Laurence, 20
storytelling. *See* narrative
"streetcar-novel." *See* novel: *"novela-tranvía"*
streetcars, 112–13, 172–75, 177, 204n. 16, 204n. 17, 205n. 9, 208n. 6. *See also* public transit
streets, 163–66
strikes, 97, 110, 204n. 5, 204n. 12. *See also* labor
Strong, Beret, 49, 53
subject, 22, 29, 39–40, 58, 80, 102; *"accidentado,"* 166; Cascardi's treatment of, 85, 193–94; modernity and the, 85; and object, 85, 167–68, 193; paradox of, 196; patient as, 156; and representation, 194; in representational art, 201n. 17; writing, 84. *See also* self; subjectivity
subjectivity, 24, 38, 40–41, 79, 173, 186,

194; ascendancy of, 155; avant-garde treatment of, 49, 61, 62, 80, 203n. 46; as basis for social and political institutions, 91; eradication of, 188, 189, 195; fictitiousness of, 187; Macedonio's reconsideration of, 49, 61, 85, 111, 192; subversion of, 80; suppression of, 187; suspension of, 59; of women, 145
suburbs, 168, 177; avant-garde attraction toward, 196. See also *arrabal*
subways, 165
suffrage, 94, 97, 104
Sur, 44, 49, 52, 106, 198n. 1
surrealism, 18, 61, 62, 106, 199n. 2, 199n. 4, 201n. 22
symbolism, European, 198n. 1
syndicalism, 99

text: liberation of, 31; privileging of, 31
theater, 77–79, 203n. 37
"theater of cruelty," 79, 88
"Therapeutics," 122–23, 154
Tiempo, El, 145
time, Macedonio's repudiation of, 193
Tolstoy, Leo, 148; "El amor sexual," 207n. 27
Torre, Guillermo de, 51
tradition, avant-garde break with, 55
traditionalism, 109
trains, 172, 173. See also public transit
transcendence, 59
transcendentalism, 180
transportation. See public transit

Ultraism, 22, 51, 55, 81, 85, 198n. 1; American or Argentine, 49, 71, 72, 75
Unión Cívica Radical. See Radicalism
unions, 100, 206n. 13
Unitarists, 109
United Kingdom, 96, 182
United States, 95, 182
unpopularity, 71–75
Unruh, Vicky, 22, 49, 50, 64, 77, 79, 80, 81, 86, 90, 196, 197, 199n. 5, 200n. 8, 202n. 27, 203n. 37, 203n. 39
urbanism, 178, 181
urbanization, 184
Uriburu government, 52

utopianism, 92–94, 101, 147, 187, 188; and the avant-garde, 201–2n. 26, 202n. 32; and concept of heredity, 126; and hygienicism, 126, 209n. 14; and libertarianism, 184; rural vision of, 181–82. See also anarchism

vagrancy, 118, 124, 196
vanguardismo, 52. See also avant-garde
Vasallo, Angel: *Elogia de la vigilia*, 210n. 1
Vecchio, Diego, 20
Vezzetti, Hugo, 153, 207n. 30, 207n. 31
Vicente de Alvarez, Sonia, 19, 193, 204n. 7
vigilantes. See police
Viñas, David, 44, 103
violence, 38–39, 40, 41, 69, 79, 92, 167, 206n. 20
Virasoro, Miguel Angel, 209n. 1
voice: Argentine, 86; poetic, 63, 65, 79, 80–81, 87, 195–96
voting, 94

wealth, 98, 99–100. See also class; poverty
Weber, Max, 179–80
"white slavery," 141
women, 119, 129, 130; abjection of, 152; association with flesh and instinct, 201n. 25; degenerative effects of city life on, 180; degradation of, 137–44, 170, 206n. 17; economic conditions of, 138–44, 206n. 21; as having criminal personalities, 150; hygienicist views on, 133; legal status of, 144–47; relationships between men and, 26–27, 119, 137, 139–44, 146, 152, 194. See also gender; sexuality: feminine
work. See labor
working classes, 97, 99, 125, 149, 165, 177. See also labor
writing, 25, 41, 103, 162; and alternative constitution of the individual, 30; "bad" writing, 70; "good" writing, 57, 71; and ideology, 163; myth of Macedonio's repudiation of, 43–44, 45, 192; professionalization of, 72, 73; relationship to nation-building, 72, 73

xenophobia, 75, 97, 99, 121, 149–50, 205 n. 11. *See also* immigration

Yrigoyen, Hipólito, 91, 92, 97, 102–6, 110–12, 119, 192, 204 n. 15. *See also* Radicalism; Yrigoyen government

Yrigoyen government, 110, 112–16, 119

Yujnovsky, Oscar, 208 n. 8

Yunque, Alvaro, 77

Zeno, Lelio: "Medicina Social e Individual," 132–33

Zukin, Sharon, 169–70